KU-764-222

# DEAD OR ALIVE

*The Skulduggery Pleasant series*

SKULDUGGERY PLEASANT
PLAYING WITH FIRE
THE FACELESS ONES
DARK DAYS
MORTAL COIL
DEATH BRINGER
KINGDOM OF THE WICKED
LAST STAND OF DEAD MEN
THE DYING OF THE LIGHT
RESURRECTION
MIDNIGHT
BEDLAM
SEASONS OF WAR

THE MALEFICENT SEVEN

ARMAGEDDON OUTTA HERE
*(a Skulduggery Pleasant short-story collection)*

*The Demon Road trilogy*

DEMON ROAD
DESOLATION
AMERICAN MONSTERS

# DEREK LANDY

# DEAD OR ALIVE

HarperCollins *Children's Books*

First published in Great Britain by
HarperCollins *Children's Books* in 2021
HarperCollins *Children's Books* is a division of HarperCollins*Publishers* Ltd
1 London Bridge Street
London SE1 9GF

www.harpercollins.co.uk

HarperCollins*Publishers*
1st Floor, Watermarque Building, Ringsend Road
Dublin 4, Ireland

1

Text copyright © Derek Landy 2021
Skulduggery Pleasant™ Derek Landy
Skulduggery Pleasant logo™ HarperCollins*Publishers*
Cover illustration copyright © Tom Percival 2021
Cover design copyright © HarperCollins*Publishers* Ltd 2021
All rights reserved.

LIMITED EDITION ISBN 978–0–00–847027–2
HB ISBN 978–0–00–838629–0
ANZ TPB ISBN 978–0–00–838631–3
EXP TPB ISBN 978–0–00–838630–6
PB ISBN 978–0–00–838634–4

Derek Landy asserts the moral right to be identified as the author of the work.
A CIP catalogue record for this title is available from the British Library.

Typeset in Baskerville MT 11/13.5 pt by
Palimpsest Book Production Ltd, Falkirk, Stirlingshire

Printed and bound in England by CPI Group (UK) Ltd, Croydon, CR0 4YY

Conditions of Sale
This book is sold subject to the condition that it shall not, by way of trade
or otherwise, be lent, re-sold, hired out or otherwise circulated without the
publisher's prior consent in any form, binding or cover other than that in which
it is published and without a similar condition including this condition being
imposed on the subsequent purchaser.

| LONDON BOROUGH OF WANDSWORTH | |
| --- | --- |
| 9030 00007 4346 2 | |
| Askews & Holts | |
| JF TEENAGE 11-14 | |
| | WW21000519 |

This boo... paper

For m... een

*In years to come, it'd be nice if Covid-19 was an easily managed affliction, or even a distant memory.*

*But right now, as we're living through it, it's robbing us of time and loved ones.*

*So this is to all the good times we've spent with the people we love, and all the great times still to come, and the loved ones we've yet to meet. If this book has a message, it's that time heals, and love is forever, and laughter is—*

*Hold on. No.*

*The message, I think, is that bad times pass, and good times are always... no. That's not it, either.*

*Maybe something about punching? There's a lot of punching in this book. Some kicking, too. And jokes. Many jokes. Man, I'm funny. I find myself hilarious, I don't mind telling you. Absolutely...*

*Wait, what was I talking about?*

# 1

This was surely going to be the greatest day in the life of Rancid Fines, and it was a Tuesday. Not the most auspicious day of the week, he supposed, but he was aware of at least a few momentous things that had occurred on Tuesdays before now.

The stock market crash, back in 1929. That had been on a Tuesday.

The *Challenger*. That had exploded on a Tuesday in 1986. He'd been sad about that. He'd never particularly liked mortals, but had always admired astronauts. He liked the way they bounced on the moon.

Elvis had died on a Tuesday, as had Buddy Holly, Ritchie Valens, and the Big Bopper.

D-Day. That had happened on a Tuesday and it had ruined everything, back when he'd been working with the Nazis. It had almost soured Tuesdays for him forever.

But he was about to take Tuesdays back. He was about to restore the most depressing day of the week to its former glory, if it had ever had any.

He checked his watch, and smiled: 4.48 in the morning would forever be known as the time the Faceless Ones returned to their rightful place as masters of the Earth.

He threw the switch. Very little happened.

"What's wrong?" asked Kiln.

"Nothing," Rancid said, hurrying over to the array and checking the connections. There were over a dozen power cables leading to and from the metal dish – any one of them could have come loose. It was an easy fix. It would be an easy fix. It had to be an easy fix.

"What are you doing?" Kiln asked.

Rancid resisted the urge to shout at him, to tell him to shut up and let him work. Now was not the time to lose his temper. This was a joyous occasion – or it would be, once it got going. Besides, Kiln was a good deal taller than him and a good deal stronger and a good deal scarier.

Rancid Fine was tall in the mind. He was strong in the heart. He was scary in the soul.

"It's a loose cable," he muttered. "It's an easy fix."

It was a nice night. Summer was a month away and the sky twinkled with stars. He was glad the Faceless Ones were going to return to good weather. He imagined that the dimension they'd been exiled to was cold and barren. He was looking forward to welcoming them back to the warmth.

"What's wrong with it?" Kiln asked, coming over.

Rancid got to his feet, staring at the array. The Crystal of the Saints – yellow, as big as both of Rancid's fists side by side, sat in its place in the centre of the dish. With the power cables connected – which they were – the crystal should have been glowing. All those sigils he'd painstakingly carved into the metal, they were supposed to be glowing, too. The whole thing should have been lighting up the entire mountainside.

"Nothing's wrong," Rancid said.

"Then why isn't it working?"

"Give it time."

Kiln frowned. "How much time?"

"As much as it needs."

"Rancid, you said it would work immediately. You said all the adjustments you'd made to the array would mean an instant connection. You said it would light up – you said there'd be fireworks."

"It just needs more—"

Kiln grabbed him by the collar of his coat and pulled him in. "I've spent every last cent I have on this project! Everything I own went into the equipment that you specified! That you designed!"

"It will work!" Rancid squealed.

"It will not work! It was never going to work! The array can't pull power out of the Crystal of the Saints because there is no power! It's a dud!"

"No!" Rancid screamed.

Kiln threw him down. "My whole life," he said, horrified. "I bet my whole life on this."

"It will bring the Faceless Ones back," Rancid whimpered.

"I don't care about them," Kiln sneered. "I don't give a damn about your gods! I was after the power you assured me was resting in that thing! With it, I could have had everything! I'd have been able to rebuild my fortune a hundred times over!"

Rancid blinked up at him. "But we... we were going to bring back the Faceless Ones."

"That was your dream, you insufferable toad."

"You were going to betray me?"

Kiln laughed. "Yes, Rancid, I was going to betray you. Once you'd proven the Crystal still had some juice in it, I was going to take it and start my life over. Your ridiculous notions of what the world would be like with the Faceless Ones in charge? Why the hell would I ever want a world like that? I happen to like this one. I happen to like mortals. They're not bad. Sure, I've killed a whole bunch of them over the years, but who hasn't?" He sighed. "But the Crystal doesn't have any power in it. You've ruined me."

Rancid got to his feet. He was short, so it didn't take long. "Blasphemer," he said.

3

Kiln didn't respond to that. His eyes were on the Crystal. "It'll be a challenge finding someone to buy it, but, so long as I sell before the news spreads that it's just one big lump of costume jewellery, I should recoup some of my losses, at least."

Rancid snatched up the Crystal, held it to his chest. "You stay back!"

"Rancid, come on. Don't be stupid."

Rancid turned and ran, tripped over a cable and stumbled, fell to his knees and the Crystal jolted out of his grip, went bouncing into the shadows.

A moment later, a figure stepped out of those shadows. Tall, slender, wearing a dark blue three-piece suit, complete with hat. The moonlight fell across the white of his skull as he looked at the Crystal in his gloved hands.

"I've been chasing you and this damn thing for far too long," Skulduggery Pleasant said.

Rancid shook his head. "No. Not you. Please, not you."

"Every time I've come close, you've managed to stay just out of reach," Pleasant continued, "whether it be by cunning or pure dumb luck. Without meaning to be rude, it was invariably the latter. Every time I've made a concentrated effort to catch you, something has pulled me away: killers, hellworlds, Remnants, alternate dimensions, ex-girlfriends... but today it is my pleasure – my absolute, unconditional pleasure – to finally say the words 'Rancid Fines, you're under arrest.'"

"No!" screamed Rancid, scrambling up again. "No! Not when I'm so close!"

He dived for the Crystal, but Pleasant tossed it over Rancid's head and it dropped into the hands of a woman in black, her dark hair falling across her face.

"So this is what we've been looking for, on and off, since I was thirteen years old," said Valkyrie Cain.

"I was looking for it a lot longer than that," Pleasant responded. "First time I even caught a glimpse of it, it was 1943 and I was crouching in the dark, surrounded by Nazis. They were talking about the massive amounts of power it could generate – but I've yet to see any evidence of that."

"Its power is limitless!" Rancid wailed.

"Nazis," Cain said, ignoring him completely, "I'd have loved to have fought Nazis. I bet you could keep on punching them and you wouldn't feel even the slightest bit bad about it."

"Nazis *were* pretty punchable," Skulduggery agreed. "Still are."

Kiln cleared his throat and held up his hands. "Thank God you're here," he said. "Rancid Fines was going to kill me."

"I was not!" shrieked Rancid.

"This guy?" said Cain. "This guy was going to kill you?"

Kiln nodded. "Yes."

"This guy right here, who needs to either stop crying or wipe his nose? This guy was going to kill you?"

"Don't let the tears or the nose fool you," said Kiln. "He's merciless."

"He certainly looks it. But I'm afraid you're under arrest, too. The Crystal of the Saints has been on the Forbidden Items list for a long time."

"It has?"

"Right there in the *Catastrophic Consequences* column."

"That does sound serious," Kiln said. "And you're not going to let me go, are you? I didn't think so. See, that presents me with something of a dilemma. You want to arrest me, and I don't want to be arrested."

"I can see how a dilemma would arise."

"So I only have one recourse. I have to resort to violence."

"Ah," said Pleasant. "Not a good idea."

Cain shrugged. "We excel at violence."

"We exceed at violence."

"You don't want to resort to violence with us," said Cain. "It won't go well for you."

Kiln nodded. "I understand what you're saying, and I appreciate you saying it. And while people a lot more powerful than I have tried to kill you before now, and I've heard about how badly that has gone for them, I can't help but think that maybe they failed because they just weren't me, you know?"

Three masked figures in black, with just their eyes visible, stepped out beside Kiln.

"Ninjas?" Cain whispered. Then, louder, "We're gonna fight ninjas?"

The first ninja took out a sword. The second took out a three-sectioned staff. The third filled his hands with throwing stars.

"Sweet blessed baby Jesus," said Cain. "We're gonna fight ninjas."

The third ninja flung the stars and Cain turned, the stars bouncing off her shoulder. He joined the ninja with the three-sectioned staff and they went after Pleasant, who started hurling fireballs, while the one with the sword lunged at Cain. The sword slashed at her, knocking the Crystal from her hands, but the blade, like the throwing stars, failed to get through her suit. Cain dodged another slash and charged, crashing into him.

Kiln crept forward, scooped up the Crystal.

"No!" Rancid yelled, diving and wrapping his arms round Kiln's leg.

"Stop that," said Kiln, trying to kick him off.

But there wasn't a power on this Earth that could dislodge Rancid Fines. "That stays with me! I'm so close to unlocking its secrets!"

"If you were ever going to unlock anything," Kiln said, doing his best to walk away, "you'd have done so by now."

The air rippled and one of the ninjas – the one currently on fire – went flying through the air like a screaming meteor.

"I will not let you take away my life's work," Rancid muttered through gritted teeth as he was dragged through the dirt and long grass.

The ninja with the sword had lost his weapon, but he was still kicking Valkyrie Cain around the place. Finally, she just blasted him with what looked like white lightning, and he slammed into Kiln.

The Crystal fell and Rancid grabbed it, kissed it, and scrambled away, leaving the fight to continue behind him.

# 2

Students lined up by year in the gymnasium, chatting among themselves, a sea of mismatched heights and weights and black blazers with different coloured piping on the lapels.

Omen Darkly made his way towards the back. The Sixth Years lounged against the wall, studiously aloof. Another month and they'd be gone, leaving their schooldays in the dust and embarking on whatever there was to embark on. Exciting times lay ahead, no doubt.

A mere two years ago, Sixth Years had seemed huge and tall and intimidatingly mature. Now Omen was as tall as most of them, even if that recent growth spurt had resulted in even more ungainliness in his movements. One day, he promised himself, he'd be able to walk into a room without being in danger of tripping over his own knees.

He joined his fellow Fifth Years. They didn't have the luxury of a wall to lean nonchalantly against, but they managed their lounging pretty well, considering. Axelia Lukt was standing with Ula and Bella, and Omen smiled at her and she smiled back, which made his heart sing. He got to his usual spot, standing beside his brother. Auger looked tired. He had dark rings under his eyes and he slouched, as if standing up straight was just too much effort. He'd been like this – disaffected – for the last three months, ever since he'd killed the King of the Darklands, and he was only getting worse.

Never walked in, and Omen searched for a sign that would allow him to figure out which gender his best friend was identifying with. He couldn't find one. Ever since Never had had his hair darkened and cut short – all except for the sweeping fringe – Omen had resorted to guessing. It hadn't worked out well so far.

Never had broken up with Auger just two weeks ago but, as usual, refused to let any of that drag her into a bad mood. He winked at Auger as she passed and Auger answered with a smile, the first smile Omen had seen him wear in ages, and Never took his place beside Omen.

"You're looking well," she said, eyes on the stage where the teachers were assembling.

"Thank you," Omen responded, surprised.

Never waited a few moments, then looked at him. "And now it's your turn to say something complimentary about me."

"Oh," said Omen. "I like your hair."

"You've already told me that."

"So..."

"Yes?"

"Are you...?"

"Am I...?"

Omen sighed. "Are you identifying as male or female?"

Never laughed. "I love how polite and awkward you get when you have to ask that. My identity is evolving, Omen. Right now, I'm not feeling particularly male or particularly female – so today I'm just identifying as me."

"And pronouns?"

"Pronouns – right now – would be *they* and *their*."

Omen nodded. "Cool."

"I'm still waiting for the compliment, by the way."

"What do you want me to say?"

"If I have to tell you what to compliment, then it won't count, will it?"

"I suppose not," Omen said. "You look nice. Is that enough of a compliment? I don't know."

"Why do you feel restricted to my physical appearance? I gave you a compliment on your physical appearance because I knew you'd appreciate that on account of how you never think you look good. But I know I look good, Omen. There are such things as mirrors and I do use them, so I know I'm looking particularly gorgeous this morning. But what about saying something regarding me as a person, rather than just a piece of really hot meat you like to ogle?"

"Was I ogling?"

"Everyone ogles me, Omen. I am intensely oglable."

"Not sure that's a word but, um, OK then... Never, you're really smart."

"Thank you."

"And confident."

"Yes."

"And I wish I could be more like you."

Never blinked at him. "Oh."

"What? Was that wrong?"

"No," Never said. "No, that was... lovely."

Omen shrugged.

The teachers were lined up and talking quietly among themselves – all except for Mr Peccant, who was glaring down at the First Years. Omen grinned. The poor First Years were so tiny and so cute and so sweet and so easily intimidated. It was actually funny how a sour look from a teacher could silence even the most—

Peccant raised his eyes to Omen and Omen looked away immediately and blushed and tried very hard not to pee.

Principal Duenna took to the stage, followed by the Vice Principal. Once she had reached the exact centre of the stage, Duenna smiled and waited for the chatter to die down.

When it didn't, Peccant stepped forward. "Shut up!" he roared, and everyone did, indeed, shut up. Peccant stepped back.

Duenna cleared her throat. "Thank you, Mr Peccant. Children, we have exactly twenty-seven days until May thirty-first, the Féile na Draíochta and the end of the school term. Your exams begin in nineteen days. You should have already received your schedules, and today marks the beginning of your revision classes."

Everyone cheered and Duenna looked unimpressed.

"Do not take revision classes to mean *free* classes," she said. "You are expected to attend each and every one – and attend them in full school uniform. There may have been some slacking under past principals, but under my watch you will behave with the dignity I expect."

There were loud, unsubtle mutterings that Duenna chose to ignore.

"While the Sixth Years and Third Years will be sitting state exams, the rest of you will be facing your own end-of-year exams, and, while it may be tempting to dismiss these as irrelevant, let me assure you that they are not. We will be paying very close attention to those of you who slack off, and there *will* be repercussions."

She cast a baleful eye over the hall, and then broke into a jarring smile.

"I'm sure all of you are excited for Féile na Draíochta – or Draíocht, to use its only approved abbreviation. That is not to be shortened to Draíochta, or the Féile, the Fleadh, the Fest, or any other inaccurate term. We want you all to have fun, but to have accurate fun. Draíocht only comes round once every seventy-two years, so I was barely older than some of you here now when I got to celebrate the last one. It was, if you'll pardon the pun, a magical time." She chuckled. Nobody else did. She turned to Peccant. "Do they know what a pun is?"

"They should," he growled.

Duenna shrugged. "Anyway, our glorious leader has decreed

11

that Roarhaven will be at the epicentre of all Draíocht festivities around the world. In his words, we shall be a beacon of light that shows the way home."

"What the hell does that mean?" Never muttered.

"And, as such, the last day of school will be a half day, after which you'll be able to go out and enjoy the carnival on the streets of our city."

Omen cheered with the rest of them. Only Auger stayed quiet.

Duenna checked her watch as the cheering continued, making sure it stayed within the time she'd allotted for it. When enough seconds had passed, she held up a hand and the hall fell silent.

"Now, a bit of housekeeping. All Magic Theory classes will be moved to the history room until Friday, and the Forging Official Documents modules will be held in the Magic Theory room. Tomorrow there will be screens set up in the dining hall over lunchtime so we can watch the acting Supreme Mage's speech live. He's announcing a new public policy, which is of interest to us all, I should imagine. Also, Mr Hunnan has asked me to remind you that you must bring your own gumshields to combat classes. You cannot ask to share one. OK, you have three minutes to get to your first class. Dismissed."

They filed out of the gymnasium, year by year, like toothpaste being squeezed through a nozzle. Once out of the doors, however, the toothpaste went everywhere, and Omen battled to get to his locker. Someone tugged at his sleeve.

"Hey, Thiago," he said, cursing himself.

"Hi," Thiago responded, thrown this way and that by the passing students – most of whom were bigger and older than him. "So, um, any news on...?"

"It's being taken care of," Omen said.

Thiago nodded, and was lost to the crowd for a glorious moment before he lunged back into view.

"Right," Thiago said, stumbling up beside him, "right, it's just it's very hard to see if anything's happening, you know?"

"Trust me on this. It's all going to be fine."

"Maybe I should talk to Auger."

"No," Omen said quickly. "The best thing to do is stay away from Auger. Don't ask him any questions – don't bring it up in conversation. Just... relax, all right?"

"All right," Thiago said, nodding. "All right. This is very important, though."

"He knows that, Thiago. I told him that. Leave it with him, and it'll be sorted, OK? Go on now, get to class."

Thiago looked like he was about to continue talking, so Omen guided him away from the lockers and let the stream of students snatch him. He took out his books and closed the locker as the bell rang. He turned to go and Never was standing there.

"Is Auger OK?" they asked. "It's just he's being very quiet lately. Like, *really* quiet. Do you know if he's OK? Have you spoken to him?"

"I speak to him all the time," Omen said, starting to walk.

"But have you spoken to him about why he's so quiet?"

"If he needs to tell me something, he'll tell me."

Never arched an eyebrow. "Yes, because that works in every single case of someone needing to talk about something difficult. He hasn't been the same since the King of the Darklands."

"Would you expect him to be?"

"No," said Never, "but that's not the point, is it?"

They took Omen's arm and stopped him. The corridor was almost empty now. "Auger killed someone. It doesn't matter if the guy he killed was a murderer who would have gone on to kill, like, everyone in the world. Auger still used that Obsidian Blade thing and wiped him from existence. He killed him in a way no one has ever been killed before. Auger's traumatised."

"He talked to a therapist about it."

Never sneered. "A school-appointed therapist, Omen. Barely

more than a guidance counsellor. If I were him, I'd be suing the school for letting it happen in the first place, and I'd be suing the High Sanctuary, and I'd be seeking compensation from Roarhaven and every damn magical community around the world."

Omen frowned. "I've never heard of sorcerers suing each other. I don't think it's a thing."

"It should be," Never responded. "You know the real problem? The real problem with this magical society of ours is that it's so small and so secretive that no one's ever really held accountable."

"OK."

"What happens when a mortal politician does something bad? They're fired because they broke the rules or they quit because they're shamed into it."

"Unless you're Martin Flanery," said Omen, smirking. "Or Donald Trump. Or that other guy."

Never ignored him. "Convention, Omen. I personally despise the notion in general, but it does have its uses, and one of the main ones is to keep a check on the people in power. We don't have that. Until a few years ago, we didn't even have a Supreme Mage. Grand Mages used to have to answer to other Grand Mages. But who does Creed answer to?"

"Mrs Creed?"

"He's not married."

"Oh. Then... probably nobody."

"Nobody," Never said, nodding. "Exactly."

"Sorry, but what does this have to do with Auger?"

"Not a whole lot. I got sidetracked."

Omen looked around. Apart from them, the corridor was empty. "We really have to get to class, Never."

"And you've got to talk to your brother," Never said. "I get that you've always seen him as this indestructible force for good, but what are you gonna do now that he's been revealed as human, eh? You think about that, Omen. You think about that."

14

And then Never teleported to class, and Omen was left standing in the middle of the corridor.

Peccant appeared beside him. "Mr Darkly," he said gruffly.

"Mr Peccant."

"You're late for class, Mr Darkly," Peccant said, walking away. "Detention."

Omen sagged.

# 3

The sound of his own breathing was starting to get to him again.

Every few months, he'd notice it, notice the way it rasped in his ears, amplified by the mask. The mask. The bloody mask. God, how he yearned to rip it off his head, to grab that ridiculous beak and just pull it all away and feel fresh air on his skin. How he yearned to scratch an itch through the suit, to rub his eyes when they were tired, to rake his fingernails across his scalp.

This feeling of intense irritation would last a few days during which his temper would grow short and his replies turn snippy. But he'd emerge, as always, with a resounding, if weary, sense of resignation. This was the mission he'd signed up for, after all. This was the cost.

But lately – as in the last three months – there'd been an entirely new reason for this dissatisfaction. He hadn't been able to show his practically-adopted daughter his smile.

He looked round. Where *was* his practically-adopted daughter?

Sebastian put down the book he'd been failing to read and went looking for her. "Darquesse?" he called. "Sweetie?"

He found her in the kitchen. Little Darquesse, the kid who'd aged two years in her first two months, and then doubled that in the third month, sitting on the floor, covered in flour.

He didn't even know he had any flour. He certainly hadn't bought any. Despite the fact that he didn't have to – and couldn't

– eat with this damn suit on, the others in the Darquesse Society had made sure the kitchen was fully stocked at all times with every conceivable foodstuff. Not that he ever got a chance to make anything. Every day, Bennet or Lily or Ulysses or Demure would pop over with home-made meals for their adorable little black-haired god. Sebastian barely had to lift a finger any more, now that the few weeks of bottle-feeding were behind them.

All in all, this unexpected bout of fatherhood hadn't been that bad since the Darquesse Society had been by his side the entire time. Along with the food preparation, Forby had hooked up the entire house with baby monitors and nanny cams, and Tarry and Kimora were taking care of babysitting duties whenever Sebastian needed a break.

And then there was Darquesse herself. He'd been there when she'd been born, had watched the pregnant Darquesse melt into and become her own daughter. The newborn had wailed and cried for a bit, but, by the time the Darquesse Society had rushed over, she was asleep in Sebastian's arms. They'd cooed and oohed, cleaned her up, dressed her, and then they'd all just stared at her. It was weird. Sweet, but weird.

By her second month, Darquesse was already walking. Two weeks after that, she was flying. Her first words were, 'The world is a vampire.' Sebastian didn't know what the hell that meant until Bennet told him it was the first line in a Smashing Pumpkins song. Most of her early proclamations were lines from songs, actually: lots of Muse in there, Nirvana, Guns N' Roses, little bit of Britney. Ulysses had a theory that these were all memories inherited from her motherself – phrases that were simply the first to rise to the surface in the vast ocean that was Darquesse's mind.

And it was a vast ocean. Before she'd given birth, Darquesse had sent out tens of thousands – perhaps hundreds of thousands, perhaps millions – of versions of herself to scour the universe, collecting information. To what end, Sebastian didn't know. But it was all locked inside the head of this blinking, flour-headed child.

He scooped her up. "You," he said, "are a mess."

Darquesse giggled.

# 4

Valkyrie moved round in a crouch, arms crossed over her chest, her steps small but quick and her eyes locked on to her little sister's. She settled and flung her hands up to either side and Alice darted in, jabbed once with her left, threw a right and then ducked a swipe and popped up to deliver three alternating upper-cuts, finishing the sequence with an elbow shot before bouncing away.

"Good," Valkyrie said, crossing her arms again, turning the pads on her hands inwards as she circled. Alice circled the oppo-site way, her gloved hands up, her elbows tucked in tight, her face flushed and her blonde hair falling out of its ponytail.

Settling again, Valkyrie presented the pads and Alice took a slight step to readjust and then repeated the sequence, her grin widening. The elbow shot came in and Valkyrie brought her hands back into her chest and straightened up, echoing the grin.

"Nice," she said. "Gloves off."

They did some stretching to cool down, then hung the gloves and the pads from the hooks on the garage wall. Valkyrie broke down the interlocking gym mats as Alice demonstrated her latest dance moves – a creature of boundless and unrelenting energy. They stored the large squares out of the way and passed into the house. Alice ran up the stairs and Valkyrie went into the kitchen.

"How'd she do?" their father asked from underneath the sink.

"Brilliant as always and getting even better," said Valkyrie, grabbing her water bottle from the fridge. "Need any help down there?"

"I've got it handled," Desmond replied, straining slightly. There was a clatter of wrench against pipe and a hiss of pain. "Ow."

Valkyrie took a swig. "They have professionals for this kind of thing, you know."

"I can fix a sink, Steph. You might have saved the world a bunch of times and your sister might be an aspiring ninja, but I have yet to meet a sink I couldn't beat. Could you hand me the next wrench up?"

Valkyrie took the wrench from his outstretched hand and found the next biggest in the toolbox on the table. She passed it to him.

"So have you saved the world recently?" he asked amid more clanging.

"Not for ages," she replied.

"What was that thing last week that your mum was telling me about? That sounded fairly serious."

Valkyrie shrugged. "It got serious, yeah, but not end-of-the-world serious. Just some psycho who'd killed a few sorcerers."

"Did you catch him?"

"We did."

"Is he in that floating prison?"

"Naw. Coldheart is being fitted with extra fail-safes to make sure it's never hijacked again, so it's still out of action. He was sent to Ironpoint. It's not any nicer."

Her dad gave a few small grunts of effort, then wriggled out from beneath the sink. He held his hands up and Valkyrie pulled him to his feet.

"Right then," he said, and turned on the tap. It rattled for a moment, and then water blasted out. "Success," he said, turning it off. "You see, daughter? I, too, have my uses."

"I never doubted it."

He turned as Alice came in. "Ah, the ninja returns. How was the training today, Little Dragon?"

"It was fun," Alice said brightly. "I did really well, I think. Stephanie, did I do well?"

"You did brilliantly."

Alice grinned and shrugged, trying her best to be modest. "Dad, when's Mom back? I have to go to dance class at quarter to three."

"She'll be back in time – don't worry. And, if she isn't, I can take you."

Alice lost her grin. "No, Dad. We're always late when you take me. Mom's on time for things. You always say we'll leave and then you go to the toilet and you take forever, and I hate walking in late, I feel so stupid, I feel like everyone's looking at me and... and..."

Tears welled up and Desmond hurried over, dropping to his knees and holding her shoulders. "Hey. Hey there. Look at me, sweetheart. Look at me. Good girl. You won't be late. Do you know why? Because your mother will be back."

"But what if she isn't?"

"Then I'll take you," said Valkyrie.

Those big eyes widened. "On your motorbike?"

Valkyrie laughed. "No, not on the bike. I'll take Dad's car. You won't be late, OK? Trust me."

Alice nodded, and wiped her eyes. "OK."

"By the way," said Desmond, "I am deeply offended that nobody trusts me to be on time for anything. I am on time for loads of things, but all anyone remembers is when I'm late, or I forget, or I've got the wrong day. I have a lot of stuff on my mind, you know. I happen to run my own business. I have employees to worry about. There's this weird cat that stares at me every time I leave the house. So I apologise if, occasionally, I'm late for something – but life gets in the way."

"Can I go now?" Alice asked.

Desmond sighed. "Sure." He stood, watching her as she wandered out of the room. After a moment, he looked at Valkyrie. "That was a close one. I mean, she's getting better all the time. The – whatever we're calling them – dark periods are getting further and further apart. But anything can set her off."

"You handled it really well," said Valkyrie, struggling to keep her voice even.

"That was an easy one. She's still buzzing from training with you, and she's got her dance class to look forward to. It's harder at the end of the day, when she's tired. But, you know, we're doing what the psychologist told us to do. We're reinforcing her, we're getting her to talk about how she's feeling... I just wish we knew what caused all this. If we did, if she'd tell us that..."

He trailed off.

"You're doing what you can," Valkyrie said.

"Yes, we are," said Desmond. "And you're helping enormously, by the way. She loves her big sister training her to defend herself. All this positivity is just what she needs."

Valkyrie nodded.

Her dad started packing away his tools. "I wonder if it's got anything to do with the magic side of things."

Valkyrie froze.

"You're the expert," he said. "Could it have? My grandfather had pretty drastic mood swings, and Gordon could be a moody so-and-so when he wanted to be – although that was always put down to an *artistic temperament*. Fergus is a permanent grouch, as you well know. Do you think the fact that we're descended from that Last of the Ancients guy means we're prone to this kind of behaviour? What about you? Have you ever experienced it?"

He looked at her, as if he needed to see how she'd react.

"I'm bright as a summer's day," she lied.

He smiled. "Yes, you are. So how about the rest of us? Do you think we're cursed to have these dark periods?"

She frowned. "Do you have them?"

He shrugged. "We all have moments where we're less than cheerful." He closed the toolbox. "Or has the magic got nothing to do with it at all? Am I blaming the Last of the Ancients for something that's really not his fault?"

If Valkyrie had been waiting for the perfect moment to tell him the truth, this was it. If she'd been waiting for an ideal opportunity to inform him that the Edgleys weren't descended from the Last of the Ancients, that they, in fact, had the blood of the Faceless Ones running through their veins instead, then her time had come. But she hadn't been waiting for such a moment. She had no intention of ever telling her family that they were descended from the bad guys, not the heroes.

So she said, "I really don't know," and her dad shrugged and carried his toolbox out to the garage.

She got home, and the vast emptiness of Grimwood House was shattered by the German shepherd sprinting towards her even as she shut the door. Valkyrie dropped to her knees and cuddled the dog, then rolled on the floor, Xena licking her face and neck, scrambling round her.

She had something to eat, sat on the couch with the TV muted, talking to Militsa on the phone, and then went to bed, Xena curled up by her knees.

# 5

Six years ago...

Twenty minutes' driving with the radio on – that's as much as he could take. It was better than last week, and he planned to be better again the following week. The radio interfered with his mind. Music stirred feelings, and he wasn't used to those. Talk radio drew his thoughts from hiding, and he wasn't used to that, either. Coda Quell was used to quiet. Talk radio had angry people, voices cracking over the airwaves. He couldn't understand angry people. He couldn't understand people, mortal or sorcerer, for that matter. They were all just bundles of contradictory emotions he struggled to comprehend.

He clicked the radio off and relaxed to the soothing hum of his truck's engine and the rumble of tyres on a dirt road.

One bit at a time, that's what they told him when he left. Rejoin the world one bit at a time.

Rejoin. He could have told them there and then that it was the wrong word to use. How do you rejoin something you barely have any memory of leaving? But he didn't tell them that, and he didn't ask that question. Because Cleavers don't ask questions.

But he wasn't a Cleaver any more. The Way of the Scythe was his way no longer. People called his kind something different now. He was a Ripper. That's the word they used. It didn't bother him because nothing bothered him. He'd had that trained out of him since he was nine years old. They called his kind Rippers and meant it as an insult. It was an attack made from a position of weakness, and it denoted fear. They were scared of people like him. They thought Cleavers should be Cleavers forever. They didn't like the idea of Cleavers hanging up the grey and walking among them.

Quell didn't understand things like fear any more. This was something else he would have to relearn.

He slowed the truck at the gate, and got out. He'd never been to Colorado before. He liked the air. It was crisp. Clean.

On the other side of the gate a jeep was parked. Its back door was open. There were fence posts inside.

A young woman appeared, came down a steep bank, leaving clouds of dust in her wake. Her dark hair was tied back into a ponytail. Her jeans were dirty and her boots were scuffed and her T-shirt was faded. Her arms were strong. She had a hammer tucked into her belt and she was carrying a broken post.

She looked at Quell, but didn't say anything. She threw the broken post into the back of the jeep, then took a bottle of water from a bag she had hidden there and took a long, long drink. She returned the bottle to the bag, added the hammer, and came up to the gate.

"You're on time," she said. "Is that the kind of person you are? You on time for stuff?"

"Yes," said Quell.

"You're a Ripper, then."

It wasn't a question so he didn't answer.

"I want training," she said. "I want the kind of training you had. Is that possible?"

"No."

"But you'll train me hard? You'll push me?"

"Yes."

"What's your name?"

"Coda Quell."

She nodded. "I'm Valkyrie," she said. "Valkyrie Cain."

# 6

She woke without opening her eyes, aware of the dog on the bed with her. Valkyrie lay like an inverted question mark, her legs hooking round Xena's curled-up form. She reached down, felt fur, gave it a scratch, and then Xena was standing over her and slobbering on to her face.

Valkyrie laughed as the big, wet tongue left a trail of saliva across her cheek, but she could only manage a few seconds of neck-licking before she had to sit up, grab the dog, and pull her down with her. Xena's tail thumped madly. That tongue lolled out of her grinning mouth.

"Such a goof," Valkyrie said to her, and Xena didn't deny it.

She filled Xena's food bowl, ate breakfast, showered, and left Xena in the huge dog run she'd built out behind the house. Then she pulled on her helmet and took the bike to Roarhaven. Militsa was waiting for her at a table outside the café she liked in the Arts District. They kissed and Valkyrie put her helmet on one of the empty chairs.

Militsa had a coffee in front of her. Her eyes widened. "I didn't order you one!"

Valkyrie smiled. "Then it's a good thing I'm a big girl and I can do things for myself." She caught the server's eye and asked for a black coffee.

"I always order you one whenever you're late," Militsa said.

"My head's just not in it today, it really isn't." She nodded to the cup in front of her. "See that? I wanted to order a macchiato, and didn't realise until after I'd paid that I'd ordered an Americano. I mean, I could have told the barista I'd made a mistake, but he looked so happy making the Americano, and I didn't want to spoil that."

"You're a complicated lady," said Valkyrie. "Busy day at work?"

"Not especially," Militsa said. "I had a class first thing, but I don't have another one till after lunch. Are you going to be watching Creed's speech?"

"I'm going to be more than watching it – Skulduggery and I are going to be there. Part of our duties as Arbiters includes providing security for the big boss – something Skulduggery neglected to mention when he invited me back. So we're gonna see it live, baby."

"You are so lucky."

"I know, right? So what has you so distracted? Necromancer stuff? I heard you on the phone yesterday talking about your old friends leaving, or something like that? I didn't mean to eavesdrop, but you were literally right beside me."

Militsa smiled. "No, no, it's not that. I mean, yes, there have been a few Necromancers leaving the Order, but I wouldn't have called them friends, exactly."

"Why are they leaving?"

"Not sure, to be honest. I haven't been inside a temple in years and I was never really into the quasi-religious aspect of Necromancy, but apparently there's been quite a radical shift in direction lately."

"Is that a bad thing?" Valkyrie asked. "Until a few years ago, the Order's teachings meant it advocated killing half the world's population."

Militsa raised an eyebrow. "Only a few years ago, was it? Val, that was *ten* years ago."

"It wasn't *that* far back," Valkyrie said. "All that Death Bringer

28

stuff, Melancholia, Lord Vile returning, the whole... Oh my God, it was. It's been ten years. I've faced some scary killers and monsters in my time, but *that* is truly terrifying. I'm getting old." A few seconds ticked by. "OK, that was your cue."

Militsa blinked. "Sorry? What was?"

"Your cue to tell me I'm not getting old."

"Well, of course you're not getting old. You're going to stay young for, literally, hundreds of years, same as me. We can stay young together, forever. It'll be dead romantic."

Valkyrie's coffee arrived. She smiled at the server and thanked her and took a sip as the girl moved off.

"Flirt," Militsa said.

"Always," Valkyrie responded. "So, if it's not the Necromancers that have you distracted, what is it?"

"I've been offered a job."

"You have a job."

"I've been offered another job."

"As a teacher?"

Militsa tucked her hair behind her ear. "Research," she said. "They want me to be part of a team."

"Researching what?"

"Magic."

"OK, well... you'd love that, so what's the catch? And who's 'they'?"

"The High Sanctuary."

Valkyrie soured. "Creed?"

"The High Sanctuary isn't just Damocles Creed. There are over two dozen different departments, all with their own heads, all with their own teams... Did you know there's an entire department dedicated to repairing the Sceptre of the Ancients after Mevolent snapped it in half?"

"Good luck with that," Valkyrie grunted.

"Yeah, anyway... they want me to be part of a team helping to research the Source."

"The Source of all magic? That Source? And what did you say?"

"I said I had to think about it."

"Right..."

"You obviously don't think I should do it."

"It doesn't matter what I think."

"Of course it does."

Valkyrie did her best to remain quiet.

"So?" Militsa pressed. "What's your opinion? You're going to blurt it out anyway over the next few days, so you may as well get it—"

The words spilled out of Valkyrie's mouth. "Creed wants to widen the Source in order to make sorcerers stronger so that, if we ever do go to war with the mortals, we'll slaughter them more efficiently."

"It's research," Militsa countered. "Important research."

"That Creed's going to use for his own ends. How can you not see what a bad idea this is?"

"This is what I've wanted since I was fifteen years old."

"That doesn't mean it'll be used responsibly. The kind of people I have to take down every day are powerful enough already. They don't need to be able to destroy more buildings or kill more innocents. They're doing fine with that as it is."

Militsa shook her head. "I knew you'd react this way."

"I'm sorry."

"Whatever," Militsa said, and glanced at her phone. "I have to get back to the school."

"Are you mad at me?"

Militsa picked up her bag and stood. "Yes," she said. "But only because you make sense. Love you."

"Love you, too," Valkyrie said, and Militsa walked off.

Valkyrie finished her coffee and rode to the High Sanctuary. A sizeable crowd had already gathered for Creed's speech, filling the Circle. City Guard officers had to clear a path for Valkyrie to get to the underground car park. She parked beside the Bentley.

Skulduggery stood watching as she turned off the engine and leaned the bike into the kickstand, swung her leg off and removed her helmet. She frowned at him as she hung the helmet off the handlebar.

"There's something different about you," she said finally. "Have you done something to your... head?"

He didn't respond.

She peered closer. "Oh my God. You have. That isn't your skull. The cheekbones are lower. The jaw is narrower. The eye sockets are rounder."

"The eye sockets are the same," he said, walking away, "more or less. But you're right – this is one of my spares. I'm in the process of polishing and strengthening my own skull, so I'll be wearing this one for a couple of weeks."

Valkyrie fell into step beside him. "You polish your skull?"

"Every few years, yes – though this is the first time you've noticed. First I soak it for eight days in a special solution to rein-force its density and to prevent any unsightly fractures from appearing. I do this for every part of me, actually, as it also serves to add significant weight to my body."

"So you have heavy bones?"

"Quite heavy, yes. For bones, I mean. The weight gives me a greater purchase in physical struggles and adds to my strength. Once the eight days are up and the skull has been dried, I go over it with a range of sanding sponges, in gradients from fine to microfine. Without getting too technical about it—"

"Too late."

"—I soak it again, leave it for twenty-seven hours, then go to work with a rotary tool fitted with a seven-eighths-of-an-inch muslin buff and a fine compound."

They stepped on to a pair of tiles that rose into the air and took them, spinning slowly, up to the High Sanctuary. The moment they stepped off, into the large marble foyer, Skulduggery continued.

"I soak it for a third time for three days exactly, not one minute longer, though this is more of a tradition than an absolute necessity. I'm sure, if one were so predisposed, the skull could be soaked for a few minutes under three days exactly, or a few minutes over – but what would be the point of going to all that trouble if you were prepared to embrace lackadaisicality at the very last moment?"

Valkyrie waited a moment before responding. "Are you done? I didn't want to interrupt in case there was more to that incredibly useless slab of information you just whacked down in front of me."

"You were curious."

"Wasn't that curious."

"Even so – now you know what I do when it's time to ensure my head remains in tip-top condition."

Valkyrie took the black skull amulet from her jeans and pressed it to her chest, then tapped it. She caught her reflection in one of the large mirrors as the necronaut suit flowed over her clothes. A different design each time it came out, dependent on her requirements, today it looked almost military-officer smart: perfect for public engagements.

They left the High Sanctuary through one of the side exits, stepping out on to the wing of the temporary stage that had been erected. The City Guard were handling crowd control while the Cleavers stood watch. Valkyrie had preferred it when Cleavers took the lead in things like this. They may have been scary killing machines, but they were *incorruptible* scary killing machines. The City Guard, on the other hand, were made up of people who were growing to love the power their uniforms afforded them.

But there wasn't much alternative to the current situation. The Cleavers' numbers had been steadily whittled down for years, seeing as how they'd been used – on occasion – as little more than cannon fodder, instead of the highly trained combatants they were. Maybe it had something to do with the visored helmets they wore. It was easier to disregard someone's humanity when you let yourself forget they had a face.

As Valkyrie watched, the Cleavers stiffened slightly, moving from standing at attention to standing at even-more attention, if such a thing was even possible, and a moment later the doors swung open and Damocles Creed walked on to the stage.

# 7

The crowd reacted like he was part rock star, part TV evangelist. They screamed, they hollered, they whistled, and when they'd run out of screams and hollers and whistles they started the chants and the slogans and the cheers, and once they'd exhausted those they went back to screaming and hollering and whistling.

The acting Supreme Mage stood there like a big, bald monolith, barely smiling. He wasn't so much soaking it all in as merely waiting for it to stop. That was something else his followers loved about him – his pragmatism. His indifference to being adored.

He hadn't even dressed up for the occasion. His massive frame was covered in a simple robe, frayed and faded. Poking out at the bottom was a pair of work boots.

When the applause finally died down, he stepped up to the microphone.

"I look out and I recognise a lot of faces," he said. "I see these faces every week – I see some of them every day – in the Cathedral. You pray with me. I appreciate that. I truly do. And I also see a lot of faces I don't know. This warms my heart. To know that our message is reaching you, to know that it's spreading, is a beautiful thing."

A fresh round of cheers and applause that he didn't let go on for too long before holding up a hand for quiet. "We live in an astonishing city. The First City of Magic, that's what they're calling it. Look around. See the person next to you? That's a mage. See the person on the other side of the street? That's a mage, too. In fact, the only people in this city who aren't mages are the ones doing the washing-up."

Laughter tore through the crowd like that was the funniest goddamn thing they'd ever heard. Creed held up a hand again.

"Was that cruel?" he asked. "Was that a cruel thing for me to say? We all know people, don't we, who insist we not be cruel to the mortals? To them, I apologise."

Someone shouted something. More people laughed.

"But even our well-meaning friends have got to admit... it's nice to be part of a city of mages. To live and work beside each other, not to be worried about hiding who we are from the stumbling, mumbling mortals. Young people, those fine young mages of Corrival Academy, they can barely remember what it was like to live like that. But I remember. Do you?"

Shouts. Roars. They remembered.

"Yes," he said, "exactly. If we were lucky, we had our communities. We had our neighbourhoods. Now? Now we have an entire city, and what a city it is. A place of beauty and wonder and, yes, magic. What's next for us? A country? A continent? A world? A world of mages... can you imagine it? Can you imagine the freedom?"

The crowd imagined it. They howled their approval.

Creed nodded. "And how did we get here, my friends? Did we get here by being meek, and quiet? Did we get here by slinking around in the shadows, fearful of the footfall of mortal man? Did we get here by talking in whispers so that mortal woman wouldn't overhear – wouldn't find out our secrets? Or did we get here by being strong, by demonstrating strength? By being fearless? By dominating?"

Oh, the crowd liked that. They liked that an awful lot.

Creed leaned on the podium as if he was leaning on a bar. "Do you know what I think? I think domination is the way to go. I do. I know how bad that sounds. You hear the word 'dominate' and you think oppression, don't you? And I'm with you. Oppression is what we want to avoid. Who knows oppression better than us, who have lived until now in a world dominated by petty mortals? But domination, if applied correctly, can be a positive force in the universe. I think we march forward from this day on, and we dominate. We have a street in some far-off mortal city? We take the neighbourhood. We have a neighbourhood? We take the city. We have the city? We take the country. Why not? Who's going to stop us? Mortals?"

They laughed. He nodded.

"You understand. You get it. I knew you would, quite honestly. You're smart people. You're aware of the world around you. You can see the way things are going. You can see the situation evolving right before your eyes. And I'm saying this not only as Arch-Canon of the Church of the Faceless, but also in my role as acting Supreme Mage of the High Sanctuary. We've done a good job, we sorcerers. We've protected the mortals and we've allowed them to thrive. It has been, let's say, an interesting experiment." More laughter. "But I think the experiment is coming to an end, if you want my honest opinion. We've given them chance after chance, opportunity after opportunity, and each and every time they have squandered that chance and wasted that opportunity. I know that a lot of us here view the mortals with huge and genuine affection. Some of them are our friends. Our family. But their short lives make them entirely unsuited to running things. If you can only expect to live for eighty or ninety years, where's your motivation to make the world a better place? But if you live five hundred years – if you live a thousand years – you're going to want to ensure that your home stays in the best possible condition."

He paused, then shrugged. "I don't know. I might be wrong. Am I wrong? I might be wrong. You'll notice that I'm not reading from a carefully worded speech." He nodded as they laughed.

"This isn't like my sermons. I'm not up here to impart unto you a grand lesson or an important moral. I'm just me, standing in front of a group of like-minded people, thinking out loud. Maybe this is the way forward, maybe it isn't. But, if it is, we've really got to lead by example, don't you think? If we want to change the world, that change starts right here – in our streets, in our homes, in our hearts. I reckon that sacrifices need to be made, and I reckon we're the ones to do it. Who else is strong enough? Who else is tough enough? This is Roarhaven! These walls held back ten thousand Warlocks and Wretchlings. These people, the City Guard, the Cleavers, they defeated both an invading army from another dimension *and* a horde of draugar. There's tough, and then there's Roarhaven tough."

Cheers. Fists pumping the air.

"So we lead by example," said Creed. "To instil discipline, we demonstrate discipline, which means we're going to be introducing a curfew. Only those with special dispensation will be allowed out on the streets of the city past nine o'clock. We already have a list of people who *do* need to be out beyond this time for work, but if you think you also qualify, and you do not receive your pass in the next two days, we'll have a Community Liaison Officer available to process your application. Bear in mind, however, that time-wasters will not be tolerated. If you apply and are found wanting, you'll be fined or jailed or both, depending on the egregiousness of your error. The curfew comes into effect tonight."

No cheers to that announcement. Some rumblings, though, mutterings of dissatisfaction that dried up when Creed cast his eye in that direction.

"The curfew is part one of our Three-part Plan," Creed continued. "The second part is in response to the – frankly alarming – lack of a faith-based culture in Roarhaven. Attendance in the Cathedral has never been higher, and for that I applaud you. But there are still so many of this city's citizens who appear reluctant to set foot inside. Turn your heads, my friends, and gaze upon the Dark Cathedral. Yes, it's imposing. Yes, it strikes fear into the hearts of the unworthy. Yes, even its name is intimidating. But it merely does its best to reflect the awe-inspiring power of the Faceless Ones themselves. If you can't bring yourself to enter a place of worship, how will you cope when the Faceless Ones make their inevitable return to this reality, and take up their rightful place as our lords and masters? We must demonstrate our worthiness. We must convince them of our love.

"To that end, we are opening nine churches around Roarhaven. All the construction that's been going on in your sectors? Churches. Opening today. The worship of all other deities, as of this moment, is against the law. Attendance is mandatory – at least twice a week. Be assured, we will be taking note of who attends and who doesn't, and also I will personally shake the hand and bestow the blessings of the Faceless Ones on anyone who comes forward – bravely but in confidence – to tell me the names of family members or neighbours or workmates who do not comply with this order. We're all in this together, my friends. Each one of us is a brick in a great wall."

The crowd applauded – some more enthusiastically than others.

"And the third part of our plan is an unfortunate necessity. This is the part I never wanted to introduce, but I think you'll agree that I have little choice. You are good people, honest people, worthy people, and I know you won't let me down. But there are others in this city who do not share these qualities. Let's be honest – these people are dangerous. Not only to others, but also to themselves. They don't know the damage they're doing to their very souls. The Faceless Ones will change everything, and those who love them will be carried gently into the new world. Those who don't will suffer, right alongside the billions of mortals. They will try to sow discord among you. They will use tricks and subterfuge to confuse you and turn you from the righteous path. They will lie to you and tempt you with promises of an easy life.

But life is hard, and it's meant to be hard, because this is the part where we prove ourselves to the Dark Gods.

"The third part of this plan will see specially selected Sensitives patrolling the streets, actively scanning for subversion. I know that this is asking a lot of you. I know that it could be seen as an intrusion. The dangerous ones out there – the dissidents, the subversives – they'll try to convince you that you're losing something if you allow this. More lies, my friends. If you are worthy, if you are good and decent, you have nothing to fear. This will scare the subversives. They'll build up walls round their minds, thinking they'll evade judgement – but these Sense Wardens have been trained to detect just that, and so any attempt to hide their thoughts will simply draw more attention to them. If you want my advice, my brothers and sisters, you won't try to hide your thoughts. Things will be easier if you comply."

Skulduggery turned his head to Valkyrie, and she raised an eyebrow.

# 8

When the speech was over and Creed had returned to the High Sanctuary, Skulduggery lifted off the stage with his hands in his pockets and flew to the rooftop of the building across the wide street. Valkyrie flew alongside him, leaving a trail of crackling energy in her wake. Flying was still something of a rare ability, and one that was regarded with equal parts envy and bitterness, so not all of the comments shouted up after them were complimentary.

They landed on the roof and looked at each other.

"That was cheerful," she said. "Bright and optimistic. I'm enthused about the future, I tell you. Enthused."

Skulduggery looked over at the High Sanctuary. "Creed's planning something."

"I didn't think it'd be possible for him to assert any more control than he already has." She shook her head. "That'll teach me to underestimate him. A curfew, mandatory worship, and thought police. I'd say it couldn't get any worse, but I hate to make the same mistake twice. I don't suppose we can count on China Sorrows waking up from her coma anytime soon and taking her job back, can we?"

"Not as far as I'm aware," Skulduggery said quietly. "This won't go down well."

"With who, the citizens of this fine city? They seemed to be pretty OK with most of it."

"The people in that audience were followers of the Faceless Ones and Creed fanatics," Skulduggery said, looking down at the crowd as it started to disperse. "They don't represent the majority of mages in Roarhaven."

"Think there'll be protests?"

"I do."

"We have to do something. I mean, we have to, right? We can't just let... *this* happen. We have to do something about Creed."

"I agree," Skulduggery said.

"He's where all our problems stem from. I've been thinking a lot lately about the vision I had."

"The one where everyone's dead or the one where Alice is the Child of the Faceless Ones?"

"The Alice one. The vision where everyone's dead has already changed so much, but I haven't had a repeat of the Alice one so, for all I know, that hasn't changed at all."

Skulduggery shrugged. "Alternatively, it may have changed so completely that it simply doesn't happen any more, which is why you're not seeing any reruns."

"I don't want to take that chance, though." Valkyrie tucked her hair behind her ears while she gathered the words she needed. "OK, so... the dilemma. The dilemma is, when Alice is sixteen, she's the Child of the Faceless, and she's going off to fight her arch-enemy, the Child of the Ancients, to decide the fate of the world. So she is, essentially, the bad guy in this scenario. And we still have no idea who the Child of the Ancients is, do we?"

"We do not," Skulduggery replied. "I haven't been able to find any reference to such a person in the usual literature."

"Have you checked for any prophecies?"

"I've checked, and there haven't been any. Keep in mind, however, that Sensitives only started seeing Darquesse in their visions a few years before she – or you – turned up so there's still time for them to tune in to this particular channel."

"But we can safely assume that, whoever the Child of the Ancients is, they're the good guy," Valkyrie said.

"I think we can."

"So my little sister is going to grow up to be the villain and, for whatever reason, I'm not around. In fact, I'm probably dead."

"We don't know that."

"In the vision, she said she missed me, and seemed really sad. That sounds pretty terminal to me."

"I wish I could tell you to put it out of your mind..."

Valkyrie dismissed it with a shake of her head. "Hey, don't worry about me. I went through a few years of being miserable, a few years where I figured I deserved to die. I have since changed my mind."

"I'm glad."

"Me too. I still have my dark moments and sometimes getting out of bed in the morning is a struggle, but on the whole I'm embracing every moment in every day."

Skulduggery adjusted his cufflinks. "The problem, as we've established, seems to be Damocles Creed. He's the one who's been searching for the Child of the Faceless Ones for the last two hundred years. He's the one with a basement full of failed experiments staring into space."

"Maybe we can use that. If we show people the thousands of Kith he's got hidden away, that might compel the other Sanctuaries to demand that he step down. You know what we need to do? We need to talk to someone who's seen what goes on in those basements of his."

"Temper Fray has seen it all."

"You know how to find him?"

"Yes," said Skulduggery, and pointed behind them. "He's over there somewhere."

Valkyrie frowned. "He's back in Roarhaven? I thought he left forever with his hot ninja girlfriend."

"He came back. Kierre of the Unveiled didn't."

"They broke up?"

"I don't know. I'll ask him to take us through what an Activation looks like, and while we're talking you can pry into his personal life all you like."

"Cool."

"But I don't know if that idea would even work. Even if we exposed what Creed's been doing, even if we show the Kith and we get Temper to explain exactly what went on, Creed – and, before him, China – has filled the top spots of practically every Sanctuary around the world with his own hand-picked Grand Mages. They're already massively unpopular with the sorcerers they govern, so sticking by the Supreme Mage won't exactly do them any harm. And there's always the risk that, by forcing Creed's hand, he accelerates towards his final objective before we can work out what it is and how to stop it. Whatever we do, we have to proceed with caution."

"OK," said Valkyrie. "So what's your plan?"

"We assassinate him."

She didn't respond for a few seconds. "You're serious."

"Yes."

"This is your idea of proceeding with caution? You want to murder the Supreme Mage?"

"I preferred *assassinate*, to be honest. It's the order China gave us, after all, when she sent us to take down Mevolent."

"Just because the previous Supreme Mage has already ordered an assassination doesn't make it OK to assassinate the current one. Is that how we deal with obstacles these days? We have an enemy and we just kill them because it's easiest?"

"I'm quite prepared to kill one person if it saves the lives of two others."

"It all depends on the life, though, doesn't it? And what does that mean? Are we going to set ourselves up to judge who deserves to live and die? I don't know about this, Skulduggery. It's a slippery

43

slope. If someone objects to our way of doing things, do we kill them, too? When do we stop?"

"We stop when Creed is dead."

She shook her head. "This is wrong. We're the good guys."

"That's exactly right. We are the good guys. That means we make the hard choices in order to protect everyone else. It's the only way to prevent your sister from becoming the Child of the Faceless Ones."

Valkyrie covered her face with her hands and thought it through.

"OK," she said, looking up, "I need to talk to Alice. Future-Alice. If I spoke to her once, I can do it again, right? There's a psychic link there so I'll figure out how to open it and she can answer my questions. If it turns out that Creed *is* the key to all this, then... then yes."

"Yes to the assassination?"

"But we'll have to be absolutely sure there's no other way."

Skulduggery nodded. "You'll need some guidance to open that psychic link."

"I'm assuming you know of someone who can help?"

His head tilted. "Naturally."

# 9

The look on this guy's face. Eyes down, probably wishing he'd turned back when he'd first seen them. His instincts had screamed at him, of course they had, but he'd kept walking because to stop was to arouse suspicion. He was hoping he'd be able to pass by quietly.

But the cops, they'd been given all this extra power and it was filling them up from the inside. It was making their muscles bigger and their chests puff out; it was lifting their chins and curling their lips. It was a power that made them swagger, made them glower, made them sneer and glare and made them tower. It was a tower power. A glower tower power. And they were filled with it.

First they slowed down and this guy, whoever he was, pretended he didn't notice and just kept putting one foot in front of the other. Then all of a sudden there was one of them in front of him and another behind and another to the side, and his back was brushing the wall and he was feeling very closed in, very pinned, very trapped.

The cops uttered a few words, each of them having a go, forcing this guy, whoever he was, to keep turning so he could answer, so he could look them in the eyes and smile and be cool and demonstrate that he'd got nothing to hide. He showed them some identification and one of the cops snatched the wallet from his hand, started poking through it, and this guy, he nodded and smiled because that's fine, that's perfectly fine, the officer was perfectly entitled to do that, even though he wasn't, not in the slightest, not even a little.

The cop with the wallet, he put that wallet away while his buddies laid hands on this guy, the scared guy, the scared guy who just wanted to get home. They put hands on him and turned him and smacked the wall with his chest and held him there as they twisted his arms and put shackles on his wrists. One of the other cops – his name was Mandrake, like the magician – reached for his radio to call it in, to get someone over here to take this guy to jail.

Temper Fray pulled the mask over his head, stepped from the doorway and walked quickly across the street. People saw him and looked away, turned away, hurried away. The cops didn't see him. Not until he'd swung that shock stick into the first cop's neck.

Oh, how he went down. He jerked to the side and collapsed like a bag of broken sticks. The next cop, the one who'd taken the wallet, he went to throw some energy and Temper broke his wrist with the lightest of light taps and the wallet-cop howled like a howler monkey and clutched his arm and bent his knees, but didn't move back for some reason. Maybe he wanted to get hit again. Temper obliged, and this time the shock stick was charged at full power so the impact took the wallet-cop off his feet.

Mandrake – like the magician – he was moving in slow motion, drawing his gun and stepping back to give himself some distance. There was panic on his face, a rush to get things done, an urgency to his movements that was jumbling everything up. The gun got stuck in the holster and he fumbled with it, and Temper struck him across the jaw before he even got close to pulling it clear. Mandrake – like the magician but really not – went twisting and falling and, when he hit the ground, the gun finally hopped free.

Temper picked up the gun, stuck it in his waistband, pulled his shirt over it.

"If I were you," Temper said to the scared guy as he uncuffed him, "I'd get out of Roarhaven for a while. Take whatever family you have with you."

"But I didn't do anything!" the scared guy protested, like that mattered. "Why did you do that? They'll think I had something to do with it! I'm in real trouble now!"

Temper placed a hand on this guy's chest, pushed him gently back against the wall. He could feel his thumping heart under his palm, and waited for the guy to lock eyes with him. "They weren't gonna take you somewhere and then release you. They weren't gonna realise their mistake because they didn't make a mistake. They're rounding up people who don't fit in any more. So either get out of the city, or find somewhere to hide. It isn't safe for people like you and me – not here. Go on now."

He took his hand away. The scared guy hesitated, then started hurrying off.

"Hey," said Temper, and threw the guy's wallet to him. "You might need this."

When Temper had left Roarhaven forever with Kierre of the Unveiled, he'd thought that forever would have lasted longer than three months. But here he was, walking down Decapitation Row and looking out for bad guys like he'd never even quit his job. Yeah, some things were different. He wasn't wearing a uniform, for one thing, and for another the folk who *were* wearing it were the bad guys. Or maybe the bad guys had been wearing the uniform for a lot longer than he thought. During his time in the City Guard, he'd known a hell of a lot of decent cops – and a hell of a lot of rotten ones. Now the rot had set in and, from what he'd heard, it had driven out most of the decent officers. In Temper's experience, this kind of rot didn't start in the basement – it started upstairs, it started at the top, and it worked its way down until the very foundations sagged with it.

Skulduggery Pleasant had set up the City Guard under

Supreme Mage Sorrows – but Commander Hoc had brought in a wave of new officers when he'd taken over and, under acting Supreme Mage Creed, the good guys didn't stand a chance.

There was still one officer left, despite all that. There may have been more, but the only one Temper could be sure of was Corporal Aldo Ruckus, the dashing-looking guy nodding to him from the window of the café.

Temper smiled at the lady behind the counter and asked for a coffee, then went and sat down.

"You're looking well," Ruckus said. "Well rested. Well fed. Retirement suits you." He had a funny way of speaking, did Ruckus. A proud son of Tennessee, he had that accent that dragged a little behind his words, so that nothing ever sounded even the tiniest bit urgent. But every single sentence, no matter how sincere, did manage to sound as if he was mocking you, straight to your face.

Temper liked him, and not just because he was a fellow American. Ruckus was a straight-shooter, and Temper could use one of those right about now.

"You saying I put on weight?" Temper asked, settling into a chair that creaked slightly.

"Just around the neck," said Ruckus. "And the gut."

Temper smiled. "Bull. The only weight I've been putting on is muscle, you goddamn moonshiner. You have any idea what it's like living with a professional assassin? She's turned me into a vegetarian."

"Damn," said Ruckus.

"Apparently, all the protein I need comes from the plants that are eaten by the animals I used to eat. It's a travesty, Aldo, I don't mind telling you."

"It sounds it," said Ruckus. "But you can still eat steak, right?"

"What?"

"Vegetarians can still eat steak, can't they?"

"No, Aldo. They can't. That's the complete opposite of what they can eat."

48

"No steak? Ever, or just on weekdays?"

"Ever. No meat at all."

"And what about chicken?"

"Chicken's meat."

"Yeah, but chickens have beaks. Vegetarians can eat things that have beaks."

"How many vegetarians have you known?"

"I used to date a vegetarian."

"And did he eat chicken?"

"Yeah. Steak too. And bacon. Can you eat bacon?"

"No, Aldo, I can't, and I don't think your boyfriend was a vegetarian."

"He said he was. Always going on about it. Either a vegetarian or a Presbyterian, can't remember which. So no steak, no chicken, no bacon—"

"Aldo, to stop you from just naming different kinds of meat, I'm gonna repeat myself: no meat. None. None of it."

"Damn," Ruckus said again.

"Like I said – a travesty."

The lady came over with the coffee. Temper thanked her, waited till she'd moved away before talking again. "And how's work?" he asked, speaking more quietly.

Ruckus's expression soured. "About what you'd expect. Lotta big talk at the lockers. Lotta big talk on the street. Lotta people getting their heads knocked."

"Must not be easy keeping your mouth shut."

"It ain't," Ruckus growled. "I swear to you, Temper, this plan you mentioned had better be a good one or I am walking outta there and never looking back."

"Well, it's a plan. I don't know how good it is, or how smart it is."

"Can't be too smart if you thought it up."

"You may have a point there." Temper sipped from his cup. It wasn't good coffee, but it'd do. He leaned forward. "I'm recruiting."

Ruckus looked at him. "From the City Guard?"

"You're about the only one in uniform I can still trust, so no. But I got two people onboard already and I'm looking for a third."

"And what are y'all gonna be doing?" Ruckus asked.

Temper paused. "Interfering," he said.

"That so?"

"You're the one told me about the arrests, even before Creed made that speech of his. Random citizens being taken off the streets, fists knocking on doors late at night, boots coming up the stairs... You know how bad it's getting."

"I do."

"So I'm here to interfere with all that."

Ruckus rubbed his chin. "And what does your assassin think of this?"

"Kierre is occupied right now. The Unveiled are trying to figure out their place in the world now that their big sister has been taken off the board. I said I'd leave her with her family. She'll join me here when they're done."

"And does she know what you're fixing on doing?"

"She does not."

"Because she'd know how dumb an idea it is?"

Temper shrugged again.

"And what do I get out of it?"

Temper grinned. "I am glad you asked. You get incredible danger out of it, my friend. You get to sneak around in the dark and protect people who don't know yet that they need protecting. You get to go up against your fellow officers in the City Guard, oftentimes violently. You get to escort good people to safety, and risk all kinds of exposure as you do so. But you, Aldo Ruckus, you also receive a special bonus, because you get to spy on the City Guard. You get to pass me vital information about their plans and their actions, thereby putting yourself in all kinds of new and added danger at all times."

"I am a lucky one."

"Aren't you?"

"And what do you hope to get outta this? What's the endgame?"

"Creed's building up to something. I don't know what it is yet, but it's something big. He started by taking people off the streets all quiet-like... now he's making it official. You think those Three Points of his are gonna stay at three? He'll introduce more and more guidelines, more and more rules, and the faithful will be fine. It won't affect the faithful one iota, and when they see it happening to their neighbours they'll be able to shake their heads and talk about troublemakers, talk about how these folk wouldn't be getting arrested if only they followed the rules. But the rules are the box that they're already living in. It's everyone else who has to worry."

"So things are gonna get worse," said Ruckus. "Big surprise there. But you still haven't answered my question. What's all this for?"

"We're gonna stop him," said Temper. "Whatever his big plan is, we'll stop it. He's turning Roarhaven into an occupied territory, and I'm building a resistance movement. So are you in?"

Ruckus's mouth shrugged ever so slightly, and Temper grinned.

# 10

Valkyrie and Skulduggery waited at the gates to Corrival Academy. Fletcher Renn emerged from the school's main doors, talking to a pretty girl with short dark hair. She grinned at whatever he was saying, then squeezed his hand and went back in while Fletcher came over.

"Nigeria, eh?" he said as he approached.

"The Sanctuary in Lagos," Skulduggery said. "Do you know it?"

"Of course," Fletcher replied, giving Valkyrie a hug. "Haven't seen you in a while."

"We're not allowed to drop into the school unannounced any more," Valkyrie told him. "Duenna really doesn't like us."

"If it makes you feel any better, none of my fellow teachers are particularly fond of her, so..." He shrugged.

Valkyrie grinned. "Who's the hottie?"

Fletcher rolled his eyes. "Do not start."

"I'm not starting, I'm just asking who the hottie is."

"Her name's Gratzia, she teaches science, and she's probably evil."

"Oh, she's not nice?"

"No, no, she's lovely," Fletcher said. "She's sweet and kind and smart and funny and, as you say, a hottie. But, purely going by my track record with girlfriends, she's probably an evil assassin or a goblin or someone who wants to remove my brain with an ice-cream scoop. I'm not getting my hopes up for any long-term relationship bliss is what I'm trying to say."

Valkyrie nodded. "Probably wise."

"Excuse me," said Skulduggery, "I hate to interrupt, but this conversation is boring me."

"Because it isn't *about* you," said Fletcher.

"That is indeed why it's boring."

"We'll talk later," Valkyrie promised him. "You can tell me all about her."

"It's a date," Fletcher said. He put a hand on each of their arms and they instantly traded their surroundings for the foyer of the Lagos Sanctuary.

Fletcher bade farewell with a quick arching of his eyebrows, and disappeared.

The Administrator looked up from his desk. "Welcome to the Sanctuary, Arbiters," he said. "Purpose of visit?"

"We're here to see Jericho Hargitsi," said Skulduggery.

"Mr Hargitsi hasn't worked here for several years," the Administrator responded. "But he lives quite close by. Please give me a moment."

He made a phone call and Valkyrie stepped back to avoid a screaming man in shackles who was struggling in vain against the two women who were hauling him in.

A young man passed and Valkyrie frowned. "Adedayo?"

He looked round and broke into a smile as he hurried over. "Hi!" he said. "Hiya! Jaysis, haven't seen you guys since... Anyway! How are you?"

"We're good," Valkyrie said, giving him a hug. "So you made your decision, then."

"I did?"

"You became a sorcerer."

"Oh!" he said. "Yeah. I mean, there wasn't really a decision to make. You're not exactly gonna talk a few gods out of ending

53

the world and then go back to normal life, are you? And it's Balogun now, not Adedayo. Balogun Blue."

"Pleased to meet you, Balogun. Are you stationed here in Lagos full-time?"

"Pretty much. Roarhaven's tempting and all, and I'd be beside my family and everyone I know, but... Nigeria's where my folks grew up, and it's where my *iyá agba* lived, so I figured I'd give it a try, like. Absorb some of my heritage." He lowered his voice. "And also I really don't like Damocles Creed."

Valkyrie nodded. "I'm with you there." She glanced at Skulduggery. "Are you going to say something?"

"Like what?" Skulduggery asked.

"Like how nice it is to see Balogun again after all this time? Maybe how it's nice to see him doing so well? Living up to the potential you saw in him? Something constructive like that. Something not insulting, maybe."

"Not insulting," Skulduggery murmured, angling his head towards Balogun. He paused for a moment, then nodded. "You're taller than you were."

The Administrator came over and handed Skulduggery a card, on to which was scribbled an address. "Arbiters, Mr Hargitsi is waiting to talk to you."

"Much obliged," Skulduggery said, tipping his hat. When the Administrator left, he looked Balogun up and down. "When we first met you, you were a confused and frightened young man with no idea what he wanted to do with his life. Now you at least look like you know where you're going."

"Thank you," said Balogun. "That means a lot."

"Where *were* you going?"

"Bathroom."

Skulduggery put a hand on his shoulder, said, "Never change," and walked off.

Valkyrie gave Balogun another quick hug and caught up with him.

They followed the map on Valkyrie's phone for close to ten minutes and came to a nice little house on a nice little street. A smiling woman answered the door.

"My name's Onosa," she said, gesturing for them to enter. "Onosa Tsira." Artwork covered the walls. Valkyrie didn't know the first thing about art, but she knew what looked cool, and this all looked cool. "I'm quite excited – I don't know if you can tell," Onosa continued. "I've never had an actual legend in my house before."

"Please," said Skulduggery, "no special treatment is required."

"I was actually talking about Valkyrie, but I suppose it's an honour to have you here, too."

Valkyrie laughed and Skulduggery pulled his left glove on tighter. "Charming," he said.

Onosa grinned, and motioned to the door ahead of them. "My husband's waiting for you in the next room. It might take him a moment or two to say hi, so don't take it personally. It's not you – he's rude to everyone."

"Thank you," said Valkyrie. "I love your house."

"That's very nice of you to say, but it's not my house. I killed the owner and stuffed his body in the refrigerator. Which reminds me, can I offer either of you a refreshing drink while you're here?"

Valkyrie's smile hovered, as if it was wondering what it was doing on her face.

"I'm joking," said Onosa. "Dear God, I'm joking. I would never do something like that. The refrigerator is far too small to hide a body. Anyway, Jericho awaits."

Valkyrie hesitated, then followed Skulduggery into the living room. Polished floorboards, muted colours, nice furniture, a glass jar on the table, and nobody else there.

"She's funny," said Valkyrie. "At least, I think she's funny. If she's joking, then she's funny and I really like her. If she's not joking, we'll probably have to arrest her and throw her in jail. But I still like her."

"You only like her because she called you a legend," Skulduggery replied.

"That's not the only reason," Valkyrie said. "She also made you look silly, which is hilarious every time it happens."

"You are easily amused."

"Of course I am," she said. "I hang around with you, don't I?" Skulduggery folded his arms and Valkyrie grinned.

"So how long do we wait?" she asked.

"I imagine we can stop waiting when Jericho walks in. It might seem strange if we wait any longer once that happens."

"It's just, she said he was here waiting for us, and he obviously isn't, so how long do we give it before you step out and ask what's keeping him?"

"Why must I be the one to ask?"

"Because I hate asking people things."

"You're a detective. Asking people things is part of your job."

"And it's the part I like the least. I'm not a pushy person, Skulduggery. I'm easy-going. I'm chill."

He tilted his head. "You are not easy-going."

"What? Yes, I am."

"I can't tell if you're being serious or not, but in case you are being serious—"

"I'm being very serious."

"You're not an easy-going person."

She stared at him. "How can you say that? I am so laid-back."

He nodded. "OK."

"Don't say that. Don't just say *OK* and move on when it's blatantly obvious you don't mean it. You don't think I'm laid-back?"

"I think you're driven. I think you're a very driven person. I think there's an engine inside your mind that propels you forward at all times, exemplified by the fact that you can't sit still for long and, once you have a mission in front of you, you do not stop until it's been accomplished."

"Well... yeah, but I do all that in a really laid-back kind of way."

"You do not."

Her stare turned to a glare. "Oh, and I suppose you're the epitome of easy-going, are you?"

"First of all, unlike you I never claimed to be easy-going. And second, yes, actually, I am."

"This is... we're getting away from the point. The point is when are you going to ask Onosa where Jericho is? That's the point. That's the... You honestly don't think I'm laid-back?"

"I honestly don't – but there's nothing wrong with being driven. I happen to value that quality."

"Still, though... I always kinda saw myself as being really chilled out."

"Yes. You're not, though."

"Apparently."

"Be right back – I'm just going to ask where Jericho is."

He stepped out of the room, and Valkyrie stood there and frowned. She took out her phone, called Militsa.

"Hey, sweetie," she said. "Quick question for you. Am I easy-going?"

Militsa laughed. "No," she said. "I gotta go – class is starting."

"Right," Valkyrie responded just before the call ended. She put the phone away and Skulduggery came back in.

"Well?" Valkyrie asked.

"He's in the jar."

"I'm sorry?"

"Jericho Hargitsi is in the glass jar on the table, according to Onosa."

They looked at it.

"He doesn't appear to be," Valkyrie said slowly.

"It *is* quite a small jar."

"And pretty empty."

"It *is* on the empty side."

"Maybe it's a metaphor. Maybe the glass jar is a glass jar in his mind, or something."

"Maybe," Skulduggery said. "Although she did say it was on the table."

"Then I'm confused. Is he a tiny, invisible man? What does he look like?"

"I don't know, actually. I've never met him. It's just common knowledge that Jericho Hargitsi is the sorcerer to talk to if you have questions about peculiar psychic abilities."

Valkyrie chewed her lip. "You know what this might be? One of those Wizard of Oz-type jobs, where you're sent off in search of something, only to discover that it's been within yourself the whole time. Like, the Lion found his courage, the Tin Man found his—"

"I know what they all found."

"Right, sorry. Anyway – maybe, if you're looking for answers, you come here, you're told Jericho is in the glass jar, but the glass jar is small and empty and, like, you suddenly have an epiphany that gives you the answers you're searching for."

"And have you had an epiphany?"

"I had the epiphany about the Wizard of Oz."

"So now you think you had the wrong epiphany?"

"I must have, yeah. Maybe if I go out and come back in it'll reset."

"Yes," Skulduggery said, "that's exactly how epiphanies work."

"Well, I don't have any other ideas. Do you?"

"You could try scanning the jar."

"You want me to read its mind?"

"We're dealing with a Sensitive, are we not? It would seem a logical place to start."

Valkyrie sighed, reached out with her thoughts, and met someone. Her thoughts instantly retracted into her head. She blinked, activating her aura-vision. A wonderful orange light swirled inside the jar. "There's somebody in there," she said softly.

The light drifted up through the neck of the jar and expanded outwards, forming a vaguely humanoid shape that hovered in the air over the table.

"Jericho Hargitsi, I presume?" she asked.

The shape floated there and something buzzed at Valkyrie's mind. She resisted at first, but then she softened, and let it in, and, when the buzzing hit the parts of her mind that formed words, she heard his voice.

"Hello, Valkyrie," Jericho said.

She smiled. "I'm not sure what's happening."

The shape shrugged. "We're just talking. That's why you came here, yes? To talk? To ask your questions?"

"Yes, I did," she answered. "Sorry. This is a bit weird."

"How do you think I feel? I live in a jar."

"I knew someone else who lived in a jar for a bit."

"Yes," said Jericho. "Let's see... a decaying man, was it not?"

"Scapegrace," she said. "Are you reading my mind?"

"I see vague images, nothing more. It's a side effect of our communication – I'm afraid I have no control over it. May I continue?"

"I suppose," she said. "Just don't pry too far."

"If I tried, you would know, and you'd block me. Can you say hello to Skulduggery for me? I've always wanted to see him in the flesh, so to speak. He does not disappoint."

Valkyrie looked over at Skulduggery. "Jericho says hi."

Skulduggery tipped his hat towards the jar. "Very pleased to meet you."

"The Skeleton Detective. It's a thrill to see him, it really is. Now then, Valkyrie, what has brought you all the way to Nigeria?"

"I'm new to all this Sensitive stuff and I really need some advice."

"But you have access to the best Sensitives in the High Sanctuary."

"And I don't exactly trust them."

"Ah," said Jericho. "Very well. Tell me what you need."

"Fifteen months ago, I had a kind of vision where I spoke to my sister in the future. I want to reopen that channel."

"I see," said Jericho. "That does sound complicated. Would you mind if I peeked inside your head, Valkyrie? I will focus in on the relevant details and you can keep track of me the entire time – but this is really something that I need as much information about as possible. You can push me out at any time."

"Sure," Valkyrie said slowly. "But tread carefully. I have things just the way I like them and I don't need you kicking over the furniture."

Jericho smiled. "You have my word."

When Jericho had finished collecting what he needed to collect, Valkyrie and Skulduggery stepped into the kitchen while he spoke to his wife. Not too long later, Onosa joined them.

"Forgive us," she said, "but Jericho gets tired easily. It takes a lot of energy just to be him, so right now he's resting. But we've discussed your situation and, while reopening this psychic link may be too difficult for you right now, we believe it may be possible for you to send your consciousness six years into the future to talk with your sister."

Valkyrie blinked. "You think I can time-travel?"

Onosa smiled. "With your consciousness, yes – not with your physical form. Have you ever tried astral projection, Valkyrie?"

"That's when you leave your body, right? No, never tried it."

"For someone of your power, this should come to you naturally, with just the lightest of prodding. Once you are in your astral form, once you leave the physical world behind you, time will fall away and you should be able to converse with your sister."

"That's... that's brilliant," Valkyrie said, and grinned at Skulduggery. "You hear that? I'm going to time-travel. Have you ever time-travelled?"

"I have not," said Skulduggery.

Her grin grew wider. "I'm going to do something you haven't done. Ha!"

"The training and preparation for this could take a few days," Onosa said, "so Jericho and I will be accompanying you back to Roarhaven. We've never been, and we've heard wonderful things."

"Maybe right now isn't the best time to visit," Valkyrie said slowly. "There's a lot of... tension. And Damocles Creed is running the show."

"Oh, we know Damocles from way back," Onosa said, waving her hand.

"You do?"

"Yes, indeed, Valkyrie. We're old friends. Practically. Almost. We tried to kill him once, but I'm sure he's forgotten about that. It was ages ago."

"Why did you try to kill him?" Skulduggery asked.

"Because we knew him."

"A good enough reason as any."

Onosa beamed. "You'll be needing us, I think. I see trouble ahead for both of you, and I think we can help."

"What kind of trouble?"

"Things aren't too clear at the moment, I'm afraid. I see vague images of violence."

"Sounds about right," Valkyrie murmured.

"And don't worry," Onosa said, "you won't have to chaperone us. We know quite a few people in Roarhaven, and I've already told them we're coming. Are you catching a Teleporter back? Maybe we can hitch a ride? I've never teleported anywhere before."

"It's not easy on the stomach," Valkyrie warned.

Onosa laughed. "I think I'll be fine."

Valkyrie gave Fletcher a call, and Onosa packed a few things while they were waiting. When Fletcher arrived, Onosa slung the bag over one shoulder, picked up the glass jar, and beamed. "I'm ready," she said.

They linked hands, Valkyrie blinked, and they were back in Roarhaven.

"Oh, dear," said Onosa, her eyes bulging. She brought the glass jar to her mouth and threw up into it.

Valkyrie stared. When Onosa stopped puking, she froze.

"My love," she said to the jar, "I am very, very sorry."

"We'll leave you to it," Skulduggery said.

# 11

It was all over the school: Bella Longshanks had been expelled for sneaking out of her room the previous night. Rumours immediately began to circulate: she'd sneaked out to meet a boy, to meet a girl, to vandalise the Devastation Day memorial – even though it plainly hadn't been vandalised – or, and this was Omen's favourite, she was part of the resistance group that had sprung up over the last few days to fight back against the High Sanctuary's new rules and guidelines. Try as he might, Omen just couldn't picture the quiet, well-behaved girl in his science class as a troublemaking resistance fighter.

It was a Sunday, which meant every student over fourteen could leave the school unaccompanied. He found Axelia on the bench beside the Black Lake.

"Hey," he said, approaching slowly, the way you'd approach an injured animal. "I heard about Bella."

Axelia was sitting forward, elbows on her knees. She shook her head without looking up. "It's ridiculous, Omen. They can't even say why they're expelling her. Yes, she was out of her room after lights out, but there were three others with her and they're not getting expelled. It makes no sense."

Omen hesitated, then sat. "How's she doing?"

"She's in tears. She's gutted. It's so unfair and there's nothing she can do about it. Her parents are coming in from Papua New

Guinea to try and sort it out, but the secretary told them Duenna is too busy to meet anyone right now. You know the worst thing? There's no one else they can go to. Duenna's only boss is, like, the Supreme Mage, and he's not going to bother with something like this. There's nothing anyone can do."

She looked up. "Unless maybe you ask your parents to say something?"

"My parents?"

"Duenna listens to them, doesn't she?"

Omen winced. "She did, until Auger fulfilled the prophecy. Now they're just like anyone else."

"But you could ask them to try."

It wouldn't do any good – he knew it wouldn't, and his parents knew it wouldn't, and the very act of asking them would highlight their very obvious and sudden irrelevance, which would not lead to warm hugs and fuzzy feelings.

"I'll ask them," he said reluctantly.

"Thank you!" Axelia responded, a smile appearing for the first time.

"It won't do any good," he said immediately, before hope had a chance to sink its hooks in. "Duenna won't listen even if I can convince my parents to talk to her, which I probably won't be able to do."

"But there's a chance, isn't there?"

"Not a big one, but... I suppose."

"Thank you, Omen," Axelia said. "Thank you."

He was seriously regretting seeking her out today.

He got back to school and went to his dorm room and stared at the homework he wasn't doing. He and Auger already had permission to leave the grounds the following evening in order to go to dinner with their parents. He could ask them about Bella Longshanks then – maybe they'd be in a good mood. Maybe they'd agree to it. He knew they wouldn't, but he was nothing if not optimistic, even when it came to Emmeline and Craddock Darkly. There was always the possibility that they might completely astonish him one of these days.

Someone knocked on his door. He told them to come in and when the door opened he stifled his groan and managed a smile. "Hey, Thiago."

Small, blond-haired, and kind of annoying, Thiago stepped in. "Hi, Omen," he said, his voice cracking even with those two words. Puberty was not being kind to Thiago. "Listen, I was talking to Auger earlier. You know, about the thing?"

Omen's smile faded. "I told you not to do that."

"I just wanted to know how it was going."

"Yeah," said Omen, "but I told you not to do that. You promised me."

Thiago nodded, not even paying attention. "So I asked him how it's going and I don't think he knew what I was talking about. He was looking at me like he didn't even understand what language I was speaking."

"What did you say?"

"I just asked him again, and he—"

"No," said Omen, "what did you say when you asked him? What did you ask?"

Thiago frowned. "Um... OK, I went up to him and I said can I talk to you for a second, and I don't think he even heard me the first few times. He looked spaced, like. Then I asked what was happening with my uncle."

"And what did he say?"

"He just looked at me. And then I started thinking, maybe Omen didn't tell him it was my uncle who was, y'know... so I explained that it was me."

"What exactly did you say, Thiago?"

"I said I'd gone to you to ask him if he could help, because my uncle's dangerous and saying that he wants to wake someone called the Witch Mother, and that the only way to wake her is

65

through human sacrifice. Then I told Auger that the rest of my family are pretending like it's not even happening and they don't seem to care that my uncle's about to, like, kill someone for no reason."

"And what did Auger say to that?" Omen asked.

"He looked at me for a while and then he nodded and mumbled something, and walked off. Is he feeling OK? He doesn't seem quite... together lately."

"Auger's fine," Omen assured him. "He's just got a lot going on right now – but the biggest thing on his agenda is finding your uncle and stopping him before he does something stupid."

"Are you sure your brother's up to it?"

"Are you seriously asking that? This is Auger Darkly we're talking about. The Chosen One. Thiago, you wanted a hero to take care of this problem for you because this is precisely one of those weird little things you hear about that grows and grows until it's something that Skulduggery Pleasant and Valkyrie Cain have to swoop in and deal with at the last second in order to save the world."

Thiago swallowed. "I don't want Skulduggery Pleasant and Valkyrie Cain dealing with this."

"I know you don't."

"They always kill the people they go up against."

"Not always, but often enough to be a worry, sure."

"I don't want my uncle killed."

"Which is why you needed Auger."

"And he's not gonna kill my uncle, right? I mean, he killed that King of the Darklands guy..."

"That was a one-off," said Omen. "He didn't have a choice. Apart from that one time, Auger doesn't kill. Your uncle will be fine. In fact, from what I've heard, Auger might even be dealing with it tonight."

"Really?"

"That's what I've heard."

Thiago considered this. "Maybe that's why he seemed so spaced earlier. He was probably getting in the zone."

"That sounds about right, yep. But, Thiago, you've got to remember what we discussed, OK? You don't talk to him about this. At all. You don't ask how it's going and, when it's over, you don't even say thank you."

"Why doesn't he want me to say thank you?"

"He doesn't want a fuss made. He doesn't want anyone to know he's still doing stuff like this."

"But he's the Chosen One."

"He *was* the Chosen One," Omen corrected. "Now he's just Auger Darkly."

"That's so weird. If I was doing things like this, saving people, saving the world, I think I'd want people to know about it."

Omen shrugged. "He's just shy, I suppose. Thiago, I have to finish my homework."

"OK," Thiago said, stepping back. "Tell him good luck from me, would you? And tell him thank you."

"You got it," Omen said, and Thiago left.

Omen sighed and closed the textbook on his desk, and lay down. It wasn't even eight o'clock, but he needed his rest. He had a busy night ahead of him.

At 2 am, with his room-mates asleep in their beds, Omen sneaked through the school. If a member of staff caught him, he wondered which kind of punishment he'd be given: expulsion, like Bella, or detention, like Bella's friends?

He climbed three sets of stairs in complete silence and reached the covered corridor that linked the four towers, at which point every footstep became a painful squeak. Scowling, he leaned against the railing to take off his new trainers, enjoying the warm night breeze on his face. The towers stood tall and dark against the sky. He peered over the edge, down into the courtyard.

Back in First Year, before he'd made any friends, Never had

tried to convince him that it was safe to dive off the balcony into the large circular fountain at the courtyard's centre. She'd insisted that it was, in fact, a rite of passage for Corrival students. He'd been so convincing that Omen had actually started to believe her – but Never had ruined it all by laughing. Declaring that Omen needed someone to protect him from himself at all times, Never had decided then and there that they should become friends with immediate effect.

Omen hadn't argued.

He hurried on in stockinged feet and found Crepuscular Vies by the North Tower.

Crepuscular was wearing a dark green suit, combining it with a matching hat and a shirt that swirled with dark colours. His bow tie was spotted, and he looked paler than usual. His cheeks were sunken, his bulging eyes tired, and his lipless mouth grinned without mirth. He'd been working hard, it seemed.

"Found him," Crepuscular said. "Remington Venture's got his human sacrifice and he's all set to kill her. What do you say, Omen? I've got a Teleporter on standby and a mortal that needs saving. Wanna go be a hero?"

"No," Omen said immediately, then sighed. "But who else is gonna do it?"

# 12

Human sacrifice, as a concept, brought to Omen's mind images of dungeons and manacles and cursed daggers clutched in the hands of robed fanatics. It did not bring to mind great tower cranes reaching over the roofs of New York skyscrapers and a control box clutched in the hand of a sweaty man with a droopy moustache.

The human to be sacrificed, in this instance, was a pretty blonde American girl, maybe around twenty-one, wearing a shimmering dress and dangling from the crane by her wrists.

"You let me down," she shouted. "You let me down right now and I don't mean drop me on to the street, I mean move me over to the roof and let me down gently without injuring me, you little creep!"

The man with the droopy moustache shook his head. "I'm sorry," he said, tears running down his face. "I'm so sorry."

Omen and Crepuscular moved through the shadows behind him, their footsteps snatched away by the wind.

"Y'know," the blonde continued, "when I walked into that bar, I looked at you and I thought *Gretchen, don't do it – he looks like a weirdo*. But I ignored that voice, Remington. I ignored it and I gave you a chance and this is what happens? This?"

"I don't want to kill you!" Remington wailed. "But I have to!"

"You are the worst first date ever!" she yelled. "Definitely in the top three!"

"Your sacrifice will be worth it, I promise you. The world will be a better place. You must believe me."

"Next time," she called, "I'm swiping left. Left!"

Remington sobbed, and held up the control box and raised his other hand to press the big red button.

Omen stepped out quickly. "Stop!" he shouted.

Remington screeched and whirled. "Don't come any closer!"

Omen held up both hands. "Remington. You're Remington Venture, right? Thiago's uncle?"

"How... how do you know Thiago?"

"I go to school with him. He asked me to check on you."

"He asked you to spy on me, you mean!"

"He's worried about you."

"He hates me!" Remington shrieked. "They all do!" His voice dropped suddenly, barely audible with all that wind. "But I'm doing this for them. I'm doing this for everyone. We're all in danger. We're all in terrible, terrible danger. I've seen it. I had a vision."

Omen licked his lips. "What did you see, Remington?"

"The Faceless Ones. They're coming back. We have weeks – six at the most. I saw them!"

"If you had a vision of impending disaster, you're obliged to alert your local Sanctuary."

"Of course I alerted the Sanctuary!" Remington yelled, waving the control box around. "I work there! The first person I told was my boss! I filled in all the paperwork, I did everything the way it should be done – but they ignored it. They told me to take a break. Said I was working too hard. Said I hadn't seen what I'd seen."

"And have you been working too hard?"

"That's beside the point! The point is the Faceless Ones are coming back and there's nothing anyone can do to stop it!"

70

"So why do you want to kill Gretchen?"

"Because he's a jerk!" Gretchen shouted.

Remington shook his head. "I don't want to kill her. You think I wanted to tie her up and terrify her? You think I'm going to enjoy dropping her seventy-three floors on to a sigil I painted with my own blood? Do you know how long it took me to collect that blood? The effort that went into stopping it from congealing? I don't want any of this! But I have to do it because this will wake the Witch Mother. We'll need her, you see. When the Faceless Ones return, we'll need people like the Witch Mother."

Omen shrugged. "I don't think I've ever heard of her."

Remington laughed. "Of course you haven't! You go to that ridiculous school with my nephew! You really think you're going to find the truth in that place?"

"So who is she?"

"How am I supposed to know?" Remington screeched. "If you don't know and you go to a school where they teach a class on Magic History, then what chance do I have?"

"But, if you don't know who she is, why do you want to kill Gretchen in order to bring her back?"

"Because I saw it," Remington said. "In a dream."

"Well, that's convinced me," said Crepuscular, stepping out beside him.

Remington yelled and jumped back, holding the control box between them like a gun.

"Hold on, hold on," Crepuscular said. "Don't do anything rash. You painted a sigil with your own blood on the ground, did you? So the girl would have to land directly on it? You sure your aim is that good?"

"I've taken it all into account," Remington said. "Wind speed. Direction. Her weight."

"He kept asking me how heavy I was at the bar!" Gretchen shouted. "That should've been my first clue, but it's so hard to find a single guy in New York who doesn't have a weird hang-up!"

She dangled in silence for a moment, then shrieked, "Guess I should keep looking!"

Remington glanced back at her and sobbed. "You hate me, don't you?"

"Yes!"

"Your sacrifice will not be in vain!" Remington cried, and went to press the button.

Omen flicked his hand, using the air to pluck the control box from Remington's grip. He dived, catching it as it fell, and heard a smack and Remington went down. Crepuscular strolled over to the main controls and brought Gretchen closer to the roof.

Omen hurried over, helped her down, untied her hands, and she flung her arms round his neck.

"Thank you!" she said. "You saved my life! Thank you!"

"Oh," he said, his voice muffled by her hair. "It's OK."

She gave him a huge kiss on the cheek before stepping back, and he felt the blood rushing to his face.

"You should've let me sacrifice her," Remington muttered. "She'd die, but the world would live."

"*She* has a name," Gretchen said, "and I am nobody's sacrifice." She lashed a kick into Remington's side. "You tried to kill me? *Me?* I have a life, you little insect! I have family and friends and you killing me would have put them through hell!" She kicked him again. "I have dreams. I've got one more year left of art college and then I'm going straight to Hollywood. I'm gonna get hired by the top animation studio on my list and I'm gonna spend the rest of my happy life making cartoons. And you wanted to take all that away from me? You wanted to rob me of that?"

Remington got to his knees and started to speak so Gretchen punched him right across the jaw and he flopped backwards.

She hissed, shaking her hand furiously. "Ow. That's my drawing hand."

"You're in art college?" Omen asked.

Gretchen nodded. "Studying animation. Why – you interested in art?"

"I think so. I mean, yes. I'd like to study it, I think – after school, like. I, uh, I wanna draw comics."

"That's cool," said Gretchen. "It's a tough field, but it's like anything – if you put in the work, you have as much of a chance as anyone. You been working on your portfolio?"

"Not really. I've been too busy, you know..."

"Saving damsels in distress?" Gretchen said, grinning. "By the way, that was magic, right? What you guys were doing?"

"Yeah," said Omen, drawing out the word. "And it's probably best if you don't tell anyone about it."

"And what happens if I do?"

"Honestly? Not a whole lot. I don't think they'd believe you, for one thing, but it isn't like we'd send the Cleavers after you or anything."

"Cleavers are scary, I take it?"

"They scare me. I'm Omen, by the way."

"Hi, Omen," Gretchen said. "This is a lot to take in."

"I'd imagine."

She nudged Remington with her foot – hard. "What happens to Laughing Boy here?"

"He'll be going to prison."

"Will I have to testify?"

Omen shook his head. "We don't really need trials when we have people who can read minds."

"That's handy," said Gretchen. "I'm taking this quite well, I think."

"You might be in shock."

"It's a possibility, Omen. I'm not gonna lie to you."

Crepuscular came over. "We have to get going," he said, hunkering down to shackle Remington's wrists.

"So you're just gonna go?" Gretchen asked. "That's it?"

"I'm afraid so," Crepuscular said.

"You should probably talk to someone," Omen suggested. "It'd be cool if you didn't tell them about the magic, but you should probably find someone to talk to about what happened. I mean, you were attacked and kidnapped, and Remington did try to murder you."

"Yeah," said Gretchen. "OK. Hey, you have a phone?"

"Uh," said Omen. "Yes."

She held out her hand and he passed it over. "I'm just putting in my number," she said. "If you need any help with your portfolio and stuff, just let me know. Cool?" She tossed the phone back to him.

"Cool," he said. "Thanks."

Crepuscular waved his hand and his Teleporter friend wandered out of the shadows. Omen put his hand on one arm and Crepuscular put his arm on the other, while keeping hold of Remington. Right before they teleported away, Gretchen gave Omen a smile.

# 13

Valkyrie thought about how best to phrase the delicate question she was burning to ask, and eventually decided on, "Did she dump you?"

Temper Fray blinked at her. "Wow."

"I figured it might be a touchy subject so I thought I'd just plunge on in," she said. "So did she?"

"No, Kierre didn't dump me. We're still together. She's just figuring some stuff out with her family and I thought I'd come back here and do what I can to help."

"Good," said Valkyrie. "I like Kierre. She's nice. She scares me, but she's nice."

"She scares everyone," said Temper.

"She doesn't scare me," Skulduggery said, joining them in the kitchen. "Who are we talking about?"

"Kierre," said Valkyrie.

"Oh," he said, "well then, yes, she does scare me. The perimeter's secure. We can talk."

It was an empty kitchen in an empty house in an empty part of the city. A few streets to the east were the mortal refugees from the Leibniz Universe. A few streets to the west were the ruins that Darquesse had left smouldering on Devastation Day. Here was the sweet spot – empty, unspoiled houses where clandestine meetings could take place without any neighbours to inform on them.

They sat, and Temper ran a finger through the thick layer of dust on the table. He wiped his hands. "OK, you wanna know about Creed's Activations. I can help you with that. I had a friend. His name was Triton. This was, like, over a hundred years ago, when I was one of Creed's favourites back in my Church of the Faceless days.

"Triton was like me – a true believer. Neither of us started out that way, but there are tricks that people like Creed use to get you wrapped up in this stuff. Before we were sent out to recruit people to the Church of the Faceless, Creed'd take us through the talking points – what to say, how to respond when they replied... He had it all down.

"The most impressive part was that he'd give us a few things we'd be likely to hear in response to everything that we said, and, in all the conversations I had with people, they always replied with some variation of those options. Creed knew how they'd respond and he'd have a response to that response, all waiting to go. Human beings are so predictable."

"Did it work?" Valkyrie asked.

"Sorry?"

"Did you recruit many people?"

Temper smiled. "No. I mean, I recruited a few, and Triton recruited maybe a half-dozen, but these were only people who'd been considering joining us anyway. That wasn't the purpose of these conversion conversations. It never is. And it's not just the Church of the Faceless – it's literally any religion. The church is home. The people around you are family. They understand you. They love you and you love them.

"So we were sent out, Triton and me, to convert others, armed with nothing but talking points and pamphlets, and we'd have to endure hellish conversations – conversations so awkward they curled my toes as I was sitting in someone's kitchen or, more likely, standing on their front step. But that's the point. Whenever we did this, whenever we had to endure the constant rejection and scorn and sheer annoyance, we'd feel a level of discomfort so profound that we started to see these people as different and separate from us, and we couldn't wait to get back to the Church, back to our people. You get me?

"When we returned, we returned from the cold, cruel world out there to the love and warmth and understanding of our tribe. Everyone in the Church knew what we'd been through because they'd been through it, too. They'd been laughed at, spat at, cursed at. We'd all experienced the pain – but in the Church we were safe."

He shrugged. "The whole thing is meant to reinforce your bond to whatever religion you happen to be a part of. It's brainwashing.

"So by this point, when Triton and I were true-believing fanatics, Creed had room upon room of Kith. We'd seen the Activation process churn them out again and again. Each person that was strapped into that chair believed with all their heart that they'd be the one. The special one. But they never were. Their minds were wiped and their faces melted off and they were led off to stand in a dark room with all the others.

"It's amazing to think back on it and remember the certainty, each time, that we were about to witness the birth of the Child of the Faceless Ones. I think it's because, after every unsuccessful attempt, Creed would tweak the process just a little – so that every attempt was seen as taking a big step closer to success."

He took a breath, and let it out. "So, Creed announced to us all that this time he had it figured. This time he'd cracked it. That meant he was gonna use one of us – one of his inner circle, those of us whom he knew had the kind of bloodline he was looking for."

Valkyrie frowned. "You were all descended from the Faceless Ones?"

"Pretty much. Now, we're talking very, very diluted streams here. Faint. Practically invisible. But sure, we all had the potential in our DNA for the Activation to take hold. Creed hadn't been willing to risk us up until that point – but he'd ironed out the creases, he said. So, he picked Triton.

"And Triton was delighted," Temper continued. "Thrilled to be a part of it. The idea that he might not be the Child of the Faceless Ones? I don't think it even occurred to him. Or, if it did, it didn't matter. Creed had convinced him – convinced us all – that to sacrifice yourself for his sacred mission was an honour beyond anything you could dream of.

"So Triton sat in this heavy old wooden chair Creed had built once upon a time, and I helped strap him in. Couldn't have him changing his mind at the last moment, no, sir. We strapped down his feet, his wrists, his chest. There was even a strap that went round his neck. I'll never forget the look on his face as we tightened the buckles. Pure happiness.

"While we were securing him, Creed came in to carve the sigils into the walls."

"What were the sigils?" Valkyrie asked.

"The main one was a form of Ensh – you know it? Ensh is from one of the newer languages of magic – and, by newer, I mean it only came into existence a few thousand years ago. The Ensh Sigil is designed to bring out someone's latent magic – it's a last-ditch attempt to provide a boost to a lagging young sorcerer right before the Surge hits. It isn't used an awful lot because it rarely has the desired effect – but Creed took that sigil and adapted it to what he needed. Now the sigil – what he called the Ensh-Arak – actively seeks out your Faceless Ones' DNA and brings it to the surface. So you either end up as the Child of the Faceless Ones or, as has happened exactly one hundred per cent of the time, you end up as a Kith."

"Back to the Activation," Skulduggery prodded.

"Yeah," said Temper. "So, anyway, once Triton was strapped in, Creed brought out the shard."

"A shard of what?" Valkyrie asked.

"A crystal, a jewel, I dunno. Creed started out with four, I think – four shards, barely more than slivers. Each one would be good for a few thousand Activations before it shattered, but he'd used up three so far. The Ensh-Arak generates the transformative kind of power he needs, and this power is then focused through the shard and directed to the... well, in this case, to Triton.

"So there we were, and the Ensh-Arak Sigil started glowing, and the energy went into the shard and then it went into Triton, and *he* started glowing. There's a radiance that starts in their chests, and it just... spreads. Every tendon in Triton's body stood out. It's like I could see every vein. His fingers were curled, his lips were pulled back, but his eyes – his eyes were wide open. It only lasts a few seconds, but in those few seconds I watched the expression turn from excitement to fear and then to pain. But by that point his eye sockets were closing over and his nose was melting into his face and his mouth was gone and... that was it. Another failed experiment."

"What happened to him?"

"I brought him down to stand with all the others. He was my friend, y'know? Least I could do. I just took him by the hand and walked him down. Everyone gave us such a wide berth. No one looked at him. No one even looked at me. It's like this blanket of shame came down over us all. For those few minutes, we were all honest with each other. We knew the Activations would never work. We knew we were killing our friends. Just like we knew that the next time Creed opened his mouth, he'd convince us all over again that this time would be different."

"And when did you start doubting him?" Valkyrie asked.

"That very day," said Temper. "A tiny doubt that I couldn't shake, that grew and spread and infected not only my belief in Creed, but also my faith in the Faceless Ones. We were doing all this for them, after all, and they couldn't protect us? Did we really have to prove our devotion at such a tragic cost?" He shrugged.

"So I ran. I joined the Church when I was eight and I left when I was twenty-two."

"And then you joined the army."

"First I went back to New York, started living among mortals again. Then, when World War Two broke out, I joined up, went overseas to fight Hitler. Never managed to find him on the battle-field, but I faced some that were just as bad."

"Creed couldn't have been overly happy with you."

Temper smiled. "He was not. I think he would've had me quietly murdered if I didn't come from such a promising blood-line – if I didn't have the potential to be what he'd been looking for. The man's a stone-cold killer, but he doesn't see it that way. In his eyes, he's doing the work of the gods. He's their faithful servant, and everything – every crime or sin or travesty – is permissible in service to the Faceless Ones."

"Which is why he must be stopped," Skulduggery said, nodding.

"I'm doing my bit," said Temper. "I'm the fly in Creed's ointment, the spanner in his works, the thorn in his side, the bump in his road, the... twig in his eyeball, the spoon in his... knife block..." He faltered.

"You should have stopped a few idioms ago," Skulduggery said.

"That's what they tell me," Temper replied, "but I never listen."

# 14

"You don't know much about astral projection, do you?" Jericho asked.

"I don't," said Valkyrie. They were in Militsa's house, waiting for Skulduggery to arrive so they could start the lesson.

"You can think of it like your soul leaving your body," Jericho said, "but your body stays alive and awaits your return. Your soul – your life force, your spirit, whatever you want to call it – is you at your very essence. In your astral form, you can travel round the world in an instant. You can visit other planets. Other universes. Not everyone can do it, and not everyone who can, can do it well. But you have a unique power inside you, Valkyrie. I could sense it long before I met you. How did you come by this power, if I may ask?"

"I lost my true name," she said.

"I'm not sure I understand."

"Well, first I got my true name sealed. Doctor Nye did that – do you know it?"

"I'm aware of the doctor's existence."

"Nye opened me up, basically, and carved a sigil on to my heart and did some other stuff that I don't understand – all while I was still conscious, by the way."

"Must have been painful."

"It was – although technically I was dead at the time. You

know the death field that's in the Necropolis? I was surrounded by something like that, except I was still walking and talking instead of, like, dropping dead. It meant that I could feel everything, but not scream about it.

"So my true name was sealed, but by that stage there was already a part of me that was breaking away from the rest of my... personality, I suppose you'd say. That part eventually broke free completely and took my magic with it."

"So you were without any magic at all?"

Valkyrie nodded. "Then a magic-sucker exploded and I absorbed that explosion and it triggered my Surge, and since then I've been flying and shooting lightning out of my fingertips and I've got a psychic thing going on and I've been able to latch on to other people's magic."

"When you say latch on...?"

"I look inside their minds and it's... it's like a series of doors that open up and I can take what's inside. I absorb what they know, and I can do what they can do. It doesn't last long, but I've been able to absorb medical knowledge and I've healed myself a few times."

"That sounds very handy."

"I might be able to do it with you," she said, "if you're OK with it. It'd save us a lot of time."

Jericho smiled. "By all means, try."

She reached out with her thoughts, and after nearly a minute she frowned. "I can't find anything."

"Because there's nothing to find," said Jericho. "I don't have a physical brain for you to search through. Seven years ago, I moved into my astral form and I went travelling, but when I returned my body was dead. An old friend of mine had killed me, and blocked my return. I have been stuck like this ever since."

"An old friend killed you?"

"Old friend," Jericho said, smiling, "new enemy. Which is why

I know so much about astral projection. I haven't really had any choice."

Valkyrie chewed her lip. "So I'm not going to be able to cheat here, am I? This is gonna take ages."

"It will not take ages for two reasons," Jericho replied. "Reason one, I am an excellent teacher, and reason two, I am sure you are an excellent student."

The doorbell rang and Militsa let Skulduggery in.

"I have arrived," he announced.

"You're late," Valkyrie said.

"I received word that Rancid Fines is still in Ireland and still trying to find someone to pay for his research into the Crystal of the Saints. I went to arrest him."

Valkyrie's heart leaped. "And did you?"

"He wasn't there."

"Who is this Rancid Fines?" Onosa asked. "Is he an archenemy? A criminal mastermind?"

"No," Valkyrie said sadly. "He's just an idiot."


Valkyrie lay on the bed with her eyes closed. Her breaths were even and deep. Her mind was calm. Skulduggery and Militsa watched, and Onosa stood beside her, holding the jar that contained Jericho.

"All right, then," said Jericho, "tell me your intent. Tell me what you want to happen. It helps when you talk about your intentions out loud. It focuses the mind, like a spell."

She nodded. "I want to contact my sister Alice. In the future."

"You want to contact your sister Alice in the future," Jericho repeated. "Good. You did it once before, didn't you?"

"Yes. I saw her when she's sixteen. We spoke."

"She must have been thinking about you as you were thinking about her. Two powerful sorcerers, two sisters – that would have formed a psychic link between you."

"I haven't been able to do it again, though."

"The link is already formed. You just have to tap into it. I can show you how to make the journey. And it will be a journey, Valkyrie. I'm going to show you how to astral project. Do you know what that is?"

"It's when your spirit leaves your body."

"Indeed it is. You will be projecting your astral self along that psychic link with your sister."

"Cool."

"First, I will show you how to leave your body and travel into the next room. What is in the next room, Valkyrie?"

"It's another bedroom."

"Describe it to me."

"The walls are blue. The bed has a... OK, I don't remember what colour the duvet is, but there's a bed. There's a chest of drawers beside the window."

"I want you to picture it in your head. Can you see it?"

"Yes."

"Now reach into it with your mind. Expand your thoughts through the wall. Find a point in the picture in your head – a point in mid-air. Direct your thoughts towards this point."

Valkyrie did exactly as he said. It was like she was falling asleep while at the same time being wide awake, alert to every sound, every smell, every sensation.

"Now allow yourself to be pulled to that point. Imagine there's a rope tied round your waist, and now it's tightening, it's going taut. It's tugging on you."

She could feel it, feel the rope digging into her hips.

"And now you're being pulled off the bed. You're weightless. You're like a balloon, and you're being pulled smoothly along."

Valkyrie opened her eyes except she didn't open her eyes. Her eyes remained closed, but she could see everything. She was still lying on the bed except she wasn't: she was floating towards the wall. She turned her head, watched Skulduggery, watched Jericho.

"When you reach the wall," Jericho said, his voice deeper now, slower, "you'll pass through it like it isn't even there."

Her feet went first, disappearing from view. Valkyrie didn't mind. She wasn't scared. She was calm. The wall came to meet her and she smiled as everything went dark for a moment, and then she was in the other room and drifting towards the point in mid-air that she'd envisioned. She reached it, and stopped, tilting slightly.

"Valkyrie," Jericho said softly, even though she could no longer see him, "I want you to look at the bed, Valkyrie. I want you to note the colour of the duvet. Once you've done that, release the rope. Let yourself return to your body."

Valkyrie imagined the rope falling away and now she was drifting back through the wall.

She turned, watching her body lie there in the bedroom. It looked so peaceful. The face was completely slack. Such an odd feeling.

She sank into her body.

"I want you to open your eyes," Jericho said. "Open your eyes now, Valkyrie. That's it."

She opened her eyes. Blinked. She felt exhausted and refreshed all at the same time.

Skulduggery loomed over her. "What colour is the duvet?"

"Blue and white," Valkyrie said. "It's blue and white."

# 15

Funny how many rooftops Temper had lurked on over the years.

It seemed to be a thing, crouching above the streets, waiting to spring into action. He knew loads of people who regularly did it – he was here with three of them, for God's sake. But in all that time, with all that crouching, with all that waiting, he had come to one simple, inescapable conclusion: rooftops weren't all that interesting.

There were exceptions, of course. He'd lurked on a few rooftops in New York that had stone gargoyles to ward off both evil spirits and menacing rainwater, and, in general, rooftops in Roarhaven were more imaginative than their regular counterparts, but no amount of gargoyles could stave off the boredom for more than a few minutes. Eventually, you had to face the inescapable fact that you were crouching on another rooftop, waiting for something to happen.

"What's your view on rooftops?" he asked Ruckus, keeping his voice down.

Ruckus narrowed his eyes, a sure sign he was giving the question some considerable thought. Finally, he answered. "This is just a guess, but... I'd say four miles."

Temper nodded, didn't say anything, and, keeping low, moved over to where Oberon Guile hunkered. Temper didn't know

Oberon well, but Tanith Low vouched for him, and both Skulduggery and Valkyrie had worked with him in the past, so that was good enough for Temper.

"Oberon," he said, "have you ever been on a really interesting roof?"

Oberon looked at him. He was a good-looking man with some grey in his dark hair and permanent stubble. "What?"

"I was thinking about rooftops," said Temper, "and it occurred to me that, by and large, they're pretty boring places to be. I'm just wondering if you have a dissenting opinion."

Oberon kept looking at him. "This is what you think about?"

"I mean... yeah."

"These are the thoughts that occupy your mind? You're the leader of this little resistance group of ours, and this is what you spend your time pondering?"

"I don't *just* think about rooftops," Temper said, a little defensively.

"I don't want you thinking about rooftops at all," said Oberon. "I want you thinking about tactics and strategies and backup plans and escape routes. Serious things."

"I think about serious things, too."

"I'm beginning to wonder if I've made a huge mistake joining up."

"You haven't," Temper said immediately. "You made the right decision. Furthermore, you're in good hands. I've got all the tactics and backup plans and escape routes worked out ahead of time. I've come at this from all angles, don't you fret."

"Got to be honest with you, Temper – I'm fretting."

Temper gave one of his most winning smiles.

"What are you doing?" Oberon asked. "You're just smiling at me. You realise you're not saying anything, right?"

"You can trust me."

"You look demented."

87

"You can still trust me, though. That's my point."

Oberon grunted, and Temper decided to quit while he was behind.

Tanith Low beckoned to him and he hurried over. She nodded at the street below.

"Grey van," she said. "See it? Been parked there all evening. Looked empty."

"There's someone inside?"

"Caught movement out of the corner of my eye, so yeah, I think so."

The grey van sat there, still and quiet. It was too late for dog walkers and too early for joggers, so the street was empty, and there were no lights on in any of the buildings. Three doorways in particular were of interest, all leading to apartments that were due for unannounced visits – the kind that resulted in people being dragged away and not coming back.

If the City Guard were to kick down those doors, of course, they'd find empty apartments – Temper had organised for all the occupants to be moved earlier that day – but he had no intention of letting it get that far. A squad of ten officers was due here at any moment, according to Ruckus, and upon their arrival the Roarhaven resistance would be on hand to offer them a quick lesson in demotivation.

They were going to kick their asses, basically, and send them running. Temper was pretty sure that'd get their message across to Supreme Mage Creed.

"Nervous?" Tanith asked.

Temper grinned. "A little," he admitted. "Not so much as for what we're about to do, but for what it'll mean."

"Ah," said Tanith, "the message."

"The message, indeed."

"And exactly *why* do we have to send a message? Why can't we just keep skulking around in the shadows, helping people escape arrest? That's been working pretty well for us so far."

"Creed knows we're out here. He doesn't know it's us, specifically, but he knows what we're doing. He'll make a speech over the next few days, denouncing us as criminals or terrorists, and he'll be able to shape the way the public see us. By announcing ourselves, we take that piece of power away from him."

"If you don't mind me saying, that's a lot of risk for low reward."

"Taking any weapon away from Damocles Creed is never low reward. You have no idea how much damage that man can inflict with just words."

Tanith tapped his arm. A man got out of the grey van, took a moment to stretch his spine and roll his shoulders, and then he spoke into his lapel. A moment later, a squad of nine officers of the City Guard teleported into the middle of the road.

The plain-clothed officer joined them, and the officers broke up into three teams of three, co-ordinated by an officer Temper recognised. There'd been rumours, back when Temper was still in the Guard, that the only friends Ferrente Rhadaman ever had were a bunch of Hollow Men he'd dress up in people clothes, but Temper never cared enough to find out how true that was. Still, he could believe it. Rhadaman was just too damn strict to be fun.

Ruckus and Oberon came over as each of the City Guard teams went to a different door.

"That's the Teleporter," Temper whispered, pointing. "The guy lugging around the extra pounds. Oberon, you take him out first."

Oberon nodded.

"Ruckus, see the big guy? That's the team you're going after. Oberon, when you're done with the Teleporter, you assist. Tanith, your group's on the right. I'm taking the middle lot. We go in, we teach the lesson we came here to teach, and we get out. Our only goal is to make them think twice about moving against innocent people. We all clear? Well, OK then." He put on his mask, and the others followed suit. "Let's go be heroes."

# 16

Tanith rang the bell at Grimwood House. A moment passed and the door opened.

"Hello, saucepot," Valkyrie said, grinning.

"Hello, chicken nugget," Tanith said, and they hugged.

Valkyrie moved back, examining her. "Where'd you get the black eye?"

"Some idiot yesterday," Tanith replied, sighing. "Took exception to something I said, or did, or kicked. I don't know – it was ages ago. He wouldn't have laid a finger on me, but I was wearing a stupid mask that wrecked my peripheral vision."

"Mask, eh? That sounds fun."

"It's not bad, I have to admit. We've got a little Robin Hood thing going on, except we don't steal from the rich and give to the poor. It's more like we clobber the uniformed and set the poor free."

"A noble pursuit."

"Ain't it just? And I can't help but notice that you're wearing your necronaut suit. Expecting trouble?"

"Not exactly," said Valkyrie, beckoning her into the house.

Tanith loved Grimwood House. She loved the books on the shelves and the paintings on the walls. She loved the statues on plinths and the weapons on display – all Gothic, all horror, all awesome. They passed what Tanith was pretty sure was a Frazetta original in a thick, gilded frame on their way up the stairs.

"I called you," Valkyrie said, "because I figured if I didn't you would never forgive me. Skulduggery and Militsa are here with Onosa Tsira and Jericho Hargitsi. They're pretty powerful Sensitives who spent most of yesterday teaching me how to astral-project."

"Ohh, cool," said Tanith. "So you'll be a ghost?"

"Yes," Valkyrie said, "but that's not the cool bit. I'm gonna be travelling when I project."

"Going far?"

"In a way, no. In another way, oh, yes." They reached the landing and Valkyrie turned to her. "I'm gonna travel into the future."

Tanith stared. "No."

"Yes."

"No way."

"Yes way."

"You're gonna be a *time-traveller*?"

"I know!" Valkyrie said, giggling as Tanith grabbed her arms. "You had to be here. You get that, right? You're the one who made me sit down and watch *Back to the Future* and *Looper* and, to a lesser extent, *Timecop*."

"This is the best thing that's ever happened. Oh, wow. Oh my God. You're doing it now? You're going to travel through time now? This is huge. This is amazing. Do I have time to pee?"

"You know where the toilet is."

Tanith charged into the bathroom.

Twenty-two minutes later, Militsa was looking deep into her eyes. "Tanith," she said, "if you don't calm down, you'll have to wait downstairs."

Tanith nodded. "I'll calm down."

"No more giggling."

"I understand."

"And you can't hum the *Doctor Who* theme tune any more."

"You heard that?"

"You weren't quiet."

"I'm really sorry," said Tanith, then looked round. "I'm really sorry, everyone. I won't be a disturbance."

"And stop making me laugh," Valkyrie said from the bed. "You're not a kid. You're a grown-up. What age are you?"

"Ninety-three."

"You're ninety-three years old, for God's sake."

"I'm really sorry, Val. I'm really sorry, everyone. Best behaviour from here on out."

Militsa glanced at the others, then nodded. "OK," she said. "This is your last chance."

"I'll be good," Tanith promised.

"All right," Onosa said. "Valkyrie, close your eyes. Calm yourself."

Valkyrie breathed deeply, her whole body relaxing with each exhalation. Tanith kept her mouth shut.

Onosa placed a curious-looking candle on a saucer beside the bed. "This is a Jericho Candle," she said. "Jericho came up with it, tried calling it something fancy, but what's the point of inventing something if you don't put your own name to it, I ask you? When it's lit, Valkyrie, you'll be able to smell it, even in your astral form, and it will guide you back to your body. There are only a handful of these in the world, and they are a lot of trouble to make, so we shall light it every hour you are gone, and keep it lit for five minutes. Time will pass at the same rate in the future as it does here in the present, so every hour on the hour you will have a five-minute window in which to return. Are you clear on everything I just said?"

"I am," Valkyrie responded, sounding like she was about to drop off to sleep.

"I will be helping Jericho manifest in this room so he can put all his focus on you, Valkyrie. Are you ready?"

"Ready."

Onosa picked up an empty jar, closed her eyes, and bowed her head. A gas began to swirl in the jar. A green gas that became a kind of liquid. Tanith had seen this before – ectoplasm. It rose out of the jar and formed a vaguely humanoid form. Jericho Hargitsi, Tanith presumed.

"Tell me your intent," Jericho said, his voice both distant and strong.

"I want to contact my sister Alice," Valkyrie said. "In the future."

"You want to astral-project?"

"Yes."

"You want to travel along the link you have with Alice, the link that has already been formed, the link that is waiting for you."

"Yes."

"This hasn't been done before," Jericho said. "Not like this. I can't tell you exactly how it's going to work. You'll have to be ready for anything, do you understand me?"

"Yes."

"I would like you to picture Alice in your head. Picture her as you saw her. Sixteen years old. Do you remember what she looked like?"

"Yes."

"Picture her. That's the Alice you want to talk to. The one in the future. The one who doesn't exist yet. You'll be moving forward in time, Valkyrie. You will lose sight of us. When this happens, I don't want you to worry. Remember, you're in control. You can come back to your body at any stage. The candle is merely here as a guide."

Tanith had a friend once who could do the astral-projection thing – even become visible for short periods of time while doing it. His favourite thing was to haunt mortals. He always got such a kick out of it.

"I want you to find your sister," Jericho was saying. "Wherever she is, whatever she's doing, I want you to find her. Time means nothing to you. Time doesn't exist. The only thing that exists is the link between you. Find the link and follow it."

"I found it," Valkyrie said weakly.

"Good," said Jericho.

"It's hard to... keep track of..."

"Nothing else matters," Jericho said. "Let the world fade away. Let your past and present fade away."

Valkyrie frowned. Shifted like she was having a bad dream.

"I need you to remain calm, Valkyrie. Can you hear me? Valkyrie, can you hear me?"

"I found her," Valkyrie whispered, her features going slack once again.

"Good," said Jericho. "Good. That's the point I want you to aim for. Keep your focus on that point. Are you ready? Valkyrie, are you ready?"

"Yes."

"Imagine there's a rope between you. It's tied round your waist. It's going taut. You're being pulled out of your body."

A flicker of a frown on Valkyrie's face.

"Let yourself go," Jericho said, his voice growing softer. "Let yourself float towards her."

"She's... so far."

"Distance means nothing to you. The rope is as long or as short as it needs to be."

"So far..." Valkyrie said, and her eye twitched.

"You're floating," said Jericho. "Floating gently along."

"Too far," Valkyrie muttered. Then her back arched so suddenly she almost came off the bed. "Too far!" she gasped.

Tanith jumped to her feet beside Militsa.

"Valkyrie," Jericho said, "you need to remain calm. You need to—"

White energy started to crackle.

"That's enough," Skulduggery said. "Valkyrie, come back to your body. Do you hear me? It's too much for you. Come back."

Valkyrie's entire body seized up, her fists bunching, her hips twisting, the muscles cording in her neck. She bared her teeth, spittle flying, as the crackling energy surrounded her, lifted her off the bed.

Tanith ran forward. Lightning flashed and she hit the far wall, fell to the ground, feeling like she'd just been kicked halfway to death. Skulduggery and Jericho were shouting. Fingers of energy scorched the ceiling. Tanith got up, staggered, shielding her eyes from the electrical storm in the centre of the room.

The energy surrounded Valkyrie, blocking her from view, and then it streaked to a point in mid-air, firing everything it had – and then it was gone.

And so was Valkyrie.

# 17

Lightning crackled.

Valkyrie shot through the air.

Screaming.

All of a sudden she stopped, but she didn't really stop. It was the kind of false stop you get when you're travelling ridiculously fast and then you suddenly slow and you think you've stopped because, compared to the speed you had been travelling at, you were practically standing still, but no – you were still moving.

Valkyrie tumbled through the air.

Her brain came back online as the ground rushed to meet her. She twisted herself upright, gave a blast of energy, but it was too much, it was way too much, and she zipped along the ground and everything was blurring and she hit the edge of a wall with her shoulder and went spinning off. With each spin, she glimpsed the sky and she glimpsed the street, like they were vying for ownership. The ground won.

She crunched into an alleyway and rolled and rolled and kept rolling until she stopped. She lay there, trying to remember how to breathe, then she sucked in a breath and turned over on to her back. "Ow."

She sat up. She shouldn't have been able to sit up, because she didn't have a body to sit up with. She also shouldn't have felt sore. She was an astral projection – an extension of her own soul.

Her soul didn't have nerve endings. Her soul wasn't supposed to feel pain. Her soul was supposed to pass *through* solid objects, not bounce off them.

Valkyrie looked at her hand. It was definitely a hand. Definitely flesh and blood.

Groaning, she stood. OK then, something had gone wrong. Maybe instead of moving into her astral form she'd done something like teleport instead. She nodded. That made sense. She just needed to find her way back to Skulduggery and the others and try again.

She blasted into the sky, landed on a roof, and froze.

She had travelled from Grimwood to Roarhaven. That was the good news. The bad news was that a hell of a lot more than six years had passed.

The High Sanctuary was relatively unchanged, but the Dark Cathedral now towered above it. The great wall around the city had been taken down – Shudder's Gate had been removed – and Roarhaven now sprawled outwards in all directions. Great spires and churches reached upwards, stretching for the heavens.

The streets were wide and well ordered, alive with people and trams and carriages that flew silently over the ground. It was eerily quiet. There were no cars. No engines. No honking of horns or wailing of distant alarms. No sirens. None of the trappings of a mortal city.

The air was clean.

Valkyrie stepped back and crouched, watching a trio of sorcerers fly by, deep in conversation. They didn't notice her.

She'd travelled into the future in her astral form and she'd somehow brought her body along with her. She hadn't a clue how the hell that had happened, but figuring out stuff like that was not her job. Her job was to throw herself head first into danger and then see what happened.

A small part of her, the cautious and sensible part, wondered if she should focus on going back to her own time and starting again, but even that small part changed its mind. She was in the future, for God's sake. Valkyrie grinned. The least she could do was look around.

She flew back down to the alley and pulled her hood up. Then she started walking.

The first time she'd walked through Dublin-Within-The-Wall in Dimension X, she'd been struck by the fashion. The sartorial choices of the sorcerers there had been ostentatious, impractical, and mostly downright ridiculous. Here, it was different. The people were well dressed and obviously wealthy, but their clothes were far more conservative.

She passed an electrical shop with huge TVs in the window. They didn't have any cables, though, so she wondered if electrical was the right word to use. It looked like everything here was run on magic.

Some of the screens were showing a big-budget action movie. An Oscar-winning actor from Valkyrie's own time ran into frame, exchanged some dialogue with her co-star, then flew into the air – young and beautiful and no special effects required.

She passed clothes shops and bookstores and cafés and restaurants. She walked through throngs of people and eavesdropped on their conversations. It comforted her to hear them gossip about friends, complain about work, laugh about dumb things they'd done. It was all so wonderfully and refreshingly normal.

Until she overheard two women talking about the 'poor wretches' caught on their way to Australia. They kept their voices down, but Valkyrie wasn't the only one to hear them. As soon as they became aware of the looks they were getting from a few passers-by, they shut up and increased their pace. One of those passers-by tapped the hinge of his jaw and a small sigil started glowing blue. He spoke softly, nodded and spoke again, tapped the sigil and it faded away.

A moment later, two City Guard officers appeared out of empty space, in black uniforms slashed with red.

The crowd parted like a stream flowing round a couple of

rocks, and the hum of voices picked up, as if everyone was intent on demonstrating the casual nature of their conversation. But the cops weren't interested in everyone else – they held up their hands, stopping the two terrified women, and closed in with sneers on their faces.

Valkyrie put her head down and kept walking.

Banners criss-crossed the streets and huge placards hovered and spun in mid-air. Draíocht. They were talking about that back in her time, too. Féile na Draíochta – the Festival of Magic – celebrated a particular confluence of factors that boosted all magic in the world from twelve noon to twelve midnight on the 31st of May. These factors only came together once every seventy-two years.

She'd tried to travel six years into the future, and ended up travelling seventy-two.

Typical.

"You're new here."

He lounged against the wall, hands in his pockets. He looked to be Valkyrie's age, but it was hard to tell with magic. He didn't have a good smile. It pinched his thin face.

"How did you know?" she asked.

He tapped his head. "The psychic blocks you're using up here. They're not allowed in Roarhaven. I don't know where they *are* allowed, but definitely not here. Our cops like to be able to make sure that the population aren't thinking subversive thoughts."

"And is that who you are? A cop?"

He laughed. "No, not me. I'm just like you – an ordinary citizen of the world with an endearing tendency to break the law every once in a while."

"By standing here reading people's minds," Valkyrie said. "You do that a lot?"

He shrugged. "A bit. I just like to peek, that's all. Never know what folks are thinking, or planning, or remembering. And you looked interesting, so I thought I'd take a quick gander. My hopes were high of seeing something fun."

"Sorry to disappoint."

"Ah, no harm done. It got us talking, didn't it? I see that as a win."

"You're taking quite a risk, though, aren't you? Confessing your crimes to a complete stranger? For all you know, *I* might be a cop."

"Are you?"

"No."

"Good. Although you do kinda have that look about you."

"What look would that be?"

"The look of authority. It's something I could never quite manage, in all honesty. How do you get a look like that, if you don't mind me asking?"

Valkyrie shrugged. "I think it comes naturally when enough people start doing what you tell them to. How long have you been in Roarhaven?"

"All my life. Where you from?"

"Not here."

"Ah, a woman of mystery! I like that! Can you tell me your name?"

"I could, but I won't."

He laughed again. "I like you! Oh, I like you! I am not a man of mystery, however, and my name is Izzaruh Rinse. Can I buy you a cup of tea? I know a place that does the best leaf blend in Roarhaven – one sip and you're floating."

"I'm not in the mood for tea," Valkyrie said. "You have a house, Izzaruh?"

"An apartment."

"I'm new in town, and I'm a bit lost and bewildered, and I just need a place to sit down for an hour or two and get my bearings. Could I impose?"

"It would be no imposition at all," Izzaruh said, his smile widening. "Come this way, mysterious lady!"

He held out his arm and she took it.

# 18

Izzaruh's apartment building was ten minutes away. In place of
a lift, there was a collection of large tiles, like back in the High
Sanctuary, and they took you up to the top floor. Izzaruh led the
way into his apartment, trying to tidy as he gave Valkyrie the
tour. He didn't appear to have any great source of income, yet
the apartment was magnificent.

"Are all apartments here as nice as this one?" she asked, standing
on the wide balcony and looking out across the city. She took her
hood down.

He shrugged. "I suppose, yeah. But I decorated it myself."

"Oh," she said, smiling. "Yeah, it shows." It was not well
decorated.

"Can I get you something?" he asked. "A drink? A coffee?"

"No, thank you. I have some questions, though. Could we go
back inside?"

"Sure," he said, and followed along. He shut the balcony
doors.

"It's so quiet," Valkyrie said.

Izzaruh nodded. "Walls and windows have been treated.
Standard stuff, but, I swear, I could run around screaming and
my neighbours wouldn't hear a thing."

"Now that is good to know," Valkyrie said, tapping his chest.

There was a flash and he hurtled backwards, nearly flipping over the couch.

"Ow!" he said, clutching the point of contact. "Ow!"

"Sorry," said Valkyrie.

He scrambled to right himself on the furniture. "What are you doing? Why'd you do that?"

"Izzaruh, I don't want you to panic, OK? I'm not going to hurt you."

He pointed with both hands to his chest and said, "Ha!" in a way that was both triumphant and defeatist.

"I mean I'm not going to hurt you any *more*," Valkyrie clarified. "Unless I have to, obviously."

"Why... why would you have to?"

"I won't have to. Forget about that part. I just need you to answer a few questions."

He paled. "You *are* a cop."

"No," she said. "I'm just looking for answers."

"What kind of answers? Why couldn't you just ask? Why did you have to attack me?"

"I am genuinely sorry about that," she said. "I just needed to demonstrate my willingness to inflict pain on you if you start to panic."

"I don't panic," he replied, indignation edging his words. He got to his feet. "I warn you – I did self-defence."

"You did, huh? Do you remember any of it?"

He held up his fists. "The basics."

Valkyrie nodded, and pushed him back down. "These won't be difficult questions, I promise. I'm not from around here and I need to get a few things straight, OK?"

"If you have questions, do what everyone else does. Ask the internet."

"And there's one of my questions," Valkyrie said. "You have the internet?"

"Of course we have the internet," he replied. "We're not some backwards little nowhere! We're Ireland, the world's capital country. We have the fastest internet connection possible. The only way it'd be any faster is if the answer appeared before the question was asked."

"That's a good line."

He shrugged. "It was in the ad. You know, with the monkey? The giraffe asks how fast is your connection and the monkey says... well, he says the line. It's got that annoying jingle at the end." He sang the next bit. "*For all your needs from A to Z, log on with us just wait and see.* Remember it? It's an awful jingle. It contradicts the very thing it's advertising, y'know? Selling instant download and upload speeds and the song ends with *wait and see.* I mean, come on. Keep your eye on the brand."

"But the internet is a mortal invention."

"No," Izzaruh said immediately. "Everyone thought it was when it first appeared, but now we know that the guy who thought it up was magic."

"I don't think that's right."

"Well, mystery lady, you're the one attacking me, so I'm fully prepared to believe you over everything that was taught to me in school."

"Who's in charge?"

"Of the internet?"

"Of the world."

"What?"

"What's your system of government?"

"Where are you from?"

"Izzaruh, unless you want me to zap you again, you'll just answer my questions."

He sighed. "Our system of government? I don't know. I mean, it's whatever the standard system of government is. Each country has its Grand Mage and the Grand Mage has their Council of Elders, and the Council of Elders have the Lower Councils and that's how countries are run."

"What about the Supreme Mage?" she asked.

He frowned. "We haven't had a Supreme Mage in, like, over seventy years."

"Damocles Creed isn't the Supreme Mage?"

"What? No."

Valkyrie nodded. That was something, at least.

"He's the pope," said Izzaruh.

"What?"

"Well, that's what we call him. Unofficially, of course. Using mortal terms for stuff like this is frowned upon. Do you know what a pope was?"

"Of course I know what a pope was."

He held up his hands. "OK, OK, I was just checking. You don't seem to know much else, so I didn't know if... Anyway, officially, he's the High Exalted One, but we all call him the pope. He's the guy in charge. The Grand Mages report to the Arch-Canons and the Arch-Canons report to him. It's a fairly simple process."

"What about Skulduggery Pleasant?"

"I don't know who that is."

"Then how about mortals?" she said. "Are there any left?"

"Do you not have mortals where you're from?"

"Izzaruh..."

"Sorry, sorry, mortals, yeah, of course we have mortals. Everyone who's born is a mortal. Then when the kids are old enough they're tested, and if they have magic they're allowed to become a member of society, and, if they don't, they stay mortal and do all the jobs that mortals do."

"So mortals are still slaves?"

"No!" said Izzaruh, like that was the most ridiculous thing he'd ever heard. "They work in service industries and manufacturing and as manual labour and they're not paid so, OK, yeah, maybe you could call them slaves. But look," he said, directing her to a large hardback book on his coffee table.

Valkyrie flicked through page after page of photographs of

exhausted people working on farms, in factories, lugging boxes and tools. She came to the section showcasing these people in cages and closed the book.

"I know what you're thinking," said Izzaruh. "Haunting, right? But isn't there something beautiful in their tragedy? A certain, I dunno... nobility in their eyes? That book has become a real rallying cry for mages who are determined to get more rights for mortals. I donate whenever I can and I'm seriously thinking about volunteering the next time someone organises something. There are some of us who do actually care."

"Uh-huh," said Valkyrie. "What about if two mages had a kid, and that kid turned out not to have any magic? Would the kid be taken from the parents?"

"Of course not. We're not barbarians. They stay with their folks until they're eighteen and then they get a job."

"So those mortals are seen as being equal to mages?"

Izzaruh hesitated. "I wouldn't go so far as to say *equal*. They're not discarded or anything, but... well, they don't have *magic*, y'know? They're kinda limited in what they can do. Listen, mystery lady, society is made up of tiers, yeah? You've got your elites at the top. They're the ruling class. Then you've got your rich and powerful. Then come your regular people, mages like you and me. Then far, *far* below us are the peasants – mortals who were born to mages. And below them are the serfs, which is most mortals."

"And what about the Faceless Ones?"

"All glory to them," said Izzaruh.

Valkyrie hesitated. "Did they come back?"

He looked at her. Kept looking at her. "Who are you?"

"I'm asking the—"

"No," he said, standing. "No. You can't *not* know this. You just can't. Who are you? Where are you from? What do you want with me?"

"I need you to stay calm, Izzaruh."

"Tell me who you are!"

"I'm not here to hurt you."

"Tell me!"

"Izzaruh—"

She reached for him and he jerked back, tripped, whacked his arm into her face as he flailed. He scrambled over the coffee table and tried to bolt, but Valkyrie jumped into his path. He backed off, towards the balcony doors.

"Who are you?" he said. "Tell me who you are!"

"My name is Valkyrie," she said, walking slowly after him. "I'm not from here, Izzaruh." She thought about telling the truth, then decided against it. "I'm from an alternate world. I'm just trying to figure this place out while I try to get home."

He stopped backing up. "You shunted here?"

"Yes."

"You're from a parallel universe?"

"Yes."

"Do I exist there?"

She blinked. "Sure."

"Do we... do we know each other in your universe?"

"Yes," she lied.

"Are we... together?"

She shrugged. "Sure, why the hell not?"

He brightened immediately. "I knew it! I felt it! You must have felt it, too, right? That connection between us? It's fate. Destiny."

"That's what it is, all right."

"Do I call you darling?"

"Uh-huh."

"And what do you call me?"

"I call you... Teddy-bear."

He smiled. "That's cute."

"It is, Izzaruh. It's sickeningly cute. So, Teddy-bear, tell me about the Faceless Ones."

"What about the Faceless Ones, all glory to their name?"

"Have they come back?"

"Of course," Izzaruh said, laughing. "They came back and they changed the world." His laugh faded. "Do you have them in your universe?"

She nodded.

"Oh, good!" he said, his smile returning. "I don't even want to think what it'd be like to live in a world without their limitless love and understanding and terrible, terrible wrath."

"It's hardly worth imagining."

"Which is why I don't. When they came back to your universe, did you have to use the Seven Pillars?"

"The what?"

"The Seven Pillars. That's what the pope – sorry, the High-Exalted One – used to bring them back. The Pillars – I always get this wrong – but I think it's the Pillars that sent out the Activation Wave, and the Wave turned ten or twenty thousand people into Kith before it found the Child of the Faceless Ones." He frowned. "Wait, no... Yes, the Pillars definitely sent out the Wave, but there was an eye involved, too."

"An eye?"

"A monster's eye, yeah. That did something important."

"And when did all this happen?"

He beamed. "Now this I *do* know because, well, everyone knows it. It happened at twelve minutes to midnight on Draíocht. We'll be celebrating the anniversary in three weeks or so. We should go. You and me. There'll be fireworks and a carnival and behead-ings and little stalls everywhere."

"Beheadings?"

He paused. "Well, yeah, but... tasteful beheadings. It'll be romantic."

Over his shoulder, through the glass doors leading to the balcony, something was flying. A huge bird coming straight for them. No, not a bird. "Izzaruh," said Valkyrie, "do you have people with wings in this universe?"

"What?" he said, frowning. "No. Of course not. Well, apart

from the harpy. You know, the bird-woman from Greek and Roman myth? Yeah, we got one of those for some reason. She's killed, like, loads of people. Why'd you ask?"

The harpy crashed through the balcony doors, screeching. Izzaruh was thrown to the ground and Valkyrie turned away from the explosion of glass and wood, and when she looked back the harpy was standing on Izzaruh's back, her great wings folding up behind her.

Black hair, long and untamed, hanging over her face. Barefoot. Dressed in rags. Taloned feet curling into the flesh of Izzaruh's back. Crouching down, clawed hand curling round his throat.

Valkyrie yelled as the harpy killed him.

She loosed a bolt of lightning, but the harpy was already moving, already dodging, already closing the distance between them. A bloodstained hand closed round Valkyrie's throat, sharp nails piercing her skin, and she was lifted, her back crunching into the wall. She brought her fists down on the arm, buckled the elbow, then she was thrown. She hit the ground and rolled, but the harpy wasn't giving her any space. A kick lashed into her side. Another cracked into her spine. She grabbed for a leg and the harpy dropped a knee into her side. Even with the necronaut suit, the breath was driven out of her.

Eyes screwed shut, trying to suck in air, her hand crackled and she poured her anger into a sustained blast of white lightning – but the harpy slashed at her wrist and Valkyrie cried out, her own blood splashing across her cheek. Hands seized her hair and yanked her to her feet and an elbow smashed into her face.

Valkyrie went stumbling. The pain darted through her skull. Her nose was broken and there was blood in her mouth and her right hand was useless, but now she had the harpy in front of her, a dark figure in her blurred vision. Now she had a target.

She roared as she unleashed an arc of white lightning. It struck home, hurling the creature away from her. Using the heel of her left hand, Valkyrie scrubbed the tears from her eyes as she stalked forward. Energy crackling, she yelled out something, no words, just a sound, just a shout, just about all she could manage with this level of pain and fury coursing through her, and the winged woman spun and Valkyrie's fury left her.

It was her. She was thinner, she had fangs, her face was etched with lines of pain and hardship and horror, but the winged woman was Valkyrie.

And, as Valkyrie recognised her, so she recognised Valkyrie and she froze, confusion flickering through the animalistic hatred.

Her cracked lips contorted.

Then the harpy shrieked and darted forward. Her right hand swept out as she passed and Valkyrie felt it drift by her throat. A moment later, she was watching her blood pump away from her and she clutched at the wound and stepped backwards, eyes wide. Her ankle gave way and she fell to her knees and all that warm blood kept coming out, flowing down her arms, splashing to the floor. She was making a sound, a gurgling sound, and her thoughts were in a distant place and all she felt was fear. This is how she died. On her knees, as she'd always known.

The harpy looked down at her with her own face, and then walked out to the balcony and those great wings unfurled. She leaped into the air and with each beat the wings propelled her upwards and then she was gone and Valkyrie was left alone.

# 19

Her blood-slicked fingers felt for the amulet, tapped it and the suit flowed off her body. She tapped it again and the suit came back, this time with gloves, this time with a zip that was already zipped right up to her ruined throat. She reached those fingers behind her, grabbing for the hood, but her fingers were numb. She pulled at nothing but air until finally – *finally* – she found the hood. Pulled it up. Pulled the mask down.

She didn't know if this would work. Didn't know if this would keep her alive.

The suit sealed itself. Her blood still pumped. Keeping both hands pressed to her throat, Valkyrie stood and fell and stood again. Her vision was failing. The only sounds she could hear were her own breathing and her own weakening heartbeat deep in her skull.

Her boots scraped along the floor to the balcony. She kept her chin tucked low, but raised her eyes to the city, searching for landmarks. There. The High Sanctuary – the only place she could be sure of that would still have a medical facility.

She focused on her magic, brought it in so that it crackled all round her, and then climbed over the balcony rail and fell.

She lost consciousness for a moment, and woke again to a spinning city. She blasted towards the building opposite, couldn't stop in time and slammed into it. She bounced off, whirling, falling, blasted again, realised she was facing the wrong way, realised she was hurtling to the street. She veered upwards at the last moment, her power sputtering out, aware of the shouts of alarm from the people below.

She hit another wall, bounced off that, bounced off the awning of a shop and flipped through the air until the street rose to slap her. More shouts. Footsteps and then faces peering down.

None of this mattered to Valkyrie. The world was darkening and there was no sound any more and it was all so very cold.

# 20

Six years ago...

She came forward with an attack, the worn wooden staff a blur. He met each strike with a block, the vibrations from every impact blending into one, such was the speed at which their weapons met.

Valkyrie shifted left, her footwork flawless. He responded in kind. She backed off. The lure was obvious, but he allowed himself to be pulled into it nonetheless, curious to see where this would lead. She slipped on the icy ground and went down to one knee, but when he swung for her head she rolled beneath his staff and twisted. She would have taken his legs from under him had he not expected the move and leaped, flipping backwards. He knocked the weapon from her hands as she rose, and jabbed the end of his staff into her solar plexus.

Quell transitioned into a relaxed stance and watched Valkyrie stagger back, struggling for breath. "That's enough for today," he said.

She shook her head. "No..."

"You need time to recover. I'll return the day after tomorrow."

She straightened. "No," she said more forcefully.

"The body doesn't work like you want it to work. You expect too much of yourself."

"I'm paying you to train me."

"And I decide how I train you," he responded.

"One more hour," she said. "We'll keep going for one more hour and then I'll see you the day after tomorrow."

He kept his eyes on her as he considered the proposal. During his time as a Cleaver, he'd had minimal interactions with anyone not wielding a scythe. Usually, these interactions consisted of little more than barked orders and official instructions, with the occasional briefing being the closest he'd come to regular conversation. Since he'd hung up the grey, he had spoken to exactly four mortals – always when they were behind a counter, looking uninterested. He liked that. It didn't overload his capacity for understanding emotions.

The only person with whom he'd interacted on any sort of deeper level was Valkyrie Cain – but he still had to work out if she was a good example of a functioning human being.

For one thing, she hated herself. This had taken him some months to realise. The constant dissatisfaction with her own progress, the endless criticism of her own abilities – at first, he'd thought these reflected an unhappiness with the training he was providing. But it had nothing to do with him, and everything to do with Valkyrie, and why she was here in Colorado in the first place.

And, for another thing, he doubted he'd ever met – in his admittedly limited experience – a person possessed of more sadness than Valkyrie Cain. He was no expert in this – or any – emotion, but it didn't escape his notice that for this sadness to be apparent to someone like him, it must be a stark kind of sadness indeed.

And it was all there as she waited for his decision, all there in her eyes.

"One more hour," he said. "On the condition that tomorrow you do nothing. You do not lift weights; you do not run; you do not work. Are we agreed?"

She got her toe under her fallen staff, and flicked it up into her hand. "Agreed."

He nodded, paused, went to speak again, but instead he whacked the staff against her head and lunged forward.

# 21

Sebastian went to the cinema.

He sat alone in the flickering dark and lost himself in a movie for two hours. It was glorious. Darquesse was at home with Ulysses and Kimora, who had been nominated as her teachers. There had been a spirited debate in the Society about whether Darquesse even needed an education, what with the vast knowledge her other selves had accumulated before her birth. They had reached the decision to go ahead with formal lessons until Darquesse herself indicated that she didn't require them. The entire reason Darquesse was putting herself through this, after all, was to experience as much of a normal life as possible before making the final judgement as to whether or not the world was worth saving.

No pressure on the father, then.

Once the movie was over, Sebastian took a leisurely stroll home. He got more than a few hostile glances and the occasional remark about his appearance, but he shrugged them all off. If you can't dress up as a leather-clad plague doctor in a city of sorcerers, then where could you? That was his philosophy.

He passed a man pushing a pram and gave him a big, understanding smile. The man couldn't see the smile, of course, and gave him a wide berth, but there was a bond there – the bond of parenthood. The bond of fatherhood.

Sebastian had never really contemplated the notion that he'd ever be a father. It wasn't something that had occurred to him. Parenthood, for sorcerers, wasn't something that had to be rushed into before a certain amount of time had elapsed. Sorcerers had centuries to contemplate starting a family. But now here he was, raising a child. Being a dad.

Thoughts of his own father intruded upon his good mood and he shut him out.

He got home, had barely stepped through the front door when Ulysses hurried out to meet him.

"You need to..." he said, and gestured.

Sebastian followed him into the living room, where a gale was blowing. Kimora stood, chewing a knuckle, while her hair whipped round her face, eyes on Darquesse who floated in mid-air, examining a portal that had opened up before her.

"That was a chair," Ulysses shouted over the wind. "That was a chair that she turned into a... a whatever that is."

Kimora looked over. "First, she turned it into a rock," she shouted. "Then a butterfly. Then she turned it into a shark. A huge, huge shark. The shark knocked over the lamp." She pointed. The lamp had indeed been knocked over. "Then it became a vortex of..."

Kimora shrugged, at a loss for words.

Sebastian moved into Darquesse's line of sight. "Sweetie? Darquesse? What's that?"

"It's a chair," Darquesse said loudly.

"Well, it used to be a chair. What is it now?"

She glanced at him, frowning in a way that said Daddy is an idiot. "It's still a chair. It just looks different. And you can't sit on it. And it lets you see into other dimensions. And take things from it."

She reached into the portal, came back with an ice cream. The portal twisted in on itself and became a puppy that floated into Darquesse's arms and licked the ice cream. As an afterthought, she looked up again. "Daddy, can we have a dog?"

# 22

Emmeline and Craddock were already at their table when Omen and Auger got to the restaurant. They rose from their chairs, each giving Omen a hug, and each making a fuss over Auger, as to be expected. When everyone was seated, they asked how school was going and generally made small talk until they'd given their orders and the serving staff left them alone.

This was the first time they'd all gone out to dinner since Auger had killed the King of the Darklands. Omen wondered how long it'd take his folks to mention that.

"A toast," said Craddock, "to the Chosen One, for killing the King of the Darklands and saving the world a full year ahead of schedule."

"That's my boy," Emmeline said. "Always overachieving."

Omen gave a polite chuckle at that, but Auger barely cracked a smile. Omen doubted either of his parents noticed.

"We find ourselves at something of a loss," Emmeline said, "as I'm sure you do, too. All your lives you've been hearing about how Auger is the Chosen One, how he has this magnificent destiny waiting for him. Your lives, and our lives, have revolved round this. The training, the preparation... I daresay at times it's been positively overwhelming."

Auger nodded.

"So now we've got to look to the future," Craddock said. "What does the Chosen One do once his destiny has been fulfilled?"

"Sleep," said Auger, and Omen laughed.

Their parents smiled. "Indeed," said Emmeline. "Sleep. After all this time, we can finally relax. Do you have any plans for what to do once you wake up, though? Have you given it any thought?"

Omen would have chipped in an answer at that point, maybe mentioned art college, but it was clear his folks were talking to Auger, who merely shrugged.

"We were talking it over," Craddock said, and Auger looked up for the first time.

"Who?"

"Sorry?"

"You were talking it over?"

"Yes."

"You were talking about what I'm going to do next?"

"Yes, and we—"

"What have you decided?"

Craddock frowned and Emmeline said, "Auger, don't interrupt your father."

"It's just, you know all that training I did?" Auger asked. "And the studying? And the work? And all those things I sacrificed? Whenever I'd complain or ask to be allowed to do something or go somewhere, you always said no, the training comes first. And, as the Chosen One, I accepted that – especially when you pointed out that after I'd fought the King of the Darklands all the pressure would be off and I'd be able to do whatever I wanted. That was the promise you made me. Do you remember?"

Craddock's jaw was clenched. This happened when he was mad.

"Yes," Emmeline said, "of course we remember. And that still holds. You'll be able to do whatever you want to do."

"Cool."

"But you must take everything into consideration," their mother continued. "We must look around and evaluate our situation and make the best, the most informed, decision."

"Right," Auger said slowly. "Only, see, now it sounds like it's less *my* decision and more *your* decision."

"Auger," Craddock said. "Nobody likes impertinence."

Omen expected his brother to hold his tongue, like he had done so many times in the past. But instead Auger smirked.

"Impertinence," he echoed. "That was one of your favourites when we were growing up. Whenever you didn't have a good response for us, you just called us impertinent and that'd be the end of it. You can't really get away with that any more, though, can you, Craddock?"

"You watch your tone, boy."

Auger laughed. "Or what?"

The serving staff came over, placed their starters on the table, and left. Auger never took his eyes off Craddock.

"This is good soup," Omen said, before he'd tried any.

Nobody else spoke.

Omen cleared his throat and picked up his glass. "I'd like to make a toast—"

"Shut up," said Craddock.

Auger's fist rattled the table. "You do *not* tell him to shut up."

Emmeline placed her hand against her chest. "I don't know what's got into you today, Auger, but that is not how we behave in this family."

"No," Auger said, "you're absolutely right. We have manners in this family, don't we? We treat each other with respect, we don't answer back, and we send our firstborn son off to die."

Omen looked down at his bowl.

"How dare you," said Craddock.

"How dare I?" Auger leaned forward. "You've made an entire business out of my date with destiny. You've elevated yourselves above all your old friends because I was the Chosen One and that made you important. You profited off the fact that I was going to risk my life and you never once even *suggested* that maybe we should all just run away before that day came. Any other parent would want to grab their kids and get the hell out if they knew there was the slightest chance of danger – but not you two. You patted me on the back and gave me a little push. And I'm not the only one you've wronged. The way you've treated Omen ever since we were born? It's disgusting."

"Ah," said Omen, "I didn't mind."

"Yes, you did," said Auger. "Remember how you used to cry yourself to sleep?"

"No..."

"Well, I do. It's a bloody miracle you grew up to be a good person, dude, it really is, because you weren't shown even the slightest bit of love."

Craddock pushed his plate to one side. "Keep your voice down."

"Shut up, Craddock."

Craddock's face went a startling shade of red.

"I'm going to make a wild guess," Auger said, leaning back in his chair. "I'm going to guess that you were about to suggest that I involve myself in something big. Would I be right? Maybe another end-of-the-world prophecy, if we could find something suitable? Just enough to keep me in the spotlight a little bit longer? Like you said, Emmeline, this Darklands thing has been concluded a whole year early. You weren't expecting that, were you? I bet you've got a load of business threads just dangling now that nobody feels compelled to take your calls. That's why you summoned us here for this delightful family meal, isn't it?"

Omen risked another peek. His parents looked pale and deflated, as if Auger had worked it all out and they no longer had any basis for outrage.

Auger stood. "I've lost my appetite. Good to see you both, by the way. Maybe this should be a weekly thing?"

He walked away from the table.

# 23

Commander Hoc woke up early, like he did every morning.

As the dawn cracked open across the horizon like a spilled egg, he stood at the huge east-facing window in his apartment and looked out over the city as it stirred to waking.

In this city, people were afraid of him. He liked that feeling.

He sat down for his breakfast, specially prepared by the cook. Not less than two months ago, he'd had to waste time making his own meals, just like he'd had to press his own uniform and polish his own boots. The bean counters at the High Sanctuary had initially refused to grant his request to bring in people to do this kind of stuff for him, but Hoc could be terribly persuasive when he put his mind to it – and terribly persuasive when he insinuated that their actions might warrant an official City Guard investigation.

They caved, because that's what spineless people do, and it made him smile every time he thought of it. Even the bureaucrats were scared of him.

It meant, of course, that at certain hours of the day his luxury apartment was filled with mortals, but this was a sacrifice he was willing to make. Besides, he kept them doing what they were good at – cooking, cleaning, and polishing – and he made sure they knew their place. He'd laid down the rules early. No speaking, no looking him in the eye, and no mistakes. Hoc couldn't abide mistakes.

Once breakfast was done, he dressed in his uniform and slid his sword into its sheath and his gun in its holster. Weapon maintenance was something he handled himself, as he just couldn't trust these mortals not to sabotage his pistol or weaken his blade. There were some things in life a police officer had to take care of *personally*.

He hung his shock stick from his belt. They were required to carry them at all times since the curfew came into effect. The citizens were being unruly.

He left his apartment and stepped into a waiting car that drove him the three minutes it took to get to the High Sanctuary. He could have walked it in ten, but what example would that have set? The people must be made to understand that the police were there to protect them, and as such had to be better than they were.

As he climbed the steps, he could feel the Cleavers watching him from behind their visors. The City Guard officer on the door knew him and let him through without checking his credentials. Hoc made a note to issue a citation for dereliction of duty later that day.

The Administrator was waiting for him in the lobby. She led him to the elevator and they rode up in silence. Hoc glanced at her clipboard, gladdened to see that she was being kept busy. Busy was healthy. A bored mind was a dangerous mind. She walked him to the Supreme Mage's office, then bid him good day and left.

The Supreme Mage's assistant was a tidy man sitting behind a tidy desk. Hoc waited three minutes until the assistant told him he could enter.

The office was stripped of any extravagance that China Sorrows had brought to it. A floor-to-ceiling window looked out over the city, and a desk sat dark and heavy in the centre of the room. Behind that desk was the Arch-Canon of the Church of the Faceless, and the acting Supreme Mage of the High Sanctuary: Damocles Creed.

It was a privilege afforded to a rare few to see him like this. The people of Roarhaven were used to seeing the Supreme Mage in the Dark Cathedral, delivering one of his famous sermons where his clenched fist would pound the pulpit and his voice would shake the foundations of the world. It was mesmerising watching him work, gazing up at him as his face contorted with righteous fury, as he spat his words like razor blades. Many a time, Hoc had watched people stumble out into the street, exhilarated beyond comprehension.

A voice came on over the speakerphone. "Supreme Mage, the Chief Medical Officer is on the line."

The Supreme Mage tapped a button. "Let her speak."

A click, and a woman's voice filled the office. "Supreme Mage, may the glory of their love shine upon you."

"And upon you," the Supreme Mage answered. "Your report."

"China Sorrows' vital signs are fluctuating slightly, but are well within normal parameters and consistently within the range we are comfortable with. She is, of course, unconscious, and brain activity is minimal, but, using electroencephalography, we have detected cognitive activity in response to verbal commands. This is a heartening sign."

"Heartening," the Supreme Mage said.

"As I reported to you last week, two of our staff are accomplished Sensitives. Unfortunately, the psychic trauma that Miss Sorrows was subjected to is still too dense to penetrate. We fear any further attempts could damage her beyond repair."

The Supreme Mage nodded, and considered, and finally spoke. "We cannot risk further harm befalling her," he decided. "Pull back from the psychic examinations and focus on her physical well-being. We shall trust that our Supreme Mage will be strong enough to recover on her own."

"Yes, sir."

"I expect another briefing at the same time next week."

"Thank you, Supreme Mage."

He cut off the call and looked up. "Commander Hoc, are you any closer to finding the dissidents we're after?"

"I believe we're closing in, sir."

The Supreme Mage sat back in his stiff chair. His shirt was simple, and would have been loose on anyone else, but his physique stretched it tight across his chest and arms. "Take me through your methods, Commander."

"Yes, sir. Because we began with no leads, we focused our attention on the friends and relatives of the people the rebels have aided."

"I don't want you to use that word," the Supreme Mage said. "To call them *rebels* gives them a robust charisma in the minds of the general public. These people are nothing but common criminals."

"Of course, sir," said Hoc. "From these friends and families, we have expanded our search. I have given a quota to my team on how many citizens a day should be brought in for questioning."

"And what have the results been?"

"Some entirely innocent citizens. Some citizens confessing to previously unconnected criminal activity. A lot of admissions of blasphemy."

"Continue."

"I firmly believe that nobody we have thus far questioned has any information about the identities of these dissidents – but I am confident that they've given us the names of citizens who might."

"I want these scum caught, Commander."

"Yes, sir."

"I want you to haul them in, do you understand me? I want the people of this wonderful city to gaze upon their faces and see them for what they are. I want them beaten. I want them broken. Humiliated."

"Sir, yes, sir."

Supreme Mage Creed observed him for close to ten seconds

without saying anything. Then he nodded. "Good. You have a solid method and you're carrying through with it. It's important, Commander, that in the job, as in life, people like us do not flounder."

*People like us.*

"No, sir," Hoc said.

The Supreme Mage pushed back his chair and stood. The immensity of the man came scarily close to intimidating, and Hoc was not someone easily intimidated. "Come," Creed said, moving to the window.

Hoc moved quickly, and stood by the Supreme Mage's side as he gazed over the city.

"These dissidents are an irritant," he said, "and your work is important. You must find them before they spark open acts of rebellion. This coming Friday I plan to announce another wave of restrictions – for the public good – that will undoubtedly lead to widespread dissatisfaction."

"Yes, sir."

"Dissatisfaction is a virus, Commander Hoc. It affects the non-believers, the wicked, and the blasphemers alike. But I have faith in you. You will put a stop to their antics and you will make them suffer. I'm not worried about that. Somewhere down there, in those streets, in those buildings, is the person I've been looking for my whole life. Someone who will change the world. Do you know what I'm talking about, Commander?"

Despite his best efforts, Hoc had heard rumours. "The Child of the Faceless Ones, sir."

The Supreme Mage smiled. "Indeed. We have been detecting traces of Faceless Ones' DNA in certain human bloodlines long before we knew what deoxyribonucleic acid even was. Someone down there has enough of the Faceless Ones' genome to endure Activation. This is not merely supposition on my part. It has been confirmed by leading psychics that I will find the Child of the Faceless Ones on the night of Draíocht, three weeks from now."

The Supreme Mage turned his head to Hoc. His eyes gleamed. "It is my destiny, Commander."

"Yes, sir."

"Thirteen years ago, Baron Vengeous revived the Grotesquery, a tormented creature, whose death cry woke the Faceless Ones from their slumber. The following year, they briefly returned to this realm – but the environment was unsuited to the forms they had taken. When the Child brings them back, we need to have made this reality as comfortable for them as it once was."

"How do you – pardon me – how do you intend to do that, sir?"

Another smile. "I'm working on it. I have whole teams of our best scientists working on it."

"Yes, sir."

"Stick by my side, Commander, and stick close. I will have need of people like you. We will drag this world into the future, and we will see it remade around us. Anywhere but by my side would not be an advisable place to be, do you understand?"

"My place is by your side, sir."

"Good man," said the Supreme Mage. "Dismissed."

Hoc snapped out a salute, turned on his heel, and marched from the office. When he entered the lift, he punched the button for the ground floor. The doors closed and the lift started moving and Hoc leaned his back against the wall and gasped.

There were a lot of different kinds of power in the world, but Damocles Creed had the most potent – he had the power of authority, the power to make people do what he said simply because he said it.

When the new world came, there would be those who stomped, and those who got stomped. Hoc was determined to learn as much from the Supreme Mage as he possibly could so that, when the new world began, he'd be doing the stomping.

# 24

"There," the doctor said, squinting at Valkyrie's throat. "Not even a mark. This is good. I'm happy with this. Are you happy?"

Valkyrie nodded and the doctor straightened, picked up her chart and scribbled something.

The Medical Facility in the High Sanctuary was pretty much the same as she remembered it. Maybe some of the machines were different, but she had no way of knowing for sure. She'd never paid much attention to machines in the Medical Facility unless they happened to be saving her life at the time.

They'd dressed her in a hospital gown. They'd removed her necronaut suit and disposed of the blood-drenched clothes she'd been wearing underneath. She didn't know where they'd put the amulet.

"OK then," said the doctor. "Try to speak. Softly at first – your vocal cords sustained significant damage."

"How's this?" Valkyrie whispered.

"Very good. A little louder."

"Water?" she croaked.

"Oh, of course," the doctor said, moving to a nearby tray. She filled a glass and brought it over. Valkyrie took a few sips.

"Better?" the doctor asked.

Valkyrie nodded. "Suit?"

"Ah, yes," she said, and pressed the hinge of her jaw. A sigil glowed. "Could you bring the patient's belongings, please?" She tapped the sigil again and it faded away. "He'll be just a moment. Now, while we wait, there are some gaps in our information. For starters – we couldn't identify you. There's no need to be alarmed; this kind of thing happens all the time. What's your name?"

Valkyrie hesitated. Telling the truth, she reckoned, would be a bad idea. She took another sip of water while she glanced round the room.

"Miss?" the doctor pressed.

"Tanith," she said. "Tanith Lamp."

The doctor hesitated. "Lamp?"

Valkyrie nodded.

A nurse came in, handed a bag to the doctor, who passed it to Valkyrie. It had her phone and the amulet. She took them both out.

"Remarkable device that," the doctor said, nodding at the amulet. "Where's it from?"

"Necromancers."

She raised an eyebrow. "That must be rare. And the gadget? What does it do?"

"It's a phone."

The doctor's eyes widened. "A mobile cell telephone?"

Valkyrie nodded and smiled and tapped the screen. It was 3:44. In sixteen minutes, the Jericho Candle would be lit back home. All she needed to do was be ready.

"My daughter would *love* something like that," the doctor said. "She's into all things retro right now. I'm, ah, assuming you have the necessary documentation?"

"Absolutely."

The doctor smiled. "You know, of course, that you're required to carry that documentation around with you and produce it on demand. Technically, that's a mortal gadget, and... well, you know the rules."

Valkyrie nodded, and took another sip of water as she swung her legs slowly out of bed.

The doctor's line of questioning was interrupted by the arrival of two City Guard officers. Valkyrie smiled politely and stood up, moving slowly, keeping her expression calm.

"Ah, officers," said the doctor, "I was just asking—"

"We'll do the asking," the male cop said. He held up a rectangle of glass, bordered by metal, about the size of a credit card, and squinted at Valkyrie through it. "Do we have a name?"

"Her name's Tanith Lamp," said the doctor.

"Miss Lamp," said the female cop, "you're one of the few to survive an attack by the harpy. I regret to inform you that your friend, Mr Izzaruh Rinse, was not so lucky. What was your relationship with the..." Her words faded when she noticed the objects in Valkyrie's hands. "You have permits for those things, Miss Lamp?"

Valkyrie nodded.

"Could we see them, please?"

The male cop frowned at the glass rectangle. "We don't have a facial match," he said. "We don't have any record for a Tanith Lamp, either."

"Miss Lamp," said the female cop, "please put the items in your hands on the bed and show us your permits. Do it nice and slow."

Valkyrie nodded, put the phone on the bed, but pressed the amulet to the back of her left hand and tapped it.

The suit spread down her arm, covering her even as she lunged. She batted down the female cop's gun as the woman drew it, grabbing her by the throat with her other hand. The male cop stumbled back, raising his weapon, but the energy that leaped from Valkyrie's eyes hurled him into the wall. Valkyrie took the female cop to the ground and slammed a hammer-fist into her jaw. She went limp, dropping her gun.

Valkyrie stood. The doctor stared, frozen.

"Thanks for saving me," Valkyrie said. "Sorry for the drama."

She grabbed her phone, stuffed it into her pocket, and ran.

She was halfway down the corridor when an alarm pierced the air. She'd almost reached the end when three cops burst through the doors.

Lightning leaped from her fingers, hurling the nearest cop into the others, and Valkyrie vaulted over them and ran on.

She ducked an energy stream. Dodged a fireball. Ran for a window.

Covering her head with her arms, she dived through, the glass smashing around her, the street hurtling towards her. As she fell, she was reminded of that line from one of Douglas Adams' books, where he described flying as the ability to throw yourself at the ground and miss.

Valkyrie rushed towards the ground, and missed splendidly.

# 25

Once she was flying, with the wind dragging her hair, she relaxed. She pulled up her hood and pulled down the skull mask so that she wouldn't have to worry about grit getting in her eyes, and flew past the towers and steeples that had sprouted from Roarhaven in the last seventy-two years. The city gleamed beneath her. In the Arts District, where once there'd stood a cinema, there was now a building with multiple floors that hovered over one another, separated by nothing but air. It was quite a beautiful structure and she glanced back at it and saw the four cops flying after her.

Her eyes narrowed, she forgot about sightseeing, and piled on the speed.

Something small passed close by. Something else zipped by her ear. They were shooting at her, firing black bullets that were getting closer every time.

Valkyrie veered left, then right, then swooped low, skimming over rooftops. They followed, still firing. The bullets splatted against the rooftops like ink.

She didn't know what kind of bullets they were, but she'd never met a bullet she liked.

Swerving upwards, Valkyrie passed over the outer wall and turned, flying backwards, sending out lightning bolts. She didn't hit any of the cops – everyone was moving way too quickly to aim – but succeeded in scattering them, so she turned again and flew on, over roads and fields and the small suburban towns that spread out from Roarhaven.

Two more cops rose from one of these towns, into the air in front of her. She looked back. The others were catching up, expecting to corral her, maybe, to chase her into a trap. Instead, she kept going straight at the cops in front. She was close enough now to see the worried looks on their faces, and in the next moment she smashed into one of them.

He squealed, went tumbling out of the sky. His partner wheeled round, wobbling in mid-air, trying to aim. Valkyrie snatched the pistol from his grip and kicked him away from her, then shot him in the leg. The bullet splatted against him, the ink spreading around his thigh in an instant. A binding sigil glowed from within the ink and the cop plunged to the ground, screaming.

Valkyrie cursed, zoomed after him, ditched the gun so that she could catch him. She dropped him the last four metres and he hit the ground beside his moaning partner and she flew on. She passed over huge farms, a crackling streak of energy in the sky that made the workers look up. As soon as one farm ended, another began, hundreds of people toiling in the fields, sheds, and greenhouses.

The cops were far behind, but all they had to do was keep following the energy trail and they'd eventually catch her. Valkyrie flew low, angling herself towards a few large packing sheds squatting between a field and a road. No one, as far as she could tell, saw her approach, and she cut the power and landed, stumbling slightly as she ran through the side door, out of the sunlight and into the cool shade of the shed and the eye-watering stench of rotting leeks.

Pallets of empty crates were crammed into one side of the shed. Pallets of full crates were crammed into the other. In between were the sorting tables, covered with the discarded remnants of weeks-old vegetables. The main doors – massive things – were wide open. Valkyrie could see hunched-over mortals pulling leeks in the field, dumping them in piles. Other mortals loaded those piles on to a trailer. Nobody talked. Nobody made a sound. The mortals all had a sigil tattooed on to one side of their face.

Walking among them were other mortals. They wore the same kind of dirty jeans as the others, the same kind of muddy boots, but they also wore shirts and ties and high-vis vests. They looked ridiculous, but their outfits succeeded in marking them out as different – marking them out as special. They barked orders and shoved their fellow mortals when they weren't working fast enough. Collaborators, Valkyrie reckoned – the kind of folk who sold out their own people to make it easier on themselves.

She resisted the urge to start blasting. She needed to find a space where she could hide and focus on getting back to her own time.

A strong wind tossed her hair.

She spun as a cop came flying in through the side door, kicking up dirt and dust as his eyes adjusted to the sudden gloom. She grabbed him while he was still in the air, swinging him round, introducing his face to the wall and then catching him with an elbow as he rebounded.

Another cop ran in, firing. The bullet exploded against her chest and the ink spread all the way around her torso even as she was diving at him. Her magic evaporated and her necronaut suit flowed back into the amulet, which dropped to the ground. She filled her hands with the cop's jacket and slammed her forehead into his nose, then stomped on his instep and, when he went down, crunched her knee into his chin. He flopped over backwards. She picked up his gun and stuffed her amulet into her jeans as she dodged into the maze of crates.

Outside, people were shouting and running, coming closer. They were inside the shed now. Valkyrie could see them as they passed through her line of sight. They couldn't see her, though. Right now, she was in the darkness.

It was a tight squeeze, but she managed to bring her free hand up to pull the ink away. She'd never had her magic bound like this before: the binding sigils she was used to dampened her abilities – but the one glowing in the ink cancelled out the necronaut suit, too. That was a heavier kind of power, one she was not a fan of. She tried to dig her fingertips in behind it, but the ink was like a second skin over her T-shirt.

The cops were arguing with each other. The collaborators rushed up, apologising, confessing that they hadn't seen anyone, but they'd heard a gunshot. It was decided that Valkyrie had sneaked out again and flown off. One cop was left behind to try and get his unconscious buddies back on their feet while the rest of them ran out to continue their pursuit of the fugitive.

And then, all of a sudden, it was quiet again. Relatively.

"Can I get you anything?" one of the collaborators asked. "Water? Are you thirsty? All we have is water. Tap water for the workers, but you can have—"

"Shut up," said the cop. "Leave me."

The collaborator left immediately, and Valkyrie heard him screaming at the workers in the fields.

The cop that had been left behind spoke again. "This is Officer Mountain. We have two officers down, in need of teleportation to the Medical Wing. I'm at, uh... I'm at a farm. One of the farms. I don't know. I don't know which one. The one with all the fields."

Valkyrie started edging back the way she'd come.

The cop was growing irritated. "I don't know, I said. It's the one beside Mortal Graves Farm. Tell the Teleporter I'm in one of the big sheds. Tell him to hurry, OK? It stinks in here."

Valkyrie peeked just as Officer Mountain, who had his back to her, tapped the sigil on the hinge of his jaw to end the call. She'd been hoping that the name had been ironic – that he was actually a small man, small and weedy and easily subdued. But Officer Mountain, it seemed, did not possess a sense of irony, and he was, indeed, as big as his name implied.

The gun in her hand would certainly alert the collaborators, and they would certainly alert the cops, so she gripped the pistol by the barrel as she stepped out. Mountain crouched by one of the unconscious cops, nudging him.

"Hey," he said, "wake up. Hey, stupid."

One swing ought to do it, providing she didn't miss. Valkyrie focused on the spot behind his right ear. An easy shot. She could be on him in two quick steps and then it'd be lights out, Officer Mountain. Definitely doable.

Valkyrie lunged and with her first step she slipped on the slimy remains of a rotten leek and crashed to the hard ground, the gun flying from her hand. Mountain whirled as he jumped up.

He looked down at her. She blinked up at him.

He laughed.

She smiled back.

Holding one hand out to ward him off in case he rushed her, she put her weight on her other hand and moved her feet back underneath her, and stood. Rolled her shoulders. "Let's try that again, shall we?"

He went to take out his handcuffs and Valkyrie stepped up and kicked him in the thigh. He hissed in pain as he moved back.

"You can't fight me," he said, like he was stunned she'd even try. "Your magic's bound. Turn round and put your hands on your—"

She kicked him again, same spot, and he snapped his hand at the air and Valkyrie hurtled into a load of empty crates.

"Ow," she moaned.

Mountain came forward, limping slightly, truncheon in hand. It crackled with power. "I don't know what you've done," he said, "or who you are, but you cannot fight me, do you understand? You can't win against me. I'm twice your size, I'm armed, and, unlike you, I can use my magic. So stop kicking me, put on the cuffs, and quit the silliness."

Valkyrie pushed a few crates off, and stood.

"Is everything OK?" the collaborator called, hurrying back in.

"If I see your face again," Mountain roared, "I'll tear it off your head."

The collaborator sobbed and ran.

"Bloody mortals," Mountain grumbled, as Valkyrie stepped into the open. "You going to do the smart thing and come quietly?"

She shrugged. "I was never much one for doing the smart thing, to be honest with you."

He shook his head. "I'm going to have to hurt you."

"You're gonna have to try."

Mountain sighed and swung the truncheon at her head.

She rammed her forearms into his arm, immediately wrapped her arm round his, grabbed his jacket with her other hand and clamped her teeth on to his cheek.

Mountain screeched and reeled as Valkyrie tore into his flesh. He tried to push her away, tried to prise her off, but she shook her head like a dog and gave an animalistic growl for good measure. She felt him slip a little on the ground and opened her jaws, and when he jerked back she slammed the heel of her hand into his chin. She did it again and again until he fell backwards. She landed on top of him and kept hitting, this time with the edge of her fist, a relentless barrage that was breaking bones and smashing teeth.

Then she ripped his gun from its holster and shot him in the belly. The ink spread instantly and she pressed the gun into his cheek – the one she hadn't torn a chunk out of.

"Don't move," she snarled, spitting blood.

"Officer!" the collaborator shouted from outside. "Officer, are you all right?"

"I will eat you!" Valkyrie screamed. "If you come in here again, I will eat you, do you understand?"

She heard the collaborator run off, wailing, and then glared down into Mountain's eyes.

"You try anything, I'll pull the trigger. You think that magic ink will care if it spreads over your mouth and nose? You think it'll care if you suffocate right here in this stinking shed?"

Blood running freely from his face, Mountain gave a small nod of surrender.

"What is it?" Valkyrie asked. "The ink?"

"Not ink," Mountain mumbled. "Transmorphic biomass inlaid with binding sigils."

"Biomass?" Valkyrie frowned. "It's alive?"

"No," said Mountain. "Yes. Not really. Complicated."

"Well, let's simplify things. How do I get it off?"

He shook his head. "Can't. Have to wait for it to peel off on its own."

She pressed the muzzle harder into his cheek. "Do I look stupid to you, Officer Mountain? Do I? You're not gonna go around with bullets like these if you don't have a way of undoing the effects. So how do I get it off?"

"Spray," he said miserably. "In belt."

Valkyrie turned him on to his belly and handcuffed his hands behind his back, then pulled a small plastic bottle from one of his pouches. She sprayed the ink on her T-shirt. It immediately began to stretch and break apart, and the moment the last strand snapped her magic returned to her.

She pulled the rest of it off, let the necronaut suit flow back over her clothes, and pocketed the spray. "Much obliged," she said, and picked up his truncheon. The sigils glowed at her touch.

Mountain muttered a curse as she came over. She pressed the truncheon into his back and he seized up as all those volts passed through his body. She pressed harder and kept it there until he passed out, then she tossed the truncheon away and checked the time on her phone.

Three minutes past four. She could still make it.

Valkyrie sat on the floor beside Mountain and did her very best to ignore the stink of the rotten vegetables.

Deep breath in. Focus. Breath out. Focus. Deep breath in. Find the candle. Breath out. Focus. Deep breath in.

There. The smell of the candle overriding the smell of the leeks. Calling her back, separating her mind from her body, pulling it out of her.

She drifted upwards, her consciousness separating from her body. Her energy started to swirl. She watched her physical form lifting off the floor after her, watched the energy consume it, felt herself break apart, felt herself becoming motes of light and matter and magic and—

# 26

—and felt the universe move around her, felt time exploding in all places at once—

# 27

—and she suddenly had physical form again, suddenly had weight and substance and meaning, and the swirl of energy slowed and she stumbled from the in-between into the now, and Skulduggery and Militsa were there to catch her.

She sagged against them, every part of her jolting and yet utterly exhausted.

"Valkyrie," Militsa said urgently. "Val, can you hear me? Are you OK? Where did this blood come from? Say something!"

"Love your accent," Valkyrie mumbled.

"Oh, thank God," Militsa said, guiding her over to the bed. Valkyrie collapsed on to it and Skulduggery waved a finger and the Jericho Candle was extinguished. It had halved in size.

"Where are the others?" Valkyrie asked.

"Tanith had to go, and Jericho was expending too much energy, so Onosa took him back to Roarhaven," Militsa said. "We didn't expect you to be gone for so long. What happened? Are you hurt? You've got blood all over your face."

"Not my blood," Valkyrie said. "I went to the future. I was there. Not as a projection. As me."

"You actually materialised?" Skulduggery asked, head tilting.

"I materialised so good."

"That is quite astonishing," he said. "Jericho will want to talk to you about that. He surmised that your unique power set might have resulted in just such an occurrence. Congratulations, Valkyrie. As far as I know, you are the world's first time-traveller."

"I rock."

"You do, indeed, rock."

"I was worried sick about you," Militsa said, kneeling by the bed.

Valkyrie patted her face. "You're sweet. Did you feed Xena?"

"Of course I did. How are you feeling?"

"I'm good. I'm fine. Just need a minute. It wasn't this bad going over. Maybe the return trip is always worse – y'know, like jet lag."

"Did you talk to Alice?" Skulduggery asked.

Valkyrie shook her head. "I don't know what I did wrong, but I didn't travel six years into the future – I travelled seventy-two."

Militsa was about to react to that piece of information when her phone beeped. She scowled. "I'm going to be late for work. Valkyrie, no more travelling into the future while I'm gone."

"Gotcha."

Militsa gave her a big kiss. "Fill me in on the details when I get home, OK? Love you."

"Love you," said Valkyrie, and Militsa ran out of there. When they heard the front door slam, Valkyrie spoke again. "Sorcerers run the world. The mortals are slaves. The Faceless Ones came back."

"When?" Skulduggery asked. "When does all that happen?"

"Twelve minutes to midnight on Draíocht."

"So we have twenty-one days to save the world."

"That's more time than we usually get."

"This is true."

They heard the dog coming up the stairs, and a moment later Xena burst into the room, tail wagging. She jumped up on the bed, jumped up on Valkyrie, and stood with her front paws on Valkyrie's chest while Skulduggery scratched behind her ears.

"Ow," said Valkyrie.

She manoeuvred herself into a seated position and waited until Xena had settled down beside her before continuing. "Creed uses something called the Seven Pillars. Don't suppose you know what they are?"

"I'm afraid not," Skulduggery said.

"Well, the Seven Pillars send out an Activation Wave that turns some twenty thousand people into Kith before finding the... before finding Alice. There's an eye involved, too. A monster's eye. That's all I could find out before I attacked me."

"Before you attacked you?"

"Oh, yes. In the future, I'm a harpy, apparently."

"A harpy? With the—?"

"With the wings and the claws and the general mindlessness, yes. I killed the guy who was helping me, and then I attacked myself. I have no idea why."

"Was I there?"

"I didn't see anyone I knew."

"Maybe I'm a robot."

"Why would you be a robot?"

"Half robot, half skeleton, then."

"Again, why would any part of you be a robot?"

"It's the future."

"Tomorrow's the future. Do you think you'll be a robot tomorrow?"

He shook his head. "We're drifting away from the point. Seven Pillars, an Activation Wave, and a monster's eye – we have three weeks to stop all this from happening."

They looked at each other.

"What are you thinking?" Valkyrie asked.

"You know what I'm thinking."

"If I knew, I wouldn't be asking."

"I know what you're thinking."

"And what would that be?"

"You're thinking about our earlier conversation."

"Which one? We've had so many."

"The one about killing Creed. The idea you opposed. Do you oppose it now?"

She hesitated. "It's become more complicated."

"Actually, it's become much simpler. Now we know, with relative certainty, that Creed is going to do something to call back the Faceless Ones in three weeks' time. This will probably involve the Activation of your sister. Our window of opportunity is right in front of us, but it has narrowed."

"You're still talking about murder."

"I'm talking about assassination."

"That's just a polite way of saying murder."

"Creed has manoeuvred himself into the most powerful position in the world. There's no one we can go to, no one who can challenge his authority, and we can't stop him any other way. Assassinating Creed is the only way we can put an end to his plans."

"I feel naive just saying these words, but doing something like this would be wrong."

"I agree."

"So we can't do it."

"I disagree. We shoulder the burden so no one else has to. That's why the world needs us. That's the sacrifice we make."

Valkyrie looked at him. Looked away.

"Damn," she muttered.

# 28

"Omen Darkly," Mr Chicane said, "we are honoured you could find the time to join our little class. Please, pick any desk you like and grace us with the unmitigated splendour of your presence. Verily, this day has become the best day ever simply because you decided to stroll in seven minutes late. Class, genuflect. Genuflect, I say!"

Omen stood in the doorway, at a loss as to how to react to that.

Spider Lee saved him by raising his hand. "What's genuflect mean?"

"Oh dear God," said Chicane. "Spider, you make me despair for the future of our species whenever you open your mouth, do you know that? Omen, why are you late?"

"I got lost, sir," said Omen.

"How long have you been a student at this school, Omen?"

"Five years, sir, but..."

"Yes?"

"But it's a big school."

Chicane sighed. "Sit."

"Thank you, sir," Omen said, and hurried to his desk.

"Door," said Chicane.

"Sorry, sir," said Omen. He hurried back and closed the door, then returned to his desk, between Never and Axelia. Never sat there, shaking her head.

"OK," said Chicane, "I've taught most of you before in various modules, and now it falls to me to guide your young, mostly stupid minds through the wonderful world of revision in these final two weeks before your exams. I'll just admit it now: I don't know the answers to any of the questions you're likely to ask me. You're going to be sitting there, studying whatever subject you want to study, and you'll invariably come to a topic that puzzles your feeble minds, and, when this happens, remember my words: if it puzzles you, it'll puzzle me. Do we understand each other? You sit there and revise and get confused, and I'll sit here and read this crime novel I've been wanting to read for ages. I'm actually going to be paid to read this crime novel. I find this hilarious. So I want zero interruptions. Zero. You can talk among yourselves if you need to, ask each other your questions, but do it in very low whispers. Are we clear? Are we all clear? Yes? Every one of us? Spider, what about you? Are you clear?"

"Yes, sir."

"So what did I just say, Spider?"

"I'm not sure, sir, I wasn't listening."

"Someone tell Spider what I was talking about, and the rest of you, open your books and, at the very least, pretend to read."

Chicane took out his crime novel, put his feet on his desk, and started reading with a great big smile on his face.

"Hey," Axelia whispered.

"Hey," Omen whispered back.

"Everything OK?"

"Why do you ask?"

She shrugged. "You looked so sad during maths class."

Omen leaned closer. "I always look sad during maths class. It's maths class."

She grinned. "Just checking."

"Oh," he whispered, before she could move back, "I asked my parents."

She frowned at him. "Asked them what?"

He made sure no one else was listening, but everyone seemed preoccupied with their own whispered conversations. "To talk to Duenna about Bella's expulsion. They're not going to do it. I'm sorry."

Axelia shrugged one shoulder. "It's OK. You tried."

"Did her folks get a chance to talk to the school?"

She gave another shrug.

"How's she doing?"

Three shrugs in a row.

"Is she still in Roarhaven?"

Axelia shook her head. "She's back in Papua New Guinea. She keeps sending me messages but, ah, I don't know. What's done is done, like."

Yet another shrug, accompanied by a smile, and she leaned away and opened a textbook.

Omen frowned.

# 29

A big part of being an adult, Valkyrie was slowly realising, was meeting people for coffee.

It was one of those skills that had to be at least attempted, if not mastered. Much like doing the taxes or clearing the moss out of the gutter. She knew there was a social-interactions class taught in Corrival that was meant to get sorcerers used to dealing with mortals. She could have used a class like that herself, just to give her practice in chatting to people. She'd grown out of the habit during her five years in Colorado, and still hadn't got back into the swing of it.

Still, meeting Fletcher Renn for coffee wasn't a bad way to dip her toe into those waters once again – even if she was dreading what she had to ask him.

Valkyrie got their coffees and a huge cookie for herself and joined him at the table by the window. The sun streamed in so they both wore their sunglasses.

"How's work?" she asked, and took her first sip. Oh, she needed that.

"Good," Fletcher said, blowing on his drink. "Three weeks left of term, we haven't had anyone try to kill a student since the King of the Darklands bashed through the wall, and there aren't any Sixth Years who want to be Teleporters, so I don't have to worry about any important failures on my record. I'm golden."

"Are there many kids who want to be Teleporters?"

"A handful. Never's the best by quite a wide margin, but that kid's a natural, same as I was."

"What's it like, training beginners?"

"The beginner classes consist of a bunch of teenagers concentrating intently on travelling from one side of the room to another without actually moving. I try to explain it to them the way it was explained to me. I was told, early on, to look at teleporting like you're stepping off the world and the planet spins without you, and then you just... step back on."

"But that's not what actually happens, is it?"

"Naw," Fletcher said, "but, if it gets them approaching it the right way, that's the important thing. When they've got a handle on it, then I'll tell them that we don't actually know how teleportation works. We just know it does."

"Kinda freaky how much of magic is like that."

Fletcher grunted. "How much of *life* is like that, dear Valkyrie."

She grinned. "Look at you, being all wise and stuff."

"Wisdom is one of the things I'm best at. How's things between you and Militsa?"

"All good, thanks for asking."

"So is it, you know... Is it love?"

Valkyrie shrugged. "It is for me."

"Good golly."

"You actually look astonished," she said, laughing. "What, you didn't think I was capable of that?"

"Not really," he admitted. "I mean, no, I knew you were capable of loving someone, but I just didn't think you'd ever meet someone who didn't annoy you to the point where you'd walk away. You haven't walked away yet."

"She's cute, what can I say? What about you? How's Gratzia?"

"She's good. Great, actually. Wonderful. It's just..."

"What?"

Fletcher winced. "She's a hundred and eleven years old."

"Wow."

"This whole thing about magic slowing down the ageing process – it makes it impossible to figure out how old someone is. And it's not like it's even consistent! Two people the same age, specialising in the same discipline, using magic at the same rate, and you'll have one looking twenty-one forever and another looking middle-aged and wobbly."

"I'm sorry, but didn't you ask Tanith out last year? She's ninety-three."

"Yeah, but she's a young ninety-three," Fletcher replied, a little sulkily. "And she's fun and funny and cool. Whereas Gratzia talks about, like, foreign films and politics and old-people stuff. You've got to remember, Val – I am incredibly immature for my age."

"That's right," said Valkyrie. "You are."

"Aren't I? I have no idea how to carry on adult conversations. You should see me in the staffroom at work. All the other teachers are talking about whatever it is they talk about and I'm just trying not to laugh because someone said the word titmouse."

"It's a funny word."

"See?" he said, groaning. "You get me, Valkyrie! Why couldn't we have stayed together?"

"Because I tend to be mean and heartless and I cheated on you."

"Oh, yeah."

"With a vampire."

"He was such an insufferable git, he really was. And you were a terrible, *terrible* girlfriend."

"No argument here," she said. "I'm better at it now, though."

"I'd hope so." He sipped his coffee, and smiled. "I'm glad we're doing this. I like chatting with you about nonsense."

"Me too," said Valkyrie. "But I'm also here to ask a favour."

He grimaced. "Why can't we just catch up and complain about stuff and insult people we used to know? Why do you always have to spoil things?"

149

"Because I'm your ex," she said, "and that's what exes do."

"So what is it? What's the favour?"

She lowered her voice. "We're going to assassinate Creed and we need your help."

"You know what the scary thing is? You could be dead serious right now and it wouldn't surprise me in the slightest. You going to eat that cookie?"

Valkyrie handed it over and he took a big bite.

"Thank you," he said. "So, you were saying? What's the favour?"

"We're going to kill Creed. We need your help."

Fletcher's chewing slowed, and then stopped. He swallowed. "You're serious."

"I am."

"You can't be. You can't just decide to kill someone and then go out and do it. That's not how things work."

"He's a bad guy. If we take him out now, all his plans and all his schemes will fail and it'll save so many lives down the line."

"He's the Supreme Mage, Valkyrie. He's your boss."

"I'm an Arbiter. I don't have a boss."

"Of course you do. He's the president of sorcerers, for God's sake. You can't just kill the man."

"We don't want to do it, Fletch, and if we had any other choice we wouldn't. But keep in mind that, yeah, he might be the acting Supreme Mage, but he's also the Arch-Canon of the Church of the Faceless. By definition, that makes him the bad guy."

"So you fight him," Fletcher said, his voice low. "You do what you always do. You don't just walk up to him and put a bullet in his head."

"We can't risk failing."

"Valkyrie, come on... What you're talking about is seriously screwed up."

"I know."

"So don't do it."

"We have to."

"You're going to do it, are you? You're going to kill him."

"No," she said. "It'll be Skulduggery."

"Of course it will. I can't help you. I won't. I'm not going to be part of a murder."

"He won't be walking up to him."

"What?"

"Skulduggery won't be walking up to Creed to put a bullet in his head. He'll put a bullet in his head from across the street. We need you to teleport him back to my side immediately after he pulls the trigger or else Creed's people are going to know that he was the one who did it."

"Valkyrie, no."

"They'll probably suspect us anyway, but the more deniability we have, the higher the chance that we'll get away with it."

"No. I'm not doing it."

"We need your help."

"I don't even know you any more."

She frowned. "What?"

"He's changed you," Fletcher said. "Kenspeckle Grouse always said he would. He said Skulduggery was a bad influence. Looks like he was right."

Valkyrie uncrossed her legs and sat forward. "You think I'm this way because of Skulduggery? You think I'm like this because he's killed people? Fletcher, I'm like this because of me. I'm like this because of everything I've done, because of everything that's been done to me. I'm a killer. You see that, don't you? I've got blood on my hands just like he has. Yes, I hate it. Yes, the guilt keeps me up at night. But *I* made me the person I am today, not Skulduggery."

"And who are you?"

"I'm the woman who does what needs to be done."

"You're doing it the wrong way."

"I'm doing it the only way that works. Fletcher, we're dealing with people who – quite literally – want to kill you and everyone you've ever loved. We're dealing with people who want to end the goddamn world. If I could stop them with words, or hugs, or whatever non-violent, non-lethal action you dream up, then I would, and I'd never hurt another living thing ever again. But, because we're dealing with people who, once again, want to end the goddamn world, I don't have the luxury of trying something that might fail. The stakes are too high when the price of failure is the apocalypse. So I punch. And yes, sometimes I kill. Because someone has to."

"And when does this stop? When do you stop?"

"When the threat's over. When the bad guys are gone."

He stared at her. "I thought you were happy. I thought Militsa made you happy."

"She does."

"Then why do you want to do something like this? If you do it, you won't be happy any more."

"It's not about me, Fletch. It's about Militsa. It's about Alice. My parents. My friends. The people. It's about the whole world. And I'll get happy again. I'll carry on, because I'll know that while I've been a part of something terrible... I'll also know it was necessary."

He shook his head. "I can't... I can't help you. I just can't."

She sank back into the chair. "Yeah," she said.

"I'm sorry."

"You don't have to be. I asked you something huge. It's perfectly fine if you can't do it."

"It's just not right."

"I get it."

"What if they find out it was you?"

Valkyrie shrugged. "Then we go on the run."

"For how long?"

"Honestly? I don't know. If China ever wakes from her coma, I'd say she'd have all the charges dropped. Maybe. I mean, maybe not. Forgiving the killers of a Supreme Mage would be a bad precedent to set."

"So you might be on the run forever," said Fletcher. "Which means you'd never be able to visit your family."

"If it happens that way, we'll figure something out."

"This isn't something you just..." He went quiet.

"Fletch?"

A glance at his watch and he stood. "I've got to take a revision class in twenty minutes. You heading over?"

She nodded. "Militsa and I are going to pop in on the folks this afternoon."

"To say goodbye?"

Her spirits sank lower. "Probably."

"Come on," he said. "Escort me back."

She looped her arm through his and they walked to Corrival.

"You want me to talk you out of it," he said suddenly.

Valkyrie frowned at him. "I'm sorry?"

He nodded, and smiled. "That's why you came to me. You're waiting for me to convince you that it's a terrible idea and that you shouldn't do it."

"I already know it's a terrible idea and we shouldn't do it," Valkyrie replied, "but we're doing it anyway. And it's sweet of you to think that's why I came to you, but I'm honestly just looking for your help in assassinating someone. There's no ulterior motive."

"You're not going to go through with it."

"Um, yes, we are."

"You're not. You're going to change your mind. Hey, don't look so annoyed – I'm glad you're going to change your mind. I approve."

"OK, one: I don't look annoyed. B: I'm not going to change my mind. And third: this is happening."

"Sure it is," Fletcher said, and grinned.

"You think you know me so well."

"I was your first kiss," Fletcher said. "There's a bond there that can't be broken."

She glared. He grinned.

Valkyrie gave another shrug. "Actually, technically, you're not my first kiss. My reflection had my first kiss."

He rolled his eyes behind his sunglasses. "Well, that hardly counts, does it? Naw, I think we both know that I was your first kiss and your first true love, and because of this I know you better than you know yourself. You're not going to kill Creed, Valkyrie. I know you're not."

"And if we do?"

"You won't."

"And if we do?"

"Honestly? I'll be astonished."

She didn't say anything to that – she couldn't bear to wipe the grin off his face. So they just walked back to the school, and every step that Valkyrie took dragged her down deeper.

# 30

Principal Duenna left the school in the back seat of a car. She saw Valkyrie waiting at the gates, but pretended not to, so Valkyrie took her sunglasses off and stared at her as the driver waited for a gap in the traffic. Duenna occupied herself with examining the car's interior. Then an opening appeared and Duenna was gone.

Students began trailing out through the school gates, loosening ties and pulling off jackets. It was a warm day. Auger's friends, Kase and Mahala, passed and said hi, and Valkyrie gave them a smile.

Militsa came out, nodded to Valkyrie. "Miss Cain."

Valkyrie nodded back. "Miss Gnosis. How was work?"

"Wonderfully rewarding," Militsa said. "Look at them all passing by. Their bright, eager faces. So quick, so intelligent, so lovely. Shall we away?"

"We shall," said Valkyrie, taking her hand.

Darkness twisted round them and they shadow-walked to Valkyrie's car.

"Little bloody terrors," Militsa said. "Gave me such a headache all day, you have no idea." She gave Valkyrie a kiss and they got in. "What've you been up to?"

"Nothing much," Valkyrie said, pulling on to the road. "Met Fletcher for coffee and a chat."

"See, when you only teach a specialised subject like teleportation, you get loads of time off. How is that fair, I ask you? So what did you chat about?"

"Just had a favour to ask. Work-related."

"Ah, so top secret."

"Pretty much. I do love you, you know."

Militsa half smiled, half frowned. "I know that, silly. What's brought this on?"

"What, a girl can't say I love you to her girlfriend any more?"

The half-smile faded. "What's happening, Val?"

"Nothing's happening." She turned the radio on.

Militsa turned it off. "You're worrying me."

Valkyrie laughed. "Don't! Don't be worrying! There's nothing going on, OK? I just wanted to say I love you, that's all."

"Uh-huh," Militsa responded. "And you're not about to rush into a situation where you're liable to get killed or anything?"

"I'm not gonna get killed. Seriously, I just wanted to say it. I was thinking of my family, and how much I love them, and that got me thinking about how much I love you, and I'm in a soppy mood, all right?"

"That's all it is?"

"That's all it is," Valkyrie lied.

"Well," said Militsa, "I love you, too."

The moment Valkyrie stepped into her parents' house, Alice threw herself into her arms, then immediately launched herself at Militsa, who staggered and laughed under the onslaught.

Desmond came out of the kitchen and pointed into the living room. "We have guests," he whispered.

Valkyrie's heart grew heavy. She wanted a couple of hours with her family, not only to distract her from the plan, but also to remind her why it was worth doing it in the first place. Still, she plastered a smile to her face and followed her father in.

Beryl and Fergus sat on the couch. Valkyrie tried to remember the last time she'd seen them. They both looked older.

"Fergus," said Desmond, "you haven't met Militsa, have you? Militsa, this is my brother Fergus and his wife, Beryl."

Fergus stood, and nodded. "Hello."

"Hi," Militsa said, all smiles, coming forward to shake their hands. "How are you both? Very good to put faces to the names."

"And that's an unusual name you have," said Beryl. "Is it traditionally Scottish?"

"It's from the Balkans, actually."

"Ah," said Beryl. "Close enough, I suppose."

"Coming through," Valkyrie's mother said, carrying a tray laden with cups, saucers, and a teapot. She set it down on the coffee table, then kissed Valkyrie and Militsa on the cheek.

"So you're a friend of Stephanie's, then?" Fergus asked, still standing.

"She's my girlfriend," Militsa responded.

Fergus's spine went stiff and he didn't answer, but Beryl froze with her cup halfway to her lips.

"I'm sorry?" she said. "I don't think I heard that right."

"Militsa and I are in love," Valkyrie said, wrapping an arm round Militsa's waist.

Beryl blinked. "You're gay?"

"Bisexual."

"I didn't know that," said Beryl, returning the cup to its saucer and then to the coffee table. "Fergus, did you know that?"

Fergus made a strangled sound deep in his throat.

"I didn't know that," Beryl repeated. "When did this happen? The last thing I heard, Stephanie, you had a boyfriend."

Valkyrie nodded. "And now I have a girlfriend. Being bisexual means I can have both."

"Though not at the same time," Militsa interjected.

"That might be awkward, yeah."

"Well," said Beryl, shaking her head. "Well. This is... Well. Melissa, why didn't you tell us this?"

Valkyrie's mum searched for an answer for a few seconds before shrugging. "I suppose it didn't come up in conversation."

"It didn't have to. You could have put it in the end-of-the-year email. Fergus puts all our important news and developments in our end-of-the-year email, just to keep everyone up to date on what's happening. Why didn't you include this in yours?"

"Because we don't do an end-of-the-year email."

"Then this would have been the perfect time to start, wouldn't it? Instead, we just happen to find out that little Stephanie is a lesbian because we just happen to call by on the same day she brings her lesbian girlfriend home to meet her parents."

"Oh, we've met Militsa plenty of times," said Desmond.

"And it's bisexual," Valkyrie said, "but whatever."

Beryl scowled at her husband. "For heaven's sake, Fergus, would you please say something about this?"

Fergus had gone a deep, deep red, and he just shook his head and kept making that weird gargling sound like he'd swallowed a teeny-tiny motorboat.

Beryl sighed, exasperated. "Fine. Then it looks like it's up to me to say what needs to be said, as usual. Stephanie, we have watched you grow from an insubordinate child to a, frankly, insubordinate adult, and I've always put it down to the idea that you might be missing something in your life. Now that I've met Militsa, I can finally see what that missing piece could be. I understand that it is probably far too early to say, but do you think there might be some wedding bells in your future, or am I just being outrageously optimistic right now?"

"Gay," Fergus blurted.

"Yes, dear," said Beryl.

Valkyrie smiled. "It's way too early to be talking about stuff like that."

"Way, way too early," said Militsa.

"Don't leave it too long, though, will you? I never have enough opportunities to wear hats these days." Beryl clasped her hands. "Oh, wait till Carol and Crystal hear about this. They'll be over the moon." She picked up her cup and saucer, and took a sip. "Ooh, delicious."

# 31

On Thursday night, Valkyrie woke, jumped out of bed and managed to get halfway to the bathroom before she threw up.

They were going to kill Creed.

They were going to kill Creed and nothing would be the same again.

# 32

The window looking across at the High Sanctuary was closed, but not locked. Valkyrie knew this, just like she knew that propped up against the wall, within easy reach, was a rifle with four special bullets. Each one of those bullets could burrow through the High Sanctuary's energy shield that was already in place. Four bullets.

Skulduggery would only need one.

When he took the shot, there would be chaos. Skulduggery and Valkyrie would join the Sanctuary detectives and the City Guard and the Cleavers and they'd scramble and shout orders and speed after suspects. Only Skulduggery and Valkyrie wouldn't stop speeding. They'd leave Roarhaven and then leave Ireland. They'd get to Australia, they'd wait, and they'd react to whatever happened next.

Valkyrie wouldn't be able to see her family. Wouldn't be able to see Militsa. Her folks would have to take care of Xena. She hadn't left any notes. Notes would be found, used against her if she was caught.

Today. It all changed today.

They stood on the edge of the stage. There was another big crowd here waiting for the Supreme Mage to announce new restrictions, to curtail their freedom even more. They sang and they chanted. If they'd known what their glorious leader was planning, they'd have only sung and chanted louder.

But Valkyrie wasn't sacrificing the life she knew for them. She wasn't sacrificing the person she was for them. She was sacrificing it all for everyone else.

Her hands were shaking. Her teeth were chattering. She felt like she was about to puke again.

She looked at Skulduggery. "How are you doing?"

He turned to her, ever so slightly. "If you're asking if I'm having doubts, no, I am not. I am quite certain that this is the most logical course of action we could take."

"But how do you feel about it?"

"My feelings are immaterial."

"Yeah," she said, "but still – how do you feel about what you're going to do?"

"Calm," he said, his voice barely audible over the crowd. "Confident. It is a regrettable thing, to take a life, but sometimes a life needs to be taken."

"And what if something goes wrong?"

"I'll improvise. How are *you* feeling about this, Valkyrie?"

"I won't be the one pulling the trigger."

"No, but you're a part of it."

They watched Creed take to the stage. The crowd went wild.

"I'll get into position," Skulduggery murmured, and went to move off.

She put a hand on his arm.

He looked at her. "Yes?"

Creed held up his hands for quiet, and started speaking. His words were dull things that didn't register in Valkyrie's ears.

"I really had better go, Valkyrie."

The words came out of her mouth. "Don't. You can't. We can't. We can't just... There's another way. There has to be another way. We just have to find it."

He put his gloved hand on hers. "We've talked about this."

"I know we have, and I agree with everything you said because everything you said was right, but you can be right and still be

162

wrong. We're not assassins. Yes, I know we went to Dimension X to kill Mevolent, but we were about to have a war and in the context of war, in order to avert it, assassination is an acceptable evil."

"This is war, too, but instead of Mevolent and his army it's Creed and the Faceless Ones."

"But we have more options here," she said. "We still have eighteen days to change the future. Skulduggery, you've been to some really dark places. I've been there, too. The people we become... It just doesn't end well. It stops being fun. That's when we know that we've crossed a line – when it stops being fun. I don't want to stop having fun right now. I'm in a good mood these days, I have a good life, I'm in love, everything's going well... Please, let's keep having fun. Please."

He was quiet for a moment. "Your way will be more dangerous," he said. "We'll have a greater chance of failing."

"We won't fail. Come on – us? We don't fail with the big stuff. We cancel the apocalypse, like in the movie with the big robots. We save the world. It's what we do."

Skulduggery sighed. She still didn't know how he did that with no lungs. "Fine," he said.

Relief flooded her veins. She grinned. "Thank you."

"But, if the Faceless Ones come back, do you know whose fault it'll be?"

"Mine," she said happily. "It'll be my fault."

They looked over at the stage as Creed spoke.

"Do we have to listen to this?" Skulduggery asked.

"No," Valkyrie said, linking her arm through his. "No, we do not."

Creed's head snapped back as a gunshot barked and he tipped over, all that muscle mass slamming into the stage and making it rumble. Cleavers sprang forward immediately, but they were still way too late.

"What?" Valkyrie said.

The window, the one Skulduggery had been planning to shoot from, was open.

Skulduggery launched himself into the air and flew over the heads of the screaming crowd.

Valkyrie hurried over to the Cleavers and sorcerers gathered round Creed. She glimpsed his face, his eyes open and unblinking, a neat bullet hole in his forehead.

It only occurred to her that maybe she should follow Skulduggery when he came flying out through the window again, shouting a warning, a moment before the window blew. The explosion caught him, sent him spinning, and Valkyrie lunged, energy crackling, leaving the stage behind her and catching him before he hit the ground.

She returned them both to the stage. His hat floated after them, into his hand.

"Thank you," he said, people running all round them. "How's the Supreme Mage?"

"Dead," said Valkyrie.

"Ah."

Skulduggery was lucky. He didn't have a face that he needed to contort into some expression of shock. Valkyrie did, however, but couldn't remember how to do it convincingly.

Skulduggery grabbed the arm of a passing Cleaver. "Secure the Council," he told him. "If someone's taking out our leaders, they'll be aiming for Creed's Advisors next."

The Cleaver hurried away, and Skulduggery put his hat on as he turned back to Valkyrie.

"What the hell, Skulduggery?"

"What the hell indeed," he responded. "Come on."

He took to the air and she followed, and they made a show of scanning the area until they landed on the roof of the building that belched smoke from one of its windows.

"So that's it," said Valkyrie. "I mean... it's done. He's dead and we didn't even have to kill him. All those doubts, all that guilt – I didn't have to go through any of it. We could have just plodded along like we were doing and Creed would still be dead."

"I resent the implication that I have ever plodded anywhere."

"But it's a win, right? I reckon it's a win."

"It's a win," Skulduggery agreed.

"Good."

"But we might be in a lot of trouble."

"What? Why? We didn't do anything. We *literally* did not do anything."

"We planned an assassination."

"Apart from that, obviously. But so what? Is it a crime to plan an assassination?"

"Yes."

She frowned. "It is? Seriously?"

"Very much so."

"That hardly seems fair."

"Nevertheless."

"But we never wrote anything down, did we? The plans are all in our heads. There's no way for anyone to figure out what we were going to do. Apart from Sensitives, I suppose. They could read our minds."

"They could read *your* mind," Skulduggery corrected. "My mind—"

"Can't be read, yeah, I remember. But I have some pretty sturdy psychic blocks in place. A casual scan isn't going to reveal anything, and there's no reason that any Sensitive would even *do* a casual scan on me because I'm an Arbiter and I had nothing whatsoever to do with the actual assassination that took place." She looked down at the stage. "It's over," she said softly. Happily. "We won."

# 33

Damocles Creed lay on the slab, covered to his shoulders in a sheet. His eyes were closed. His face was slack. He had a pretty large entry wound in his forehead, and an even bigger exit wound round the back of his head.

Valkyrie looked at the coroner and said, "Give it to us straight, Doc – is he gonna make it?"

Doctor Peculiar arched an eyebrow. "You could at least pretend to be distraught that our Supreme Mage is dead, Detective Cain. It's a little thing called decorum – perhaps you've heard of it?" He tapped his pockets. "Has anyone seen my pen? I swear, if I've dropped it into another bullet hole..."

He peered into the wound. "Well, good news on the not-having-dropped-anything-into-the-bullet-hole front, bad news on the where-is-my-pen front. Stay here. I'll be right back. Do not move the body." He pointed at Skulduggery when he said this, and hurried out, passing a Sanctuary detective on the way in.

"Did I miss it?" Detective Waverly Cardigan asked. "Did I miss the examination?"

"It hasn't started yet," Valkyrie assured him. "How you doing, Waverly?"

"I'm terrible," he said miserably. "I'm awful. I can't do this. This is a murder investigation. I'm not good at those. I've investigated three murders in my career, and two of those remain unsolved."

"But at least you solved the other one," Valkyrie said.

He shook his head. "That's unsolved, too."

She frowned. "So all three remain unsolved?"

He sagged, impossibly, further. "When you put it like that, yes." He looked up suddenly. "But you two. You can take charge of this, right? That's why you're here, isn't it? You're Arbiters – you can decide which cases you want to look into, and this is the assassination of the Supreme Mage, for God's sake. You *have* to investigate this!"

Skulduggery tilted his head. "You're really not as bad a detective as you think you are, Waverly."

"No, I am. I'm a terrible detective. I'm useless! I'm literally the worst! But no one else wants it because of the huge, unbearable pressure that'll be put on by people who will demand answers. I'm not the one to give them those answers, Skulduggery, even if I could find them, which I won't be able to because, again, I'm a terrible detective."

Skulduggery looked at Valkyrie. "What do you think?"

It was important, she recognised, not to appear too eager. "I don't know," she said. "I mean, shouldn't this be a City Guard investigation? We really didn't like Creed, and that's pretty common knowledge. I don't think it'd look great to the general public if we're the ones investigating."

"You have to," Waverly said. "This is perfect for you. This is a political assassination, so there has to be some grand conspiracy at work here, and that's what you two handle, like, every other month. You save the world!"

Valkyrie made a face. "But, as you said, there'd be an awful lot of pressure..."

"But you're used to that," Waverly said, sagging. "I'm not up to the job. Look at me. What if I have to chase somebody? I can't run very far. And what if I have to get into a fight? If you're tracking down an assassin, you have to at least know karate or something. I'm just not suitable. If we were all in TV shows, you two would be in the fast-paced American detective show, and I'd be in one of those British shows where everyone's old, and all the murders take place in garden centres. Please. Please don't make me do this."

"Maybe we can advise..." Skulduggery said slowly.

Waverly brightened. "Yes? You will?"

"Maybe," Valkyrie said, her tone cautious. "Let's not get too carried away here, all right? What do you know so far?"

Waverly could barely contain his delight. His eyes twinkled. "About what?"

"About the murder, Waverly."

"Oh! Yes, well, not much. We know somebody shot Damocles Creed. We know they shot him in the head. We've been searching the room where – the crime scene – but we haven't been able to find much yet, on account of there not being much of a crime scene left after the explosion. We recovered the rifle in the rubble, though, and traces of the explosive, but we haven't yet found the assassin's body."

"Did you *expect* to find the assassin's body?" Skulduggery asked.

"Well... it would have been nice."

"I'm confused. Do you think that after the assassin killed Supreme Mage Creed he... exploded?"

Waverly went quiet. "No," he said, a blush rising. "He probably rigged the bomb to go off to hide his retreat and destroy evidence."

Skulduggery nodded. "Probably. Waverly, you haven't asked me any questions yet."

Waverly blinked. "Why would I?"

"I flew into the tower right before it blew up."

"Well, yes, I mean, I know that. Everyone knows that. But I imagine, if you'd seen anything while you were in there that might be useful, you'd have told me."

"That's not really the point, though. I'm a witness. You should be interviewing witnesses."

"Oh, God, you're right, I should," said Waverly. "But that's why you two should be leading this investigation! Detective Cain can interview you. Or you can interview yourself! I'm sure you'd be quite ruthless."

"None more so."

Peculiar came back in, wielding a pen. "Ah, Detective Cardigan! I thought that was you. What are you doing here?"

"I'm, uh, I'm leading the investigation."

"Into what?"

"The... this," he said, indicating Creed's body.

Peculiar paused. "I see. And are you sure this is a good idea?"

"No."

"Does the Sanctuary or the City Guard have anyone else they could possibly use instead of you?"

"Apparently not."

Peculiar chewed his lip. "You know, if you happened to miss my initial examination, maybe everyone would be fine with you entrusting it to the Arbiters here."

Waverly blinked. "If I missed it?"

"If you happened to miss this examination, yes."

A smile spread across Waverly's face. "Yes," he said. "If I got lost on my way here. If I'm not here right now..."

They watched him back up, then tiptoe out of the door.

"A nice man," Peculiar said, putting on a surgical mask, "but not very good at his job. Now then, before you ask, yes, the bullet that killed him would seem to be the same calibre as the gun they recovered at the scene. I'll be able to verify that when I dig it out of him. How that bullet got through the shields, I can't say, but I would imagine it has some rather significant sigils carved into it."

He pulled on a pair of latex gloves. "The autopsy is perfunctory at this point, but I can guarantee you that death was instantaneous and he felt no pain. People like to hear that the recently deceased felt no pain, apparently. I don't understand it myself, but then my job isn't to understand what people like to hear. My job is corpses. Lots and lots of corpses."

"You're a strange man, Doctor," Valkyrie said.

"Maybe so," Peculiar replied, flexing his fingers, "but I've always found more comfort in the dead than the living – as I'm sure you can appreciate."

She frowned. "Why would you say that?"

Peculiar picked up a scalpel, waved it in Skulduggery's general direction.

"Oh," Valkyrie said. "Yeah. Him."

Skulduggery grunted. "*Him* has a name."

She gave him a smile, then turned back to Peculiar. "Had you met our beloved Supreme Mage while he was alive?"

"People don't like to meet me, generally speaking," Peculiar replied. "They avoid me if at all possible – until, of course, they don't have a choice in the matter. I prefer it that way. It means I don't have any preconceived ideas of who they were, what they were like, if they were serious or funny or happy or sad... None of that means anything when they're lying here on my slab. I get to know the real person once they're open. I get to note the condition of the heart, the liver, the kidneys. I get to catalogue the contents of their stomach. How heavy the brain is. Did you know that the brains of geniuses weigh approximately the same as the brains of idiots? There is absolutely no discernible difference."

"That's good to know."

"I've always thought so. In the end, we're all just chunks of meat, are we not? Meat and bone, of course."

Skulduggery nodded to him. "Just happy to be included."

The coroner smiled at Valkyrie. "I wonder what I'll find when I open you up, Detective Cain."

She blinked. "I actually have no idea how to respond to that."

Knuckles rapped lightly on the door as it opened, and Waverly stepped back in. "Hi," he said. "Sorry. I was leaving the building and a gentleman was approaching so I let him in. It's only just now occurring to me that I didn't ask for any identification or—"

A man in robes swept past him into the room. His pale face was lined. His dark eyes glittered as they settled on Creed's body.

"I'm sorry," said Peculiar, "but who is this?"

"I don't quite know," Waverly answered.

"I have come," said the man, pointing at Creed, "for him."

Peculiar nodded. "And are you related to the deceased?"

"I will take him with me," the man said, coming forward.

Skulduggery stepped in front of him. "Before any of that," he said in his friendliest of voices, "why don't we have a chat? Who are you?"

The man smiled at Skulduggery. "I am Uriah Serrate, Herald of the Dark, Harbinger of Doom, and Emissary of the Everlasting Death."

Skulduggery nodded. "Hi, Uriah. I'm Skulduggery and that's Valkyrie."

Valkyrie smiled. "How do you do?"

"I'm Waverly," said Waverly.

"And I'm Simon," said the coroner. "Simon Peculiar. Doctor Simon Peculiar, actually, since I didn't go through an entire weekend course at Coroner's College to be known as 'Mister'."

"I have come for him," Serrate said, pointing at Creed once more.

"And what do you mean by that, exactly?" Skulduggery asked. "What are you going to do with him once you have him?"

"Such matters are none of your concern."

"I'm afraid I'm going to have to insist on an answer to my question. Valkyrie, do you have any questions for him?"

"I do," Valkyrie said. "Uriah, did you have anything to do with the Supreme Mage's death?"

"I didn't kill him," Serrate said. "I've come to help."

Valkyrie winced. "Bit late for that."

"You don't understand," said Serrate, "but you will."

He went to move past Skulduggery, but Skulduggery blocked his way again.

"I see," said Serrate, and moved so fast Skulduggery was already flying backwards before Valkyrie had even realised he'd been struck.

Energy crackled round her hand as she raised it to fire, but Serrate grabbed her wrist with one hand, and her throat with the other. Without pause, he lifted her off her feet and flung her away from him. She hit the wall and bounced painfully.

The air rippled and Serrate catapulted back, flipping over an empty slab. Skulduggery pushed at the air again and Serrate grunted as an invisible hand smacked into him from above. Skulduggery tossed a fireball that exploded across Serrate's arm, then pulled his gun and clicked back the hammer.

"Don't move," he said.

But Serrate moved.

Skulduggery fired into a swirling mass of shadows and Serrate leaped from the gloom behind him, slamming his fist on to Skulduggery's arm. The gun fell. Skulduggery twisted and Serrate ducked from under his grasp and spun, and as he spun his hand filled with shadows that became a staff, a staff with a long, wide blade at one end, a blade formed from darkness, and it launched Skulduggery across the room.

Necromancer.

Valkyrie jumped up and let loose her lightning, but the shadows rose to meet it, and Serrate backed up until he was beside Creed's body. The darkness swirled and then both of them were gone.

# 34

Valkyrie sat back and watched Commander Hoc pace behind his desk, his fists clenched, his teeth grinding, a not-insignificant vein popping out on his forehead.

"And?" Hoc said angrily.

Skulduggery tilted his head. "And what?"

Hoc stopped pacing and glared. "And what happened?"

"I told you what happened," Skulduggery said. "Someone stole Creed's corpse last night. A Necromancer with a glaive."

"I'm going to need a more detailed report than that," Hoc said, practically seething now.

"Ah," Skulduggery responded, "I see where the problem lies. You think this is a report. You think I'm reporting to you. Both of these things are laughably wrong."

"I am the Commander of the City Guard!"

"I'm aware of that, as it's the post I relinquished after I set up your entire police force. You're welcome, by the way. But Valkyrie and I are Arbiters. You have no authority over us, and you certainly don't outrank us. Nobody does. That's one of the best things about being us."

"One of many," Valkyrie added.

"One of many, indeed," said Skulduggery. "We came to your office today as a courtesy – because we are nothing if not courteous – but please be aware that this visit marks the end of our co-operation."

Hoc continued to glare, and Skulduggery and Valkyrie stood up.

"I suppose you're right," Hoc said.

This was an unexpected reaction.

"The Arbiter Corps was designed to be completely independent, after all. You pick your own cases; you go after whoever you want." He shrugged. "And I probably do owe you a debt of thanks for setting up the City Guard. It can't have been easy. I know how long it took, and I do appreciate it."

Skulduggery waited, and Hoc smiled.

"It's healthy, now that I think about it, to have two agencies, both dedicated to upholding law and order, but neither reliant on the other in the slightest. You are absolutely right to say that I have no authority over you."

Skulduggery waited some more.

"Just as you have no authority over me," Hoc continued. He pressed a button, and a crumpled man in a crumpled suit came in. He wasn't quite as tall as Valkyrie, but he carried with him an air of someone not to be messed with.

"Detective Cain," said Hoc, "I don't think you've met Detective Rylent."

Rylent gave a nod to Valkyrie that could only be described as curt, before his gaze settled on Skulduggery.

"Rylent was one of the City Guard's top detectives," Hoc said. "Possibly the very best, actually. Certainly, he was the best when Skulduggery brought him onboard."

"Detective Rylent," said Skulduggery.

"Detective Pleasant."

"I thought you were working exclusively for the African Sanctuaries."

"I was," said Rylent, "until Commander Hoc offered me this assignment."

Skulduggery nodded. "In that case, welcome back."

"Thank you."

"Since we're both investigating this, we could work together if you like. Pool our resources."

"I work best alone," Rylent said.

"I thought the same way," said Skulduggery, "until I met Valkyrie. Maybe if we work together you'll see the benefits of teamwork and change your approach to the job."

Rylent scratched his jaw. "Mmm. Maybe I should work with someone. Maybe you're right. I'll tell you this, though – whoever I work with, it won't be you. I hate you with every fibre of my being and I won't rest until I have your skull mounted on my mantelpiece. I don't even collect trophies, but I'll collect your skull. Maybe I'll have it stuffed with potpourri. Get some use out of it. I don't know. I haven't decided."

Skulduggery nodded. "Potpourri would be nice. We'd better be going."

Rylent nodded. "I'll see you soon."

Skulduggery held the door for Valkyrie and followed her out. She didn't say one word until they were on the street and far away from the City Guard headquarters.

"So?"

Skulduggery looked at her. "So what?"

"So who's this Rylent guy?"

"A detective," he said. "A good one. Worked for various mortal police forces in America since 1912 before I convinced him to come to Roarhaven. If anyone's going to find the connection between us and the assassination, it's Rylent."

"What connection?" Valkyrie asked. "Yes, we planned it, but nobody knows that except for us and Fletcher, and Fletcher's not going to tell anyone."

"You're forgetting one other person who knows what our plans were."

"Who?"

"The assassin."

"What? The assassin doesn't know what..." Valkyrie faltered. "The assassin fired from where you were going to fire, using the rifle you were going to use. He, she, or they knew what we were planning."

"Yes."

"Which would mean we're in a whole lot of trouble. Right then – we'll have to find the assassin ourselves and control what we can from then on."

"I was thinking the same thing."

"Where do we start?" she asked, and continued before he could answer. "Probably with the rifle. That's the most obvious way someone could have figured out what we were planning – they knew you bought a sniper rifle. So we go talk to whoever you bought it from – before Rylent does."

"Good idea."

They started walking.

"And why doesn't he like you?"

"What makes you think he doesn't like me?"

"Something he said about putting potpourri in your skull."

"You heard that?"

"I did. Because of my ears. So what did you do to make him not like you?"

"Nothing," said Skulduggery. "Well, something. He's still angry with me over the death of another detective – a friend of his. He reckons it was my fault."

"And was it?"

"Seeing as how I killed him," Skulduggery said as he unlocked the Bentley, "yes, probably."

# 35

Tributes were pouring in from every Sanctuary around the world, apparently, with everyone saying how great Damocles Creed had been. What a leader. What a visionary. How the world will be a dimmer place without him.

Omen was as shocked as anyone at the assassination, but over the last three days he'd come to the conclusion that the world would probably be better off without Creed in it. Maybe now the Church of the Faceless would lose some of the hold it seemed to have over its followers – though he doubted it.

It was right before lunch, and Omen had slept through breakfast – something it was only possible to do on Sundays – and his belly was rumbling as October Klein passed him in the corridor.

"Your brother's being weird again," she said, and walked on.

Omen took a detour on his way to the Dining Hall and knocked on Auger's door. There was no answer, so he stepped in. The curtains were still drawn. There was no one here. Then his eyes adjusted.

"Hey," he said.

Auger didn't respond. He sat in the corner, on the floor, arms resting on his knees, staring at nothing.

"Auger," Omen said softly, hurrying forward and crouching beside him. "Auger, what's wrong? What happened?"

Auger blinked, looked up at him, and his blank face creased into a smile. "Hey."

"Are you OK?"

"I'm good."

"Why are you sitting on the floor?"

He frowned, the question puzzling him, then he smiled again. "My chair's full." His chair, beside his desk, was indeed full, stacked with textbooks and notepads.

"You wanna maybe sit on your bed?" Omen asked. "Or stand?"

Auger shrugged, and Omen pulled him to his feet, then opened the curtains.

"Nice day," said Auger.

"They're saying it'll rain later."

"Rain's never far away in Ireland. What time is it?"

"Lunchtime."

"Have you seen Never?" Auger asked suddenly. "She hasn't been round as much. I don't know if I've upset him or what, but..."

"Dude, you and Never broke up."

Auger blinked. And nodded. "Yes. I know that. I'm just wondering if you've seen her, wondering how he is."

"Never is Never," said Omen.

Auger grinned. "Yes, she is." He stretched his spine, and groaned.

"How long were you sitting there?" Omen asked.

"Don't know. Wasn't really paying attention."

"I, uh, I talked to Mum last night," said Omen. "She rang. She's wondering why you're not answering her calls."

Auger laughed. "So she talks to you just to ask why she's not talking to me. I swear, Omen, I have no idea why you even bother with those two any more."

"It's a chore, all right. But I suppose I'm used to it."

"You shouldn't be. You shouldn't have to be."

"Is everything OK? I know I've been asking that a lot, but I don't think you're being entirely honest with me. There's obviously something going on with you."

Auger sighed. "I could never keep anything from you, could I?"

"No," said Omen, "but I don't have to be your twin to see that something's not right. Ever since you fought the King of the Darklands—"

"Ever since we fought him."

"OK, ever since we fought him and you killed him, you've been... different."

"Imagine that."

"Auger... I never want to know what it's like to kill someone. I never want that weight hanging over me. I don't think I could handle it. So thankfully I have no idea what it feels like to do that, even when you have to, even when the fate of the world depends on it.

"But you're free now. For the first time ever, you don't have a prophecy telling you what's expected; you don't have people depending on you; you don't have that pressure... I mean, that's gotta be kinda liberating, right?"

"I suppose so," said Auger.

"You should let yourself be happy."

"Being happy would be nice. How do you manage it?"

"Well, I've never had that sort of pressure on me, so I have a head start."

"Yeah," said Auger, "but you've also grown up with parents who basically ignored you your entire life. How do you manage to stay positive with all that weighing you down?"

"I don't know. I try not to think about it."

"That's not exactly the healthiest way to deal with it, though."

Omen didn't know what to say, so he smiled and shrugged.

Auger collapsed on to his bed. "We have rotten parents."

"Yeah."

"Say it."

Omen laughed. "We have rotten parents."

"I don't even know who I am," Auger said. "My life and my personality revolved round the prophecy. They prepared me for that, yes, they did, but they didn't prepare me for anything beyond it. They built Auger Darkly to be a cog in a great machine, and, now that I've done what I was supposed to do, the machine rolls on and that cog is no longer needed. So Auger Darkly is no longer needed.

"I mean, look at us, dude. Auger and Omen. The Darkly brothers. Practically every other sorcerer around the world comes up with a brand-new name that sets them apart from everyone else. What did we do? We took Emmeline's name."

"Because we're a Lineage family."

"What does that even mean?"

"It's... you know what it means. It's a bond that some sorcerers want to maintain."

"It's a way to control us."

"We both decided to be Darklys."

"We think we decided, but come on – they were pulling the strings. They wanted to establish and then reinforce the Darkly brand. Even our first names weren't our choice. Remember the way that they'd keep repeating certain words, all about destiny or fate? We thought we came up with them all by ourselves, but they'd been planting those names in our heads since we were kids. They wanted us to be Auger and Omen."

"Well, that's not quite true, is it? They wanted you to be Augur, but you decided on only one 'u'."

"My one moment of rebellion," Auger said, "misspelling my name. I thought that small act of defiance meant something, but it didn't." His voice softened. "None of it means anything."

"What's all this about?"

Auger sat forward. "I think I'm going to change my name."

Omen stared at him. "What?"

"I don't want to be Auger Darkly, ex-Chosen One, any more. I want to be someone else."

"But we're the Darkly brothers."

"We'll still be brothers. Nothing will change that. But I'm going to renounce the Darkly name."

"What does that mean?"

"I'm leaving."

"Leaving where?"

"School, for a start," said Auger. "Then Roarhaven. And probably Ireland. I want to go places. Meet people. I want to have a life."

Omen struggled to come up with any coherent argument. "But what about your education?"

Auger smiled. "I reckon I've learned enough to get by."

"But what are you going to do?"

"Travel. Get a job."

"With what qualifications?"

He laughed. "We've been taught to forge every kind of mortal document there is. We've been trained to survive and thrive in whatever environment we find ourselves in. I'm gonna be fine."

"But what about your Surge? You should stay in school until your Surge, or at least until—"

"Actually," Auger said, "it looks like I'll be getting that a little earlier than most."

"What?"

"The doctors at the High Sanctuary said I've got all the hallmarks of an approaching Surge. Fluctuating levels, biorhythmic spikes, the whole lot. They reckon that the power boost we're all going to experience on Draíocht will be enough to set it off."

"So you're gonna have your Surge in, what, just over two weeks? But you're only sixteen!"

"Ex-Chosen One, dude."

"Does that mean I'll get my Surge as well?"

"Don't know. Are you experiencing spikes in your biorhythms?"

"I have no idea."

"Then you're probably going to have to wait another few years."

"I hope so," Omen said. "I don't want my Surge. I have no idea what I want to specialise in. What are you going to specialise in?"

"I'm going to be a Healer."

Omen blinked. "You?"

"Why are you surprised?"

"I... I don't know."

"I'll tell you. It's surprising because my whole life has been about fighting. It's been about inflicting pain on others. I just want to flip it around. I want to help people."

"Wow," Omen said slowly. "That's... that's perfect."

Auger smiled. "I'm glad you approve. What about you? What are you going to be once you leave this place behind?"

"As far as magic goes, I have no idea. There are so many disciplines, and I'm so bad at them all."

Auger laughed. "And what about other stuff? Don't you want to apply to art college?"

"How do you know about that?"

"Because I'm your brother, dimwit. Of course I know. When we were kids, you were always drawing your own comics, coming up with your own superheroes. Who was that guy, with the wings?"

"Hawkman," said Omen, "but I kind of stole his name from DC. Stole his wings, too. But everything else was mine."

"I always thought the comic thing was pretty cool."

Omen shrugged. "I don't know how the folks would react to art college, though. But I met this girl, Gretchen, and she said she'd help me with my portfolio."

"A girl, eh?"

"Not like that. She's older than me. And American. Sophisticated, you know? But she's pretty cool. I'm going to send her some of my stuff and see what she thinks."

"Good man," said Auger. "And, if the parents don't approve, so what? Think how great it'd be for both of us to strike out on our own. Our parents don't deserve our loyalty. You should renounce your name, too."

"But I really like my name," Omen said. "It's the one thing about me that I do like. When are you going to tell them?"

"After I've had my Surge. That's when I'll pack my bags."

"I really don't want you to go."

"I'm going to miss you like crazy, Omen. You're the best brother a guy could ask for, and my best friend. But I think if I stay I'll be driven to hurt more people. Maybe kill someone again."

"Are you, like, renouncing violence, or something?"

"I think so. There's something inside me. I noticed it in the days after I killed the King of the Darklands. I don't know how to describe it, but it's like this... emptiness. If I don't do something drastic, I think the emptiness will grow. Take over."

"Then it sounds like you're doing the right thing."

"You should have this, then," Auger said, getting up. He went to his desk, pulled open a drawer, and took out a collapsible baton. "This is my favourite," he said, snapping it to its full length, roughly as long as his arm. The sigils etched into it started to glow. "Easily concealed shock stick with three settings. *Three*. The lowest is enough to give a decent jolt, and the highest will pretty much knock out any regular-sized person. Your mileage may vary."

He thumped the end against the wall and the baton telescoped in until it wasn't much longer than his fist. He handed it over.

"Why would I need this?" Omen asked, taking it, testing its weight.

Auger raised an eyebrow. "You think I don't hear what you're getting up to? I may be a little out of it, a little distracted these days, but I pay attention when it comes to you. That Thiago kid?"

"Ah," said Omen.

"You're doing all this stuff, walking into danger, risking your life, saving people – and you won't even tell them that it's you being the hero."

"I'm not doing it to be a hero."

"Oh, I know. I'm aware. People have always called me brave, but any time I've fought a bad guy or saved an innocent life, I've always known that people would hear about it. It got to the point where I was wondering if what I was doing could be counted as brave and selfless or whether it was just me having to live up to my reputation. But you... Dude. You're out there being an anonymous hero. That's something that never even occurred to me."

"You're making me sound cooler than I am," Omen said. "Thanks for this, though." He put the baton into his back pocket, and, as Auger slid the drawer closed, he caught a glimpse of the Obsidian Blade, the knife that Auger had used to kill the King of the Darklands. Auger had told him, had told everyone, that the weapon had snapped off completely, rendering it totally useless – but Omen saw the single sliver of black blade that remained attached to the handle.

The drawer closed. Auger knew that Omen had seen it. He looked at him and didn't say anything.

Omen didn't say anything, either.

# 36

Five years ago...

He found her crying.

The gate opened and he drove his truck through, parking beside her mud-splattered Land Rover. Usually, she was already walking to meet him by this stage, no matter if it was raining or snowing or freezing. Today spring was beating back the chill in the air, but the door to the farmhouse didn't open and Valkyrie didn't come out to meet him.

So Quell walked up the steps and stood at the door, fist raised to knock. Inside, he could hear her crying. Great racking sobs of unfathomable sadness.

He looked at the door for the longest time, and realised his fist was still raised to knock. He pulled the door open instead, and went inside.

She was in the kitchen, sitting on the floor, her face hidden in her hands, her shoulders juddering with each sob. She sounded hoarse, like she'd been doing this for a considerable amount of time.

She'd heard him come in – he knew she had, she was too alert not to have – but she didn't seem to care. That was OK with him. Quell didn't know how to process other people's embarrassment.

He thought he should be helpful and he didn't know where

the handkerchiefs were, so he picked up a hand towel from beside the sink and brought it over to her. She accepted it without speaking, used it to wipe her eyes and her nose and her face. Over the next few minutes, she brought herself under control and leaned back against the cupboards, red-rimmed eyes coming to rest on nothing. Calm now. Quiet now.

She held her hand up and he took it and pulled her to her feet. She stood so close to him he could smell the peppermint on her breath.

"No training today," she said, and kissed him.

He kissed her back.

# 37

It was a lovely day in Dublin.

Denton Peccadillo dumped a wooden chessboard in the skip behind his shop. He had a beard – closely cropped – and his forehead was big and rumpled, as if it was struggling to push his hairline back as far as it would go.

"Don't like chess?" Skulduggery asked, emerging from the shadows.

Peccadillo cursed and jumped back, his hands going to his chest. "Jeez! Don't do that! You scared the life out of me!"

"Sorry," said Skulduggery.

"Sorry," said Valkyrie, at Peccadillo's shoulder.

He cursed again and spun, then leaned against the skip for support. "You two, I swear to God. You two..."

Valkyrie pulled the chessboard out of the skip. "What's wrong with this? Is it broken? Doesn't look broken."

"It's a dud," Peccadillo said, lips twisting. "Guy who sold it to me said it was the Oberite chaturanga board. You know about the Oberite chaturanga board?"

"I do," said Valkyrie, "but why don't you tell me what *you* think those words mean, and I'll tell you if you're right?"

"Chaturanga is the game chess evolved from," Skulduggery said, taking the board from her. "And the Oberites were a group of West Slavic tribes who fought alongside Charlemagne."

"Recently?"

"Not very."

"The chaturanga board is supposed to be able to show the outcome of any violent encounter," Peccadillo said. "From the lowliest bar brawl to the most sophisticated military engagement, if you know how to read it, you can see the future while you play. It's never wrong. But this? This is not it."

He took the board out of Skulduggery's hands and tossed it back in the skip.

Valkyrie shook her head sadly. "Did you pay much for it?"

"Yes," said Peccadillo.

"It's so unfair when a good, honest person such as yourself is cheated out of their money. It makes me so mad to think of all those other black-market dealers of stolen magical items who are going about their day, happy and smiling, and you're here, sulking like a little baby, because you were too stupid and greedy to bother checking whether this latest illegal thing you did was in any way intelligent – which, obviously, it was not." She put a hand on his shoulder. "You're one of the good ones, Denton. Don't let this latest setback get you down. You'll always be a hero to me."

Peccadillo shook her hand off. "What do you want? Why are you here? I have a business to run, in case you've forgotten."

"A criminal business," Valkyrie pointed out.

"With a legitimate front," said Peccadillo, "so I have to be actually in the shop in case anyone actually wants to buy something."

"And why haven't you relocated to Roarhaven like everyone else?"

"Not *everyone* else," Peccadillo countered. "There are some of us out there who still care about quality, and service, and the fact that it's easier to run a criminal business in Dublin or London or Chicago than it is to run it in Roarhaven. Do you know how much money I'd have had to put into psychic defences? Do you know how much effort I'd have had to go to each day so that the Sense Wardens couldn't randomly read my mind as they drove by? Don't let the propaganda fool you. You might be free to be who you are in Roarhaven, but you are not free to do as you please."

"You poor, oppressed little man."

"Whatever you came here for, just get on with it."

"We want to talk to you about that item you sold me," Skulduggery said.

"The item?" Peccadillo repeated. "Oh, you mean the gun. You mean the rifle you bought. Yes, I remember it now. I remember it because I'm not an arms dealer. I don't generally sell people guns. That's not my business."

"And yet you sold one to me."

"Only because you forced me to," Peccadillo responded. "But I told you – I said when I handed it over – I said no returns. You remember me saying that?"

"I do, as it turns out."

"Then you agree that there's no way you're getting your money back."

"I don't want the money back, Denton. I just want to know who else you told about it."

Peccadillo frowned. "Told? I told no one. I don't tell other people about the things I sell and who I sell them to. If I were to get a reputation for that kind of carry-on, it would be extraordinarily bad for business."

"So you didn't tell anyone?" Valkyrie said. "Not one person? Not your buddy down the pub? Not your low-life contacts? Not your boyfriend or girlfriend or partner?"

"No one," said Peccadillo. "Not even when the acting Supreme Mage was assassinated."

A strange sort of silence descended for a moment – a silence heavy with implication. With threat.

"Why would that make you mention it?" Valkyrie asked.

"It wouldn't. It didn't. But if, for instance, I'd been talking to someone about the news of the day, and the murder-in-broad-daylight of Damocles Creed came up in conversation, as it undoubtedly would, then I may have been compelled to remark upon the type of weapon that was probably used. In this case, a rifle of some description. I may then have been compelled to mention that I had happened to procure and sell such a weapon to one Skulduggery Pleasant, not three days earlier.

"If this conversation had taken place – which it didn't – then perhaps I would have remarked upon the sheer coincidence at play, to which my friend – my hypothetical friend – would have said that he didn't believe in coincidences. Surely a laugh would follow, as I asked my – non-existent, remember, and entirely hypothetical – friend if he sincerely believed that the great Skeleton Detective himself, along with the shall-we-say *notorious* Valkyrie Cain, had used said rifle to carry out the assassination of our dearly beloved Supreme Mage? To which my friend – my non-existent, hypothetical, and all-round imaginary friend – would smile, and then chuckle, and then dismiss the very idea from his head."

"I'm so glad we got that straightened out," Valkyrie said, her eyes crackling with power.

Peccadillo paled.

"What about your contact?" Skulduggery asked.

"Sorry?"

"Your contact," he repeated. "The person from whom you procured the rifle. Like you said, you're not in the business of buying and selling weapons. Did this purchase raise any eyebrows?"

"Perhaps," Peccadillo said, after a slight hesitation. "But nothing I couldn't handle."

"I do not doubt your eyebrow-handling abilities in the slightest," said Skulduggery, "but, if you didn't tell anyone about the rifle, then maybe your contact did. We're going to need a name."

"Ah. That... that would be verging precariously close to sharing information that is not mine to divulge."

"Your principles are as admirable as they are arbitrary, Denton, but I'm afraid I'll have to insist."

Peccadillo mused on it. "So this could be seen as, perhaps, me doing you a favour, right?"

"Perhaps."

"And favours being what favours are, if I do you a favour, you're obliged to do a favour for me, yes?"

"What do you need done?"

"There's this... thing," said Peccadillo. "This object. This item. Whether it's valuable or not, what it's used for or isn't used for, that doesn't matter. You don't need to know that. For the purpose of this favour, all you have to know is that this object exists, and it's in the possession of a worm of a man. Absolute worm. Now, I know where this worm of a man is, but as I am currently lacking in the loyal henchmen department I need a couple of tough customers – such as yourselves – to facilitate the recovery of said object."

"You want us to steal something for you," said Valkyrie.

"Not steal," said Peccadillo. "Just take."

"Does this item belong to you?"

"No, but it doesn't belong to this worm of a man, either. Just because it's been in his possession for years doesn't mean it's his."

"And where is this object located?" Skulduggery asked.

Peccadillo chuckled. "First, I need your word that you'll bring it back to me."

"That all depends on how far we'd have to travel."

"Meath," said Peccadillo. "It's barely a forty-minute drive, just off the motorway. I have the name of the hotel and the number of the room he's staying in – but he's leaving tonight, so time is of the essence. I would go myself, but, like I said before, I am very busy. Once I have the object in my possession, I'll give you the name of my contact and you can go and make your case and I hope everything works out. What do you say?"

"No," said Skulduggery.

Peccadillo's face fell. "What? Why not?"

"Because you've already told us who your contact is."

"I did no such thing!"

"You said we could go and make our case, implying some deference would possibly be required, which rules out the usual criminals and lowlifes, and elevates it to crime-boss status. There's only one crime boss worth anything these days, which leads me to conclude that you bought the gun from Christopher Reign."

Peccadillo froze for a moment. "Not necessarily," he mumbled.

"Good talking to you," Skulduggery said, walking for the car. Valkyrie grinned and followed.

"But what about the favour?" Peccadillo called after them. "What about procuring the object for me?"

"The object," Skulduggery said, "is the Crystal of the Saints, the worm of a man is Rancid Fines, and you've already told us that he's in the City View Hotel, room five two eight."

"But that's not fair!" Peccadillo yelled.

They got in the Bentley.

"How'd you know all that?" Valkyrie asked, buckling her seat belt.

Skulduggery started the car and pulled away from the kerb. "Fines would want to remain largely anonymous, so a big hotel would be desirable – preferably a big hotel used primarily for business people on overnight stays, which means it would be relatively empty during the day. The City View in Meath is such a hotel, and it's one we could get to within forty to fifty minutes, it's just off the motorway, and, if I were a paranoid little man, that's the one I'd choose. Providing you get the right room on the top floor – number five two eight – you can see who's coming from every window long before they get close."

"How are you an expert in hotels? Do you spend a lot of time in hotel rooms that I don't know about?"

He shrugged. "I don't sleep. Researching hotels is but one of the ways in which I fill my time."

"You will never not be weird, will you?"

"I'm just being me, Valkyrie."

"That's exactly what I mean," she said, and turned on the radio. Skulduggery immediately turned it off.

She sighed. "Christopher Reign isn't going anywhere, so I assume we're off to visit our good friend Rancid, yes?"

"I thought we might stop by."

"I swear to God, if we don't get him this time..."

"We will," said Skulduggery. "I've got a good feeling about this one."

# 38

They left the motorway, drove deeper into the countryside and found a place to park. The City View Hotel stood out among all those flat fields and meadows, like whoever had built it was planning on building a city round it and then just... forgot.

Because Valkyrie left a trail of lightning behind her every time she flew, she wrapped an arm round Skulduggery's waist and they rose straight up, disappearing into the clouds. It was cold up there, so she tapped the amulet and her suit spread over her clothes.

Redirecting the wind round them as they moved, Skulduggery got them to the hotel in less than a minute. They then descended on to the roof, where Valkyrie tapped the amulet again and her suit flowed away.

Skulduggery held his hand out towards the fire door and made a fist, and the door popped open. They walked in and Valkyrie closed it behind them. It had probably set off an alarm at the front desk, but they'd be nowhere near by the time someone came to check.

They got to room 528 and Valkyrie knocked. "Housekeeping," she called. She knocked again.

When there was no answer, she gripped the handle and gave it a little jolt of energy. The lock buzzed unhappily and she opened it, walked in.

It was a pretty standard room, as far as hotel rooms went.

There was no sign of Rancid Fines and no sign that anyone was staying there.

"Are you sure he's here?" she asked.

Skulduggery pulled out a small bag of rainbow dust, took a pinch and sprinkled it in the air. It swirled in multicoloured drifts.

"That's a yes," she murmured.

They followed the trail out of the door and over to the lifts, Skulduggery sprinkling the dust every time they came to a junction. They got in the lift, pressed the button for the ground floor. The lift stopped at each floor going down and more people joined them until Valkyrie was squashed up beside Skulduggery in the corner.

They reached the ground floor and the doors opened and voices and chatter and laughter flooded the lift. Valkyrie and Skulduggery were the last ones out, and Valkyrie's eyes widened when she saw the huge sign in the foyer.

"A magic convention! Skulduggery, look! It's a magic convention!"

"You seem strangely excited," he responded.

"I love magic!" she said, turning to him. "Love it! The card tricks where you sign a card and fold it up and then they cut open, like, a lemon, and inside the lemon is your folded-up card...! How do they do that?"

"Do you want me to tell you?"

"And then, when they ask you to think of something, and you think of it, and they write it down and show it to you, and it's the same thing you were thinking of! How do they do *that*?"

"I'll tell you if you—"

"Magic, Skulduggery. It's magic."

His head tilted. "It's not, though."

"OK, but, in a way, isn't pretend magic more real than real magic?"

"No. Just the opposite, in fact."

They watched people file into the convention hall and wandered over.

"Can you do card tricks?" Valkyrie asked.

"I don't."

"But can you?"

"Yes."

"Will you show me one?"

"No."

She scowled. "When did you learn to do card tricks?"

"Sleight of hand is a useful skill to develop, and has applications in a variety of settings."

When he was sure that nobody was watching, he sprinkled a little dust.

"He went into the hall," Valkyrie said, her smile broadening. "And recently, too, judging by the strength of the colours. We have to follow him."

"Or we could wait until he comes out," Skulduggery said.

"I don't think that's a good idea. I think it'd be better if we go in and, you know, actively search for him. Since when do we wait around, anyway? We go in, find him, finally get the Crystal of the Saints, and then – if we're lucky – arrive back in Roarhaven in time to question Reign."

"You just want to see magic tricks."

"With everything that's inside me," Valkyrie said, and led the way to the doors.

"Hello," said the girl in the *Magic Convention* T-shirt and the colourful nails. "Could I see your tickets?"

"Yes, you could," Valkyrie said, answering her smile with one of her own. "Check in your back pocket."

The girl looked excited. "Really?"

"Have a look."

The girl checked her jeans, and then her face fell. "I can't find anything."

Valkyrie blinked. "I'm sorry?"

"My pockets are empty."

"But... but that's where our tickets were. Could you check again?"

"Of course," the girl said, and checked, and then shook her head sadly. "I'm really sorry."

Valkyrie slumped her shoulders. "I worked ages on that trick."

"Are you sure it was me you, you know...?"

Valkyrie stared. "You mean there's someone else walking around with our tickets in her back pocket?"

"It... it's possible."

"Oh my God, I'm such an idiot. I just wanted to show off to the cute girl and now I've lost our tickets and we're not even gonna be able to get into the convention."

"Oh, no, it's OK, you can still go in," the girl said, blushing, and hopped to one side. "Go on. It's fine."

"Really?"

"Go on. I'm sure the trick would have been brilliant if it had worked!"

"Thank you!" Valkyrie gushed. "Thank you so much! And I love your nails."

"Oh, thank you! Aren't they gorgeous? My sister-in-law does them. Acrylics."

"I wish I could have something like yours, but..." Valkyrie held up her hand. "Short nails."

"Long fingers, though."

"At least there's that," Valkyrie said, and gave her a little wave. "Thank you."

"Enjoy yourself," said the girl.

"I will," said Valkyrie, flashing her a smile.

"You are shameless," Skulduggery muttered as they entered.

The hall was packed with gawkers who thronged the carpeted aisles between stalls selling a wide variety of bargain magic books, marked decks, tarot cards, and pamphlets on how to unlock smart-phones. Valkyrie grinned at everyone as she followed Skulduggery through the crowd, pausing at a silly-magic stall with floppy wands and malfunctioning equipment, then hurrying to catch up with him only to pause again at stalls showcasing specialist equipment, mini guillotines, liquid forks, boxes for illusionists, and something called an invisible deck kicker. The men and women behind the stalls called to her, showing her whatever they were selling, inviting her to pick a card, any card, to check out their puzzle cubes, to inspect these coins or wallets or this perfectly innocent vase.

They passed a booth that checked lung capacity for escapologists. "Oooh," said Valkyrie, "can I have a go?"

"No," Skulduggery said.

"But I want to see how much I can breathe."

He sighed. "Fine. I'll meet you over by the close-up magic stall."

Valkyrie gave him an enthusiastic thumbs up and he used his façade to roll his eyes, then weaved through the throng of people until he was lost from sight.

There was a queue for the lung-capacity test and Valkyrie got bored so she wandered away. She giggled for a few minutes at a young man who showed off by shooting great gouts of fire from his sleeves, accompanied by only the faintest traces of lighter fluid in the air, before joining the crowd marvelling at a man with a waxed moustache levitating a cheap plastic ball. It was pretty good, she had to admit, and everyone watching was seriously impressed. Amateur magicians of all ages stared in awe, trying to figure out how he was doing it.

When the demonstration was over, the guy sold out of the plastic balls he was selling alongside a folded pamphlet. Valkyrie waited until the last of the punters were turned away, disappointed and empty-handed, and the man – the Great Fernando – collapsed into his chair to count his money.

Valkyrie perched on the corner of his table and smiled at him. "Hey," she said.

The Great Fernando looked up, clearly about to tell her he was sold out. He changed his mind quickly, though, and answered her smile with one of his own.

"Hello there," he said, stuffing the rest of the money into his cashbox and sliding it into the bag at his feet. "I don't think I've seen you at one of these things before. I'm sure I'd remember."

Valkyrie laughed. "My first time," she confessed. "I've always been a big fan of magic, though. That was brilliant, what you were doing."

The Great Fernando shrugged. "It's all about misdirection and timing, my dear. Do you partake?"

"Of magic?" she said. "A little."

His smile broadened. "It's always good to see a girl interested in the magical arts – we get too few, even today. Have you performed?"

"Onstage? No, I'd be way too shy."

He stood and moved a little closer, so they didn't have to raise their voices to be heard. "What you need is some experience. I find the best way to rid oneself of the jitters is to step out in front of a crowd and wow them with your talent. You'd be a hit, young lady. Believe me. How tall are you, by the way?"

She stood, and smiled down at him.

"Oh, my!" he said. "Oh, that is impressive!" He raised his hands, stroked the corners of his moustache as he pondered something. "I never offer this," he said, "because traditionally I am a one-man show... but I would be willing to take you under my wing."

Valkyrie's eyes widened. "You would?"

The Great Fernando nodded. "How would you like to be my assistant? It's an almost archaic notion in this day and age, but if approached in the right way – ironic, almost postmodern – I believe it could work. Would you like to be my assistant?"

"I don't know," Valkyrie said, frowning. "What would I have to do?"

"Accompany me onstage, help with setting up the gags, occasionally – perhaps – taking a more active role in the performance."

"Would I have to be sawn in half?"

He laughed. "If we have to perform such a hackneyed trick, we'd be in dire straits indeed!"

"What would I have to wear?"

"Something very tasteful," the Great Fernando assured her. "Something with sequins, a bow tie, some high heels... Something tasteful. Are you aware of Zatanna?"

"From the comics?"

"That's her," he said, beaming.

Valkyrie nodded. "That is all very intriguing, Fernando – and very tempting. If you were anyone else, I'd say no – especially to the outfit. But after seeing that levitation trick... You are an immense talent."

He nodded. "Immense."

"How did you do that, by the way?"

The Great Fernando laughed. "My dear girl, a magician never reveals his secrets – you know that! Of course, if you were to agree to be my assistant, I'd have to share everything I know with you."

"The plastic balls you sold," said Valkyrie, "is there anything special about them?"

"Between you and me? Just plastic balls I picked up for next to nothing in a toyshop."

"You sold them for quite a profit."

"And that is the first lesson of magic – you take the ordinary, and you transform it into something amazing."

"The pamphlets that go with them – I bet they don't even explain the trick, do they?"

He laughed again. "And that's the second rule of magic – convince the audience to expect one thing, and deliver something quite different."

She picked up the plastic ball he'd been using. "Can I give it a try?" she asked.

"By all means," he said.

"Levitate," she said to the ball. Her hand crackled and the plastic sizzled and burned away to nothing. The Great Fernando froze.

"Well," Valkyrie said, "at least I made it disappear. That's something, right?" She brushed the residue from her palm. "Is this how you make a living? You go to magic conventions, use actual magic, then scam the mortals out of their money?"

Fernando swallowed. "I *do* know you."

"Maybe."

"I know your face. I know... Oh, God," he said. "You're Valkyrie Cain."

"And you're an Elemental con artist."

He shook his head. "No, no, Miss Cain. Not a con artist. How can I be a con artist if I'm demonstrating actual magic? In fact, it could be argued that I'm the only one at this convention who *isn't* a con artist."

"Nice try, Fernando, but these people are *expecting* to be tricked. If you show them the real thing and tell them they can do it, too, that's the con. I could arrest you right now."

It may have been Valkyrie's imagination, but it looked like even his moustache drooped.

"Or," she said.

He perked up. "Or?"

"We're looking for someone, Fernando, a man named Rancid Fines. You know him?"

"Don't know the name, no. I'm sorry. I'm not really one of the elite, you know?"

"Elite?"

"The Roarhaven crowd," Fernando explained. "I wasn't invited to go and live there."

"You don't have to be invited. You can apply."

"I did," he said. "Apply, I mean. But the application was rejected. I'm just, I'm not that powerful, and I wouldn't contribute that much, and the only thing I know about is card tricks."

"Can you actually do any card tricks?"

"Not very well," he said miserably. "But there's another sorcerer staying at the hotel, if that's who you're talking about. Small guy? Nervous?"

"Sounds like him."

"He came over yesterday after seeing my demonstration. I guess I gave the impression that I had more money than I do, because he was asking about the circles I ran in, and if I knew anyone who might be interested in funding his research. He was quite disappointed when he figured out that I was a nobody."

"You know where he is now?"

"Saw him heading into the performance about twenty minutes ago. They have a magic show? They do it every year. It's quite good, actually. Anyway, that should be finishing up around now, so you'll probably catch him coming out. It's in one of the smaller halls – the East Hall, I think."

"What's your name, Fernando?"

"Fernando."

"Your full name."

"Oh. Fernando Marvellious."

Valkyrie blinked. "I'd arrest you for being a con artist, but I think you've already punished yourself enough with that name."

He sagged. "It's true. I have."

"Be good, Fernando. Or I'll find you."

He swallowed nervously and she left him. She waved to Skulduggery and he joined her as she headed over to the East Hall, arriving just as people were filing out of the door.

"There's our man," Skulduggery said, and Valkyrie craned her neck until she saw Rancid Fines splitting off from the main group. He had a satchel over one shoulder – big enough to hold the Crystal.

But, just as they were about to walk over, someone else detached themselves from the main group, walked right up behind Rancid and said something to him. Rancid stiffened, and the newcomer gripped his arm and steered him towards a side door.

Valkyrie picked up the pace, Skulduggery right beside her. It was only as Fines was being forced out through the door that the newcomer glanced round and Valkyrie saw his face.

"Oh, damn," she whispered, as she locked eyes with Silas Nadir.

# 39

They followed Nadir as he dragged Rancid into a deserted car park.

"What are you doing here, Silas?" Skulduggery asked. "I wouldn't have thought a magic convention would be of any interest to a serial killer."

"That's because you don't know me," Nadir responded. "I've always been a big fan of mortal magicians. Houdini, David Blaine, Paul Daniels – the greats. And, if you take one step closer, I'll kill this guy. One more step. That's all."

"We'll stop walking forwards if you stop walking backwards," Skulduggery said.

Nadir shook his head. "You stop walking, and I keep walking. See, I'm the one with the hostage. I'm the one with the power here."

"But, if you kill the hostage, you lose the power, and then I shoot you. See how that works?"

Nadir sneered. "I'll kill him and then shunt away before you can even draw your gun."

"Then why haven't you shunted away already?" Valkyrie asked. "That's what I would've done. Unless, of course, you can't. The land this hotel was built on was flattened out a bit, am I right? Something like that? So in any parallel dimensions you might travel to, the ground wouldn't be this flat. Maybe there's a hill right where we're standing. Am I close? I bet I'm close. The thing is, as a Shunter, you have to know exactly what you're shunting into, or else you might shunt straight into a mound of dirt. I'm right, amn't I?"

"I bet you are," said Skulduggery.

"I bet I am, too."

Skulduggery pulled out his gun. "You take one more step, Nadir, and I'll shoot you."

"You'll have to shoot through this pipsqueak!" Nadir snarled.

Skulduggery shrugged. "I'm OK with that, actually."

Rancid blinked. "I'm sorry?"

"I'm just a little tired of chasing him. A little bored of it, to be quite honest. If I have to shoot him to shoot you, I will gladly shoot him."

"That's hardly fair," said Rancid.

"Just keep walking," Nadir snarled.

"I don't think I will," said Rancid, and he straightened his legs and stopped co-operating as Nadir pulled him back.

Nadir dragged Rancid Fines for about a metre or so before he started to lose his grip, and Rancid slid slowly and awkwardly to the ground. "You little jerk!" Nadir snapped.

Rancid lay on the ground, as stiff as a slice of stale cheese.

"Silas Nadir," said Skulduggery, "you're going back to prison."

A minibus pulled into the car park and Nadir grinned. "I don't think so," he said.

The door hissed and then opened with a rattle, and the passengers disembarked and stood there, frowning at the scene before them.

"Help!" Rancid shouted. "They're mugging me!"

"We're not," Valkyrie assured them.

"I'm definitely not," said Nadir, moving backwards.

"Help!" Rancid screeched.

The passengers stepped slowly closer.

"Now, just hold on a second here," the guy out front said.

"They made me do it!" Nadir yelled, pointing at Valkyrie and Skulduggery before sprinting away.

Skulduggery held up his hands in a calming motion. "Everyone just relax."

"Look!" someone cried. "He's holding up his hands!"

For some reason, this sparked the group into as close to a frenzy as it was going to get, which amounted to little more than raised eyebrows and nudges, but it was enough to convince Rancid that it was safe to scramble up and stagger through them. He lunged dramatically into the minibus. "Save me!" he pleaded, and the door rattled closed and the bus pulled a U-turn and took off.

"We weren't mugging him," Valkyrie told the passengers as they neared. "Look at us. Look at my friend's suit. Why would we try to mug someone?"

That sowed enough doubt to halt the group's progress, but the minibus was already out of the car park at that stage, and Silas Nadir was gone.

# 40

In the warmth of the early afternoon sun, Omen found Axelia on one of the benches in the courtyard. A handful of students passed the last few minutes of lunch break lounging around the fountain, accompanied by nothing but the murmur of conversation and the gentle plashing of the water.

Axelia didn't look relaxed, though. Her face was tight. Pensive. He sat, and the words flowed out of her.

"Something's wrong with me," she said. "I can't focus on anything. I can't study, can't pay attention in class, my mind keeps wandering whenever I try to revise. I can't even read a book. I have to read the same line five times before it even goes in. I'm distracted, like, all the time, but I've got nothing to be distracted by."

"Sure you do," said Omen. "Look around – look at the world. You got protests, demonstrations, inequality, police brutality, Flanery in the White House, you've got Damocles Creed being assassinated in broad daylight, and everything is scary and upsetting and nobody's happy. Added to all of that, exam stress."

"But I don't have exam stress," she said. "Our exams will be easy, so long as you've been doing the work all year."

Omen nodded. That's why he was in so much trouble. "But you've got other sorts of stress that this place brings. I mean, it's only been just over a week since your best friend got expelled."

Axelia grunted.

Omen frowned. "Bella's not your best friend?"

"I guess she is? Or she was? But... to be honest, I don't know why I hung out with her at all. She was very irritating."

"Was she?"

"You didn't think so?"

"I didn't really know her," said Omen, "but I always thought you two got on really well."

"It just goes to show what a good actor I am. Maybe I should audition for the school play this year."

"I don't think Corrival does school plays."

"Then I probably won't get the part," she said miserably.

"Axelia, why are you telling me this stuff? Don't take it the wrong way, but don't you have other friends? What about Ula?"

"Ula's mad at me. I don't know why." She stood up. "At least I can still talk to you, right?"

"Absolutely," said Omen.

They chatted a bit, and she left, and Omen checked the time, then left the courtyard and went looking for Ula.

On his way, he saw a First Year hurtling round the corner, and a hand reached out from the throng of students and snagged him.

"Where are you running to?" Filament asked, forcing the child to walk backwards until he was pressed up against the wall. The First Year's friends appeared, smiles on their faces until they saw what was happening to their classmate.

"Eh?" Filament urged. "Where are you running to?"

The First Year obviously didn't know how to answer that.

"Filament," said Omen, slowing as he passed, "come on, they're just having fun."

"There's no running in the corridors, Omen, you know that." Filament loomed over the boy. "Did *you* know that?"

The First Year nodded.

"Then why were you running?"

The poor kid looked as if he was going to start crying at any second, so Omen hurried over, his hand closing round Filament's wrist. "Dude, let him go."

Filament frowned. "I'm a prefect, Omen. Making sure the First Years are safe is part of my job. The way they run, they're going to hurt themselves or someone else."

"You don't have to grab him, though."

"You didn't have to grab me, either, and yet you did."

Omen gave a laugh. "I suppose I did. All right then, let's both let go at the same time, what do you think? One, two – now."

He released his hold on Filament, but Filament held on to the First Year for a few more seconds – just to demonstrate his authority – and then turned his full attention to Omen. Predictably, a few of the students in the crowd went, "Ooooooh." Omen laughed again.

"I have a responsibility to the welfare of the students in this school," Filament said.

Omen's smile turned to a grin. "Seriously? You're a prefect, not a City Guard."

"I have been given a set of duties, Omen – all the prefects have. Maintaining order is number one."

"He was just playing."

"This isn't about him," Filament said. "He was playing a little game with his little friends and he ran when he should have walked. It's against the rules and he could have hurt himself, but it's no big deal. But you, Omen, what you did – that is a big deal."

"What did I do, Filament?"

"You assaulted a prefect."

A thousand responses rushed into Omen's head, but he ignored them all. "You're right," he said. "I shouldn't have done that. That went way too far. I'm sorry, Filament. I'm genuinely sorry. I won't do it again, I promise."

For a moment, Filament looked confused, like he was expecting some big confrontation, but the need to have his authority recognised trumped any little games he was hoping to play. He nodded. "Don't let it happen again."

Omen smiled. "You got it. Hey, you seen Ula around?"

"She's still in the Dining Hall," Filament said, a little reluctantly.

"Thanks," Omen said brightly, and hurried off.

Ula had commandeered one of the smaller tables in the Dining Hall and had filled it with textbooks. Omen hesitated before approaching.

"Hi," he said. "Is this seat taken?"

"That depends," Ula responded, not looking up. "Are you going to ask me out? Because I have a girlfriend."

"I – no, this isn't anything like that."

"Are you sure?"

"Positive. Can I sit?"

"No."

"I just need a word."

"That's great," said Ula, "but you can't sit. My girlfriend's sitting there. She's real."

"I'm sorry?"

"My girlfriend. She's real. I'm not making her up."

"I wouldn't have thought you were."

"Do you want to know her name? It's Ula."

"That's your name."

"It's her name, too." She looked up. "What, do you think an Ula can't go out with another Ula? Do you think they'd get confused over which one is which? Do you realise how stupid that sounds?"

"It does sound pretty stupid, all right."

"You can sit if you want," she said, "but I have to warn you that my girlfriend Ula is sitting there."

"I'll be quick," Omen said, and sat, and there was a squeal and something moved and he leaped up and Ula burst out laughing and there was someone else laughing, too, someone sitting in the chair, someone invisible.

"Jesus," Omen muttered, hand on his chest, feeling his thumping heart.

The bubble of invisibility collapsed into the cloaking sphere held by the grinning Sixth Year girl in the armchair. "Hi," she said. "I'm Ula."

"Hi," Omen said, amused by the amusement.

"I told you she was sitting there," the first Ula said.

"Are you allowed to have that?" Omen asked, eyes on the sphere.

"Technically, no," the second Ula said, "but technically, we're not allowed to do a lot of things, which I've always thought is a bit unfair, so I decided that my last few weeks of school will be different. This is me rebelling."

"Um... are you studying?"

"I'm rebelling while studying, yes. Is there a rule that defines how you're supposed to rebel? Because I'd sure as heck rebel against that rule."

"Omen," the first Ula said, "I'm trying to spend quality revision time with my girlfriend before the term ends and she goes back to China, so can you say what you need to say?"

"Yes," Omen said. "It's about Axelia."

Ula's face soured. "What about her?"

"I was going to say that she's your friend, but I get the impression things may have changed."

"Just a little."

"What happened?"

"What happened, Omen, is that Bella was expelled, and, after a few days of soaking up the sympathy of having her best friend leave, Axelia has pretty much forgotten all about her."

"Any reason why?"

"None – but she's not answering Bella's calls, she's not responding to her in the group chat... She's just shut her out of her life."

"That doesn't sound like Axelia."

210

"Well, it is."

"And how is Bella?"

"Angry. I mean, yeah, she doesn't know what the hell is going on with Axelia, but she's angry with the school, angry with Duenna, angry with whoever let this happen."

"Has Duenna given a reason yet why she expelled her?"

"They just said her behaviour has been getting worse and her work has been deteriorating – which is a load of crap, because her work was never that great to begin with, but whatever."

"Why exactly did she get expelled?"

"She sneaked down to the kitchens, herself and, like, three others, at two in the morning. They were all caught, but the other three just got detention." Ula's phone beeped. She looked at it. "That's Bella now," she said, and started tapping on the screen.

"Say hi for me," said Omen.

Ula frowned at her phone, tapped out a response, read the reply, and her frown deepened.

"Everything OK?" Omen asked.

Ula murmured a response, her fingertips dancing on the phone.

Omen waited for nearly a full minute, then smiled and nodded. "I'll be going, then."

"Not yet," Ula said. "Ula, can you get me a cup of water? I'm parched."

"Get it yourself," said Ula.

"Please? I'm on the phone."

"It's a mobile phone. You can take it with you."

"But I'm texting."

"You can text and walk, I've seen you."

Ula sighed, took her eyes off the screen for a moment. "I have to tell Omen something."

Ula narrowed her eyes. "Is it super-top-secret?"

"It is."

"Then I don't want to know." Ula stood. "Water?"

"Yes, please."

"Omen..."

"Oh, nothing for me, thanks."

She looked at him weirdly. "I wasn't offering. I was going to warn you not to take my seat while I'm gone." And she left.

"Ula's awesome," said Ula, still tapping. "Bella's being cagey."

"About what?"

"She wants me to ask Axelia if she's looked into *that thing*. I asked her what *that thing* is. She said she saw something odd while she was headed down to the kitchen that night. She won't tell me what it was, though."

Omen frowned. "She saw something unusual and the next day she was expelled?"

Ula tapped her phone and didn't respond.

"That sounds dodgy," he continued.

Ula nodded, and put on an inexplicable London accent. "It sounds well dodge, mate, innit?"

"Maybe I should ask Axelia about it."

"Go right ahead," Ula said in her normal accent. "I'm a bit too mad at her to ask polite questions. Oh, Omen, if I don't get to speak to you before the term ends—"

"That's still two weeks away."

"—I just want to say have a nice summer."

"Right," said Omen. "Thanks. Bye, Ula."

"Bye, Omen."

"Bye, Ula," Omen said to the other Ula as she returned with a cup of water.

"Whatever."

# 41

Martin Flanery sat in the Oval Office and wallowed in horrible silence.

He preferred when things were happening, when the TV was on, when people were cheering, when they were chanting his name. But this was a quiet moment, and he resented it with every fibre of his being.

It was all coming apart. He was the most powerful man in the world and he was terrified that he was about to lose it all.

The election was six months away and he was ten points behind in the polls. Every single thing his team advised him to do went wrong – and all of the great and genius moves he instigated himself were then fouled up by the incompetence of the people around him. Ever since Crepuscular Vies had walked out on him, he'd been floundering. It wasn't fair. It just wasn't fair.

He got up. "I'm going to the Residence," he said to whoever was listening, and ignored the voices that trailed after him, reminding him of appointments and meetings and calls, like any of that stuff was important. He was the President of the United States, for God's sake. He decided what was important.

He got to the Residence and slammed the door and sat on the toilet. With the remote in hand, he flicked through the news channels on the TV he'd had installed, found those that were nice to him and closed his eyes, letting their reassurances wash over him. Yes, he was doing a good job. Yes, the people loved him. Yes, he was probably the greatest president of all time.

He felt himself relaxing. He allowed himself a little smile, and opened his bowels.

"You look happy."

Flanery shrieked and twisted and fell sideways off the toilet, clutching at his pants, trying to pull them up over his knees. A tall man stood in the bathroom doorway wearing a double-breasted blazer and a cravat. He had neatly combed blond hair, a wide smile that showed no teeth, and small, round spectacles.

"Pardon me," the intruder said, "I don't mean to make you uncomfortable. When you're ready to talk, I'll be out here. A mutual friend suggested we talk – one Crepuscular Vies? He intimated that we might have some things in common."

A slight bow, and the man – a British man – stepped away, leaving Flanery to pick himself up off the floor. He did his best to clean up and restore some dignity, but before he left the bathroom he glared into the mirror.

Vies had a knack for keeping Flanery off-balance. That wasn't going to happen this time, not with this guy. He didn't know what kind of magical wizard he was or what he could do or what he could offer, but Flanery was determined to assert himself as the one in charge. He was the President, after all.

He straightened his tie, and walked into the living room, where the British guy was examining the bookcase.

"Have you read any of these?" the man asked, trailing a finger along the spines of a long row of books.

"I've read all of them," Flanery lied.

Another smile – all lips, no teeth. "And which is your favourite?"

"I like them all. They're all good."

"They're very thick books, bound in very impressive leather. I like a man who reads. It shows an intelligence, a curiosity, and a capacity for empathy that is so important in this day and age, wouldn't you say?"

"I would. What are you—?"

"My name is Perfidious Withering, Mr President, So very pleased to make your acquaintance." He came forward and Flanery stuck out his hand to shake, but Perfidious hesitated. "Did you wash your hands, Mr President?"

Flanery reddened, and Perfidious politely retracted his arm.

"As I said," he continued, "Crepuscular Vies suggested I speak to you to see, perhaps, if we share common ground."

"You're a wizard, then?" Flanery asked gruffly. It was important to be the one asking questions. To ask them gruffly was even better.

"I am," Perfidious said. "Since 1922, I have been heavily involved in various avenues of research and experimentation. Along the way, I have encountered some rather unique individuals whom I think would be something of a boon to you, sir, going forward."

Flanery frowned at him. "In what way?"

Perfidious indicated a chair. "May I sit?"

"Sure," said Flanery. He wondered if he should sit, too – but feared it would look like he'd been waiting for Perfidious to sit first. If he sat now, he'd look weak.

"You had an arrangement with Abyssinia," Perfidious said, "a war that would eliminate her enemies and secure you a second – and perhaps third – term. All of your mistakes would be wiped away and you'd have the whole country – the entire world – cheering you on as you led them to victory against the evil sorcerers."

Flanery wondered if standing like this made him look subordinate. Perfidious was sitting in a comfortable chair, his long legs crossed, while the President of the United States stood before him like an errant schoolboy or a rattled employee about to be fired.

"Abyssinia, obviously, tried to betray you," Perfidious said, "and, once Crepuscular Vies left, you have been cast somewhat adrift, would I be right in saying?"

Flanery put his hands behind his back and paced slowly, like he was putting serious effort into thinking. "Perhaps," he said eventually.

"Then tell me, Mr President – what is it you want?"

"I want to win."

"Ah, yes, the election. At this point, the only way you'll get a second term is if you can find a way to cheat on a frankly enormous scale. But I'm not talking about votes, sir. I'm asking you what you want."

Flanery made a decision. He sat – but on the very front of the chair. He perched. "It's not about what I want," he answered.

Perfidious waited.

"It's what the people want," said Flanery. "It's what drives them, not me. What are they scared of? How can I make them feel like they've got some power? That's what got me the presidency, and that's what'll keep me the presidency."

"And, by extension, keep you out of federal prison," Perfidious said with a chuckle.

Flanery didn't find that funny. "I wanted to go to war with your kind because the best kind of enemy is the enemy you can't see. It's not about what country they're from or what colour their skin is or what religion they are or their accent – the best kind of enemy is the one that's already here, in America. It could be your friend or your neighbour or the person in the office you hate or it could be your brother-in-law. That's the kind of enemy America needs right now."

Perfidious smiled that smile. "A multipurpose enemy," he said. "An enemy that will fill whatever role you need it to fill. Mr President, you are a surprisingly insightful man."

Flanery shrugged.

"I have someone I'd like you to meet."

# 42

Kimora and Ulysses sat on the couch and told Sebastian they could no longer teach Darquesse.

"Oh," Sebastian said.

"Honestly, we could have stopped weeks ago," said Ulysses. "Her understanding of abstract concepts has leaped forward exponentially. We've, um, we've been feeling pretty stupid, to be frank. Compared to her intellect, we're... pebbles on a beach."

Sebastian hesitated. "Yeah..."

"You already knew this," Kimora said.

"Darquesse mentioned it to me a while back," he responded. "She didn't want to say anything in case she hurt your feelings."

Kimora sat forward. "In case she...? Sebastian! This is huge!" Now Kimora was on her feet and pacing. "She didn't want to hurt our feelings! She considered how we would react to this news and she decided, independently, that she didn't want to offend us! This is empathy, Sebastian! Real human empathy!"

"I suppose it is."

"This is amazing! It worked! It actually worked! We're helping her come to an understanding about... about humanity!"

Kimora went on like that for a bit and Ulysses joined in, and they made some calls and soon all of the Darquesse Society members were in Sebastian's living room, talking excitedly about this new revelation. Sebastian agreed and nodded along with everyone, but of course this reaction came as no surprise. Darquesse herself had predicted it weeks ago.

They fell silent when Darquesse walked in. Sebastian looked at her, surprised. She had aged in the last few hours.

"Hey," he said. "What age are you now?"

"Ten," she answered. She gave a little whistle, and the puppy came trotting in, sitting obediently beside her feet. "You're all talking about the lessons, aren't you?"

"Yes, we are," Kimora said. "Your daddy told us you don't need them any more, but you didn't want to hurt our feelings. That was really nice of you, to think of us like that. Really super nice."

"You're a good little girl, aren't you?" Ulysses said. "A good little girl."

Darquesse nodded.

Kimora laughed. "Maybe we should ask you to teach us sometime."

"You wouldn't understand any of it," Darquesse said.

Kimora's laugh dried up a little. "No," she said. "We probably wouldn't."

Darquesse walked up to Sebastian. "Dad, I think I need a friend."

The puppy trotted after her and Sebastian ruffled its ears. "The doggy isn't enough of a friend for you?"

"Not really," Darquesse said. "He's only a chair. I think I need a person-friend. Someone my own age. Someone I didn't make. A girl or a boy. Just for a little bit. Just to see what it's like."

Sebastian glanced at the others. They looked hesitant. "I don't know if that's a good idea, sweetie. Real people are delicate. You can't turn them into puppies or chairs or portals into other dimensions."

"I won't, I promise."

"You can't change them at all, though, or take them anywhere, or show them any of your powers."

Darquesse frowned. "What powers?"

"Your magic, sweetie."

"Oh! Yeah, I know that."

"I think it'd be safer if you just stayed here, though."

"No, it's OK," Darquesse said.

Sebastian reached for her way too late, and clutched at empty space as she disappeared.

"Oh, God," said Bennet.

# 43

Alice Edgley tapped furiously on the tablet's screen and the points chimed and flashed in the way that was guaranteed to make her dad shake his head and wonder what was wrong with good old-fashioned computer games where you shot people in the face. Alice had never played one of those games and wasn't too eager to start. She liked collecting golden rings and racking up points. She'd already beaten her record today and was on a winning streak.

Someone knocked on the patio door. A girl, around her age, with long black hair. She reminded Alice of someone, but she couldn't quite figure out who. She had a face Alice liked.

Leaving the tablet on the couch, Alice opened the patio door. "Hello," she said.

"Hello," the girl replied. "Would you like to play?"

Alice looked back at the tablet, then at the girl. "Yes," she said.

And they had a wonderful afternoon together.

# 44

"Missed him again," Valkyrie muttered. They hadn't spoken at all on the drive to Roarhaven. Now that they were passing through Shudder's Gate, she found her voice. "Maybe we're just not meant to ever catch Rancid Fines. Maybe the universe has decided that, no, we can't scratch that particular itch."

She looked up. "Has this ever happened to you before? There's a bad guy and, no matter how hard you try to bring him in, it just doesn't happen?"

"Absolutely," Skulduggery said. "And when that occurs it is both infuriating and aggravating. But usually it happens because the bad guy is too powerful, or too clever, or too paranoid. Or even too lucky. But Rancid Fines... Rancid Fines is just..."

"Uncatchable," Valkyrie said.

"No one's uncatchable," Skulduggery responded immediately. "We will catch him. I vow to you here and now, Valkyrie Cain, that we shall catch Rancid Fines, on my honour and on your honour."

"Don't you be bringing my honour into this."

"Then just on my honour."

"Unless we do catch him and then it can be on both of our honours. But you know what's worse? Silas Nadir caught him. Silas Nadir the *serial killer* caught him, and we didn't. That's just... that's insulting."

"As a wise man once said—"

"You, right?"

"—never underestimate a heart of evil—"

"I bet it was you."

"—for in that heart you can—"

"It was you, wasn't it?"

"Yes, it was me," Skulduggery said impatiently, "but I'm just trying to make the point that Nadir must have heard that the Crystal of the Saints is worth money to the right people and everyone knows Rancid has had it since the 1940s, so Silas's greed would have been a strong motivator. If we were after Rancid Fines out of greed, we'd have caught him by now."

"Maybe we should be after him because of greed."

"Ours is a nobler pursuit."

"But a longer one."

They parked outside Christopher Reign's nightclub and walked right in under a sky that was heavy with clouds.

"Excuse me," a young woman said, hurrying over. "Excuse me, you can't be in here. We're not open yet."

"We're here to see Christopher," Skulduggery told her, not slowing down. "We have an appointment."

"I'm his assistant," said the young woman. "I handle all his appointments, and I know for a fact that you don't have one."

"Sure we do," Valkyrie said, following Skulduggery through the bar area. "We called ahead. We talked to Betty."

"There is no Betty here."

Valkyrie frowned. "Are you not Betty?"

"I'm Acantha."

"Acantha!" Valkyrie said, snapping her fingers. "That was it! We talked to Acantha and arranged an appointment. You should speak to her."

"I am her!"

Valkyrie frowned. "Then why are you speaking to us?"

They reached the office and walked in.

"Mr Reign," Acantha said in the run-up to an apology, but Reign waved it away.

"It's OK, Acantha. These two have a habit of barging in and acting tough. You can go back to what you were doing."

Acantha nodded. With a glare at Valkyrie, she left, closing the door behind her.

Christopher Reign was a handsome man, an American, who sat behind his desk in his expensive suit and looked at Valkyrie and Skulduggery and didn't smile. "The Dynamic Duo return to my establishment," he said. "Remind me, though, which one's Batman, and which is Robin?"

"I'm Batman," they both said together.

Skulduggery looked at Valkyrie. "You're clearly Robin."

She raised an eyebrow. "Excuse me? I clearly am not. I said at the very start of this whole thing, I am not your sidekick."

"Well, I can't be Robin. I'm in charge."

"It is so nice that you think that."

"And then there's the age thing. Batman is older."

"That still doesn't make you Batman and me Robin. If anything, that makes me Batman and you some old guy who hangs round Batman." She clicked her fingers. "Alfred! You're Alfred! You're old and you have manners and you bring me tea in the Batcave!"

"None of that is what happens."

Valkyrie nodded, satisfied, and looked back to Reign. "I'm Batman. This is Alfred."

"Uh-huh," said Reign. "And who does that make me? The Joker?"

"Naw. You're one of the lesser-known bad guys. You have a funny name and a single annoying quirk that's become your whole gimmick. You got knocked out very early in the fight, basically."

"Y'know something? Despite it all, and despite myself, I actually enjoy it when you two call round. You are nothing if not entertaining."

"I'm glad you think so," said Skulduggery. "How's business, Christopher?"

"I can't complain."

"The criminal enterprise going well, is it?"

"I wouldn't know anything about no criminal enterprise, seeing as how I'm a simple bar owner, struggling to get by in today's economy. Where we went wrong, as a culture, was to link our economic prosperity to that of the mortals. Where was the sense in that?"

"We all use the same currencies," Skulduggery said, taking off his hat, flicking a speck of lint from the brim.

"It makes us vulnerable," Reign responded. "Opens us up to forces beyond our control. Plus, how much time, effort, and expense goes into running our money through the fake corporations as it leaves Roarhaven? It's a flawed system, my friend. A flawed system."

Skulduggery nodded to Valkyrie. "I'll let you take this one."

"Thank you," she said, and smiled at Reign. "I have no idea what either of you are talking about, but my God, it's boring, so can we skip to the reason we're here?"

"By all means," said Reign. "Although I must advise you that I have a business meeting scheduled for right now, and I have to go."

"I'm sure you can delay that for just a minute, though, can't you? For me?"

"For you?"

She gave him one of her smiles.

He smiled back. "You're cute."

"Thank you."

"But not nearly cute enough to delay me from business," he said, getting to his feet.

"You sold a rifle to Denton Peccadillo last week," Skulduggery said.

Reign didn't move. "Allegedly," he said.

"You allegedly sold him a rifle. This rifle was then allegedly used to assassinate Supreme Mage Creed. You have heard about the assassination, I presume?"

"I caught something about it on the news, yeah."

"That makes you a conspirator."

"That makes me a conspirator if A: I sold him the rifle, and B: I knew what that rifle was gonna be used for. But, as I did neither of those things, I don't see how I could be implicated in any of this at all."

Reign was choosing his words carefully. There was wariness there. No cockiness. No teasing. He was purely on the defensive, the way criminals got when their crimes were laid out in front of them. There was no hint of him knowing anything about Skulduggery or Valkyrie's involvement. Whoever had discovered their assassination plans, it wasn't Christopher Reign.

Valkyrie glanced over at Skulduggery, knowing he'd come to the same conclusion.

The door opened and a man came through – trim, greying hair, a face she'd seen before in the corridors of the High Sanctuary.

"Ah," he said, stopping when he saw them.

Valkyrie frowned, waiting to hear what a Sanctuary official was doing in the office of a gangster. The man stood there and smiled. An easy smile. Well-practised.

"This is awkward," said Reign, sitting back down.

The man came forward, hand out to shake. "Detective Cain," he said, "what a pleasure to finally meet you. I've passed you in the High Sanctuary on many occasions, but I was always too intimidated to introduce myself. You have quite the reputation, young lady! Thoroughly deserved, of course! The good bits, anyway. Not the bad bits. My name is Savoir Fair."

She looked at him. Looked at his hand. Didn't shake it.

He dropped it back by his side, looking as happy as if they'd embraced. "I know Detective Pleasant, of course. No introductions necessary there, eh, Skulduggery?"

Skulduggery ignored the question. "Why are you here, Savoir?"

"As Business Liaison, it's important to me that local business owners can put a human face to their dealings with the High Sanctuary. I find it helps lessen the intimidation they would otherwise be feeling."

"I am easily intimidated," Reign said, shrugging.

"Do you have time for a spot of dinner?" Savoir asked. "I'm just here to check in with Mr Reign on the wants and needs of his establishment, but after that I'm free! What do you say — Gregario's?"

"We'll have to decline your kind offer," Skulduggery said.

Savoir chuckled. "And am I surprised? No, I am not! It's not easy, is it, Detective Cain, to get by his tough-talking exterior?"

"I don't eat dinner," Skulduggery explained.

Savoir waved a hand. "Then you can just have the salad. Honestly, Skulduggery, I'd almost think you didn't want to spend any time with me! Worried about the stories I'd tell, are you? Detective Cain, did he ever tell you of the time he was responsible for my wrongful arrest? It sounds serious, I grant you, but it was, what, five years ago? Six? So long ago that I've quite put it out of my mind!"

"Yet here you are," Valkyrie said, "talking about it."

"Indeed," Savoir said, infinitely cheerful. "So! Dinner?"

"We're busy," Valkyrie said. "And we're leaving."

"So soon? Ah, well, maybe tomorrow? Or next week, perhaps? Say, Tuesday?"

"Christopher," Skulduggery said, "we'll be in touch."

"I'll be waiting," said Reign, and watched them walk out.

# 45

The grey clouds had opened as they were walking back to the Bentley. It was still warm, so Valkyrie didn't bother with the necronaut suit, trusting in Skulduggery to divert the rain before it hit her.

"Savoir Fair was a low-level Sanctuary official with a nasty habit of accepting bribes when I arrested him," Skulduggery said, as they got in the car. "He spent a few days in a cell, long enough to regret his life choices, and promised China that he'd never do it again."

"And she let him keep his job?" Valkyrie asked.

"That part surprises me, too."

They pulled out on to the road. The windscreen wipers whirred enthusiastically.

"Business Liaison doesn't sound like a low-level position," Valkyrie said.

Skulduggery nodded. "He's been moving up in the world. It's something I've been keeping my eye on, figuratively speaking."

"And do you think he's discussing legal or illegal matters with Reign right now?"

"If you're asking whether Savoir's connected to anything that's been going on, I doubt it. But there are pies and he has fingers, so I can't be sure at this early stage."

"Do you believe what Reign said? That he had nothing to do with the assassination?"

"I do, actually. I also believe that he has no idea of our connection to it."

Valkyrie nodded as they pulled up at a set of traffic lights. "Same here. Where does that leave us?"

"Just because we believe Reign and Peccadillo when they say they're not involved doesn't mean we're right. We need a Sensitive to scan them both – preferably without them realising."

"That rules me out, so."

"You *are* less of a precise scalpel and more a butcher's cleaver, this is true."

"Oh," she said, "cheers for that."

Pedestrians hurried across the road in front of them. One of them, a man with his hood up against the rain, stopped, patting the pockets of his long coat like he'd forgotten something. Then he turned, and Valkyrie registered the black helmet he wore even as his coat opened and he brought up the assault rifle.

Skulduggery tried to lunge in front of her as the man opened fire, but the seat belt held him back. The first bullets made spiderwebs in the windscreen and tore into Valkyrie's chest. Skulduggery jerked against his seat, bone splinters spraying from the holes in his jacket.

Valkyrie turned, shielding her head with her left arm, like that was going to do anything. Her other hand scrambled for the lever down the side of her seat and she yanked it and the seat flattened, dropping her back. The whole world consisted of the roar of gunfire and the sound of the dashboard being chewed up. There was glass in her hair. Blood in her mouth. Blood all over her.

Skulduggery couldn't get his seat down. His arm had been shot off. Another hail of bullets snapped into his shirt, pulverising his sternum. Valkyrie grabbed him, pulled him down.

Her ears were ringing so much it took her a moment to register that the gunfire had stopped. He was reloading.

Skulduggery slid his revolver from its holster with his good hand as Valkyrie dug her fingers into her pocket, tried dragging the amulet out, but it was stuck there. The way she was lying twisted her jeans, made them too damn tight. Skulduggery sat up, fired twice through the windscreen. The gunman returned fire and the revolver dropped from the hand Skulduggery didn't have any more. Bullets came through the ruined dashboard, punching into Valkyrie's legs. She turned involuntarily and her fingers tapped against the amulet.

The necronaut suit flowed out from within her pocket, shredding through her clothes, covering her in time to stop the next round of bullets from puncturing her flesh. She pulled up the hood. Dragged down the mask.

Her vision darkened. The pain was blossoming, making her moan. She opened the car door, fell out on to the street.

The gunman walked over. She tried to get up. He emptied the rest of the clip into her torso. The suit saved her.

There was a sound. A new sound. Like a car alarm.

Valkyrie collapsed on to her back. The rain splattered against the lenses of her mask. Focusing through the pain, forcing her body to co-operate even as it was shutting down, she made energy dance between her fingertips.

The gunman stood on her wrist, pinning it to the ground.

He let the assault rifle swing back on its strap, let it disappear into his coat, and brought out his next weapon.

A sledgehammer.

He removed it from its strap, tapped the head lightly off Valkyrie's mask, then raised it high above his shoulder. She looked up at him, saw her own face reflected in the black visor of his narrow helmet.

Then that sound again, like a car alarm but louder. A siren.

The gunman looked away from her, and she followed his gaze as a City Guard patrol car roared in from the adjoining street and screeched to a halt in front of them. Valkyrie wanted to laugh in relief, but all she could manage was a cough that sprayed the inside of her mask with blood.

The patrol car sat there, engine running, siren wailing. The gunman stood there, one boot on her wrist, that sledgehammer poised and ready to burst her head open like a grapefruit. She doubted the mask would save her from an impact like that. The Roarhaven cops had saved her life. Then the siren was switched off, and the patrol car drove slowly on, disappearing round the corner.

Valkyrie's strength left her. She looked up at the hammer and thought about all the people she loved.

There was a roar and Skulduggery flew from the open door of the Bentley. He crashed into the gunman, who staggered back, dropping the sledgehammer. It missed Valkyrie's head as it hit the ground. Barely.

Skulduggery rose off the street. His left arm was missing below the elbow. His right arm didn't have a hand. Both trouser legs flapped in the rippling air. He was roaring. Screaming with rage.

The gunman observed him. Moved his right foot back a bit. Then he kicked, a perfect roundhouse kick, that took Skulduggery's head clean off.

Valkyrie tried to cry out, but her lungs weren't working the way they were supposed to. She tried to sit up, but her body wasn't obeying the way it was supposed to. She could only lie there, tears streaming from her eyes, watching as Skulduggery's skull came to a rolling stop beside her.

The gunman picked up the sledgehammer, raising it as he stood over the skull.

Valkyrie pointed at him, making a finger-gun. Closed one eye to aim. Magic flowed through her arm and leaped from her fingertip, hitting the gunman in the chest and flinging him back.

There were people now, passers-by and drivers getting out of their cars, and they were hurrying forward, their hands filled with flame or energy or whatever they could find, whatever they could carry. The gunman saw this, saw them meaning to surround him.

He turned to look at Valkyrie – she could feel his eyes on hers, even through that visor – and then he backed away and ran.

Valkyrie stopped trying to sit up. She blinked at the sky, at the grey clouds spilling rain. She couldn't feel her hands. Couldn't feel her legs. Despite the suit, she was cold. Dying. She managed a smile. Wouldn't be the first time.

She breathed out and didn't breathe in again.

# 46

Valkyrie woke in the Medical Bay in the High Sanctuary.

A doctor leaned over her, his hands glowing warmly. She felt sick. Weak. Her body buzzed, pins and needles everywhere, quickly rising from uncomfortable to a level that made her wince.

"Welcome back, Miss Cain," said the doctor as he worked. "My name is Locke. I haven't seen you in here before – apparently, you prefer Reverie Synecdoche's clinic, is that true? I can't say I blame you. She's a lot nicer than I ever manage to be. But, rest assured, I can heal you just as well as she can."

A nurse came over, injected something into the IV bag.

"Don't look so alarmed," said Locke. "Your injuries are traumatic and a lot of work needs to be done. It would be best for you if you weren't conscious through any of it."

Valkyrie's mouth was so dry, her words emerged as a croak. "Will I die?"

He paused. Looked at her. "Hopefully not," he said, and then it all went dark and so, so quiet.

# 47

She woke again and someone was in her room.

"This is terrible," said Savoir Fair. "Shocking is what it is. It makes you think, doesn't it? One day you're walking around, strong and proud and intimidating, and the next you're lying in bed, completely vulnerable." He came closer. Looked down at her. "Why, if I were so intentioned, I could kill you right now and you'd have no way of stopping me. Absolutely no way. None. At all."

He shook his head, and moved back.

"Fortunately, I'm not a killer. I'm a concerned public servant is what I am. I heard about what happened and I rushed straight over. Plenty of doctors and nurses and security personnel tried to stop me but, well, what good would it be to work in the High Sanctuary and not be able to throw your weight around once in a while, eh?"

He chuckled, then suddenly looked concerned. "But seriously, how are you? No, no, don't talk. You're far too weak. Let me do the talking, yes? It's what I'm good at, after all."

He cleared his throat.

"I assume that Skulduggery has told you next to nothing about me – would I be right? I think I would be. In which case, I need to tell you a little story. Are you comfortable? Then I'll begin. Sorry – a little storytelling humour there. A few years ago, as the

High Sanctuary was being established, I came onboard in a supervisory capacity. It was never my intention to stay working here beyond eighteen months or so, but I was good at my job and I liked being a part of something important, you know? Something that mattered. Sadly, there was a mix-up along the way and Skulduggery arrested me along with a bunch of other bewildered people. It was a mistake, obviously, and I was released, but, as a consequence of those mix-ups, a man was killed. A Sanctuary detective, actually, name of Somnolent."

Savoir hesitated. "This is, unfortunately, where it gets awkward. I have a recorded confession of Skulduggery Pleasant admitting to Somnolent's murder."

Valkyrie watched him.

"I intended to go straight to the City Guard with this confession, but Skulduggery was Commander at the time and, to be honest with you, I thought that this would get buried – maybe even buried alongside me." He chuckled again, this time without humour. "Skulduggery left soon after and Hoc became Commander and I could have gone to him, I suppose, but there was a lot happening for me around then, both professionally and personally, and I had a change of heart."

He fidgeted with his tie for a moment. "I have a confession of my own, Detective Cain. I was running with a somewhat disreputable crowd – something I'm not proud of – and I was looking for a way out. This was exactly what I needed.

"Two years ago, I asked Skulduggery to investigate some of my supposed friends. I fed him information and, once he'd gathered the evidence he needed, he arrested them. One by one, over the last few years, they've been going to prison. I think you've helped with some of them, though I doubt you were aware of how your partner came by the incriminating evidence.

"Now, I know what you're thinking. You're thinking I blackmailed Skulduggery into doing this. And you know what? You're right. I did. But I couldn't go to Hoc, I couldn't tip off the City

Guard, because I needed whoever was investigating to basically delete my name from all the files as they went along. I've made some big mistakes in my life, Detective, and I'm just trying to turn over a new leaf. I needed someone to take my old associates down – someone who wasn't going to involve me. Does that make me a bad guy? Anyway, most of that crowd, that disreputable crowd, are in prison. There's only one prominent member left – and that's Christopher Reign. Unfortunately, I can't allow Christopher to be arrested. He would immediately know who'd betrayed him, and my life and the life of my family would be in danger."

Savoir leaned over the bed again. "I need him killed," he whispered, "and I need you to do it. I asked Skulduggery, but he declined, and now I'm in that awkward position that no blackmailer wants to be in – when the person you're blackmailing refuses and you have to carry out your threat. Valkyrie – can I call you Valkyrie? Valkyrie, I don't want to release Skulduggery's confession. He's helped me out so much in the last few years and we're right at the end now, we're at the final stage, and I don't want it to have been for nothing."

He shook his head. He looked miserable. "And, of course, if I release the confession, my involvement will come to light, and I'll probably go to prison, too. But this is the only course of action I have. I'm desperate, Valkyrie, and, as I'm sure you know, desperate men are dangerous. Do you need something? A sip of water, perhaps?"

She didn't even try to respond.

"I can tell by your expression that you're reluctant to help me with this," he continued, "but here's the twist. You see, this isn't just about me and my sordid past, and it isn't just about the murder Skulduggery confessed to and the blackmail and the arrests... It's also about the assassination. Christopher Reign hired the man who killed the acting Supreme Mage. He's responsible for it – and he's responsible for putting you in the assassin's sights.

A true professional, from what I understand, and, now that he's been set on this course, the only way to save Skulduggery – to save yourself – is to kill Christopher Reign."

He looked away. "That wasn't easy for me to say. I... I have to go. Please consider my words."

She couldn't move her head so didn't see him leave, but she heard the door close and knew she was alone.

# 48

"Did you hear?" Never asked as they filed into the dormitories.

"Hear what?" Omen asked.

"Skulduggery and Valkyrie were shot this afternoon."

Omen frowned. "What?"

"Ambushed, from what I've heard. At least three gunmen."

"Are they OK?"

"I don't know," said Never. "Don't know anything apart from they were shot. I think, though, that if it had been serious we'd know. I mean, it'd be everywhere, right? People would be talking about it."

"We are talking about it."

"Oh, yeah. Besides, what harm can bullets actually do them, you know? Skulduggery's already dead, and Valkyrie wears that necromancer suit. Bullets bounce off her."

"Yeah," Omen said doubtfully. "OK. Yes, they're probably fine."

"Maybe you should text them, though. Just to check."

Omen nodded, taking out his phone as Never wandered off towards his room. Omen tapped out a quick message and sent it as Axelia bumped his shoulder with hers.

"Hey," she said, "you hear?"

"About Valkyrie and Skulduggery? Never told me. Have you heard if they're hurt?"

She shook her head. "All I heard is that they're being taken care of by High Sanctuary doctors."

"So they're hurt?"

"I mean... I guess."

They walked on a bit.

"You OK?" she asked. "Omen?"

"I'm fine. And they'll be fine. They're always fine."

Axelia smiled. "You're the one who knows them, so I'll trust your judgement. Night."

She started to walk off.

"Axelia, hold on. Um... I spoke to Ula yesterday."

"Oh, yes?"

"She was chatting to Bella, and Bella was wondering if you'd looked into that thing she'd told you about."

"Ah, Omen, seriously, it's nice that you're trying to patch things up between Bella and me, but sometimes friends just grow apart, and there's nothing much you can do about it."

"But did you look into it?"

"I haven't looked into anything, to be honest."

"What did she want you to—?"

"Omen, come on. What's the point?"

He looked at her, and didn't say anything for a bit.

She raised her eyebrows. "Hello?"

"Axelia," he said slowly, "I think you've been mind-mugged."

"I'm sorry, what?"

"I don't know what else to call it. I think someone has attacked you psychically, and stolen some of your memories."

She laughed. Then stopped. "Are you being serious?"

"What did Bella ask you to look into?"

"Omen, please, just—"

"What did she ask?"

"It doesn't matter."

"You can't remember, can you?"

"I can remember, I'm just not sure what you're talking about."

"You can't focus."

"So?"

The corridor was emptying so their voices carried further. He took her arm, led her closer to the wall.

"You can't focus," he said softly, "can't study, can't work. You keep forgetting things. Your mind keeps drifting. I keep asking you what Bella wanted you to do, but you can't answer. I think someone wiped that out of your memory, and everything else is just damage, like aftershocks following an earthquake."

"Omen, why would anyone do that to me? I've had one adventure in my life, and that was with you and Never. It was fun. It was scary, and fun, and quite painful. But I'm not on an adventure now."

"Bedtime," said Miss Ether as she passed.

Omen waited till she'd moved out of earshot. "Bella saw something. The night before she was expelled, she saw something unusual on her way to the kitchen. She told you about it – and then she was kicked out of school."

"OK," said Axelia.

"Do you remember that?"

"No," she said, "but it was a while ago. I don't remember every single thing I talked about a while ago."

"I think you'd remember this, though. Wouldn't you? If I told you I'd seen something weird, and then I was expelled, wouldn't you at least remember what I'd said?"

"I suppose I would," Axelia said, frowning.

"Bella's been your friend for years. Don't you think you should be more upset that she's gone?"

"We've been growing apart."

"Have you, though? Think about this. Really think about it. Have you been growing apart, or is this just a line that keeps popping into your head?"

Axelia faltered.

"You should miss her more, shouldn't you?"

"Yes."

"And the fact that you don't—"

"Is suspicious," said Axelia. "And you think I've been mind-mugged? Who would do that?"

"Bella saw something, and she was expelled. That's one way to silence her. But she told you, and maybe they couldn't expel you. You hadn't broken any rules, and they might have reckoned that they could get away with one unreasonable expulsion, but two might be pushing it. So they wipe your mind, instead. It's clumsy, but it does the job, because now you're silenced, too."

"Wait," said Axelia, "when you say *they*, you're talking about Duenna?"

Omen shrugged. "She's the one who expelled Bella."

"So Bella saw Duenna do something? What, though?"

"I don't know – Bella wouldn't tell Ula. It can't be too bad or else Bella would have told her folks and they'd have gone to the City Guard."

"But the City Guard are controlled by the Supreme Mage," said Axelia. "Maybe she didn't trust them."

Omen nodded. "You'll have to ask Bella. She might not tell Ula, but she'll tell you."

"It's weird," Axelia said, "I really don't want to talk to her. Like, I have this huge feeling of *couldn't be bothered*, which, fair enough, now that you mention it, is obviously a psychic suggestion – but wow. I really don't want to communicate with her at all."

Omen held his hand out. Axelia sighed, unlocked her phone and handed it to him. He found Bella's number, dialled it, and handed it back.

Axelia blanched. "You're making me talk to her?"

"Your reluctance isn't real."

"It is for actually talking on an actual phone. I hate talking on the phone. It's why nature gave us fingers, you know, so we can text." Nevertheless, she held the phone to her ear.

"Bella," she said, breaking out into a false smile. "Hey. Hi. It's me. Hi. Sorry for calling so late." She paused while Bella said something. "It's Axelia." She frowned. "No, Axelia. Axelia Lukt. From Corrival." She listened for another moment, then the call was disconnected. "She doesn't know who I am," she said quietly.

Omen felt the blood drain from his face.

"They got to her," Axelia said. "They got to her, Omen."

# 49

Militsa brought her a fresh set of clothes, and Valkyrie dressed slowly, with much moaning.

Her body ached. The internal trauma had been repaired and the bullet holes healed. Two would leave scars just below her left shoulder blade, but apart from that, all that was left were bruises.

When she finished dressing, she clipped the amulet to her belt for easy access. No more digging around in tight pockets while she was getting shot, no sirree. She was a girl who learned from her mistakes – usually just in time to make brand-new ones.

She thanked Doctor Locke and the nurses, and held Militsa's hand as she walked out. Skulduggery was waiting for them in the lobby. He had the black three-piece on today, with a crisp white shirt and a tie that matched the red hatband.

"Looking dapper," she said to him. "Are you shorter? You look shorter."

"I can assure you that I am exactly the same height I was yesterday," he responded. "The replacement bones I keep in storage have been precisely measured. My suits are far too well tailored to risk a misalignment."

"And how's the head?"

"It's sitting on a shelf in my home and looking ever-so-slightly the worse for wear. I'm wearing my actual head today, as you have probably noticed."

"I definitely noticed that."

"Do you have any idea who attacked you?" Militsa asked, not taking any of this with the good humour in which it was intended.

Valkyrie rolled her shoulder to get rid of approaching stiffness. "Savoir Fair claims it was Christopher Reign who sent the gunman after us, but we don't know who the gunman is. Not yet, anyway."

"We know he's a Ripper," Skulduggery said, "probably based in America."

Valkyrie looked at him. "We know that? How do we know that?"

"The helmet he wore is standard gear for Rippers, but when he lifted the sledgehammer to turn my head to dust I saw the label on the lining of his coat. Three Ghosts Tailoring – an American company specialising in armoured clothing. Not as good as Ghastly's, obviously, but adequate, and not entirely unstylish. I knew they'd never tell me *who* they'd made coats for – discretion is a must, after all – but this morning, while you were recovering, I phoned them and intimated I might be in a tailoring emergency so they managed to fit me in. Fletcher teleported me over there and, while they busied themselves, I sneaked a look at their books. The books were in code, obviously, but the one they use is what is commonly referred to as the Shugborough Code, so not a terribly difficult one. The coat's owner was identified only as Client Forty-three, but there was a note inside the margin which listed an address in—"

Valkyrie held up a hand. "It's OK. I believe you."

"I could go on."

"I know you could."

"It gets quite impressive."

"It usually does."

"He came very close to killing you," Militsa said. "I mean, I am right, aren't I? I know you're both joking around, but he almost shot Valkyrie to death and, from what I know of you, Skulduggery, he came prepared to smash your bones. What happens when enough of you gets smashed to dust? Remind me?"

"I die," Skulduggery said, not a little reluctantly.

"Exactly," Militsa said. "You die. This guy would have killed you both on that street were it not for the fact that the citizens of Roarhaven all have magical powers and they came to save you. I really don't know why you're making jokes about this, I really don't, but right now I've got to get to work, so I'll try to figure it out over lunch."

They watched her walk off.

Valkyrie glanced at Skulduggery. "We made her mad."

"We did."

"We possibly joke too much when people try to kill us."

"Possibly."

They didn't say anything for a bit.

"It's just," she continued, "we tend to be really funny."

"You see, this is it," Skulduggery said as they started walking. "If we weren't as funny as we are, I'm sure we'd take things a lot more seriously."

"Quick wit is a curse."

"It's not a blessing," he agreed.

"I have to say, though, I'm a little chuffed that all those people came to save us."

"Me too."

"I thought they'd just let us die."

"You especially."

"Because of the Darquesse thing."

"That's primarily the reason, yes – although now that I think about it, they were probably coming to save me, and you just happened to be there."

"That makes sense." Valkyrie winced. "So, uh, how's the car?"

They took the elevator down to the car park and found the Bentley sitting on burst tyres. The bonnet was pockmarked with dozens of bullet holes. The windscreen was gone. The dashboard was unrecognisable. The steering wheel was broken. The seats were in tatters.

"Oh, God," said Valkyrie.

"Yes."

"Look at all that blood."

"Yes."

She stared at the passenger seat in horror.

"How am I even still alive?" she whispered.

Skulduggery shook his head. "I'll never get that out of the leather."

"What?"

"What?"

"That's my lifeblood there, Skulduggery. We're talking pints of my lifeblood that pumped out of my body."

"And a lot of it splashed on to the carpet in the footwell. That's the original carpet that came with the car in 1954, by the way. Ruined. Completely ruined."

She glared. "I'm sorry for your loss."

"Yes, well," he said, "it's a bit late now, but thank you."

"You're welcome. So is it fixable?"

"Not with magic," he said. "She's been worked on by many gifted mechanics and engineers over the years, but she's been through so much that she can't take any more. Magically speaking."

"So she'll have to be fixed the old-fashioned way?"

"If it's possible."

"What'll you drive in the meantime? I swear, if it's the Canary Car or the Purple Menace or something stupid like that, I'm not setting foot in the thing. I'm just not doing it."

He started walking, his footsteps echoing. "I've taken another car out of storage – just until the Bentley is back on her wheels or I decide on something else."

"Is it as nice as the Bentley?"

"That's firmly a matter of opinion."

"Is it as rare?"

"More so."

"Seriously?"

He gestured ahead of them.

It was black and gleaming and long, a cross between the sleekest Batmobile ever made and a speedboat. The bonnet ornament was of a woman leaning forward, with something like wings billowing out behind her. The grille was massive, the bumpers curved, and it had a fin on its sloping rear. A *fin*.

"What is it?" Valkyrie breathed.

"*She* is a Rolls Royce Jonckheere Aerodynamic Coupe," he told her. "She was originally a 1924 Rolls Royce Phantom 1. I first saw this one's sister in Nanpara, in India. It was a car that the Raja had, shall we say, acquired, but he was dissatisfied with certain elements, most notably the convertible aspect that had been commissioned. Between us we came up with this art-deco design. He bought one for me because, back then, that's what rajas did, and I accompanied both cars to Belgium to be remodelled. The Raja's car was improved upon, and my car was improved upon again. She's not technically a Phantom any longer, but she retains the name."

"The doors are round," Valkyrie said.

"Oval, actually."

"It has a fin. Why does it have a fin? Does it go underwater?"

"It's a stabilising fin. For driving at speed."

The door was hinged at the back instead of the front. She opened it. The interior was red leather.

"Oh my God," she whispered.

The steering wheel was transparent.

"Oh my God."

The gearstick was a lacquered human bone.

"Oh my God." She looked at him. "One of yours?"

The overhead light hit the brim of Skulduggery's hat, casting his skull into darkness. "No," he said. Then he brightened. "Would you like a lift back to Militsa's?"

"Can I drive?"

"Most assuredly not," he replied, and got in.

# 50

Unsurprisingly, the Phantom drew just as many stares as the Bentley had. It was an astonishingly smooth ride, however, and the seats were comfortable, and when the windows were shut it was incredibly quiet.

"You have something to say, don't you?" Skulduggery asked, switching on the headlights as he drove.

"Yes," Valkyrie answered.

"Savoir Fair didn't just stop by your hospital bed to tell you that Reign sent the Ripper after us. He told you about Somnolent."

"Is it true?"

"That I killed him? It is."

"Savoir called it murder. He said you confessed."

They stopped at the traffic lights and Valkyrie found herself tensing.

"Did I forget to mention?" Skulduggery said. "Bullet-resistant glass. Armoured body. This is the car to drive when you're in danger of being ambushed."

"You couldn't have made the Bentley bulletproof?"

"And ruin the aesthetic? Some things are not worth sacrificing." The lights turned green and they started moving again. "When China was setting up Roarhaven as the city it is now," Skulduggery said, "she asked me to help. You had just gone to

Colorado and, frankly, I was at a loss. I needed purpose. A project, if you will, in the same way that you were a project."

His head tilted. "Although you were never a project. You were always exactly who and what you were." His head tilted back. "China's true power, as you well know, is not magical. Her true power lies in manipulating people, in getting them to do what she wants. In order to establish Roarhaven as the city it needed to be, she required someone with a badge and a gun to arrest anyone who opposed her plans."

"That was you."

"I agreed to set up the City Guard, I agreed to keep the peace, and I eventually agreed to act as China's enforcer. It's not something I'm especially proud of, but it was a job that needed doing. I reasoned that a short spell of dubious morality was worth it, providing the end result was a better society for everyone. That's how I excused it, anyway.

"The City Guard weren't detectives. They were police – they maintained law and order. As such, they left the detecting to the High Sanctuary. That's changed now, as the City Guard has assimilated most of the detectives, but back then I had no authority over someone like Somnolent. He was a big man, a quiet man, and a great detective. I liked him enormously."

"Why did you kill him?"

"He was investigating China's activities. He knew she was strong-arming a lot of people to get her own way. He suspected that not everything she was doing was entirely legal. He was getting close to building the type of case that not even China, as Supreme Mage, could sweep away. So I went to see him. To talk. To persuade him to drop it.

"Somnolent jumped to the wrong conclusion. He thought I'd come to kill him, and so he attacked."

"And you killed him."

"Yes. I embellished the scene in my confession, just to make Savoir believe he had more of a hold over me, but it was a justifiable case of self-defence, so long as you ignore the circumstances leading up to the confrontation."

"So you've been letting Savoir blackmail you?"

"He wouldn't share the information he has any other way, and I've been using it to put some genuinely bad people in prison. We've reached the end of the list of his – now only Reign is left, but Savoir won't give me the evidence I need to act."

The Phantom pulled up outside Militsa's house.

"And when Reign is put away?" Valkyrie asked.

"Then I arrest Savoir."

"How do you feel about what happened with Somnolent?"

Skulduggery turned his head to her. "I was forced to kill a good man, Valkyrie, in order to save my own life. It's not something I have an easy time living with."

"Could he have killed you?"

"If I'd let his attack continue, he would certainly have killed me, yes."

"Then I'm glad you defended yourself," she said. "What's the plan for tomorrow?"

"I think Christopher Reign is due another visit."

"Cannot wait," she said, and got out.

Militsa was reading a book on the sofa when Valkyrie walked in.

"I heard back from some friends of mine," Militsa said. "I asked them to look into the Necromancer that stole Creed's body. They say he walked out on the Order a year ago, maybe a little more. They asked around, but no one seems to know him that well. They certainly don't know where this Herald of the Dark, Harbinger of Doom stuff is coming from. He was a pretty low-key Necromancer, as far as anyone can tell."

"The mystery continues," said Valkyrie. "Thanks for trying."

"Sure," Militsa said, and went back to reading her book.

"You're still mad at me, then," Valkyrie said.

Militsa sighed. "I'm not mad at you."

"You seem mad at me."

"This is just how people get around you, sweetheart. You should be used to it by now." Militsa slipped a bookmark between the pages and closed the book. "I'm not mad, OK? I'm relieved. You're still alive."

"Yay me."

"But I'm also exhausted because dealing with you is like... I don't know what it's like. I understand that people try to kill you all the time. I understand that a part of you might be used to it. But at the same time... Val, someone tried to violently kill you and they came very close to succeeding. This has to be affecting you. It has to be messing with your head. You might not be in shock, but... you have to be traumatised by this. You just have to. If you're not traumatised, then you're not human."

"Right," said Valkyrie.

"And you can deal with this however you want to deal with it," Militsa said quickly. "Whatever you need to do to cope, you go ahead and you do that. I'm here to talk or to listen or to just, I don't know, hold on to you, because while it's great that you're joking around with Skulduggery... maybe joking around with Skulduggery is not the healthiest way to deal with it. You know? I don't want to pressure you to do anything you don't want to do or say anything or..." Her shoulders slumped. "I'm babbling, but basically if you want to cry and wail and scream, you can cry and wail and scream on me and I won't mind one little bit."

"You are the best girlfriend, you know that?"

"I had my suspicions."

"My hands shake," said Valkyrie.

"They do?"

She nodded. "Out of nowhere, like, they'll just... tremble." She held up her hands. "They're not doing it now, obviously, but I promise you, they shake. And my teeth chatter. Actually chatter. And I get panicky. You know that horrible feeling when your heart just starts pounding and you're feeling like you're being attacked, or you're about to be attacked? All the hairs stand up on the back of your neck? And that horrible... the cold feeling rises. Here?" She rubbed her belly. "It's like when I'm in a small space. When I'm trapped. The fear that pushes all of the other thoughts to one side."

"How long does it last?"

Valkyrie shrugged. "A few minutes."

"Has it happened around me?"

"Yeah."

"And you hid it?"

"I always just walk out of the room when I can feel it coming on. I don't want to worry you, I suppose, but it's also... I don't know. I've been through this. I've had all these anxieties for the past few years and I'm dealing with it now. I don't, or I didn't, want you to know that I might slip backwards."

"Do you feel like you might?"

"No. But it's always possible."

"Next time, don't walk out, OK? Let me help you."

"OK."

That night they were watching TV and Valkyrie stiffened, but she didn't leave the room. Militsa noticed, wrapped her arms round her, wouldn't let her pull away as she cried.

"It'll pass," she told her, holding on tight. "This feeling won't last forever. It always passes. Always."

Her words were lifebelts that swirled through the rising sea of panic, and Valkyrie grabbed on to them, moving from one to the next. They stopped her from flailing. Stopped her from drowning.

When it was over, she collapsed against Militsa and Militsa kissed the top of her head.

# 51

Just after eleven the next morning, Valkyrie and Skulduggery strode into Reign's nightclub.

Acantha stepped in front of them. She wore a white suit with a red shirt. "Can I help you?"

"We'd like a word with your employer," said Skulduggery.

"My employer isn't in today, unfortunately. I'll let him know that you stopped by, though."

"I'll just check that he hasn't popped in without you knowing," Skulduggery said, moving past her towards the office.

Valkyrie went to follow, but Acantha stood firm. "What are the names again?" she asked. "Skeleton Man and the Sidekick, isn't that it?"

"That's exactly it," Valkyrie said, giving her a smile instead of a slap. "When will he be back?"

"Mr Reign? Who knows? He's taking a personal day. I thought you two were dead. It's all over the news. Weren't you gunned down in the street, or something equally common?"

"Gunned down in our car," Valkyrie corrected, "and then the street."

"Oh, my mistake."

"Like that outfit."

"I'm sorry?"

"You're forgiven."

Acantha smiled coldly. "I'll tell Mr Reign you dropped by."

"Tell him we're very eager to talk to him."

"I'll say desperate, just to make sure he knows who it refers to."

Skulduggery came back, nodded to Valkyrie, and they walked towards the exit. She thought of a great insult and turned to deliver it, but Skulduggery held her arm and kept walking.

"I don't like her," Valkyrie said as they emerged into the sunlight.

"I couldn't tell."

"Can we arrest her for something?"

"Only if she's committed or is intending to commit a crime."

"Is being annoying a crime?"

"Sadly, it is not."

They got to the Phantom. Detective Rylent was peering through the window. He straightened when he saw them.

"I thought this was in the Petersen Museum," he said.

"That's her sister," said Skulduggery.

Rylent nodded approvingly. "She's a thing of beauty, she truly is. Shame about your other one. Is it salvageable?"

"I've got people working on it as we speak," Skulduggery replied.

"I've always liked that Bentley. Gets a lickin' but keeps on tickin', isn't that what they say?"

"Depends who they are."

"Much like you two," Rylent continued. "Attacked like that in broad daylight – that has to be galling."

"Also painful," said Valkyrie.

"But galling, too," Rylent insisted. "Apart from the injuries you sustained and the damage to the Bentley, the impact upon your reputations must be considerable. I mean, for so long around here, the two of you were thought of as something approaching invulnerable. No matter who you went up against, you just didn't stop – it's like you were propelled towards victory by sheer determination alone. But now, after you were caught flat-footed, ambushed at a traffic light and very nearly killed without even mounting any kind of defence... your legend has been tarnished, wouldn't you say?"

"Maybe so," Skulduggery said. "In which case, it's a good thing we don't live our lives according to what other people think of us."

"Now that," said Rylent, "is a healthy approach to failure. Would you agree with your partner, Detective Cain?"

"Totes," she said.

Rylent nodded. "I'm assuming you're here as part of your investigation over who tried to kill you. Any leads?"

"Not yet," Skulduggery said.

"I suppose it doesn't help matters when you write down all the names of the people who might want you dead and you realise there are so, so many of them. At this point, is there anyone who doesn't want the two of you dead?"

"We do seem to have trouble making friends."

"Yes, you do. Now, detective to detective, do you think the attempt on your lives has anything to do with the assassination of acting Supreme Mage Creed?"

"Why would it?"

Rylent scratched his chin. "Well, that's the thing about mysteries, isn't it? You don't know the whys until you've got the whos and the hows and the whens... But eventually it all comes spilling out into the light. The connections between events. Between people."

"Why are you here?" Valkyrie asked. "Do you think Reign had something to do with Creed's murder?"

"Maybe he does," said Rylent, "but I'm actually here to talk to you two about the assassination, if you've got a moment to spare. I've been reviewing the footage from that day. It's taken a while because there were so many cameras around. It's terrifying when you think about it: how easily we've given up our privacy. Big Brother's watching and we're all OK with it, apparently."

Skulduggery tilted his head. "Is there something in the footage you wanted to ask us about?"

"Yes," said Rylent, "yes, there is. Right before the Supreme Mage was shot, the two of you appeared to be having an argument."

"We were?"

"It appears that way. Can you remember what you were talking about?"

"Of course," Skulduggery said. "I can remember everything."

"And?"

"And I'm afraid it's none of your business."

Rylent paused. "I see."

"Do you suspect our involvement in the assassination?"

"No, no, of course not. Nothing like that. You're Arbiters, for God's sake. You're trusted."

"OK then."

Rylent continued. "It's just, I had a friend of mine go over the footage. He's deaf, which is by the by, and he's really good at reading lips. Most of it we missed because, as luck would have it, the camera is behind Valkyrie, and you yourself don't have any lips to read. But my friend caught some of what Valkyrie was saying, enough to figure out that she was trying to convince you of something."

"Indeed she was," Skulduggery said, "and in the end she was successful."

Rylent nodded. "And then the Supreme Mage was killed."

"You seem to be linking the two events."

"Not at all. I'm merely remarking that the one followed the other."

"In an effort to make a point?"

"Merely passing comment. Although, that being said, I did notice something that might be considered suspicious. Damocles Creed is shot. The Cleavers react almost instantly, with the City Guard close behind. The crowd enters a moment of – how do I put this? – stunned silence before it reacts. There's screaming, shouting, crying, orders being issued, commands being barked... and then there's you two."

"What about us two?" Valkyrie asked. "We couldn't have anything to do with it – we were on camera the whole time."

"Yes, you were. And, the moment Creed is killed, you both look up at the exact window the shot came from. You don't look around, you don't scan the buildings, you don't search... you both look at the same place."

Valkyrie went cold, but kept the annoyance in her voice. "If you're hoping we can identify who the shooter is, you can forget it. I just saw movement and that's it."

Rylent smiled. "That's not what stirs my curiosity, Detective Cain."

"You think we knew where to look," Skulduggery said.

"I do."

"And yet, as Valkyrie has just mentioned, she noticed move-ment, which is why her eyes were drawn to the window in question. As for me, I have no eyes, but I can assure you that when I turned, it did take me a moment to pinpoint where exactly Valkyrie was looking. Once I saw the shadow move across the curtain, I flew straight there in an attempt to apprehend the assassin."

"You truly are the hero Roarhaven needs," said Rylent. "Well, that answers all the questions I have so far. Thank you for being so truthful with me – it will not be forgotten."

"You're welcome," Valkyrie said, her words dragging across concrete.

"But as this is an ongoing investigation," Rylent continued, "I must ask you not to leave this reality without first alerting me or the High Sanctuary. Standard procedure, I assure you."

Rylent raised a hand, and a City Guard patrol car pulled in, the door already opening.

"Detective," Valkyrie said, "before you go?"

Rylent turned to her. "Yes, Detective?"

"Maybe you could check something out for us down at head-quarters. Only if you wouldn't mind."

"By all means."

"Thank you. When we were being shot, when we were almost killed, one of these patrol cars came speeding up, stopped right beside us. Then it drove off. It just left."

Rylent's eyes hardened. "That right?"

"That's right," she said. "Maybe you can ask around, see who was driving. See why they drove off."

"I'll be sure to look into it," Rylent said, and got in.

The patrol car pulled out on to the road, and, when it turned the corner, Valkyrie's necronaut suit flowed over her clothes. She pulled the skull mask down over her face, and, when Skulduggery tilted his head at her, she shrugged.

"He's got a lip-reader reviewing CCTV footage," she said.

"You are a sneaky one, Valkyrie Cain."

"Thank you." She leaned against the Phantom. "So it looks like he's on to us."

"Please don't lean on the car."

"It's bulletproof and armoured. What damage am I going to do by leaning against it?"

"Let's just get into the habit," Skulduggery suggested, "of not leaning on any car. It doesn't have to just be this one, but we could start with this one, and carry on from there."

She sighed, and stood away from the Phantom.

"See?" Skulduggery said. "Isn't this a fun new habit? And Rylent suspects – he doesn't know. There's a big difference. Unfortunately, he does hate me with a fiery passion, so that will work against us insofar as he will be unrelenting in his dogged pursuit of what he perceives as justice."

"Why can't people like you?" Valkyrie asked, shaking her head.

"People love me," Skulduggery responded. "Who doesn't like me, apart from Rylent?"

Valkyrie weighed up the pros and cons of the impending discussion. "Never mind," she said. "Everybody loves you."

"You had someone in mind, didn't you? Who is it? Is it Tanith?"

"Why wouldn't Tanith like you?"

"Valkyrie, I'm as mystified as you are."

"Can we please focus on the fact that Rylent thinks we had something to do with the assassination?"

"We did have something to do with—"

"Can we focus on the fact that he knows that?"

"As I said, he suspects, and, as long as we stay a step ahead of him, a suspicion is all it will ever be. We have other things to be occupying our time."

"Yeah, I suppose," she said. Then, "I have to go back to the future."

His head tilted. "Why would you have to do that?"

"We've got to know if the future's been averted. We didn't go through all of this just to *hope* it worked. I have to check to make sure."

"You need more training before you go."

"I got there no problem last time."

"You need to master the art of keeping your physical body here and only sending your astral form. Your astral form can't be hurt – or at least it can't be hurt quite so easily. I'll ask Jericho to take you through the basics again."

"We don't have time for that."

"You mean you don't have the patience."

"Patience is boring."

"Valkyrie, please promise me that you won't travel into the future without more training."

"I promise that I'll try to promise that, but I can't promise that my promises aren't lies."

"Dear God. Do you even know what you're saying any more?"

"Not all the time, no."

# 52

Five years ago...

He watched her move through the plywood corridors, gun held close in a two-handed grip, barrel pointed slightly down. He triggered a target as she reached a corner and she put two centre-mass and kept going. Another target popped out behind her and she spun, fired twice, dropped the empty magazine and slid in a fresh one as she pivoted and carried on.

She moved well. Economically. Covered the angles. Didn't hang around, but didn't rush forward, either. Most importantly, all her shots were on target. Her image moved from one screen to the other and that's how he followed her, on the monitors, as she made her way through the course like she'd taken this route a hundred times. But this was a new route, one that he'd only set up that morning. Tomorrow they'd be back on the range with the heavier weapons, but she still had some surprises in store today.

She came to a locked door, stepped back, and kicked it in. Three targets in here and flickering lights and she did what she was supposed to do without fuss, taking them down with the bullets provided. He watched her face on the screen. Grim but satisfied. Job done, test over. She nodded to the camera, but he didn't stop the flickering lights. He pressed another button and heavy-metal music blasted from hidden speakers and Valkyrie turned, frowning.

A Ripper crashed into her from behind. Quell watched her bounce off the wall, letting the Ripper grab her, throw her, kick her as she rolled. She came up to one knee and he kicked again, but Valkyrie had reversed her grip on the pistol and she hammered it into his knee. The Ripper tore the gun away from her and she charged into him, and Quell turned off the monitors.

He left the makeshift hut they'd built that housed the control room and walked to the plywood city. It had got cold again. The summer had been hot, but winter was here and making itself known. He'd noticed Valkyrie getting quieter the closer to Christmas it got. She was missing her family. Missing her baby sister.

The music tore at him as he neared. He didn't like much music, and heavy metal was far too angry, anyway, but it was effective. It did what he needed it to do.

He waited by the workbench outside the door, his hands stuffed into the pockets of his coat. He wondered if he'd allowed himself to get soft, and tried to remember if the cold had bothered him as much when he'd worn the grey.

The door burst open and the Ripper walked out. Valkyrie came next, blood all over her face, breathing heavily and holding her ribs. The Ripper nodded to Quell and Quell nodded back, and the Ripper walked on.

"That was sneaky," Valkyrie said. "That was like all those times you made me think the fight was over and then you'd attack me again."

"You keep saying how you want to be tested," Quell responded.

"So you had your friend jump out at me?"

"He's not my friend. Having him attack you when you don't expect it trains you to expect it when no one's attacking you. It's why I let you think the lesson is over when there's still more to learn."

She used her T-shirt to wipe some of the blood off her face. "He beat me," she said.

"OK."

"You didn't see?"

"The point of it wasn't so you'd win," said Quell, "the point of it was so you'd fight. And you fought. That's what matters."

She looked at him and didn't say anything, then wiped her face again. "He's not staying for dinner."

"He wouldn't even if he were asked, and he wouldn't be asked."

"You cooking or am I?"

"It's your turn."

"I've just been beaten up."

"Even the vanquished have to eat," he said, and held out his hand.

She took the gun from her belt and passed it over. He removed the magazine and started to strip it down at the bench while she shrugged into her jacket. Usually, he'd insist that she clean the gun herself, but he was hungry, and wanted her to start dinner as soon as possible. She didn't move on to the house, though. She just stood there, looking at him. He didn't need to raise his eyes to know that.

"I love you," she said.

He paused, and looked up.

"You don't need to say it back, or anything," she continued. "It's just something that I needed to say. No big deal."

She walked to the house to start dinner. Quell went back to cleaning the gun.

# 53

Valkyrie went for a run, following the trails through the woodland that bordered Grimwood House. Xena ran alongside her, occasionally disappearing into the trees and then bursting out again. They didn't pass a puddle that the dog didn't splash in.

They got to the stream and followed it to the north before veering off again, piling on the speed, going uphill now. When they approached the house, Xena peeled off, having run enough for one day. Usually, Valkyrie would continue on for another few laps, but today she followed her dog inside.

She showered, ate something, and let Tanith in when she rang the doorbell.

"Thanks for inviting me over," Tanith said. "Have I ever told you how much I love this house? The fact that Gordon Edgley himself wrote some of his best books here, that he came up with some of his greatest ideas while pacing these very floors... it's inspiring, it really is. And you know why else I love it? Because I get to sit with my friend and chat about our love lives and the state of the world and make jokes and reminisce about the good times and have absolutely no ulterior motive for—"

Valkyrie interrupted her with, "I'm going to time-travel again and I want you to keep lighting the Jericho Candle."

"And there it is," Tanith said, nodding. "The ulterior motive

I knew was lurking round the corner, just lying in wait for me to—"

"I told you on the phone that I had an ulterior motive."

"Lying in wait, Valkyrie."

Valkyrie rolled her eyes and headed into the living room. Xena was curled up beside the couch, evidence of the run already dried on to her fur. She barely raised her head when she saw Tanith.

"What a good guard dog you are," Valkyrie said to her.

Xena whined a little, then went back to sleep.

"Why do you need me to help?" Tanith asked. "Why not ask Skulduggery? Or Jericho himself?"

"Because neither of them would approve of the journey."

"And why do you think I would? Skulduggery is hugely, massively irresponsible. We all know that. Are you actually saying that I'm more irresponsible than he is?"

Valkyrie hesitated. "Probably?" she said at last.

"Yeah, you might be right," Tanith responded, shrugging. "What are you after?"

"I want to see if the future's changed," Valkyrie said. "I want to make sure that Alice is OK. I'm just going to check, I swear. The moment I see that everything's cool, I'm coming back. I doubt I'll be gone even an hour."

"But you still want me to light the candle on the hour, every hour?"

"For five minutes each time, yeah. Just in case."

Tanith regarded her for a moment without speaking. "Will it be dangerous?"

"Not at all."

"Val..."

"It shouldn't be," Valkyrie said. "I mean, it's time travel, so I suppose there is a risk, but I need to do this, and I need your help."

Tanith sighed. "No longer than an hour."

"I shall do my best," Valkyrie said, grinning.

"Wait, now you'll do your best? What happened to you doubting it'll even take an hour?"

"It's time travel, Tanith. Who knows what could go wrong?"

Clad in her necronaut suit, Valkyrie lay on the couch as Tanith lit the Jericho Candle. She folded her hands on her stomach and closed her eyes. Focused on flattening and narrowing her thoughts. She breathed in the candle's aroma and it filled her head.

"Tell me your intent," Tanith said softly.

"I want to travel into the future," Valkyrie told her, her voice dull.

"Why?"

"So I can see if it's been changed."

"Picture Alice in your head. Picture her as she'll be as a sixteen-year-old. Time doesn't mean anything. You've proven that. You've done it before. Find the link that connects you. Let your past and present fade away. You're looking for Alice. Alice is the only thing that matters."

She found her. Faint at first, like the feeling when you're being watched, then stronger. More assured.

"Imagine the rope between you," Tanith said from very far away. "The rope's going taut. It's pulling you forward. Let it, Valkyrie. Let it take you."

Valkyrie rose up out of herself, could see all four corners of the room at the same time. Could see Tanith beneath her and yet above her and beside her, could see Xena kicking softly in her sleep, and could see her own body as it lifted from the couch, white energy crackling around it.

The dog looked up as the lightning storm intensified, and then Valkyrie broke apart as her body broke apart, and she became billions upon billions upon billions of streaking, shrieking atoms that tore through time and she felt the universe, she felt it all around her, she felt it and she felt something, someone, reaching out to her, and then all those billions upon billions upon billions of atoms slammed into the same space and she became herself once again, her legs pumping, the ground under her feet, and when she had eyes again she opened them and ran straight into a wall.

Valkyrie bounced off. Fell back. Lay there.

"It's her," someone said.

She blinked. Sat up. She was on the pavement outside a clothes shop, and everyone was looking at her. She tried smiling as she got to her feet.

"Sorry," she said. "Had a bit of a..."

They backed off. They knew her. This was bad.

She was about to fly off when an energy stream struck her shoulder, spinning her round. "Hey!" she shouted. "What the hell?"

A wall of air sent her staggering, a fireball exploded across her back, and now they were all at it, the crowd closing in, and Valkyrie snarled, energy crackling round her hands. The citizens of Roarhaven hesitated. There was some jostling, and a man was shoved towards her. She went to blast him and he flinched.

"Please!" he cried.

The fear in his eyes, the plainness of his clothes... he was mortal. A servant or lowly assistant. But there was someone behind him, a woman, and she grabbed this mortal's wrist and swung him with inhuman strength and he crashed into Valkyrie like a baseball bat made of flesh and bone.

Valkyrie went down, rolling, gasping, and she saw multiple pairs of gleaming black boots running in. Her wrists were twisted behind her back and forced into shackles, and when her magic was dampened they hauled her up. The wind rushed in and she kept rising, the cops carrying her over the heads of the crowd. Her legs dangled, her arms feeling like they were going to pop out of their sockets.

Over the city she was taken. It hadn't changed since her first trip here. It was still vast, still gleaming. Nothing had changed. Killing Creed had done nothing.

The High Sanctuary rose in front of them and they rose to meet it. The cops touched down on a balcony and the doors swung open and they pulled her through into a room of masks, rotating slowly on waist-high podiums.

"On your knees," said the cop, stamping on the back of her legs. Valkyrie winced as she went down.

A man in a luxurious robe swept in. His long hair was dark, with ribbons of silver running through it, and he wore several rings on his fingers. "This is her?" he said, with haughty contempt. "This is the one that evaded capture eleven days ago?"

"She fits the description, Grand Mage," said the cop.

The Grand Mage grunted as he examined her. "She certainly looks like trouble," he said. "Where did you find her?"

"Arcadia Street, sir. She teleported in, as far as we can tell, but it wasn't like any teleportation I've ever seen."

"I want her questioned, I want her talking, and then I want her executed." The Grand Mage reached down, moved Valkyrie's hair away from her face. "We cannot have mages attacking mages in broad daylight. It could stir feelings, and we don't want..." He faltered.

The Grand Mage paled. Backed away.

"Grand Mage?" the cop said. "Are you OK?"

"He's just a little shocked," a woman said as she entered the room. "Shocked at the identity of your prisoner, and the fact that none of our esteemed police officers have actually recognised her yet."

She was pretty, and tall, maybe a little taller than Valkyrie. Dressed in jeans and trainers. Her T-shirt was faded and her arms were thick, well muscled. Her blonde hair was short – kind of punky. She looked to be Valkyrie's age.

The cops and the Grand Mage lowered themselves to their knees, their heads bowed.

"All hail the Faceless Ones," the Grand Mage said, "and all hail the Child of the Faceless Ones."

"All hail them," Alice responded, her smile directed at Valkyrie, "and all hail me."

# 54

At a gesture from Alice, the Grand Mage scrambled up and scurried out, bowing all the way, and the cops hurried after him. Alice came over. She didn't say anything for a bit, just stood there, smiling.

"It is you, right?" she said at last. "You're not Darquesse, or any of your weird assortment of other selves? And you're not from an alternate universe or anything?"

"It's me," Valkyrie said, standing.

"The same Valkyrie I know?"

A nod.

"And yet – not the harpy. It's you. Actually you." She reached out – poked Valkyrie's arm. "By their divine glory... this is brilliant! But how? How'd you manage it? How did... Right, I'm gonna ask a question, and, if it's stupid, it's OK to laugh at me, because I'd laugh at me, too. Valkyrie – did you travel through time to get here?"

"I did."

Alice whooped with joy. "I knew it! I knew it! The moment I saw the footage of the harpy leaving that apartment, and then you following her out? And then, quite magnificently, falling? Not only did I know it was you, the real deal, but I knew you'd managed to come here from the past. I just did. I knew it." She paused. "I saw you, didn't I? Years ago, right before I went off to fight the Child of the Ancients? That wasn't just my imagination? That really was you in that vision?"

A nod.

"And now you're here. In the flesh. You have to tell me how. I've got to try this! Not now, of course. You don't have to tell me right this second. I'm just... I'm excited, as you can tell."

"Explain the harpy."

"Ah," said Alice. "Yeah, OK, you probably need a few details filled in, what with you being a time-traveller and everything. That's cool. I think you already know that the Edgley family legend didn't get it quite right. Do you? We did have major magic in our bloodline, and it was assumed that we were descended from the Last of the Ancients, but actually..."

"We're descended from the Faceless Ones," Valkyrie said.

"Oh, good," said Alice, "you *do* know. I was so worried. Spoiler alert, you know? Did we have those back in the old days? Were spoiler alerts a thing? I forget. Anyway, Damocles Creed had been searching for the Child of the Faceless Ones for centuries. He had no idea that he'd been searching for our family all that time.

"He'd developed a process, what he called Activation, that was designed to trigger dormant genes. If he Activated someone like me, my power level would skyrocket and he'd have found what he was looking for. If he Activated someone who might have had *some* weak traces of Faceless Ones' heritage, but those traces weren't as strong as you'd find in someone from our family, they'd turn into Kith – faceless people who just stand around doing nothing. Not even thinking. There were other side effects for other people, but that never really became much of an issue because in your time, on Draíocht, at twelve minutes to midnight, Creed performed a Mass Activation."

"Creed did that?"

"Yep."

"He was alive on Draíocht?"

"Well... yes," Alice said, puzzled. "I mean, he still is."

Valkyrie frowned. "He's alive? How? He was assassinated."

"Was he?"

"I was there."

"I think I remember something about that," said Alice, "but what I can say for certain is that he was definitely alive for the Mass Activation."

"How mass?"

"The Activation Wave he unleashed would have spread outwards in all directions," said Alice. "The moment it Activated someone with the genes it was looking for, it'd retract. If it didn't find them, it would continue until it covered the planet."

She stepped closer. "Those without enough of the Faceless Ones' genome would have been transformed into Kith. That's roughly a million people. But those without any trace of the Faceless Ones' genome at all would have – and there's no polite way of saying this – melted down to puddles of biological soup. That's, what, seven and a half billion people? Eight billion? That's ridiculous, right? Imagine risking that."

She stepped back again. "Anyway, the Wave didn't get that far. It turned a few dozen people in Roarhaven into Kith and killed a few thousand – which was incredibly sad – and then it met you and it retracted, like it was designed to do.

"But, of course, when it met you, you resisted, because that's what Valkyrie Cain does, right? She resists. You fought the transformation, and that's where it all went wrong. See, there aren't only three major outcomes when you're dealing with Activation. It isn't just skyrocketing power *or* a catatonic state *or* complete body-melt. There's a fourth major outcome if someone of our bloodline resists like you did. You were warped. I don't know why this resulted in you turning into a bloody harpy, though. Magic, eh? It does weird things sometimes that we just don't understand. Of course, if we understood every little thing about it, it wouldn't be magic, it'd be science."

She paused again. "Well, no, it'd still be magic, but it'd be magic that we understood. The point is, you fought the Activation and so the Wave changed you physically, and it also changed who you are. Your mind snapped.

"Creed couldn't use you, obviously. He needed the Child of the Faceless Ones to fight the Child of the Ancients to decide the future of the world – but you were way too unstable. But, since he now knew that it was in our bloodline, he found me, and Activated me. I didn't resist, and I suddenly had all this magic."

"And you did battle with the Child of the Ancients," Valkyrie said.

"Yes, I did."

"And you won."

"Winning is what I do. I learned it from you."

"Who was it?" Valkyrie asked. "Who did you fight?"

Alice smiled. "I'm afraid I can't tell you that. If you go back to the past, that knowledge could change what happens."

"*If* I go back?"

"Think about it, Val. All you have to do is stay here – with me. I mean, you obviously belong in your own time. *Obviously.* But how about you stay here until Draíocht passes, or you travel back after it's over, or however time-travel works. Basically, you miss the Mass Activation. You're not there when the Activation Wave rolls out. It doesn't find you, it doesn't warp you, you don't grow wings and you don't try to kill me every chance you get. The harpy *is* quite vicious. I mean, you know that, but she absolutely hates me. Seriously. She can't stand me. Attacks me every chance she gets. I've tried to speak to her, but she's not one of life's great conversationalists. She communicates mostly in shrieks and grunts. That said, she's not stupid. We haven't been able to catch her in all this time, so she's doing something right. Anyway, sorry – so what do you think of my plan?"

"But if the Wave doesn't find me," Valkyrie said, "then it'll continue spreading. More people will be turned into Kith and a lot more people will die."

"Yes," said Alice, "but then it'll find me, and, when it finds me, it'll stop. Then I'll be who I'm meant to be and then you'll be free to travel back to your own time. It's perfect!"

"It's not."

"Maybe I'm not explaining it right."

"You're explaining it fine – but, if the past doesn't happen how it's already happened for you, then everything will change. Your history will be different."

Alice's smile dipped a little. "Oh, yeah. Damn."

"I have to go back," said Valkyrie.

"Just... just hold on, OK? You just hold on here. I need to talk to a guy. I won't be long." She went to move away, then turned back and hugged her, impossibly tight. "I can't believe it's you."

When Alice broke off the hug, she had tears in her eyes, and she laughed. "I'm being silly."

"Not at all."

"It's just so good to see you – exactly how I remember you. It's a miracle. The Faceless Ones are smiling on us today. It must be so weird for you, though! Looking into your sister's face, but older."

"It's... odd, yes. You're, what, eighty-two?"

"Crazy, huh? I'm so old!" Alice laughed. "You stay right here, OK?"

"OK, but, Alice, I need to get home."

"I get it. I do. I just have to figure something out." She walked over to the door, but stopped before she left. "Oh, and I'm not Alice. Not any more."

Valkyrie blinked. "Of course. Sorry, yes, you'd have taken a name. Obviously. So what do I call you?"

"Malice," her sister said, smiling. "You can call me Malice."

# 55

The door to Rangle's dorm room was open. Omen went to knock, but Axelia walked right in.

"Hey, Rangle," she said. Rangle sat back on his bed, strumming his guitar. He had the kind of easy smile that people liked. He was an OK-looking guy, but when he smiled he was gorgeous.

"Axelia," he said, and nodded to Omen. "Darkly. What's up, man?"

"Nothing much," Omen said, trying to match his cool. "Well, actually, no, a lot's up. We need your help."

Rangle raised an eyebrow. "Do tell?"

Axelia sat on the bed opposite. "Someone's wiped my memory," she said. "I need you to poke around and figure out what they don't want me to remember."

A moment passed, and Rangle nodded. "No."

Omen frowned. "No?"

"No way. Not doing that."

"But you're the best Sensitive in—"

"And I don't want to be," Rangle said. "I've got no interest in reading people's minds for the rest of my life, or having visions, or talking to the dead, or whatever. I want to play music. When I get my Surge, that's what I'll be focused on. Making beautiful music. Rockin' out, man."

"But right now—"

"You know who's good at this Sensitive crap? Trophonius Sooth. Ask him."

Axelia made a face. "Trophonius Sooth is disgusting," she said. "He tries to read girls' minds without their permission. There's no way I'm letting that creep anywhere near my thoughts."

Rangle chewed on his lip. "Yeah," he conceded, "he is kinda gross."

"Rangle, please. I wouldn't let anyone into my head unless it was an emergency."

He thought about it, then sighed. "Fine. Sit over there and no one make a sound. This always gives me a headache so, Omen, could you get me one of those pain leaves?"

"Sure," Omen said. "Be right back."

When he returned, Axelia was sitting with her eyes closed. Rangle put his finger to his lips and Omen nodded, tiptoed over, and gave him the leaf. Rangle folded it up and popped it into his mouth and started chewing.

Omen stood back against the wall.

Nothing happened for ten minutes.

"OK," Rangle said, "I think I can see what's wrong. There's a whole load of... I don't know how to say it. Scattered memories, maybe. Things aren't in order."

"Stay away from the rude stuff," Axelia said.

"I'm trying."

"What do you mean, you're trying?"

"I think it would be easier if you didn't keep thinking rude thoughts."

"It's very hard to not think about something if you've been told not to think about something."

"Can you at least try?"

"I am trying."

"Because this stuff is everywhere."

"Oh my God..."

"Try to empty your mind," Omen said, remembering the

lessons with Miss Wicked. "Or just focus on something nice, like a meadow. Picture a meadow. There's a tree there. It's sunny and warm. Maybe you can hear something – a stream – in the background."

"That's good," Rangle murmured. "Keep doing that."

"The sky is blue. There's a single cloud, small and fluffy and white, but all it does is make the blue sky seem even bluer."

"I need some help here," Rangle said. "Start thinking about what we're after."

Omen nodded. "In this meadow, there's someone walking towards you. It's Bella. She's walking slowly. She's smiling. You're happy to see her. She gets closer and she says something. She tells you something. Can you hear what she's saying?"

"No," said Axelia.

"She's walking closer," Omen said. "Still smiling. She's pleased to see you, and you're pleased to see her, too. She keeps talking. What is she saying?"

"This is good," Rangle said. "I can hear her."

Axelia frowned. "I can't."

"Bella saw someone heading towards the West Tower," Rangle said. "Two people. Two men. One of them wearing shackles."

"Did she see who it was?" Omen asked.

"I don't think so," Rangle answered. "Now she's talking about being called into Duenna's office. She's pretty annoyed at getting caught."

"What about the people who did this to me?" Axelia asked.

Omen nodded. "Can you skip forward, Rangle? This would have happened over a week ago."

Rangle stuck the tip of his tongue between his teeth for a moment while he worked. "OK," he said, "I'm here. I'm Axelia."

"Weirdo," Axelia muttered.

"I've been called into Duenna's office," Rangle continued. "I don't know what I did. I'm curious, and confused, and nervous. The secretary's desk is empty. I'm... I'm wondering if I should wait or just knock on the door – but the door's opening. Someone – I think it's Duenna – tells me to come in. I'm walking towards her and... that's it. There's a blank space after that, and the next thing I can see is I'm in the Science Block, heading to class." He opened his eyes.

So did Axelia. "I can't remember any of that."

"You'd need a proper Sensitive to go in there to see if they can repair the damage," Rangle said. "I wouldn't even know where to start."

Axelia suddenly looked worried. "Do you think the damage can be repaired? I mean, I haven't been able to concentrate since it happened. I will get better, won't I?"

"I'd imagine so."

"You'd imagine?"

"Axelia, I'm not an expert."

"You'll be OK," Omen said, a hand on her shoulder. "If it doesn't get better by itself, I'm sure there are a thousand ways to fix it."

"Yeah," Axelia said. "Yeah, you're right." She straightened up. "So – Duenna did this to me."

"Maybe not her exactly," said Rangle. "I got the impression that there was someone else in the office when you walked in."

"But she's involved."

"I think we can assume that," Omen said.

Axelia looked at Omen. "So what do we do now?"

"Hey, hey," said Rangle, "discuss this away from me, if you please. I have no interest in whatever madcap adventure Omen Darkly gets into this week."

"I don't get into adventures," Omen said, blinking.

"Yeah, right," said Rangle, picking up his guitar. "Away, peasants. I need to strum."

# 56

Valkyrie stood when Malice came back.

"I talked to one of the guys in the R&D department, name of Guadalupe," Malice said, getting straight to it. "He's our top expert in time manipulation – or, well, he's our top expert ever since Destrier left."

"Destrier left?" Valkyrie said, raising an eyebrow.

"Just up and vanished one day," said Malice. "Didn't tell anyone he was going, didn't leave a forwarding address. Just... went. But Guadalupe isn't bad at all. If anyone knows anything about time-travel, it'd be him. So – you're worried that if you miss the Activation Wave it'll change your future, also known as my past. Guadalupe agrees."

"I thought he might."

"But it won't change it in any major, universe-altering way. He said, in theory, reality will do its best to correct itself and get back on track, so, while this time period won't be *exactly* as it is now, it will be *pretty much* as it is now – maybe even to an unnoticeable degree. So we're good."

"No, we're not good. Alice—"

"Malice."

"Sorry. Malice, even if this time period is only unnoticeably different, it's still different. So the person I'm talking to right now, the you I'm talking to, will be a different you if we change the past."

"Yes," said Malice, "but Guadalupe is working on that."

"Working on it how?"

"If he brings in some of the other departments in the High Sanctuary, he reckons he can come up with a sigil that will provide protection from any changes to the timeline. *I'll* have this sigil and *he'll* have it, and whoever else he'll have to tell. We're keeping this on the down-low, if you know what I mean."

"How does he expect it to work?"

"I'm not entirely sure – he started talking science fiction so I tuned out. But, from what I could gather, it'll let me remember two timelines at once – kinda like when you absorb your reflection's memories, you know? Anyway, from what he tells me, time passes in your timeline at the same rate it's passing here. How long since you arrived?"

"I've been here a day."

"Then a day has passed for your friends back home. We have another, what, eleven days until Draíocht? Valkyrie, all you have to do is stay here another eleven days and we'll have changed everything. Eleven days is nothing! I can take you on a tour round the world! You have no idea of the changes we've made. Wait till you see America. You'll love it, you really will. It's one big theme park."

"Alice—"

"Malice."

Valkyrie sagged. "Sorry. Yes. I don't know why this is so difficult for me. It even rhymes."

"That's one of the reasons I picked it," said Malice. "It's close enough to my given name so that our folks would be happy with it. Well, maybe not happy, but... OK with it. I swear, I was so close to picking Aforethought as a surname, you have no idea. Either that or Springs, or In-Wonderland, but I decided no, I couldn't do that. You should never take a name that will make people chuckle."

Valkyrie didn't say anything to that, and it took Malice a moment to figure out why.

"Ah," she said, "yes. Mum and Dad."

"I assume they're..."

"Gone. Yes."

Valkyrie had a curious feeling – like a part of her, deep inside, had broken off and fallen somewhere dark and deep.

"They died peacefully, if that makes it any better," Malice said. "I made sure of that. Everyone had the same order – you do not harm these two mortals. I took care of them – don't worry. Right until the end."

Their parents were still alive in Valkyrie's time, still alive in the present, but the fact that right now she was standing in a world in which her mother and father were dead was enough to make her choke up.

She cleared her throat, shook her head. Back to business.

"Malice, the Faceless Ones are the bad guys. You must know this."

"That's what I thought as well, until I let them into my heart. You know what that's like, don't you, to feel that kind of power? You had it with Darquesse. It elevates you. It's better than peace – it's better than love... It's wonderful."

"I've seen what the Faceless Ones do to people."

Malice shook her head. "You don't understand. Yes, they'll attack when they're threatened, but so do you. So does everyone. But look around – see the world they've made. Valkyrie, you're my sister and I love you, but you'll never make me regret bringing the Faceless Ones back. They're a part of me. They'll be a part of you, too – if you'd just let them in."

"But we're the good guys. We're supposed to help people. To save people."

"I do help people. The world is a much better place now than it was in your time. It's cleaner and healthier and the people are happier."

"What about mortals?"

"What about them?"

"They're slaves."

"Not all of them," Malice said defensively. "There are three types of mortals, and only some of them are slaves. But others have paying jobs and make a valuable contribution to society."

"And the rest?"

"Sorry?"

"You said there were three types of mortals. Peasants and serfs I know about. What's the third type?"

"There is no third type. I meant to say two types of mortals."

"What's the third type?"

"I told you, I meant—"

"What happens to the other mortals?"

She sighed. "Food," she said.

"What?"

"Some have jobs, some are slaves, and some are food. Their souls are nourishment for the Faceless Ones."

"Jesus."

"We don't exactly advertise it, you know? I'm well aware that it could be seen as cruel to some people, but it's what they were born for. They're not like us. Mortals are stunted people. Sorcerers have been able to touch the divine, but mortals don't have the capability. Tests have been done, carried out by the Nye Institute, and it's been proven that mortal souls aren't like ours. An argument could be made, in fact, that they don't really have souls. Not proper ones."

"You're talking nonsense."

"I'm speaking as plainly as human language allows."

"What happened to you?"

"I told you what—"

"No," Valkyrie said, "I mean what happened to you? When I spoke to you in my vision, you told me you were about to change. What did you mean?"

Malice shrugged. "I was Activated when I was ten, and after that I spent every moment learning and training and preparing.

The day I fought the Child of the Ancients, I was finally able to access the full power of the Faceless Ones. It saved my life."

"But it changed you."

"I had to give myself over to it, yes."

"What does that mean?"

"Do I really have to explain it to you, of all people? Magic changes everyone who uses it – most of the time in tiny little ways. But, for people like us, the change is a lot more drastic. Before Darquesse became her own person, she was a part of you that you'd access when you needed her. That's kind of like what happened to me."

"Who did you become?"

Malice shrugged. "I became me. A better version of who I was. Someone who could do what had to be done."

Valkyrie shook her head slowly. "Maybe you're right," she said.

"I am," said Malice. "I've been right a lot, so I'm used to the feeling, and I'm feeling the feeling right now."

"OK," Valkyrie said. "OK, I'll... I suppose I'll trust you. I'll go back and the future will—"

"I can't let you go home," said Malice. "Not until after I've been Activated. I know you. You won't exactly sit by and let it happen, now will you? You'll try to change history because you think it's the right thing to do. That's what you're planning on, isn't it?"

"I'm not going to interfere with—"

"Oh, wow," said Malice, "you are a terrible liar."

"Fine," Valkyrie said. "I have an opportunity here to stop all this from ever happening so that you can grow up to have a proper life."

"A proper life? Like yours?"

"No," said Valkyrie. "Not like mine."

"You'd make me stay mortal? That's what you're saying, isn't it? You'd deny me magic."

"You won't need magic," said Valkyrie. "You'll be happier without it."

"You cannot honestly believe that. Look at me! Don't I look happy to you? Or does this not count, because it's not the right kind of happy? Because it's not a happiness of which you approve? You're such a hypocrite. You know who should have given up magic once upon a time? You. Way back when you first realised that you were gonna grow up to be Darquesse, you should have walked away. Why didn't you?"

"You're right, I should have walked away. I agree."

"No, no," said Malice. "Answer the question. Why didn't you?"

"I thought I could change what—"

"That's not the reason."

"How do you know what the—"

"Why didn't you?"

"I'm trying to tell you."

"Why didn't you walk away?"

"Dammit—"

"Why didn't you walk away, Steph?"

"Because I was having too much *fun*," Valkyrie said, almost blurted. "But magic has killed me," she continued, back in control. "It's killed my friends. It's tortured me. Changed me. I had to kill you – I had to kill my own baby sister – because I was involved in this craziness. If I could go back and change it all by walking away, I would. But this is as close to an opportunity as I'm going to get. I just want a chance to save you."

"And I want a chance to save you," said Malice. "Because I lost you. Because you changed. Because that isn't fair. All I'm doing now is correcting something – now that I have the power to do it. But I don't want to take anything away from you. I want you to stay as strong as you are. I want you to join me, Valkyrie. This is paradise. This is Utopia. I don't get why you can't see that things are better now."

"Not better for mortals."

"Like I said: stunted people."

"And what about the sorcerers?"

"We're having a great time."

"And what about the sorcerers who opposed you?"

"Nobody opposes us."

"So everyone went along with this from the start?"

Malice sighed. "OK, we have our troublemakers – every society does – but there's no one fighting us. There's nothing to fight, Valkyrie. There is no war here. It's done. The Faceless Ones returned. The world changed. It settled. Even the heathens are careful now with what they say. The Blasphemy Laws make sure of that – if you speak against the Faceless Ones, you're put to death. That's the way it has to be. I mean, there were gods walking among us and those people were still denouncing them. How does that work? When you can see the gods with your own eyes, when you can reach out and touch and feel their warmth, their love – how can you continue to hate? I don't understand it. I never will."

"There must be someone still fighting. There has to be. You're walking around with an armed escort, for God's sake. If this is a Utopia where everyone's happy, why do you need guards?"

Malice chewed over that one. "Because of him."

"Who?"

"Who do you think?"

Valkyrie's eyes widened. "Skulduggery. Where is he?"

Malice shook her head. "You don't want to talk to him."

"But he's alive? I mean, he's still around?"

"The person you knew, the Skeleton Detective, is gone. The person he is now is... different."

"I need to see him."

"He's not the same."

"I don't care how much he's changed. When he sees me, he'll be himself again, OK? Trust me."

"Please, Valkyrie, forget about him. He's the past. You and me here, we are the future."

"Where is he, Alice?"

"Malice."

"Where is he?"

"This isn't a good idea."

"I have to see him. Where is he?"

"I don't know where he is," Malice said, irritation clouding her features. "Nobody does."

"But he's fighting back."

"If you mean he's regularly attacking the members of a peaceful society, then yes, he is. He's a bad loser, do you realise that? He lost, the Faceless Ones reclaimed their home, and he's never been able to get over it."

"But you can't stop him? Even with the Faceless Ones on your side, you can't even find him?"

"Try not to look so excited, OK? He's developed an annoying habit of anticipating everything we're about to do. It makes it very difficult to kill him."

"Sounds like Skulduggery, all right."

"Oh," said Malice, "he's not."

"Sorry?"

"Skulduggery," she said. "He's not Skulduggery Pleasant any more. He left that name behind a few years after you grew wings, after he retreated from everything except violence. Remember that old guy who kidnapped me when I was a kid?"

"Cadaverous Gant?"

Malice nodded. "They were friends, apparently. Well, kind of friends. I don't know the details."

"Skulduggery was corrupted by a man named Smoke and changed sides for a while," Valkyrie said. "They hung out. Skulduggery found Cadaverous amusing."

"Well, there you go. He named himself Cadaver after his best buddy Cadaverous, just to mess with me, I think. Just to remind me that once upon a time I'd been in trouble and he helped save me."

"And that's it? Just Cadaver? He doesn't have a second name?"

Malice didn't say anything for a bit. "No, there's a second name. It doesn't mean anything, though. It's not proof that the old Skulduggery is still in there, the fact that he named himself after his two best friends."

"Cadaver Bespoke?" Valkyrie asked.

"Cain," said Malice. "Cadaver Cain."

That's when the wall exploded.

# 57

Before Malice could react, she was hit with binding bullets. Black ink exploded across her belly. Another round hit her shoulder. A third hit her thigh. Upon impact, all that ink spread outwards, wrapping round her torso, her arm, her leg. Sigils glowed.

Skulduggery strode through the rubble in a tattered suit, his hat cocked at an especially jaunty angle, throwing down the rifle loaded with the binding bullets and pulling his revolver.

No. Not Skulduggery. Cadaver.

Malice snarled. "It's only a matter—"

He shot her in the head and Valkyrie yelled.

"It's OK," Cadaver said, putting away the revolver and taking Valkyrie by the arm. "That won't keep her down for long." He led her to the window. A gesture, and the glass exploded outwards.

Behind them, shouted commands. Running feet.

"Before we go," he said, and hugged her, "it is so, so good to see you again, Valkyrie."

Then he picked her up, and they flew.

# 58

The wind over the vast city parted for them, making for a smooth, quiet ride.

"She'll be OK?" Valkyrie asked. "You shot her in the head."

"Your sister will be unconscious for thirty-seven minutes and then she'll awaken with nothing more than a headache," Cadaver said. "She's the Child of the Faceless Ones, Valkyrie – bullets only slow her down. Oh, could you possibly do me an enormous favour? There's a cloaking sphere in my inside pocket. If you would be so kind..."

"Sure," Valkyrie said. It was awkward with the handcuffs, but she reached in, found the sphere and twisted both sides and a bubble of invisibility enveloped them. They suddenly altered course and flew on over Roarhaven. "Is that how you've evaded capture?" she asked.

"Sorry?"

"The sphere. Is that why they haven't been able to find you?"

"One of the reasons," he said. "You're looking healthy, Valkyrie."

"Thank you."

"A bit heavier than I remember."

"Careful."

"I only mean that you're more muscular."

"Still careful."

"Though I'm glad to see your vanity is unchanged."

"You know how I'm here?"

He nodded. "You're a time-traveller."

"You know *why* I'm here?"

He turned his head to her slightly, and she could have sworn his skull grinned. "Oh, yes," he said.

They touched down on the edge of a forest and Cadaver led her to a contraption that was little more than a pair of bucket seats and a steering wheel.

"What the hell is that?" she asked as he dragged a covering of light branches off the canopy.

"It's a car," he said.

"And where's the rest of it?"

"This is all that's needed. Hop in."

"No."

He took out a pocket watch, glanced at it. "Valkyrie, Tanith will be lighting the Jericho Candle in exactly eleven minutes, and Malice—"

"How do you know about—?"

"And Malice," he interrupted, "once she wakes, will be able to track those handcuffs you're wearing. My point is, we don't have time to be picky about our transportation."

"But where's the Bentley? Or the Phantom? Even the Canary Car would be better than this."

"The Bentley is gone. The Phantom is missing. The Canary Car was, sadly, destroyed in a fire that I believe was started deliberately – possibly by the car itself. Besides, nobody drives anything with an engine any more. These days, everything is powered by one's own magic."

Valkyrie scowled, and took her seat beside him. The moment he touched the steering wheel, the whole thing lifted off the ground and the canopy closed over, sealing them in a transparent bubble. They moved off silently, skimming over the grass.

"I hate it," she said.

"I hate it, too. It's better for the environment, though – not that the environment needs any help."

"Magic solved that problem, eh?"

"Within four months."

They crested a hill, picking up incredible speed.

"OK," said Valkyrie, "this part's actually fun."

"There's an upside to everything, it seems."

She looked at him. "Cadaver Cain, eh? What was wrong with Skulduggery Pleasant? I liked Skulduggery Pleasant."

"It just felt right," he said. "I was embarking on a new chapter in my life. A new adventure, as it were."

"I see," she said. "An exciting, fun new adventure, or a grim, joyless new adventure? Because Cadaver Cain sounds a little grim and joyless, if you ask me."

"It suits my purpose."

"You don't seem particularly surprised to see me."

"Don't I?"

"You do not."

"I knew you'd be back, Valkyrie," he said. "I have faith in you."

"At least one of us has. So what's it been like here? Alice gave me her version of events—"

"Malice," Cadaver corrected.

"—and now I'd like to know how it really is."

They veered on to a trail and, astonishingly, picked up yet more speed.

"After Malice was Activated," Cadaver said, "things went down-hill. For a start, Creed had figured out a way to widen the rifts to the Source. Suddenly every sorcerer on the planet was stronger – more powerful. As you can imagine, this led to some rather reckless behaviour, and suddenly the reality of magic was the lead story in every newspaper and on every website and news channel. There were riots, shootings, terrorist attacks... and that was just the initial mortal response.

"The Sanctuaries, under Creed's instruction, struck back –

taking out the mortal leadership, imposing order... and asserting control."

"So from my viewpoint," Valkyrie said, "all this happens in the next few months?"

"Seven weeks was all it took for us to take over the world," Cadaver said. "I say *us* but, of course, there were plenty of mages fighting by the side of the mortals, and that continued for years. It was a long, drawn-out war – but compared to the war against Mevolent it was over in a heartbeat. We put our faith in the Child of the Ancients. The power at his fingertips... it was extraordinary. Then Malice turned sixteen and she killed him."

He went quiet for a moment.

"That was the sign, I suppose – the act that proved to Malice that she was now strong enough to do what Creed had been pushing her to do."

"Bring back the Faceless Ones," Valkyrie said.

"Billions of mortals died. The rest – slaves. This world is, despite its reclaimed beauty and vitality, hell. But, now that you're here, we can change history and prevent it all from happening – but the first thing we must do is get those shackles off."

They slowed, pulling up behind the ruins of a small house. The canopy opened around them.

"Is this where you live?" Valkyrie asked, trying to sound upbeat as they stood.

"No."

"Oh, thank God. I didn't want to say anything in case you did live here, because, I mean... wow. What a dump."

"This is only my summer home."

She froze. Nodded. "Oh, that's cool. I like it. It's very open, you know? Lot of light."

He tilted his head. "You're still funny."

"You're not."

"Lies," he said, and pulled camouflage netting over the thing-that-wasn't-a-car, then led the way into what had once been inside, but now – without a roof – remained an outside. He indicated a circle drawn on the ground. Around the circle, sigils were carved into the old concrete. "Step inside, if you please."

Valkyrie checked the time as she stepped into the circle. One minute until Tanith lit the Jericho Candle back in her time. She pocketed the phone and Cadaver took out his lock picks as he knelt, and went to work on the cuffs.

"So what's the plan?" Valkyrie asked. "How do we change history?"

"We stop Creed," Cadaver said, his lock picks clinking softly. "Without his plans, without the structures that he put in place, without the secrets only he knew, none of this would have happened. None of what I've lived through would come to pass."

Ignoring, for a moment, the fact that Creed's dead," Valkyrie responded, "what will happen to the people here? What will happen to you?"

"The versions of the people here will never get the chance to exist. There'll be different versions. Happier versions, I hope. China Sorrows would definitely be happier. As for me, I'll blink out of existence and be replaced with a more well-adjusted version. Whatever happens, I'm prepared to sacrifice it all in order to bring back everyone and everything that has been lost. Otherwise, what's the point? What's the point of the struggle, the constant pressure to win, the refusal to stay down, to admit defeat...? What does it all mean, Valkyrie? What does any of it mean?"

"I really hope you're not expecting an answer."

"Before you came along," he said, "before we met at your uncle's funeral, I was asking these same questions. I'd been around for hundreds of years and then, all of a sudden, the war was over. Soldiers became Operatives. I became a detective. The mortals were safe from evil sorcerers and it was our job to keep it that way. But all that death, all that pain and destruction and loss and trauma... what was it for? Was something new and grand forged in that furnace? Did we advance in great leaps and bounds because of it? Did we grow? Evolve? No. After centuries of fighting, we looked around, figured out what the normal was now, and we went back to it."

The handcuffs clicked open and dropped, but Valkyrie frowned. "My magic isn't coming back," she said.

Cadaver stepped out of the circle. "Yes," he replied.

"Why isn't it coming back?"

"It will in a moment. When I allow it."

Frowning, she tried following him. An invisible wall stopped her. "I don't get it," she said.

"The years can change a person, Valkyrie. They changed you. They certainly changed me."

"Am I... Am I trapped?"

"You seem to be, yes."

"Why have you trapped me, Skulduggery?"

"I'm not Skulduggery," he reminded her.

"OK then – why have you trapped me, Cadaver? We're friends."

"We *were* friends," he said. "Then you turned into an evil harpy and now, every time we see each other, you try to kill me. That can sour a relationship, it really can."

"But I'm not her. You can't blame me for something I haven't done yet."

"I can and I will," Cadaver said. "But that's not why I've trapped you. By now, Tanith will have lit the Jericho Candle. In a moment, I'm going to expel you from this time period and you'll use the candle to guide you home. You won't have a choice in the matter, I'm afraid."

"Why?"

He gestured, and a gust of wind cleared the rubble and dust from the ground beside the circle. "Things have obviously not worked out well for me. For you, either, come to that. Someone needs to stop Creed's Activation Wave."

"That's what I'm going to do."

"No," he said. "Unfortunately, you're going to fail. I have to be the one."

"I'm sorry?"

He lay on the floor, placing his hat on his chest. "I'm going to be hitching a ride with you, Valkyrie. I've been experimenting with my life force over the last few years, but I've never actually possessed anyone before. I hope this isn't too uncomfortable for you, but if it is – apologies in advance. Are you ready?"

"Wait. Stop. What do you mean? What's going to happen?"

"Just close your eyes," he said. "Can you smell the candle?"

"I'm not going anywhere till I get a—"

He tapped a sigil on the ground beside him.

The circle powered down and Valkyrie's magic came back and then, before she could even move, it surged unexpectedly. It surrounded her, blinding her, the aroma from the Jericho Candle filling her senses, but there was something else in here, something new, a force, an entity. Cadaver.

Her lightning took her apart and she lost all sense of who she was and she became nothing but streaks of light and energy, rushing back to her own time.

# 59

The page rasped as it turned and Tanith's eyes flowed with the words. She'd read this story before, but it was one of her favourites, a delightful oddity she'd discovered in Gordon Edgley's second collection of short works. It was about a man who thought he was a butterfly who thought he was a man. In the end, fluttering against a window, a cat caught him and ate him, and it turned out he'd been a butterfly all along.

Her phone buzzed, and she read the message from Oberon and grinned, and had just sent off a reply when the lightning started to crackle overhead. Xena jumped up, watched the light-show intensify, and left the house through the doggy door.

There was a flash, and Valkyrie fell from the ceiling. Tanith caught her, grunting a little, then grinned as she set her down.

"Welcome home. You OK? Val?"

Valkyrie blinked at her. "Yes," she said. "I'm fine." She tried standing. She was wobbly at first, but quickly regained her balance, and straightened.

"You're not tired?"

"I'm... hungry," Valkyrie said, and walked out.

Tanith followed her into the kitchen, where Valkyrie picked up an apple and stared at it. Then, with her eyes closed, she brought it slowly to her mouth and bit into it. The apple crunched. The look on her face was pure bliss.

"You doing OK there?" Tanith asked. "You two wanna be alone or something?"

Valkyrie chewed, and swallowed, and smiled. She looked over. "Would you like to know a secret?"

"Secrets are my favourite things to know," Tanith said, and came forward when Valkyrie beckoned.

Valkyrie put her hand round the nape of Tanith's neck and pulled her in gently. There was a moment when Tanith was sure that Valkyrie was smelling her hair, and then she whispered, right into Tanith's ear, "I'm not Valkyrie."

A charge of energy went through her and Tanith stumbled back, gasping. Valkyrie examined her hand, watched the energy dance. "This will take some getting used to," she said.

Tanith's whole body buzzed and her thoughts came in a jumble.

"It's different," Valkyrie said. "Touching things. It's different. Before, I could only really feel pain. But this... this is spectacular." She touched her own face, her hair, felt her own biceps. "Well now," she said, and laughed. "Having muscles again is... nice." She stepped up to Tanith and closed her fist.

The punch caught Tanith right on the cheekbone and sent her to the floor, and Valkyrie howled with pain and clutched her fist and laughed.

"Oh, that is satisfying!" she cried. "That is alarmingly satisfying!"

Still shaking her hand, she moved in again. "One more time," she said. "I swear, just one more—"

Tanith sprang backwards, catching Valkyrie in the chest with her boot as she did so. Valkyrie went down and Tanith picked up a chair.

"Now then," she said, "I don't know who you are or what you want, but if you think I'm gonna let you walk around in my friend's body you're even dumber than the situation I currently find myself in."

She cracked the chair into Valkyrie's back as she tried to get up, then hunkered down beside her. "From the sounds of things, you haven't had a human body in quite some time, right? So you're getting used to all these new sensations? Let me save you some trouble. The only sensation you're gonna be feeling from now on is pain." She stood, whacked her with the chair again, then dropped it on her.

"What are you?" Tanith asked. "You a ghost? A Remnant? What do I need to do to get rid of you? Would a Soul Catcher do, or will I need a good old-fashioned exorcist?"

Valkyrie moaned, and turned over. "I'd forgotten," she said, "what it's like to be winded."

Tanith looked down at her. "Sucks, don't it?" she said, and kicked her in the face. Valkyrie rolled over, arms up, covering her head, laughing with the pain, and Tanith took a pair of handcuffs from her belt.

She went to snap them on, but Valkyrie turned, grabbed Tanith's wrist, swept her feet from under her. Tanith hit the ground, face first, and Valkyrie lunged on top of her, one arm wrapped round her head, her knees on either side of her hips. Tanith bucked madly, almost throwing her off but not quite, and now Valkyrie had her hooks in deeper. She had both hands on Tanith's arm and Tanith felt her elbow about to break and her shoulder about to pop and Valkyrie wrenched back and Tanith screamed.

# 60

Valkyrie was trapped in a little box in a corner of her mind.

She tried to move. Tried to make her body obey. It didn't listen to her. Cadaver Cain was controlling things, totally and utterly. She couldn't even blink. She couldn't even do that.

Her thoughts couldn't stretch beyond the box she was in. At the least – at the very least – she wanted to be able to sink into his memories like she'd done so many times before with other people, to open the doors in their heads and take a peek. But the walls of this box, the walls and the floor and the ceiling, they were impenetrable. And yet...

She felt his presence all around her, felt the shifting moods of delight at being in a flesh-and-blood body once again. The joy at taking a bite from that apple. The indescribable happiness that came from being in a fight, of feeling the many different kinds of pain.

He was used to one kind, she knew that much – a pain that came whenever the integrity of his aura, his life force, was disrupted. But that was a clumsy pain, dull and functional. It had none of the flavours of his fight with Tanith. The rattling pain of a kick to the head. The sharp pain of a knee to the ribs. The juddering pain of a head smacking into the floor. These were the flavours he missed.

She saw through eyes he controlled as they flew over Dublin

City. She heard the laughter as the cold wind tore at their hair. She felt them pile on the speed.

By the time they reached Cemetery Road, she could feel their body's hunger. They landed outside Skulduggery's house, beside the Phantom, and Skulduggery opened the door. Valkyrie felt something new at that moment – a wariness. It absolutely stood to reason that the only person Cadaver Cain would be wary of was Skulduggery Pleasant.

"You visited the future again, didn't you?" Skulduggery asked as they stepped inside.

Their eyebrow arched. "How can you tell?"

"The very fact that you came here to tell me in person. What was it like?"

"Unchanged."

"Killing Creed didn't work?"

"Killing Creed didn't even kill Creed. I'm thirsty."

"You know where the fridge is."

They led the way into the ridiculously sparse kitchen and took a water bottle from the fridge. They leaned against the counter as they drank.

"So Creed's alive in the future?" Skulduggery asked.

They nodded, licked their lips, put the water bottle away. "The Activation Wave still happens. Alice still becomes the Child of the Faceless Ones. And you..."

"What about me?"

"You become Cadaver Cain. I met him. We have a potential ally, and he has no interest in the future he's living in."

"I'm not surprised."

"He doesn't particularly like sorcerers any more. He never did, of course, but then he never liked any large groups of people. But sorcerers, as you can imagine, have fallen in his estimation."

Skulduggery nodded. "Understandable."

"I thought so, too. So, whatever he can do to disrupt that future from ever happening, he's willing to do it."

"Even though it'd wipe him from existence?"

"Stopping Creed's Activation Wave would erase that future, yes, but Cadaver has been working on a way to survive such an eventuality."

"Now this is interesting," Skulduggery said. "How's he going to manage that?"

"By not being in the future when it gets erased," they said. "He believes that he would be protected by a naturally occurring temporal bubble that would shield him from his own collapsing timeline, allowing him to continue to exist in another."

Skulduggery tilted his head. "I'm assuming he has good reason to believe all this?"

"He's spoken to enough experts on time-travel theory now to be an expert himself."

"I see."

"I'm glad."

A moment passed.

Valkyrie felt her body sigh. "My speech patterns gave me away, didn't they?"

"From the very beginning," said Skulduggery.

"I was going to adopt Valkyrie's patterns," they said, "but it felt... cheap, somehow. Disingenuous."

"Says the person who's hijacked her body."

They laughed. "Honestly? I just couldn't bring myself to say 'like' that many times."

"Oooh," said Skulduggery, "she's going to hurt you for that one."

They raised their hand to unleash the lightning but Skulduggery was on them. A fist to the cheek and an elbow to the jaw and their head was grabbed and sent smacking into the wall.

Skulduggery went for a choke, but they turned, pinned his arm, jammed their hip against his, tried to flip him. He countered and then they countered his next move and he countered that and back and forth it went, the fight beating its own rhythm, and then Valkyrie's lightning sent him spinning back.

"You realise you can't win, yes?" they said. "No matter what, you're not going to attack me with everything you've got – because I'm her. You don't want to hurt her. Whereas I am rather ambivalent about hurting you."

Skulduggery got to his feet slowly. "I'm not going to let you take her."

"I hate to be the one to tell you this, old me, but you're not in a position to be deciding anything for anyone. Besides, I've already taken her." They spread their arms wide. "What a nice vehicle she makes. So strong. So healthy. So powerful."

Skulduggery moved and they blasted him with their eyes. He hit the ground and then the wall and lay there, his clothes smoking.

"It really is a wonder, to be quite honest with you," they said. "I'd need some time to practise, obviously, but her ability to adopt other people's abilities? Simply astounding. You should try it, you really should. Would you like to take her for a test drive? I can show you how."

"Sure," Skulduggery said, sitting up, "that sounds like a great idea. You pop out of her and I'll take over."

Valkyrie felt her lips widen in a smile, and they threw Skulduggery a pair of handcuffs and hopped up to sit on the worktop. "Put those on," they said.

Skulduggery stood. "That's a bit presumptuous of you. You may have me at a disadvantage, but you haven't come close to beating me."

"I had you beaten the moment I stepped into this house," they responded, showing Skulduggery his own gun.

Skulduggery patted his empty holster. "That was sneaky."

Valkyrie smiled. "The hand is quicker than the eye – even for those who don't have eyes." They clicked back the hammer and pressed the muzzle to their head. "Shackle yourself or I'll shoot."

Skulduggery went quiet for a moment. "No," he said, "you won't."

"Won't I? You think I value her life too much? Still? After all these years?"

"Maybe you do, maybe you don't. But I'd say you value that power you're so enamoured with. Valkyrie has the potential to be the most powerful sorcerer who's ever lived. You're not going to throw that away just to win a fight with me in a kitchen."

"I am disappointed in you, Skulduggery, I really am. You're making some pretty staggering assumptions there. Your refusal to do what I command hinges on the admittedly understandable belief that Valkyrie's body is my ultimate destination. But you'd be wrong. Is it wonderful? Undoubtedly. Is it an absolute pleasure? Indescribably so. The power, the sensation, the sheer physicality of it... It's so close to being addictive, it truly is.

"But two things prevent me from viewing this form as my new home. The first is Valkyrie herself. I have her tucked away in a corner of my mind, but I like to be alone with my thoughts. I don't like the idea that one of these days she'll get out, because of course she will. You know it and I know it. This is Valkyrie Cain we're talking about. She'll find a way."

"And the second thing?" Skulduggery asked.

"I'll tell you that once the handcuffs are on. You have to the count of one until I pull this trigger."

Before they could speak again, Skulduggery picked up the cuffs. He put them on.

They laid the gun on the worktop beside them. "The second thing that prevents me from viewing Valkyrie as home is that, quite frankly, she *isn't* home. I need my own place. Somewhere I'm familiar with."

"Ah," said Skulduggery.

They shook their head. "There you go again, making assumptions. No, I do not want to jump into you. You're already there, and I have no immediate way to exorcise you from your own form."

"*Ah*," said Skulduggery.

They chuckled. "Now you have it. Lead the way, if you please."

They followed Skulduggery out of the kitchen and into the

library. He opened the middle bookcase on the far wall and they walked into the room with all those bones on the glass shelves. With Skulduggery standing in the corner, they picked out every bone they needed, assembling them carefully on the floor. When it came to the skull, they hesitated.

There were three on display. Two were perfectly fine. The third was the one Skulduggery had been wearing when they'd been ambushed by the Ripper. There was a bullet hole through the cranium and the entire left side was now held together with metal staples. Hairline fractures ran from the right eye socket to the jaw.

"This one," they said, taking it off the shelf. "This one has distinction. This one has history."

They laid it atop the spinal column, then stepped back.

"All right then," they said, and blasted Skulduggery with white lightning.

He cried out as he went down and Valkyrie immediately felt Cadaver leave her body. Her thoughts expanded to fill her head even as she toppled backwards. She hit the wall, cracking the mirror, and slid down, blinking quickly. Dimly, she was aware of the bones on the floor clicking together, aligning themselves to form a skeleton.

Skulduggery was trying to get up. Valkyrie was struggling to remember how to control her limbs.

Cadaver Cain sat up. He opened his jaw wide, then clacked it closed. He turned his head, moved it up and down, then thrust his hands out and the air rippled as he floated up off the ground, to his feet.

"Home at last," he said.

A wave of his hand and Valkyrie slid across the floor to join Skulduggery in the corner. She tried to resist, but Cadaver threaded her arms between Skulduggery's, cuffing her wrists.

"Be right back," he said, and left the room, his feet clacking lightly.

Valkyrie took a deep breath, then struggled to her knees. It took a minute. "Skulduggery. Hey, Skulduggery."

"I hear you," he said, shaking his head. "Welcome back."

"Come on, get up. Maybe we can rush him."

Moving awkwardly, they managed to stand.

"I don't think we'll be rushing anyone," he said.

"What do you think he's doing?"

"Probably seeking out my best suit to steal."

"It's not stealing if it belongs to me," Cadaver said, walking back in. Instead of a suit, however, he just wore trousers, shoes, a shirt, and a long coat. All in black. No hat. No tie.

"You're not wearing a tie," Skulduggery said, shocked.

"That's right," Cadaver responded.

"I see. I'm interested, though – what year is it *exactly* that I turn into a savage who has abandoned proper suit etiquette?"

"You stop caring about ties when your favourite one burns while still around your neck."

Skulduggery shook his head in disgust. "I'm ashamed of you. If those Croatian mercenaries could see you now..."

Cadaver tilted his head. "Croatian...? Oh! With the neckties, of course. What a fun group they were. Couldn't speak a word of French, of course, but that's neither here nor there. As for our situation as it currently stands, rest assured that I'm not going to kill you. Either of you. You are not my enemies and I, despite my recent actions, am not yours."

"So why are you doing this?" Valkyrie asked.

"I wish I could explain everything to you here and now," Cadaver said, "but events must unfold how they unfold. Enjoy freeing yourself from the shackles."

Then he bowed slightly, and left.

"God, he's annoying," Skulduggery muttered.

# 61

"Good morning."

Sebastian screeched and jumped back, his coat flapping, his hat falling off. It tumbled over the side of the building, then rose back up, floating through the air. He put one hand on his chest, feeling his heartbeat, and used the other to pluck the hat from the air and put it back on his head. "Thank you."

"I didn't mean to scare you," Darquesse said from where she sat, right on the edge of the roof.

"Don't worry, you didn't."

She frowned. "Then why did you scream?"

He paused. "OK," he admitted, "you scared me. But I forgive you." He sat beside her. "Good morning to you, too. You didn't come home last night. Did you find a friend?"

"Yes, and I played with her for ages. We had a sleepover. Her parents didn't know about it, but that just made it more fun."

"You didn't... didn't turn her into anything, did you?"

"Of course not. I promised."

"Thank you."

"You're welcome. What were you looking at?"

"Ah, nothing much," he said. "Just the city. The people."

"All their little lives," she said.

"Yeah." Sebastian hesitated. "Do you think about that at all? The lives that other people lead?"

She tapped her head. "It's in my brain."

"What is?"

"Their lives. All of their lives are in my brain. So I suppose I'm always thinking about the lives that other people lead – or part of me is."

"Is this from when you had all those other parts of you?"

"They're called aspects," she said, nodding.

"And you keep all those memories in your mind?"

"Not all of them," said Darquesse. "The human brain isn't built to think the kind of thoughts I do."

"Then where do you keep them?"

Darquesse shrugged, and fluttered her fingers round her head. "Everywhere. Outside and inside me. It doesn't matter." She looked at him, suddenly concerned. "Or, not that it doesn't matter, it does matter, but I don't think the same way as you do and as other people do, so I'm a little bit different. It doesn't mean that I'm better than you, it just means that I'm different."

He smiled. "That sounds fine. And I'm glad you're different. Aren't you?"

"Sometimes."

"Not all the time?"

"Earlier, when I was playing, I wanted all my life to be like that. I wanted to be the same as everyone else so I could have fun every second. But then I remembered that other people aren't happy every second, so that wouldn't make any sense. I felt a bit better after that."

He frowned. "Are you not happy?"

"Mostly I'm happy."

"But then sometimes you're not?"

"Yes."

"Why is that?"

She gave a long sigh. "I have to decide if I should save everyone. On some days, I think yes, I should save every single person and thing. Then I think I should save only the good people, and every cat and dog and fish and bird and all the animals and trees and plants and furniture and all that stuff. But then, on other days, I don't think I should save anyone, or anything, because I remember that a person is the same as a piece of dirt or a rock and that it makes no difference if they're alive or not. On those days, I get sad."

"I don't blame you. I'd get sad, too."

She nodded.

Sebastian let a few moments go by. "Do you think you *will* save the world?"

"I don't know. I haven't finished thinking about it. Maybe if I keep remembering all the cats and dogs and the baby sheep and the deer and polar bears, and if I remember all the things I like and love, maybe then I'll *want* to save the world."

"That's a good idea," said Sebastian. "Just keep thinking about the things you love."

Darquesse nodded again, and got to her feet. "I'm going home now. Will I take you?"

"I'll walk, actually. I like walking. Demure and Tarry should be there, though. Be nice to them, OK?"

"OK, Dad." She vanished – but reappeared a moment later. "Dad?"

"Yes, sweetie?"

"I think I'm going to call you Sebastian from now on."

His smile faded. "Oh. OK. Why?"

She shrugged. "Because you're not my dad. I don't have a dad. And because I think it'll be easier to let you die if I stop calling you that."

"That's a good idea," he said dully, and she vanished again.

He stayed up on the roof for another fifteen minutes, trying – and failing – to shake the feeling of dread that was rising up his spine. He made his way down to street level and walked home. He couldn't even enjoy the odd looks he was getting.

When he got home, he found Tarry in the hall, sprawled face

down, his blood following the cracks between the floorboards. The house was quiet, the air so very still. Sebastian stepped over the body and moved into the living room. Demure was on the couch, her eyes open, her top sodden with blood and punctured with three small bullet holes over her heart.

His flesh rippling, his head light, Sebastian swept through the ground floor quickly and quietly, making sure it was empty. He took a knife from the kitchen and climbed the stairs, resisting the urge to scream Darquesse's name.

There was no one upstairs, either. With trembling fingers, he took out his phone, called Bennet.

"She's gone," he said. "She came back home but she's not here. Somebody took her. They killed Tarry and Demure and they took her. She's gone."

# 62

The Darquesse Society met in Lily's house. She insisted on making cups of tea for everyone, and passed them round with trembling hands. Sebastian put his cup on the coffee table.

"Who talked?" Ulysses said.

The rest of them looked at him.

"Someone must have said something," he continued. "We all agreed, we all promised, that we wouldn't tell a soul about what was happening with Darquesse – not to our wives, husbands, friends, no one. No one. So no one could have known that Darquesse was a kid. No one could have known that she could be snatched. Unless one of us told someone."

"I didn't tell anyone," said Kimora.

"I have no one to tell," said Forby.

"Maybe Tarry or Demure told someone," said Lily.

Ulysses glared. "That's convenient – blaming the only people who can't defend themselves."

"What? I'm not doing that!"

"You just did!"

"I didn't mean it that way!"

"You told someone, didn't you?"

"I didn't! I swear!"

"Lay off her, Uly," said Bennet. "For all we know, you told someone."

"I keep my promises," Ulysses shot back.

They argued like this for another few minutes. It was ugly, and unsightly, and a little embarrassing. They weren't very good at arguing, because none of them really suspected the others of being at fault. They simply needed someone to blame, just until they comprehended what had happened.

Unfortunately, they couldn't wait that long.

"Stop," said Sebastian, getting to his feet. "Just stop. We're all confused; we're all in shock. We've just lost two of our friends. We're going to have to deal with that at some stage, but right now we have to focus on finding Darquesse. Bennet, tell everyone what we were talking about."

Bennet nodded. "We found binding sigils throughout the house, hidden behind pictures and furniture and stuff. It looked... I mean, I'm no expert, but it looked recent, y'know? Like they'd only been carved a few days ago."

"We think whoever did this waited until they were sure Darquesse was home," Sebastian said. "They knocked on the door. Tarry answered. They killed him, probably activated the sigils then. They killed Demure in the living room. There were signs of a struggle in Darquesse's bedroom, so we think that's where they grabbed her. They'd have had to shackle her, and then carry her out. The back door was open. I think they either had a van or a Teleporter waiting."

"We should call the City Guard," Kimora said.

Ulysses shook his head. "Under no circumstances."

"We don't have to tell them who she is. We just have to tell them that a child has been kidnapped."

"For all we know," Sebastian muttered, "it was the City Guard who did this."

"Then what do we do?" she demanded. "You're the leader, Sebastian, so lead. What do we do?"

He didn't answer.

"Brilliant!" Kimora said. "Great! Wonderful!"

"Kimora..." said Lily.

"What? What, Lily? We have a missing child and we can literally go to *no one* for help, because everyone apart from us would view her as the real threat! And we don't have a clue as to what to do about it! So, what? What do you want? What do you want to say, Lily?"

Lily had gone quite pale. "I was only going to ask if you wanted a drop of milk in your tea."

Kimora started crying. "I'm sorry, Lily."

"I'm sorry, too, Kimora," Lily said, already in tears, and they hugged. Forby started crying next, and Ulysses hugged him. Sebastian left the room.

"We need leadership," Bennet said, coming after him.

Sebastian motioned for him to close the door.

"I don't think it was the City Guard," Sebastian said.

"But you're the one who—"

"I know I suggested it, but if it had been them they would have come with overwhelming force. There wouldn't be a door left on its hinges."

"OK," said Bennet, "so who was it?"

"Apart from us, only one person has any idea what we're doing. Only one person would know enough to keep tabs on us."

Bennet frowned. "Tantalus."

"The Society started in his living room, right? It was all him until you guys voted to kick him out and bring me in. And we know he's capable of murder because he tried to kill me that time."

Bennet snarled. "Tantalus."

They pounded on his front door and shouted his name, and then Ulysses broke the door down and they stormed in.

"Who's there?" Tantalus cried from deeper in the house. "Help! Please! I'm in here! Help me!"

They found Tantalus in his basement, shackled to a pipe. The look on his face changed from hopeful desperation to one of pure guilt.

Nobody said anything.

Sebastian turned to go.

"No!" Tantalus cried. "Wait! You can't leave me here!"

"You took her," Sebastian said.

"I... what? I don't know what you're... OK. Yes, I took her. Of course I took her! You had no right keeping her to yourself!"

"How did you know it was Darquesse?" Bennet asked.

Tantalus sneered. "I saw her, you moron. All I had to do was keep an eye on you all and look through a few windows. I saw you all, with your stupid happy faces. It was obvious what had happened! You'd found her. You'd found Darquesse and you'd brought her back and you hadn't even bothered to tell me about it."

"You weren't part of the group."

"I started that group!"

"Stop, Tantalus. Just stop. We're not going to let you rewrite history. We started the group. The group started the group. Then we voted you out because nobody liked you, and you tried to kill Sebastian."

"Who's Sebastian?"

"The Plague Doctor," said Kimora. "You tried to kill the Plague Doctor."

"And then you started spying on us," Ulysses said.

"Yeah, I spied on you," Tantalus said, and lost his scowl. "Could you get me out of these shackles now, please?"

"Not yet."

The scowl came back. "Yeah, I spied on you. I watched you keep Darquesse for yourselves."

"But how did you know about her becoming a child?" Bennet asked.

"Because she disappeared, you idiot. I didn't see her any more. Instead, I watched the lot of you cooing round a baby – a baby that aged, like, ten years in the space of a few months. I figured it out, Bennet! I used my brain!"

Sebastian walked forward. Tantalus held his shackled hands towards him, but Sebastian ignored them and hunkered down. "Where is she?"

"Let me out and I'll tell you."

"Where is she?"

"Did you not hear me? I said let me out and I'll tell you."

Sebastian's hand closed round Tantalus's throat. "Answer the damn question or we'll walk out and leave you here."

Tantalus gagged and strained, and Sebastian leaned in, tightening his grip.

He took his hand away before he killed him, and Tantalus gasped.

"I don't know! I don't know where she is!"

"Who has her? Who did you call?"

Tantalus was making too much of a big deal out of his choking. He coughed and spluttered and wheezed, playing for time, trying to come up with good excuses.

"Were you there?" Bennet asked, in a quiet voice. "When she was taken, were you there?"

Tantalus shook his head.

"Did you tell your friends to kill Tarry and Demure?"

Tantalus stopped wheezing. He stared. "What?"

"Your new friends killed Tarry and Demure before they took Darquesse," Sebastian said. "You didn't know about that?"

"They... they wouldn't have done that."

"They shot them."

"They wouldn't have done that!"

"Well, they did," said Bennet. "I know you didn't think much of Tarry, but Demure was a friend of yours, wasn't she? Or as close to a friend as someone like you can have?"

"I... I liked Tarry, too."

"You got them killed," Sebastian told him.

"No."

"Who did you call?"

Tantalus was going through something. His face contorted, shifting between confusion, revelation, and grief. Sebastian didn't have time for any of that.

"Who did you call?"

"Someone I know," he said. "Or... knew. I used to know him. Granton Bicker. He was a, a thug from the old days. Violent. Not too bright. I thought..."

"You thought you could control him."

Tantalus nodded. "He brought in a friend – Gobemouche. Another dummy. I told them what I wanted. What I needed. I didn't tell them who she was – I didn't say anything like that. I paid them to go in and not hurt anyone and just take the girl and bring her here and..."

"And they shackled you to this pipe," Sebastian finished, "and left. Where did they go?"

"I don't know."

"What are they planning to do?"

"They're going to sell her. They know she's powerful, and they know they'll get a good price for someone like that, but they don't... they don't have a grand scheme, or anything. They're really not that smart."

"That might be so," Sebastian said, straightening up, "but they're smarter than you."

# 63

"This is how Bella got expelled," Axelia whispered as they crept through the darkness. "This is probably not the smartest thing in the world, what we're doing. Do you think it's smart?"

"No," Omen whispered back. "Not even remotely."

"Where's Never? I thought Never was going to be here."

"He will," said Omen.

"Do we have a plan?"

"Yes. We look around, see if we spot anyone."

"For how long?"

"For as long as it takes. Or an hour. I'm pretty tired."

"And what makes you think we'll see anyone?"

He shrugged. "It's been two weeks since Bella saw what she saw. That was a Saturday night – this is a Saturday night."

"So you think the mysterious figures only come out on Saturday nights?"

Omen sighed. "I don't know, Axelia. I'm just trying something. It's probably a stupid idea, but—"

She looked at him sternly. "Hey. There are no such things as stupid ideas."

"Just stupid people," Never said from beside them, making them both jump.

"Do not do that," Omen scowled. Never was dressed all in black.

"I love your catsuit," said Axelia.

"Thank you. I feel like a ninja when I wear it. How's the sneaking going?"

"Pretty good. Shall we continue?"

They continued. They did a few patrols near the towers, but as the hour wore on it started to get less and less fun. Just as they were about to head to bed, they heard something.

A voice.

Keeping to the shadows, they crept through the corridor, stopping when they came to the junction.

Two figures disappearing round the next corner.

They hurried after them.

The one in charge was tall and thin. The other one had his hands bound behind his back. He was speaking, but his words were muffled by a gag. The tall one shoved him onwards and he nearly fell.

It was Chicane. It was Mr Chicane. It was a teacher.

The other guy, the one in the cuffs, the one who kept rubbing his chin against his shoulder, Omen didn't recognise. He managed to dislodge his gag.

"Please," he said, the words rushing out of him, "please just let me go, I won't tell anyone, I won't tell a soul, I don't even know who you are so I wouldn't be able to identify you and I'm terrible with faces, even if I saw you in a line-up I'd never be able to point you out, please, I have a family, I have a wife and children and I love them so much, please—"

Chicane didn't bother answering – he just hit him, right in the gut, and fixed the gag back into place as the handcuffed guy struggled to recover.

He led him on to the West Tower. A section of wall opened. Inside was something like an elevator shaft, except it was perfectly cylindrical and made of a polished metal that flickered with a reflected blue light from somewhere far below. The handcuffed man peered over the edge, and whimpered.

Axelia gripped Omen's wrist. They looked at each other, eyes wide. Omen turned to Never, and Never nodded. They didn't need to come up with a plan. The plan was obvious. Teleport over there, grab the handcuffed man, and get away.

But, before Omen had even placed his hand on Never's shoulder, Chicane shoved the handcuffed man into the shaft.

Omen froze. Axelia froze and Never froze. The handcuffed man screamed as he plunged out of sight and then there was a moment, just the slightest of moments, when the light in the shaft turned red and the scream turned agonised, and then it was cut off, and the soft blue light flickered again.

The wall started to close over. Chicane waited until it had sealed before he turned to leave.

Never teleported them away before he saw them.

# 64

"He killed him," Axelia said. "He murdered him. Mr Chicane murdered that guy."

"I never trusted him," said Omen. "Remember that? Remember me not trusting him?"

"I remember," Never said.

"But you said he was OK. He murdered someone and you said he was OK."

Never scowled. "First of all, and I think this is important, that's not the order in which those things occurred. I said he was OK, and *then* he murdered someone. But, due to recent events, I've obviously changed my mind about him."

"How could you think he was OK?"

"Because he rarely made us do any work," Never responded. "Because he could be kinda funny if the mood took him. Because he's good-looking without being *too* good-looking. There's something weird going on with his eyes: they're either too close together or they're not close enough together, and he has a goofy smile, but all in all he's perfectly all right for a teacher, in the looks department. But, again, let me make this perfectly clear, due to recent events and with more information having come to light, vis-à-vis the murder we just witnessed, I've changed my mind about Mr Chicane, and now I hate every single thing about him. Are we clear on where I stand now, Omen?"

"I suppose," Omen muttered.

"Good."

"What do we do?" Axelia asked. "We can't go to Duenna – she's involved, somehow. Can't go to the cops, either – they might be involved, too. Everyone's involved."

"Not everyone," said Omen. "Not Skulduggery and Valkyrie."

"And there are teachers we can trust," Never said. "Miss Gnosis, and Miss Wicked. Hunnan. Peccant."

Omen frowned. "Can we trust them?"

"Just because Peccant doesn't like you—"

"I'm not even talking about Peccant. I'm talking about the others. Just because we like them as teachers doesn't mean they haven't been pretending to be good people, like Chicane. I don't think we can trust any of the staff – not until Skulduggery and Valkyrie check them out." He thought about this. "OK, we can probably trust Miss Gnosis, because Valkyrie's dating her, and she wouldn't date a bad guy."

"Disagree," said Never, "but, fair enough, I'd say Gnosis is cool."

"I'll talk to Skulduggery and Valkyrie. Nobody say anything to anyone about this until then. Chicane doesn't know we saw him, so, if we just continue on with our lives as normal, we'll all be perfectly safe. Probably."

# 65

Four years ago...

He struck and she blocked, spun, went to sweep his ankle and
then abruptly brought the blade round, the tip whistling by his
cheek. He hadn't taught her that move. She was improvising
freely, wielding the scythe as an extension of her own body.
Impressive.

She came forward in a flurry, sunlight glinting. Quell blocked
and parried, careful not to step beyond the Combat Circle, waiting
for an opening. He saw it as he always did – the slight raising of
an elbow, and the gap that resulted – and he stepped in and
whacked the snath section of the scythe into her ribs.

Or that's what he expected to happen.

But Valkyrie had lured him in, offering him an opening that
wasn't really there to begin with, and she blocked and pressed
down, hooked her foot behind his and twisted. Quell would have
tumbled out of the Circle had he not been able to get a hand to
the ground and cartwheel away from the edge.

The puppy watched from the shade the truck offered, one ear
perked up, the other folded over.

They fought on, snath clashing with snath, blade clashing with
blade, constantly moving, pivoting, lunging, and retreating. And,
as they fought, Quell started to wonder about all those times

Valkyrie had exposed her ribs for that strike. He started to wonder if it was, as he'd assumed, a weakness in her defence, or if it had been a ruse all along. He realised he'd built his entire offensive strategy round that weakness, and a new feeling came over him: a slow kind of sadness.

He pushed her back. She swung for his head and he held his scythe out flat, and she stopped a whisper from his neck. She drew the weapon in, flipped it, held it flat, and they bowed to each other.

She was panting slightly, and sweating in the sun. So was he.

"I can't teach you anything more," Quell said, taking her scythe into his other hand.

Valkyrie frowned. "But I haven't beaten you."

"Nor will you," he said, walking out of the Circle. He laid the scythes in the back of his truck and tossed her a bottle of water. "You can't beat me, and I can't beat you – not without killing you."

"There's still more to learn."

"There's always more to learn, but I can't teach you that."

She took a big gulp, then upended the bottle over her head. "So what now?"

"Now I go," he said.

She watched him, water running through her hair and down her face. "You're leaving?"

"You paid me to train you. I've trained you. You're a better unarmed combatant than you were. You're better with weapons. You're bigger, stronger, and faster than ever. I can't do anything more for you."

"But you haven't just been training me," she said. "We've been living together, Coda. We're... you and me, we're a thing. We have a relationship. Are you seriously saying that's over just because you can't think of anything else to teach me?"

Her anger was rising.

He was confused. "That was our arrangement."

"We made that arrangement before you moved in with me."

"But the arrangement hasn't altered."

She stared at him, then looked away. He stepped forward, reaching for her arm, but she slapped his hand down. She hunkered, scratching behind the puppy's ears. "When do you leave?" she asked.

He hesitated. "I didn't expect to finish training you so soon, but I've been offered a job in Spain that I'll be able to take on now. I'll be leaving tomorrow."

"Training someone?" she asked. "Or killing someone?"

"Protecting someone. I'm sorry, Valkyrie. I didn't mean to upset you."

"No less than I deserve," she responded, and gave him a bitter smile. He wasn't used to seeing her smile, bitter or otherwise.

# 66

"Stop hugging me," said Tanith, her face mashed into Valkyrie's shoulder.

"No," said Valkyrie, holding on even tighter. "Not until you forgive me."

"But it wasn't you who attacked me. It was Cadaver Cain."

"But it was my body that broke your arm."

"Dislocated my shoulder," Tanith corrected. "And it's fine now. Really. You can stop hugging me."

Militsa walked in. Froze. "I can come back later, if..."

"I'm not letting go until Tanith tells me that she forgives me," Valkyrie said.

Tanith sighed. "Fine, fine, I forgive you. Will you let me go now?"

"No."

"Why not?"

"Because I don't believe you."

"Val, I forgive you because I know it wasn't you. I've been possessed as well, remember. I know what it's like."

Valkyrie squeezed one more time, then stepped back. "I really am sorry."

"And I really do understand. I've got to go, though. Oberon's waiting."

"He's so dreamy."

"Yes, he is."

"Give him a big kiss from me."

"I'm still in the room, you know," Militsa said.

Tanith winked at Valkyrie, and left, and Militsa came over.

"How you doing?"

"I'm good," said Valkyrie. "I'm fine. Have you seen my boots?"

"Beside the door, where they're meant to be. Val, I meant how are you doing?"

Valkyrie resisted the immediate urge to blow the question off, and took a deep breath before answering. "I'm not great," she said. "I didn't like Cadaver controlling me, obviously. It's... not nice. And a violation. And it's horrible seeing these hands hurt the people I love. I'm just ridiculously grateful that he didn't hurt you."

"Has this changed how you think about Skulduggery?"

"No," she answered. "It's pretty clear, the difference between them. I'm just mad that I wasn't able to, like, access his thoughts or figure out his intentions or anything like that. Though it means that he wasn't able to peek into my thoughts, either, which is a relief, I suppose. But I am OK, sweetheart. I'm not great, but I'm OK."

Militsa nodded. "Thank you for sharing that with me. Do you feel better?"

"I do. Wow. Talking about things actually helps."

"You sound so surprised," Militsa said, and laughed. "Want a cup of tea?"

"I can't. I have to head out. It's the start of the Week of Mourning."

"Oh, of course," Militsa said, filling the kettle. "Yes, rest in peace, Damocles Creed, wherever your body is right now. Hey, do you think it'd be seen as disrespectful if I did a little dance outside the Dark Cathedral?"

"Probably."

"Then I think I might stay home."

"Good idea," Valkyrie said, and went to get her boots. She came back to put them on and Militsa's phone beeped. She read the screen, frowning slightly, before pouring boiling water into a mug. "Everything OK?" Valkyrie asked.

"Ah, just more Necromancer talk," Militsa said. "Something big is gonna be announced later today."

"Is this anything to do with what you were saying about the change in approach the Order seems to be taking?"

"I really don't know. I should know, but I haven't been inside a Necromancer Temple in years."

"Good," said Valkyrie. "They're creepy."

"But I loved them. I never felt connected to the religious part of it all, but at the same time I always felt like I was on the verge of something special when I was studying. Like I was part of something bigger than me."

"So why haven't you been back?"

Militsa took a sip of her tea. "I've... changed. I think. Maybe. Or maybe I never suited that life, but I wanted to, so badly, that I convinced myself that I belonged."

"You don't come across as overly... Necromantic, I have to admit."

There was a hesitation. And then, "So what if I've made a huge mistake? What if Necromancy isn't for me? I mean, having the Surge so young is just dumb, when you think about it. Your twenties are when you're supposed to be figuring out who you even are – and yet we've got to decide on a magical discipline for the rest of our lives when we're eighteen, nineteen? How are we supposed to know? It's stupid."

"I agree."

"The Surge puts us on a path and we don't know where it leads. It's ridiculous. So, if I no longer agree with all of the Necromancy teachings, what does that mean for me? I'm stuck at this power level? I'm never going to rise any higher? Get any stronger? I'm never going to gain those insights I've been promised?"

Valkyrie's boots were on and she stood, choosing her words carefully. "Do you care?"

"Pardon?"

"I mean... OK, the insight thing is something you'd care about, but do you really care about getting stronger? You barely use Necromancy as it is."

"It's the principle of the thing, you know? But yes, you're right. I don't do battle or anything. Don't get in fights. I shadow-walk a lot, though."

"That's only because you hate public transport."

Militsa sighed. "I don't know what's wrong with me lately. I think I'm having a mid-life crisis."

"You're twenty-eight."

"Some other kind of crisis, then. I'm questioning my station in life, my Necromancy... and it's not helping that the research people keep pestering me for an answer to their job offer."

"You haven't turned it down?"

"Not yet. I'm not going to take it, obviously, but... I don't know. Turning it down just means I'd be closing a door I've been wanting to walk through since I was a kid. I don't think my inner child could handle that right now. Why does everything have to be so complicated?"

"See, that's why I prefer punching people. It's very straightfor-ward. You see a face, you punch it. There is beauty in simplicity."

"Maybe I should take a leaf from your book."

Valkyrie kissed her forehead. "You let me be the idiot who does battle and gets into fights. You've got a curiosity about the world and about magic that's going to lead to great things."

"You're not just saying that because I'm super-cute and you love me?"

"I swear. Now I gotta go."

"Be safe."

"I'm going to a memorial," Valkyrie said, laughing. "How much trouble can I get into?"

*

The High Sanctuary had designated Sunday to be the start of a Week of Mourning over the loss of their acting Supreme Mage, and, as the crowd of sobbing sorcerers began to file into the Dark Cathedral, Valkyrie wondered how so many normal people could be so devoted to such an incredibly bad man.

"I feel I need to apologise again," Skulduggery said.

"You didn't do anything wrong."

"Technically, I did possess you."

"Cadaver Cain possessed me and, technically, he isn't you. Not yet. We have no idea what drove you to become him, but I'm betting that, whatever it was, it wasn't fun. The point is, apologising once was enough. Now can we get back to work? We only have nine days to save the world."

He nodded. "Very well."

"So, as it stands, Creed still somehow sends out the Activation Wave at twelve minutes to midnight on Draíocht, even though he's dead. That's fine. It makes no sense, but let's be honest, stranger things have happened. Maybe it's Zombie-Creed, or a Creed from another dimension, or a clone or a reflection, or simply an imposter. However he manages to come back, what exactly will he need to do to send out the Wave?"

"According to Temper," Skulduggery said, "for one-on-one Activations, leaving aside the chair and the restraints, all that's required is the Ensh-Arak Sigil to generate the power and the shard of a particular yet mysterious jewel to focus it. But, for something on the scale of what your sister described, hundreds – perhaps thousands – of Ensh-Arak Sigils would be needed to even approach the power required, and then that energy would then have to be focused through something a lot bigger than a shard."

Valkyrie pulled her hair back into a ponytail to cool down in the sun. "And how is he going to get all this? He couldn't manage it alone, right? Maybe he had someone else helping him – maybe they're the one we've got to deal with now."

Skulduggery didn't answer.

"Hello?"

"Of course," he said quietly.

"Are you working something out in your head again? You've got to explain these things to me, OK? We've talked about this."

He took out his phone, opened an app, and drew a sigil on the screen. "This, crudely, is the Ensh-Arak," he said, tapping his finger at each point where the sigil changed direction. "There are seven points that the construction of this sigil hangs upon."

"Seven Pillars," Valkyrie said softly.

"So long as these points are perfectly placed, the sigil itself could be as big as it needs to be."

"And how big would it need to be?"

He put his phone away. "Come on."

They joined the back of the queue. At the entrance, two black-armoured Cathedral Guards stepped in front of them.

"We're full," one of them said. He was gruff. Valkyrie decided to call him Gruffy.

"Surely you can fit in two more," Skulduggery responded. "I'm quite narrow, and my partner's shoulders may appear broad, but she's very good at turning sideways."

"I've been practising," Valkyrie said happily.

"What business do you have here?" Gruffy asked.

"We wish to pay our respects," Skulduggery answered. "Maybe offer up a prayer. Damocles Creed wasn't just your Supreme Mage, you know. He was ours, too. Valkyrie, in particular, worshipped the man."

Valkyrie nodded. "Worshipped."

"She was devoted to him, to be honest."

Valkyrie nodded again. "Devoted."

"She has a collection of his toenail clippings that she likes to take out when she's sad and give them a quick lick."

Valkyrie nodded a third time. "Devoted."

"Also," said Skulduggery, "we're Arbiters, and we're investigating the assassination, so, if you wouldn't mind, we'd like to get past."

The Cathedral Guards glanced at each other, then reluctantly moved aside.

Beyond the entrance, across the marble floor, were the doors into the Cathedral's nave. Valkyrie and Skulduggery hurried after the last of the mourners as the doors were swinging slowly shut. Before they reached them, and when they were sure they weren't being watched, they took their cloaking spheres from their pockets and twisted the hemispheres.

The bubble of invisibility enveloped Valkyrie and she veered away from the doors, heading instead for the arched passage that led to the rest of the Dark Cathedral. The personal sphere, about the size of a golf ball, didn't last as long as its bigger cousin, and it needed more time to recharge between uses, but it rendered her perfectly invisible and for that she was grateful. Skulduggery's sphere rendered him perfectly invisible, too, however, so she walked slowly in case she barged into him.

She got through the passage, waited for Cathedral staff to pass, and switched on her aura-vision. Skulduggery's life force glowed a healthy red down the other end of the corridor, and she caught up with him. Once their invisibility bubbles intersected, he popped into view beside her.

"Do you know how to get to the basement from here?" Valkyrie asked.

"Not really," he answered. "I always sneak in through the secret tunnel. I'm sure we'll be fine."

"The spheres are only going to last another minute."

"Another minute is all we'll need," he said.

# 67

Fifteen minutes later they were totally visible and staring at a wall.

"I thought you said you recognised that corridor," Valkyrie said, keeping her voice down. "I thought you said it would take us to the stairs."

Skulduggery nodded. "And I maintain that it still would, were this wall not in our way. But all is not lost. I can get through this."

Valkyrie frowned at him. "No."

"I've done it before."

"Still no."

"I took Tanith with me and she's still around, isn't she? It's relatively perfectly safe." He held out his hand.

She glowered, and took it, and he pressed his other hand to the wall. It cracked and crumbled, and he pushed his hand through. Then his whole arm disappeared up to the shoulder.

"Follow me," he said, and stepped in.

Valkyrie stopped thinking about it and just stepped in after him.

She passed into absolute darkness, filled with the rumbling of a thousand boulders all around her, and before she could even begin to panic light broke through and she was stepping out again. She waited until she was clear before gasping. "Oh, thank God."

"You should really have more faith in me, you know," Skulduggery said.

She smiled at him to apologise, then frowned. "Where's your hat?"

He felt for the hat that wasn't there, then looked back at the wall. "This isn't a problem," he said, reaching in. "Not a problem in the slightest. Ah, here we are."

He pulled out half of his hat. The other half remained in the wall.

Valkyrie stared. "Are you serious?"

"My poor hat."

"That could have been me."

"Look what happened to my hat."

"Skulduggery – you could have left me in there."

"Look at my hat, though."

She snatched it from his hand. "You could have left me in there, Skulduggery. You could have lost me halfway through the wall as easily as you lost this hat!"

"I didn't lose all of the hat," he said, a little defensively, and started walking.

She stalked after him. "So you'd have pulled half of me out?"

"I lost focus midway through. Lesson learned."

"How?"

"How what?"

"How did you lose focus midway through a wall? We took, literally, two steps. How did you lose focus after one step, Skulduggery? What was so distracting about all that darkness that you lost focus?"

"I remembered something funny I said yesterday."

"Tell me you're joking."

"I'm not joking. I was yesterday, though, and that's what I was thinking about. You look angry."

"Do I?"

"Would it help if I told you the funny thing I said?"

329

Valkyrie stared. Glared. "Sure," she said. "Tell me the funny thing, Skulduggery."

He paused. "No," he said at last, "I don't think it'd be a good idea."

"I want to hear it."

"I don't think you're in the mood to hear it, and because of that, if you do hear it, it'll just make you even madder than you are now."

"That's actually pretty smart thinking."

"I'll wait until tomorrow, when you're in a better mood. Then you'll be better able to appreciate my wit."

"Sometimes, I swear to God, I could kill you."

They took the stairs down. With each level, it got colder and quieter and darker. The stairs went from being polished and sleek to rough stone. And still they went down.

"This next one," Skulduggery said, his voice low.

They reached the bottom of the steps and emerged into a huge, brightly lit cavern. A huge, brightly lit, empty cavern.

Skulduggery grunted as they moved forward. "The last time I was here," he said, "this entire place was filled with Kith."

"Creed must have found somewhere else to store them," Valkyrie said, approaching a circle carved into the cavern floor. It was maybe four strides across, and dotted with sigils. "Know what this is for?" she asked.

"Probably something to do with this," Skulduggery said, looking up.

Directly over the circle there was a hole, the exact same size, in the ceiling.

"Wonder how far up it goes," Valkyrie said.

Skulduggery clicked his fingers, summoned fire into both hands, and rose off the ground. Valkyrie waited till he was a fair distance above her before blasting off after him. It wasn't easy, flying slow, but she kept pace with him well enough, her crackling energy dancing with the flickering light of his flame on the tunnel's curving wall.

Less of a tunnel, she realised, the higher and higher they went, and more of a chimney.

Shafts of sunlight pierced the darkness as they neared the top. Skulduggery squeezed through one of the narrow windows and Valkyrie flew towards a ledge and grabbed it, then hauled herself up.

The wind chilled her as she looked out over Roarhaven from the Dark Cathedral's tallest tower.

"Well," she said, "this is curious."

"I think this is a Pillar," Skulduggery said. "If I'm right, there are another six in Roarhaven, just like this one."

"So the Pillars are chimneys?"

"This isn't a chimney, it's a... Think of it as a gun barrel, designed to channel an extraordinary amount of power. It's the city, you see?"

He took out his phone and pulled up a map of Roarhaven, then marked their position with a tap of his finger. "The Dark Cathedral itself has the first Pillar. It's designed to fill with energy and then, presumably, link up with the other six." He made another dot on the map. "The second Pillar is probably here, in the High Sanctuary." He tapped twice more. "These Pillars here, on either side, probably around Carnivore Row and the Garment District. Then these two... somewhere on Suture Street and Razorblade Alley. And this one here, down at the bottom, that has to be Corrival Academy. It has to be." He tapped it, and they looked at the seven dots on the screen.

"The streets line up," Valkyrie said quietly.

Skulduggery moved his finger from dot to dot, drawing the sigil along the streets and laneways of the city. "That's how it'll be done," he said. "The Seven Pillars will carve the sigil into Roarhaven itself."

"But to focus that amount of power," said Valkyrie, "they'd

need something a lot bigger than a little shard of a jewel or whatever."

Skulduggery nodded. "A lot bigger."

"And where does this monster's eye that Izzaruh mentioned come into it?"

"I don't know," Skulduggery said. "Not yet."

They flew down to the street and walked back up to the Cathedral. Gruffy the Cathedral Guard frowned at them as they passed.

"*Déjà vu*, eh?" Valkyrie said, smiling. They retraced their steps but, instead of sneaking off into the bowels of the Dark Cathedral, they slipped into the back of the nave. It was vast, and packed full of true believers, with curved tiers of pews radiating outwards from a platform on which stood the pulpit. A walkway linked the platform to the stage behind.

They were just coming to the end of a prayer. Even so, Valkyrie and Skulduggery still got their fair share of disapproving scowls.

A priestess emerged from one of the doors on the stage, and the congregation fell silent. She crossed the walkway, reaching the platform, and stood at the pulpit.

"Nine days ago," she intoned solemnly, "our Arch-Canon, our Supreme Mage, was murdered. He had become too dangerous to those who feared his message. He had to be silenced so that he could not lift us from this quagmire, this misery. He died for us. He gave his life in service."

People were sobbing. The priestess nodded. And smiled.

"But Damocles Creed is no ordinary man. He is the voice of the Faceless Ones, here on Earth. He is their prophet. And he will not die!"

The priestess left the platform down some steps Valkyrie couldn't see, her words echoing round the Cathedral. The worshippers in the pews looked confused. Then the doors on the stage opened, and everyone sitting on those pews gasped.

"Damn," Skulduggery said softly, as Damocles Creed walked out.

# 68

The gasps turned to whispers, and the whispers grew to shouts, and the shouts became cheers, and then there was a tidal wave of sound that washed over the crowd and crashed on to the pulpit until Creed held up his hands for silence, and silence followed.

He smiled.

"Hello," he said, and the Dark Cathedral trembled with the roars of the crowd.

Valkyrie flicked the switch in her head that altered her vision and watched him standing at the pulpit, burning with a healthy orange.

"It's him," she whispered. "He's real. It's actually him."

"Thank you, my friends," Creed said, his voice booming with strength. "Thank you for your prayers, for your tears, for your sorrow and your mourning. As I recovered from my injury, you gave me strength. All of you.

"Nine days ago, someone tried to kill me. You all saw it. You were there. A coward fired a bullet into my head."

The audience booed for an excessively long time.

Creed swept his arm back, guiding their eyes to the Necromancer standing on stage. "But this man, Uriah Serrate, used his Necromancy to bring me back so I could continue my work. Death itself is not strong enough to keep me. Death itself bows before a true servant of the Faceless Ones. Uriah, I thank you for guiding me through the realms of death, back to the warm embrace of my people."

The audience cheered, chanting Serrate's name.

"I have someone else to thank for my recovery," Creed continued. "It is only by the blessings of the Faceless Ones that Uriah sought me out, and only through their might, and their power, and their love, that I stand before you. To the Faceless Ones, I say thank you, thank you, one hundred thank yous."

The crowd roared, and Valkyrie turned to Skulduggery.

"I have questions," she said.

Skulduggery held his hands out, forming a bubble round them where they could talk without being overheard by whatever listening devices had been installed in Creed's office.

"Do you know what our mistake was?" Skulduggery asked. "Our mistake was not cremating the body immediately."

"We should have broken into the High Sanctuary and taken the Sceptre," Valkyrie said. "Then we would've found out if it works and I could've turned his remains to dust."

Skulduggery nodded. "Try reviving a pile of dust. Try getting a pile of dust to make a speech. No one would listen. Would you listen to a pile of dust making a speech? I wouldn't. I doubt it'd have very much to say. Nothing relevant, anyway."

Hoc came in and Skulduggery let the bubble dissipate.

"Did you know?" Skulduggery asked.

"Did I know what?" Hoc snapped. "That the Supreme Mage was alive? No, Detective, I did not, and I have some questions that demand answers, especially concerning this Necromancer. We don't know who he is or what he wants and we cannot trust him. I'm suspicious. I am very suspicious."

"You almost sound angry, Commander," Valkyrie said.

"Oh, I am," said Hoc. "I very much am."

The doors opened and Damocles Creed walked in, followed by Uriah Serrate.

"Supreme Mage," Hoc said, falling to his knees. "Bless the Faceless Ones for your return!"

Creed stared at him. "Get up."

Hoc jumped to his feet.

"Detectives," Uriah Serrate said, bowing, "I must apologise for my behaviour the last time we met. I feared you would not allow me to take the Supreme Mage's body and do what I knew must be done."

"And what exactly did you do?" Skulduggery asked.

"He brought me back to life, as I said," Creed told them. "He healed my injuries and reunited my soul with my physical body."

"After nine days," Valkyrie said. "You were dead for nine days. Your brains had been blown out the back of your head for nine days. This wasn't just CPR he performed on you. You were beyond help."

"No one is beyond help," Serrate said.

"And what do you get out of it?" Skulduggery asked. "I can think of far better people to bring back to life than Damocles Creed – offence intended, Supreme Mage. Why him, Mr Serrate?"

"I need help," Serrate said. "My people need help. They need a new home."

"And who are your people? I'm assuming it's not the Necromancers, because they have plenty of homes."

"I am a Necromancer," Serrate responded, "but I am not of the Necromancer Order. Nor are my people, who are suffering. I'm here to change that. I'm here to save them. I am Herald of the Dark, Harbinger of Doom, Emissary of the Everlasting Death, and the King of the Dead."

Valkyrie went cold. "Which dead in particular?"

"The dead of Meryyn ta Uul. The City Beneath. The City of the Dead. The City Below. It has many names, but the one it is best known by is the Necropolis. I believe you are familiar with it."

"I've... I've been there."

"You've walked its streets quite recently," said Serrate. "You entered the death field with only your necronaut suit to protect you, searching for a fragment of your sister's soul. A noble endeavour."

"And you're their king?" Skulduggery asked. "Since when?"

"It is a recent appointment," said Serrate. "They had been searching for leadership for decades, but their home was attacked quite recently. Tens of thousands of souls have been frozen, turned to glass. There are but thirty thousand left."

"Attacked how?" Skulduggery asked.

Valkyrie braced herself, waiting for him to describe how she had panicked and lost control of her power, waiting for him to fill in the blanks in her memory that she couldn't access and didn't want to.

"By a power surge nobody could have foreseen," Serrate said, not even glancing at her. "Their home in ruins, they needed a leader more than ever, and they called upon me. Reluctant as I was to take on the responsibility, I felt it was my duty to help. So I became their king, and promised that I would find them a new home."

Skulduggery looked at Creed, then back at Serrate. "Where do you propose this new home be located?"

"Here, of course," said Serrate. "In Roarhaven."

Valkyrie found her voice. "I don't get it," she said. "You want to turn Roarhaven into the new Necropolis?"

"Not all of it," Creed said. "Just the section that still remains damaged from Devastation Day."

"You're actually considering this," Skulduggery said.

"I am doing more than considering it," Creed responded. "I have agreed to it. The operation is already in motion."

"And you think that's safe, do you?"

"Uriah assures me that he has the knowledge to erect a boundary that will keep death on one side, and life on the other."

Serrate gave a single graceful nod. "The boundaries will be

up by Wednesday night, at which point my fellow Necromancers will immediately facilitate the transport of the souls from Meryyn ta Uul to Roarhaven."

"You're going to shadow-walk thirty thousand souls from Scotland to here?" Skulduggery asked.

"With enough Necromancers working together, we are confident that we can establish a tunnel from one location to the other, yes. In a show of gratitude, Supreme Mage Creed will allow the Order to establish a temple in Roarhaven."

"That'll make the Necromancers happy," said Valkyrie. "It'll look like they've been forgiven for trying to kill half the planet."

"Supreme Mage," said Hoc, trying to smile, "surely this is an incredibly precarious operation you're talking about. Nobody living can enter the Necropolis – it's a realm of death."

"We are all aware of the unique properties the Necropolis possesses, Commander."

"Yes, sir, of course, it's just... I've never heard of anyone seriously suggesting that such a place could ever co-exist within a living city. How can we be sure the boundaries hold? How can we be sure that the, the death field doesn't spread through the streets?"

"Uriah assures me he has every eventuality accounted for," said Creed. "That's enough for me. And, if it's enough for me, Commander, surely it is enough for you?"

Hoc swallowed. "Yes, sir. Of course."

Skulduggery slapped him on the shoulder. "Good man, Hoc. That's exactly the kind of backbone we need in this moment of lunacy."

"Shut up," Hoc growled.

"A question, Supreme Mage," Skulduggery said, holding up a finger. "What makes you think you can believe Mr Serrate here? Granted, he's brought you back to life which, I'm sure, predisposes you to give him the benefit of the doubt, but what do you really know of him?"

"I know all I need to."

"And you're quite comfortable putting the well-being of the city in his hands?"

"Quite."

"Then I'm sure you won't mind if we ask him a few questions about his background, his activities, his training – just to reassure ourselves, you understand."

Creed waved a hand. "None of that will be necessary, Detective. I have made my decision."

"That's what I thought," Skulduggery murmured.

# 69

Omen ordered a Coke and sipped it while they waited. The café was small and, apart from Omen, Axelia, and Never, devoid of customers. The owner glared at them from behind the counter, as if he resented their presence. Which was kind of weird.

"So," Axelia said, in a blatant attempt to dispel the silence, "are either of you ready for the exams?"

"I'm not," said Omen. "I'm not at all. For ages they were always, like, months away, and then they were weeks away, and then days away..."

Never frowned. "You do realise that's how time works, right?"

"It's just, the exams were always at some point in the future, and so long as they stayed at some point in the future that was fine. I had time to study. To do the work. I just didn't expect them to suddenly start tomorrow."

"So you've been caught unawares," Never said, "by something you've known was coming since forever?"

"Exactly."

"Well," said Never, "I've known it was coming, and I know how time works, but I'm still not ready. My only consolation is that we're not in Sixth Year. If this was the Leaving Certificate exams we were facing, the last exams we were ever going to take in school, I'd be ever-so-slightly panicked right now."

"I'm going to fail," Axelia said.

"No, you're not," Omen responded. "What are you talking about? You're super-smart."

"I haven't been able to study since Duenna's Sensitive did whatever they did to my head. I haven't been able to focus." She started whispering. "And also we witnessed a murder! We shouldn't have to take exams if we've just witnessed a murder!"

"That's true," Never said, nodding. "I agree with that. Roarhaven's just getting too bizarre. I mean, we watch our teacher murder a guy, and then the Supreme Mage comes back to life. What the hell? How are we supposed to get any work done? And did you hear about the dragon?"

Omen almost spat out his Coke. "There's a dragon?"

"It was on a news report on the Network last night. A bunch of sorcerers in Norway have been sent out hunting after a dragon was spotted eating sheep, or cows, or whatever they have in Norway."

"Bears," said Axelia. "And elk. And little foxes that are so cute. Is the dragon eating the little foxes?"

"The news report didn't say," Never replied. "My point is, the world is weird and it's getting weirder and we're expected to do exams? Totally ridiculous."

All three of them straightened up when Skulduggery and Valkyrie walked in. Skulduggery gestured, and two extra chairs slid towards the table. They sat.

"Sorry we're late," Valkyrie said. "Skulduggery had to go home to change his suit because he lost his hat in a wall and he couldn't possibly not wear a hat for an hour or two."

Skulduggery looked at her. "You sound annoyed."

"You didn't have to change your entire outfit just because you picked up another hat."

"But it's an ensemble."

"The suit you had been wearing is the exact same shade of blue as this one."

"Not the *exact* same."

"It's the same colour, Skulduggery."

"If you ignore the subtle difference."

"You'll have to order something if you want to stay here," the owner said from behind the till.

"Right," Valkyrie said, sighing. "I'll have a cappuccino, please."

The owner's scowl deepened. "Don't do cappuccinos."

"An Americano, then."

"Don't do those, either."

"Espresso."

"No."

"Do you serve coffee?"

"Yes."

"What kind of coffee?"

"Black coffee, or black coffee with milk."

"A black coffee, then." Valkyrie said.

"All out of black coffee."

"What *do* you have?"

"Black coffee with milk."

"You have black coffee with milk, but no black coffee on its own?"

"Yeah."

"Then I'll have a black coffee with milk, please."

"OK."

"And hold the milk."

"OK."

She smiled at them all. "Sorry about that. Omen, you—"

"All out of milk," said the owner.

Valkyrie looked over. "So what? I asked you to hold the milk."

"I can't hold it if I don't have it."

"Just give me the black coffee."

"I don't have black coffee."

"Give me the black coffee with milk without the milk."

The owner paused. Considered it. "No," he said at last. "You can have hot chocolate or water or a fizzy drink or a juice. The only juice we have is grapefruit, but we're all out of that."

"I won't have anything, thanks," Valkyrie said, turning back to the table.

"If you're not going to buy anything, you'll have to leave."

"Well, Jesus, what's the cheapest thing you sell?"

"Probably tap water."

"Then I'll have a glass of tap water."

"Do you want it cold or lukewarm?"

"Cold."

"It only comes lukewarm."

Valkyrie bit her lip. "That's fine." Her hand crackled with energy, but she smiled, and the crackling faded. "Omen," she said, "you witnessed a murder last night, is that right?"

"Uh, yes, we all did," Omen said, indicating his friends. "We were all there. Like I told you on the phone, we saw Mr Chicane push a guy into... Well, a hidden door opened in the West Tower and he pushed him in and he... It was a long drop, basically."

"Did Chicane see you?"

"No."

"We looked into his past," Skulduggery said, "and we're fairly certain he is who he says he is."

"But we saw him kill that guy," Axelia said.

"Undoubtedly, he left some things off his CV, such as the killing-people thing. But it seems he did attend the university he says he attended – part-time, at least – and he did do the things that are listed in his file. So he's a real teacher."

"Who kills people," Valkyrie added. "But, apart from verifying the facts, we couldn't find out much else about him. We contacted some of the people he has down as references, and they've worked with him, but not for any great length of time."

"Everything about him, in fact, seems to be part-time," Skulduggery said. "There's nothing permanent about him. Nothing settled."

"That's true of a lot of serial killers, isn't it?" Never asked.

"It is," said Skulduggery. "But we don't think he's a serial killer

– or at least not *only* a serial killer. We're interested in his connection to Principal Duenna and, obviously, his method of murder."

"Pushing," said Omen.

"I'm referring more to the shaft the victim was pushed *into*, as per your account."

"Oh. Yeah."

"We sneaked into the school and examined the wall," Valkyrie said. "It looks perfectly normal."

"It opened up, though," Axelia responded, eyes widening. "I swear."

Valkyrie smiled. "We believe you. It just means a stronger kind of magic is at work here – which makes things even more interesting."

The owner came over, put a chipped glass of cloudy water in front of Valkyrie. "That'll be eight fifty," he said.

She looked up at him. "Eight euro and fifty cents? For tap water?"

"Yes."

"For dirty tap water?"

"The tap water is fine. It's the glass that's dirty."

"The glass is chipped."

"It's dirty, too."

Valkyrie nodded. "I'm not paying."

"You have to."

"No, I don't."

"I've already poured your drink. I can't put it back in the tap."

"You can pour it down the drain."

"I'm not pouring eight euro and fifty cents down the drain. It's wasteful."

Valkyrie stood. "And I'm not paying eight fifty for dirty water in a dirty glass."

Now the owner was looking up at her. "It's also chipped."

The café door opened and Miss Gnosis came in, walking towards them with a raised eyebrow. "Making more friends, sweetie?"

"Always," Valkyrie growled.

"Could I have a tea, please?" Miss Gnosis asked sweetly.

The owner shook his head. "Don't have tea."

"That's OK," Miss Gnosis said, "I'll wait." She pulled up another chair.

The owner frowned. "Wait for what?"

"Sorry?" Miss Gnosis said.

"What are you waiting for?"

"I'm waiting for my girlfriend to sit down. Valkyrie?"

Valkyrie hesitated, then sat.

"Thank you," Miss Gnosis said, and the owner wandered back to his counter, his frown deepening. She turned to Omen and his friends. "Now then, are you all ready for exams tomorrow?" When none of them responded, she sighed. "So, instead of studying, the three of you are here without a textbook between you."

"We're traumatised," Never muttered.

"Speaking of which, you're sure it was Mr Chicane you saw last night? Absolutely certain?"

"Positive," said Never.

"Do you know him well?" Valkyrie asked.

Miss Gnosis shook her head. "Barely at all. He seemed to be a nice enough guy. A bit boring, maybe. He's a modules teacher so he's not a permanent member of staff, and I know some in the faculty have been getting annoyed because of all the days he's missed."

"Tell us everything," Skulduggery said to Omen. "Actually, wait, before you do, a little heads-up, as it were – there's another me running around. It's me from the future. It's a long and complicated story, but he calls himself Cadaver Cain and he's me, but he looks nothing like me – his skull is completely different, so you should have no trouble telling us apart. But, just to be sure, when we meet from this moment on, you'll know it's really me if I say, *It's a cold day in hell. Wear your mittens.* Understood?"

"You from the future?" Never said.

"Yes."

"From how far in the future?"

"Seventy-two years. And I know what you're thinking, but no, I am not a robot."

Axelia frowned. "Why would you be a robot?"

"Because it's the future. Why wouldn't I be a robot?"

"I don't understand."

"I travelled to the future for good and reasonable reasons," Valkyrie said, "and I accidentally brought Skulduggery's future self back with me. That's the whole story."

"You can time-travel?" Omen said. "People can time-travel now? Can I time-travel?"

"No, you cannot, but what you can do is tell us about this murder you witnessed and everything that led up to it."

Omen hesitated.

"Is it me," said Never, "or does the fact that we witnessed a murder sound really boring now that we're sitting at a table with a time-traveller?"

"Omen," said Valkyrie. "Speak."

"So, um, OK," said Omen. "Axelia's friend, Bella, was expelled because she saw someone acting suspiciously in the West Tower two weeks ago. She told Axelia about it before she left, but then someone wiped Axelia's mind."

"Well," Axelia said, "not all of it. I just can't remember what Bella told me, and also I was finding it hard to care about any of it."

Miss Gnosis frowned. "You're going to have to get that checked out, Axelia. I don't wish to alarm you, but this is a potentially serious issue. It's obviously done some damage, and, for all we know, it could still be doing damage. I'd like Miss Wicked to take a peek, see if there's anything she can do."

Axelia looked worried. "And if there's not?"

"Then you'll have to seek medical help. I know this sounds

scary, and I'm probably being overcautious, but it's better to be safe than sorry, isn't it?"

Axelia nodded.

"Good girl."

"Do you know who did it?" Valkyrie asked.

"I don't," Axelia said. "All I know is that it happened when I went to see Duenna in her office."

"I never liked Duenna," Miss Gnosis muttered.

"You'll have to keep an eye on her," Skulduggery said. "You're the only one in a position to do so."

"I think we can bring Arabella Wicked into this, though, can't we?" Miss Gnosis asked. "We can trust her."

"Best not," Valkyrie said. "The more people who know, the greater the chance of someone else finding out."

"You just don't like her."

"I neither like nor dislike your beautiful ex-girlfriend who's still in love with you and who happens to be taller than me," Valkyrie said.

Miss Gnosis nodded. "That's convincing."

"I have a question," said Never. "Now that we've told you what's been going on, and what we saw, you can go in and arrest everyone, right? You're Arbiters – you can arrest whoever you want."

"We could," Skulduggery replied, "and we could get a Sensitive to poke around inside their heads, and that might get us the answers we need. But more than likely Chicane and Duenna and whoever wiped Axelia's mind—"

"Again," Axelia said, "not all of it."

"—would have some significant psychic blocks in place. Getting through them would take time, time in which any co-conspirators might accelerate whatever plans they have in motion. The best thing to do at this stage is to uncover as much as we can before we start hauling people in."

"By co-conspirators," Axelia said, "you mean the Supreme Mage, don't you?"

"Acting Supreme Mage, and I do, yes."

"I have another question," said Never. "Is it true, then? Creed actually came back to life?"

Valkyrie grunted. "It's true."

"And he's OK? He's not a zombie or something weird?"

"He appears to have been returned to full health," Skulduggery said. "As annoying as that may be."

"So what are you going to do about Chicane?" Omen asked. "What's your next step?"

Valkyrie glanced at Skulduggery before answering. "Actually... it might not be as simple as that. You might have to take the lead on this one."

Omen looked at her. "Usually when I bring you something like this, you immediately run in and start hitting people."

"And that is still our favourite method of operation," Skulduggery said, "and, if we weren't expecting to be embroiled in a ridiculous amount of trouble in the next few days, we would surely storm this particular Bastille."

"I don't know what that means."

"The Bastille is a small island nation off Paraguay," Valkyrie informed him.

"It most decidedly is not," Skulduggery said. "Omen, our primary reason for meeting with you today is to actually ask for *your* help."

Omen swallowed.

"As you know," Skulduggery continued, "whenever there's the slightest chance of danger rearing its ugly yet strangely alluring head, we tend to advise you to run in the opposite direction."

Omen nodded. "And I've appreciated that, I have. I've discovered that I'm just not cut out for action and adventure."

"Yet now we must ask that you run *towards* danger."

"Oh," said Omen.

"Run towards it," said Valkyrie, "but not *into* it. Run alongside it, maybe."

"Yes," Skulduggery said. "If you could somehow manage to be danger-adjacent at the very most, that would be ideal. You are aware of the Kith, yes? Damocles Creed is planning an Activation on a grand scale on Draíocht, in nine days' time, that will send out a wave of energy that will transform a million people into Kith, and kill some seven billion more, in his search for the Child of the Faceless Ones."

Axelia went pale. "He's going to kill seven billion people?"

"We're going to stop him," Valkyrie assured her.

"But that's what he's planning to do?"

"The killing-seven-billion thing is more of a side effect than an actual goal, but yes."

"Right," Axelia said quietly. "OK, this might seem very childish and stupid and immature, and you might all laugh at me, but I seriously think that if we call my parents they'll know what to do."

"Hey," Miss Gnosis said, looking her in the eyes, "trust Valkyrie and Skulduggery, OK? They've saved the world a lot, and they'll do it again now. We're going to be fine."

"This is very true, Axelia," said Skulduggery. "If anyone can do it, it's probably us. But we are, as we said, going to need your help. To generate the Activation Wave, Creed will use Seven Pillars to form a massive sigil in Roarhaven called the Ensh-Arak. He'll also need some way to focus that power, and a monster is involved, or at least the monster's eye is, so that's something else we'll have to watch out for. Is everyone clear so far?"

"What kind of monster?" asked Never.

"We don't know," said Valkyrie.

"What's the monster going to do?"

"We don't know that, either."

"How is Creed going to focus the power?" Miss Gnosis asked.

"Again, we don't know," said Valkyrie. "Everyone seems to be focusing on what we don't know – how about focusing on what we do?"

"Good idea, Valkyrie," said Skulduggery. "Those Seven Pillars are in the High Sanctuary, the Dark Cathedral, locations on Carnivore Row, Razorblade Alley, Wallow Street, Suture Street, and Corrival Academy. We need to ensure that at least one of these Pillars is sabotaged."

"And seeing as how you're in the school anyway," Valkyrie said to Omen, "we figured you could focus your efforts there."

"I'm sorry," said Never, "but what does a Pillar look like?"

"When it's active," Skulduggery said, "it will most likely be a massive column of energy, so it will need adequate space."

Valkyrie said, "The one we found in the Dark Cathedral was basically a gigantic chimney rising up through the middle of the whole building – so that's what you'd be looking for."

"The West Tower could be a gigantic chimney thing," Omen said, eyes widening. "So does that mean the stuff that's going on with us is linked to what's going on with you?"

Skulduggery nodded. "Very likely."

Never frowned. "But, if the West Tower is the Pillar, why is Chicane throwing people into it?"

"We don't know," Skulduggery admitted. "We don't know much, as you've probably realised. A lot of this is pure speculation."

Omen straightened in his chair. "I don't think I can blow up the school based on speculation."

"What?" Valkyrie said quickly. "No. No blowing up the school. We don't know how Corrival becomes a Pillar, so you've got to find that out. And, when you do, you need to find a way to put it out of action. Destroy the Pillar, Omen, don't blow up the whole school."

Omen sat back, relieved.

"So while these *schoolkids* are doing that," Miss Gnosis said, "what are the wildly irresponsible adults going to be doing?"

Valkyrie nudged Skulduggery. "I think she's talking to you."

"We'll be continuing our investigation into who tried to kill us and how they're connected to this whole thing," he said. "There's also the slight possibility that we may be arrested on a charge of conspiracy to commit various and sundry crimes, but I can't be sure about that one."

Miss Gnosis glared at Valkyrie. "Arrested?"

"*Possibly* arrested," Valkyrie clarified, "which is completely different to *definitely* arrested, but a close relative of *probably won't be* arrested, so you really have nothing to worry about."

The door opened and Detective Rylent walked in with a load of City Guard officers trailing after him.

"Ooooh," Valkyrie said, "yeah, we're definitely getting arrested."

# 70

Valkyrie and Skulduggery stood and faced the cops as they approached.

"Detective Rylent," Skulduggery said, "how are you this fine evening?"

"Skulduggery Pleasant, Valkyrie Cain," Rylent said, "you're both under arrest for conspiring to assassinate acting Supreme Mage Damocles Creed."

"What an outrageous accusation," Skulduggery said, not sounding the least bit outraged. "You've brought a lot of officers with you just to take us in."

"Yes, I have."

Skulduggery nodded. "It won't be enough."

Skulduggery lunged and Valkyrie dived and the world became a shuddering, shaking maelstrom of fists and snarls. The cops blurred into one entity with many faces that reared up just to be smashed down. They grabbed at her and she grabbed at them and her suit absorbed a whole lot of damage and she inflicted a whole lot more damage and someone yanked her hair and lightning leaped from her fingers and leaped between the cops and then she was stumbling over writhing bodies and running for the back of the café, through the kitchen, Skulduggery right behind her. There were cops coming through the back door and she launched herself at them, energy crackling, hitting them like a cannonball and flying out of the door, veering upwards, landing on a rooftop with Skulduggery dropping down beside her.

Valkyrie peered over the edge at all the City Guard Elementals using the air to boost themselves upwards. "I thought you shared your flying techniques with the world."

"I did," he said.

"Then why can't these idiots fly?"

"Because flying is difficult."

A City Guard cop powered off the pavement below and went screaming by them. "As you can see." They ran to the other side of the roof. "We need to get back down to street level. They'll be expecting us to fly out of here."

Something poked Valkyrie in the back at the same time as a shot rang out.

"Snipers," she said.

Skulduggery boosted them from rooftop to rooftop, bullets whining through the air around them. They dropped between buildings, Valkyrie nearly twisting an ankle as she landed. A patrol car screeched to a halt in front of them and both doors on the passenger side opened wide.

"Hello there," Cadaver Cain said from behind the wheel. "Would you care for a lift at all?"

They hesitated, and glanced at each other, and then Skulduggery got in the front and Valkyrie slid in the back.

"Seat belts," said Cadaver as he pulled out on to the road.

# 71

They passed cop cars screaming the other way, and when they were clear Cadaver cut off the siren and slowed to a reasonable speed.

"Engine cars are fun," Cadaver said. "I'd forgotten just how much of this time period was enjoyable."

Skulduggery pressed his gun into Cadaver's head. "Pull over."

"This might not be the best time for that," Cadaver said, tapping the accelerator to give them a little boost that took them across the next junction just as another patrol car raced by. "I understand and acknowledge that you won't believe me when I say this, yet I have to say it in order to get you to the point where you *do* believe me, so... I'm here to help."

"You have a funny way of helping," Valkyrie growled.

"By saving you from being arrested?"

"We didn't need saving," Skulduggery said.

"On the contrary, they would have surrounded you within two minutes. You would have fought them, of course, until you realised the only way to escape would be to seriously injure officers of the City Guard – and you won't be prepared to do that for at least another week."

"You're a psychic now, are you?"

"Me? Not at all."

"I meant," Valkyrie said, sitting forward, "that if you're here to help, attacking us is a funny way of showing it."

Cadaver nodded. "I apologise for that."

"Oh, well, that's OK then, all is forgiven." She glared. "Care to explain yourself, or is the apology all we're getting?"

"After I lost you, Valkyrie, I lost myself," Cadaver said. "All the pain and all the darkness that swirled round me, that drove me to take on the name of Lord Vile – it came back. I left Skulduggery Pleasant where he belonged – in happier times, with better people. I became someone new – someone strong enough to survive a planet ruled by the Faceless Ones.

"They were right, you know – all those fanatics who assured us it would be a better world. We used to think that if the Faceless Ones ever returned they would destroy everything, even their disciples. But they didn't. They trampled on cities and burned entire countries and billions of mortals died and the billions that didn't die became slaves, but they remade the world, and they allowed sorcerers to build a paradise for themselves.

"The Sanctuaries crumbled, of course. They fought back initially, but once it became clear that the Faceless Ones couldn't be defeated and the changes they'd made couldn't be reversed, the fighting slowed, and then stopped. Sorcerers I fought beside just gave up and joined the enemy. I heard all their excuses. They wanted to continue the struggle, but from the inside. They wanted to topple the new world order through peaceful means. They wanted to save the mortals by making the fanatics understand that we're all one race. That's how they justified it."

"And what about you?" Valkyrie asked. "You were living right alongside them."

"I was an oddity," Cadaver said. "An amusing sideshow attraction. I couldn't effect change, I didn't have the resources and I didn't have the support. I couldn't hurt the Faceless Ones in any way, so I just went after the sorcerers, but they caught me again and again. They punished me, then released me. Eventually, I promised not to kill any more mages, and they left me in relative peace, so I was just as bad as the Sanctuary sorcerers who changed sides. I capitulated, exactly like they did."

Valkyrie could feel her anger dissipating. "I mean... OK, that's a horrible story."

"Ah," said Cadaver, "but it's not over yet. I sank further and further into darkness, and I started to remember things. Memories that had been hidden from me for so long came to the surface."

"Memories of what?" Skulduggery asked, lowering his gun.

"My time as Lord Vile."

"I remember everything from that time."

Cadaver laughed. "Even if I didn't know the truth, that still wouldn't have convinced me, Skulduggery. There are blank spots in your memory – some small, some gaping. You've always wondered why." He pulled the car into a side street. "We'll need to change vehicles."

He got out. Skulduggery and Valkyrie did, too, keeping a wary distance as they followed him to a van.

"Skulduggery," he said, tossing him the keys, "you'll have to drive. I don't have a façade in this form." He climbed in the back.

"I don't like this," Skulduggery muttered, and got behind the wheel.

Valkyrie hesitated, and went to sit beside Cadaver, where she could keep an eye on him.

When they were on the road again and headed for Shudder's Gate, Cadaver continued his story.

"You're wearing your necronaut suit, Valkyrie. Those suits were designed by Necromancers for Deep Venturing – the exploration of dead dimensions. The vast majority of dimensions that Shunters manage to find are devoid of any life at all, let alone intelligent life – but there are universes out there where life is simply not possible. Not because of any atmospheric condition or inhospitable environment, but because death itself permeates every molecule, every atom. Those suits allow Necromancers to study death from the inside. Of course, when I was a Necromancer, I didn't need such a suit."

"You went Deep Venturing?" she asked.

"I walked on dead worlds, Valkyrie. You have no idea what it's like to stand on a world and know with absolute certainty that you are the only person in the universe. It's both incredibly humbling and wonderfully self-aggrandising."

"I'm sure you managed to come down more heavily on one side than the other."

That made his voice smile. "I did, as it happens. But a most curious thing happened while I was exploring these vast, empty universes. I felt someone watching me."

Skulduggery activated his façade as they approached the gate. "Can you just skip to the end of this story and summarise?"

"My," said Cadaver, "I can be grouchy, can't I?"

"Yep," said Valkyrie.

"How I tell the story is as important as why I tell the story, younger me. It's all part of the experience. And, seeing as how this is exactly how you tell stories to other people, it might be useful for you to be on the receiving end for a change."

"If there's one thing I've learned," Valkyrie said to Skulduggery, "it is not to interrupt you. Just keep your mouth shut as much as possible and you'll eventually reach the end."

"The two of you are ganging up on me," Skulduggery muttered. "I don't like it."

They passed through Shudder's Gate without anyone trying to stop them, and drove on.

"I encountered beings known as the Viddu De," Cadaver said, "a race of dead gods who had fled from the Faceless Ones. Weakened, practically powerless, they were trapped in their dead realm. They spoke to me. They told me of their history. They showed me their secrets. To the Viddu De, time means nothing. They exist within death, and within death all things happen at once. Within death, it's possible to see the hand of fate at work."

Skulduggery nodded. "Just vague enough to not make any sense whatsoever."

"I have to admit," Cadaver said, "it's not easy explaining concepts that sometimes defy language. To be plain about it, the Viddu De allowed me – allowed Lord Vile – to see all possibilities at once. That's why he could never be taken by surprise on the battlefield. That's why he was never beaten."

Skulduggery tilted his head. "You're claiming that you could see the future."

"Yes. That's why I left the Necromancer Order. It's why I chose to fight alongside the man who'd murdered me and my family. It's why I fought on the same side as the man who murdered... well, you know what I'm referring to, don't you, Skulduggery? It's also why I betrayed Abyssinia. That's not over yet, by the way. The consequences of that partnership? It's not over for you."

"Man," said Valkyrie, "I love it when people get cryptic. There's nothing I like more than being confused. So tell me this, Cadaver, if you could see the future, why bother joining up with Mevolent if you were just going to abandon him a few years later?"

"Because life is a complicated journey."

"Uh-huh. So is it why you went back to being Skulduggery?"

"It is, indeed. I had to block all memories of the Viddu De, of course. I knew what the next few centuries held for me, but I needed to be able to make the decisions I would make without interference."

"That had nothing to do with why I hung up the armour," Skulduggery said.

"How would you know if those memories are being blocked?" Valkyrie asked. Even though he was facing the other way, she could feel his disapproval in the way he tilted his head. "Sorry," she mumbled.

"The decisions I made as Lord Vile have led me directly to this point," Cadaver said. "I saw how the war against Mevolent would end. I saw my life afterwards. I saw Valkyrie, and I saw the changes she would bring to me and to who I was. I saw the Activation Wave turn her, and I saw myself alone in the world the Faceless Ones remade. I saw my lowest moment, my darkest moment, and I knew that was when I would remember. I set that knowledge to one side for all those centuries, but it was there, just waiting for me to be ready for it."

"Just like you were ready for me to travel into the future," said Valkyrie.

"Yes."

"This is all part of a plan."

"Somewhat ironic, isn't it? I've always hated plans. I always felt they made you predictable. I've changed my mind about that."

"If you could see every possible future," Skulduggery said, "then why would you let the Faceless Ones win?"

Cadaver tilted his head. "They haven't won."

"They returned, didn't they?"

"Yes," said Cadaver. "But that doesn't mean they've won."

"So you can still see every possible future?" Valkyrie asked.

"Yes. Every decision branches out endlessly and I have to decide which branch I want to take."

"It sounds complicated," Skulduggery said.

"It is."

"But you manage."

"It was overwhelming at first, but I've learned to master the skill."

Now that Roarhaven had been left in the rear-view mirror, Skulduggery pulled the van into a field and they all got out. Valkyrie and Skulduggery stood together. Cadaver faced them.

"And what do you want?" Skulduggery asked. "What do you get out of all of this?"

"I'm like you," he said. "I want to avert the future. I'm going to stop Creed's Activation Wave."

"We did stop it," Skulduggery said. "And then Uriah Serrate

brought Creed back to life. But, now that you're here, you can supply us with a quick step-by-step guide on how to avoid this particular apocalypse, yes? And you can answer all of our questions. For example, how does Creed focus all this energy the Pillars will generate? And what monster is involved, and how, and what makes its eye so special?"

"The only thing I can tell you," Cadaver responded, "is that the key to altering the future is preventing the Activation Wave from being triggered."

"So, out of everything that you say you know, the only thing you can tell us is the astonishingly obvious thing that we'd already decided on?"

"The future needs to unfold how it unfolds."

"Isn't that a tad risky, though?" Valkyrie asked. "Focusing on only one aspect? Wouldn't dismantling the entire project be safer?"

"Not even remotely." Cadaver tapped his skull. "I've looked into the future, remember. In effect, this has already happened. I just have to wait for the universe to catch up with what I've seen. The trick is for you to continue as if I'm wrong. The only way events unfold as I've seen them is if you do everything in your power to save the day. Pretend, Skulduggery, that you don't trust me one little bit."

"That will be so difficult for me," Skulduggery said.

Cadaver laughed again. "It's so good talking to you. I've seen it, obviously, I've seen these moments, but the actual words we exchange hop around, they change, they never quite settle... so it's good to hear them out loud. Live, as it were. Good conversation is so hard to find in the future. Everyone's a true believer. It's all so incredibly boring."

Valkyrie raised her hand. "Can I ask a question?"

"Of course," Skulduggery and Cadaver said at the same time.

Valkyrie kept her eyes on Cadaver. "Since you're the future version of Skulduggery, has this already happened for you? Do you remember this from Skulduggery's point of view? Do you remember looking at yourself right now and thinking, *God, he's annoying?*"

Skulduggery glanced at her. "That's exactly what I'm thinking."

She shrugged. "I know."

"It's a curious sensation," said Cadaver. "I can't remember what happens next, but I do remember it once it's happened."

Valkyrie frowned. "But we can all remember something once it's happened."

"Yes," said Cadaver, "but I remember it twice."

"This is very confusing," said Valkyrie.

"It's like when you absorb the memories of a reflection," Cadaver said. "You know what that's like, of course."

"Yeah," she said. "It never stopped being weird."

"And that is my cue to leave," said Cadaver. "You have things to do and so do I. I can't give you any advice, I'm afraid, or events would veer off course. All I can say is that I'm excited to work with you both." He lifted off the ground. "You can keep the van for as long as you need it," he said, and flew away.

"I don't trust him," Skulduggery said.

"I've noticed."

They got back in the van, reversed out of the field, and started driving towards Dublin.

"I was at my lowest ebb when I decided to abandon the name Skulduggery Pleasant the first time round, and it led to years of death and destruction as Lord Vile. Now he tells us that at some stage in the future I get low enough to abandon the name again, but I manage to stay a good guy?"

"You don't think it's likely?" she asked.

"I know me, Valkyrie. If I were to lose you in the way that he lost you, if I were to live in a world ruled by the Faceless Ones with no hope of fighting back, no hope of effecting change, no hope of anything... If I go dark a second time, I stay dark. I know that in my soul."

"So we don't trust him," she said. "But, if we're right and he's a threat, then how are we going to beat him if he knows exactly what's going to happen? It'll get very complicated."

"Then we'll keep it simple," Skulduggery said. "He's from a future that we're already changing simply because we know it's coming. When you first saw him in the future, was he wearing a hat?"

"Yes," she said. "Navy blue with a black band."

"Like the one I have at home?"

"It's hard to tell. You have so many navy blue hats with black bands."

"So in order to change the future, even slightly, all I have to do is decide to get rid of all my navy blue hats with black bands. It's just like how prophecies are mere possibilities of what might happen. Our knowledge of the future changes the future."

"OK," said Valkyrie. "That's... reassuring. I'm reassured."

"I'm glad."

"Are you going to throw out all of your navy blue hats with black bands?"

"What? No. Why would I do that? They're good hats."

# 72

Sebastian knocked on the front door and a large man with many muscles answered.

"Hello," said Sebastian.

"Who are you meant to be?"

"My name is Sebastian. I was wondering if—"

"Why are you dressed like that?"

"It's fancy dress."

"Oh."

"Are you Mr Bicker?"

"Yeah. What do you want?"

"I believe you've kidnapped a little girl and I'd like her back, please."

Bicker's expression didn't change. "You think I did that, do you? You think I kidnapped someone?"

"And murdered two people."

"You think I kidnapped a little girl and murdered two people and you knock on my door and what are you gonna do? You gonna ask for the kidnapped little girl to be returned?"

"Yes."

"And there's no one with you," Bicker said. "You come here instead of going to the City Guard and having them bust my door in. Why haven't you gone to the cops, you weird little freak, if I'm such a bad and dangerous man?"

"I'd really prefer if we could resolve this without the authorities knowing about it."

"Uh-huh. I bet you do. Why is that, though? Is it because the kidnapped little girl is one of the most powerful new sorcerers on the planet?"

"Oh, she's a lot more than that."

"You had her. You lost her. We have her. We're gonna sell her. Do you know that there's this Crenga out there, and it's paying all kinds of ridiculous money for mages with rare powers? Dunno what it's doing with them and I don't care. But that's where this little girl is going."

"Do you have her? I'd like to see her, please."

Bicker scratched his head. "I don't get it. I don't get your whole thing here. You think you can take me down, is that it? You think you can take down me and my friend?"

"Is Mr Gobemouche here also?"

"He is. You've been talking to Tantalus, haven't you? Did you let him out of his basement?"

"No," said Sebastian. "He's still there."

Bicker laughed. "Good. That's funny. That's good. Well, you want the little girl? You stay right there and I'll fetch her for you."

"I don't think you will."

"You stay right there," Bicker said, and walked back into the house. Sebastian waited until he had disappeared into another room before stepping in after him.

The house was pretty basic. No effort or imagination had gone into the décor. If Sebastian's mask allowed him to smell, he was pretty sure the place would reek of socks and stale sweat. He took the shock stick from beneath his coat and moved to the wall, right beside the door Bicker had gone through. He waited a moment.

Bicker came back in, holding a pistol, and Sebastian brought the stick down, shattering the bones in his wrist. Bicker roared, stumbling against the doorframe, clutching his arm. Sebastian watched him. Turning the pain into anger, Bicker lunged and Sebastian dodged, tapping the shock stick against his temple. Bicker powered onwards for a few steps and fell, face down and unconscious.

Sebastian waited, listening for running footsteps. Instead, he heard music. He followed it to a door.

He knocked.

"Yeah?" came the voice from inside.

He knocked again.

The music was turned down and then the door opened. A second muscular man – Gobemouche, presumably – frowned at him. "Huh?"

Sebastian kicked Gobemouche in the groin and whacked him over the head with the shock stick. Neither blow particularly bothered the man.

*Uh-oh.*

Gobemouche took hold of Sebastian's coat lapels and threw him – *he threw him* – the entire length of the hall. As Sebastian came to a rolling, sprawling stop on the floor, the thought occurred to him that maybe he should have spent a little longer trying to find out Gobemouche's discipline.

"I don't want to hurt you," he said as Gobemouche advanced. Gobemouche laughed.

The door to the utility room splintered beautifully under Sebastian's weight and momentum. He landed on top of the washing machine. As Gobemouche reached for him again, Sebastian kicked out, his two feet slamming into Gobemouche's face.

Again, no more than a mild flicker of irritation in response.

"I'm here for the girl," Sebastian said.

"I'll take you to her," Gobemouche said, grabbing hold of Sebastian's ankle and swinging him against the wall. Pain exploded across his shoulder as it crunched, and he fell awkwardly, Gobemouche still gripping him.

Then he was dragged out into the hall, passing his hat along the way. He hadn't even noticed it come off. He didn't bother struggling as Gobemouche pushed open a door. *Oh, great, another basement.* Down they went, each step a new kick in the back, until Gobemouche flung Sebastian across the cold concrete floor.

Darquesse looked down at him. Her wrists were shackled, the chain looped behind a pipe. They did like to shackle people in basements, these guys.

"Hi," Darquesse said.

"Hey," he wheezed.

"Have you come to rescue me?"

He nodded.

She looked away. "Oh, good."

Sebastian stood up, turned to Gobemouche. "OK," he said, "you probably don't realise this, but everything's going according to my plan."

"That so?"

"I got you to take me down here, didn't I? So please, make it easy on yourself. Give me the key to the shackles here and then stand aside. I didn't want to hurt your friend and I don't want to hurt you."

"You got a lucky shot," Bicker said, coming down the steps. He held his broken wrist close to his chest. In his other hand, he carried the gun. "Now it's my turn."

He went to a bench on the other side of the cellar, started searching clumsily through metal boxes.

"Was it you?" Sebastian asked.

"Was it me what?"

"Did you kill my friends?"

"Yeah," said Bicker. "That was me." He found what he was looking for, and popped a dried leaf into his mouth. He closed his eyes, waiting for the pain to subside.

"You didn't have to do that," Sebastian said.

"I know," Bicker replied, his eyes opening slowly. "But what

I've come to understand – in all my years of involvement in the shadier side of life – is that it's always better to kill witnesses. Always. Without exception."

"You didn't kill Tantalus."

Bicker laughed. "Tantalus isn't a witness. He's a conspirator. You – you're a witness. So I'm gonna have to kill you."

"Do you think I came here without backup?" Sebastian asked. "If we don't walk out of here in the next few minutes, my associates will—"

"Your associates," Bicker interrupted, sounding confused. "Oh! Oh, you mean those three idiots?"

Beneath his mask, Sebastian paled.

"The three idiots who came in while Gobemouche was kicking the living daylights out of you? The morons who walked right up to me just as I was picking up this gun? Those associates?"

"What did you do with them?"

"They're upstairs," said Bicker. "Handcuffed together. I'm sorry, were you actually relying on those losers?"

"Let them go."

"Well, obviously, I'm gonna kill them. That's just a given. I mean, what's the difference between killing one of you, and killing four of you? It's just numbers by this stage."

"Can you kill this one now?" Gobemouche pressed. "I need to use the toilet."

"Right," Bicker said, "sorry." He pulled a face at Sebastian. "He's got a small bladder."

"Come on!" Gobemouche said. "There's no need for that! Just kill who you need to kill and get it over with. And I don't have a small bladder. I have a normal-sized bladder. It's just a little weak, that's all, and I've been drinking a lot of water lately in an effort to lose weight."

"Sorry, man," Bicker said.

"You always do this," Gobemouche muttered. "You always embarrass me."

"I'm sorry, I said."

"Just kill him, would you?"

"You know what?" Bicker said. "I'm a really bad shot when I use my left hand – I'd probably miss, or shoot him in the leg, and then he'd start screaming and all the blood would get everywhere and... I think you should do it." He held out the gun.

Gobemouche stared at it. "You serious?"

"Yeah, I'm serious, you big ox."

"You'd let me kill him?"

"I figure you've earned it, don't you? You're the one who dragged him down here, after all."

Gobemouche took the gun. Held it in his hand. "Thank you," he said softly.

"No big deal."

"No," Gobemouche said, "it is a big deal. This isn't just about a gun. This is about everything. This *means* everything. So thank you."

They looked at each other.

"You kill him good," Bicker said, smiling.

Gobemouche aimed right at Sebastian's head and Sebastian braced himself and Gobemouche pulled the trigger and nothing happened. He pulled the trigger again and – again – no bullet.

Sebastian looked at Darquesse.

"Sebastian isn't my father," she said, "because I don't have a father, but he's the one I picked to raise me. And I don't like the idea of you shooting him."

Gobemouche handed the gun back to Bicker. "I think it's broken."

"You shouldn't kill people," Darquesse continued. "I've killed people. I've killed lots of people. I didn't care about the people I killed because to me it was like stepping on grass."

Bicker frowned at her. "What are you on about?"

"You don't stop to consider the grass's feelings. You just step on it. That's how I feel about killing people. But you... you *are* people, and even I know that you shouldn't go around killing other people. It's wrong."

Bicker popped out the magazine with some difficulty due to his broken bones, checked it, and then reloaded and handed it back. "Try it now," he said.

Gobemouche racked the slide and prepared to fire and the gun disappeared. "Uh," he said. "What?"

The gun reappeared, floating in the air before Darquesse. It turned into a shock stick and drifted over to Sebastian, who took it.

"That's impossible," said Bicker, speaking softly. "You're bound. Your magic is bound."

"My magic could only be bound if you'd put shackles on me," Darquesse told him.

"But we did," said Gobemouche.

"A few years ago, I was all set to destroy the world, and a few people got together and made me see stuff so that I thought I *had* destroyed the world. That was clever. That was very clever. And that's what I did to you. You never put those shackles on me. You only thought you did."

The shackles disappeared and Bicker and Gobemouche stepped back, their hands up.

"How were you going to sell me," Darquesse asked, "if you didn't even know who I was?"

"Spare us," said Bicker.

"Like you spared Tarry? Like you spared Demure?"

"Please..."

Darquesse folded her arms. "Relax. I'm not going to do anything. Sebastian, however, is going to beat you up."

"I am?" said Sebastian.

She nodded. "But if you can beat up Sebastian, you get to go free."

"I've got an injury," Bicker said, and gasped. He shook his wrist, a grin spreading across his face.

"You healed him?" Sebastian muttered. "Why did you heal him?"

"It has to be a fair fight," said Darquesse, "or else it doesn't count."

"But two against one isn't fair."

"Which is why the shock stick delivers ten times the damage."

"And we go free?" Bicker said. "We beat him, we go free and you don't do anything to us?"

"That's the deal."

"One at a time," Gobemouche asked, "or both together?"

Darquesse shrugged. "Whatever you want."

Sebastian groaned and went to meet them. He gripped the shock stick tighter, and the carvings lit up with energy.

Gobemouche charged and Sebastian dodged left, whipping the stick into his shin. The big man flipped all the way over and crashed to the ground, and Sebastian cracked him over the head and he went rolling into the corner.

Bicker stared. Sebastian stared.

Bicker ripped his shirt open and something pressed against his chest from within – a face, a snarling, snapping face – and Sebastian hurled the shock stick. It hit Bicker between the eyes with a flash of energy and threw him back into the wall. He collapsed, and the gist faded away.

Sebastian took a moment, making sure everyone who was supposed to stay down stayed down, then turned to Darquesse. "You could have saved them," he said.

She looked puzzled. "They're still alive."

"I mean Tarry and Demure. You could have saved them. Why didn't you?"

"I didn't know what was happening until it had happened."

"With Tarry, fair enough. He answered the door and they shot him. But you heard the gun go off, right? You had plenty of time to stop them from killing Demure."

"I was in my room. And my magic was bound."

"The moment you heard the gunshot you would have known what was happening. You would have sensed how many there were and what they intended to do. At the very least, you would have had time to climb out the window and get your magic back."

"I was confused. I didn't know what was—"

"Do you know what I think, Darquesse? I think you were bored and you let it happen to see what they'd do. That's why you let them kidnap you." She didn't say anything to that. "And that's why you let them kill Demure. Because you don't care what happens to other people."

"I stopped them from shooting you."

"And then you set them on me. I could have been killed."

"I wouldn't have let that happen."

"See, Darquesse, the thing is I don't know if I believe you."

She looked away, her lower lip trembling, and then vanished.

# 73

The first day of exams had gone pretty well, all things considered. Omen had found the exam hall without a problem, he'd been on time, he'd brought along everything he was supposed to bring, and his desk hadn't burst into flames or anything dramatic like that. On the downside, he hadn't known the answers to most of the questions, and he was pretty sure that the answers he did know were wrong.

Every silver lining, he concluded, had a dark cloud within it.

He was just happy that he'd been able to concentrate long enough to write *anything*. That detective, Rylent, had questioned them all so thoroughly that, by the time Omen fell into bed last night, he was doubting his own name. Axelia and Never had been similarly shaken, but none of them had talked. Axelia said Rylent had hinted that maybe he'd get a Sensitive to find the answers she was keeping from him, but she'd reminded him of the laws against poking through the minds of minors and he'd backed off.

Omen had dragged his friends into enough trouble recently, so, when he woke at two in the morning and decided to go and check on the West Tower, he went alone. He wasn't planning on hanging around – a quick peek and then back to bed, that was his intention. It's not like he was expecting to see anything suspicious, after all.

So, of course, he saw Mr Chicane dragging a struggling man towards the hidden door in the wall. Of course he did.

Omen didn't have time to call anyone, didn't have time to raise the alarm, didn't have time to do anything except sprint forward in an attempt to stop the struggling man from being pushed in.

He got halfway there when Chicane gave the final push and the man disappeared over the edge and screamed all the way down.

At the same time, Chicane heard Omen's footsteps and turned, frowning at him, and instead of slowing and stopping, Omen put on a burst of speed and barrelled into the teacher, sending him flying.

But Omen got tangled in his legs and tripped, and suddenly Chicane was hauling him off the ground.

"Mr Darkly," Chicane said in his ear, "what are you doing out of bed at this hour?"

Omen twisted with an elbow to the ribs and swung a punch, but Chicane saw it coming and wrenched Omen's arm behind his back.

Omen dropped to one knee, absolutely certain that the tiniest increase in pressure would pop his arm out of its socket. "We're on to you!" he cried. "Skulduggery Pleasant and Valkyrie Cain – they know you killed that other guy! They know about the Activation Wave and the Pillars and everything!"

"Do they now?" Chicane said. "That is interesting."

"You... you better let me go."

"I don't know if I can do that," said Chicane. "I'm in quite the dilemma, Omen, I really am. Do I kill you? I've put so much work into this whole thing, so much effort... And my boss will not be pleased if I let you mess it up. Honestly, and this is nothing personal, but I really think you should probably die tonight."

His free hand closing round the back of Omen's neck, Chicane brought him right to the edge. Far below – far, far below – a blue light flickered in the dark.

"No," said Omen. "Please."

"I know what you're thinking," said Chicane. "You're thinking, *That drop is going to kill me.* Well, I assure you that it won't. You'll barely get halfway down before your body is vaporised. And I know what you're thinking now. You're thinking, *Oh, God, oh, God, I'm going to die.* Well, that's not entirely right, either. Yes, your physical body will burn away to nothing, but your soul, Omen, your magic, will be sucked into a whirling tornado of energy. Doesn't that sound fun?"

Omen shook his head violently.

"Oh, you're just saying that because you don't want your consciousness to evaporate. It's perfectly understandable, but I'm afraid you must face the consequences of your—"

Omen waved his free hand and a blast of air hit Chicane and sent him stumbling over the edge.

Omen stared.

"Help."

Omen took a step, and leaned over.

Chicane clung to the thinnest sliver of a ledge. "Please," he whispered.

"Oh, God."

"Don't let me die, Omen."

Omen dropped to his belly, thrust his hand down and grabbed Chicane's sleeve. He tried to pull him up, but it was way harder than it looked in the movies. People were heavy.

"Don't let me go," Chicane said. His voice was quiet. Terrified.

Omen heaved. It didn't do much good.

"I know I intended to kill you just a few moments ago," Chicane said, "but don't let that stop you from putting in the effort to save me now. You're a good kid, Omen. A decent young man. If you let me die here, you'll never forgive yourself. I'd hate for that to weigh on your conscience."

"That's... really nice of you," Omen said, straining.

"The recent attempt on your life notwithstanding, as a teacher, I really care about your future well-being."

"Please stop talking."

"I'm just trying to motivate you. Like any good teacher should."

"You're a... wow, you're heavy... you're a terrible teacher."

"We can talk about that later, Omen. Right now I need you to pull me up."

"I can't."

"Then I'll climb up over you. Are you secure?"

"Not really."

"That's unfortunate," Chicane said, and flung his other arm up. His fingers dug into Omen's shoulder. "Don't let go now," he said, and started climbing.

Omen focused on not moving as Chicane clambered over him. Once he was on solid ground, he let himself roll, coming to a stop on Omen's legs, and lay there, panting. It struck Omen that he was in a potentially very bad situation. He locked eyes with his teacher, and Chicane sat up. They got to their feet – slowly – Omen's back to the open shaft.

Chicane looked at him. "So what do we do now?"

Omen swallowed. "You hand yourself in, I think."

"That's an option, yes. Not a particular favourite, I have to admit, but definitely an option. That'll be option one. Option two is I push you – which would solve two of my most immediate problems at the same time. Problem one is that I can't very well have a gawky teenager spoiling plans that have been years in the making, now can I? My boss... he would literally kill me. And problem two is that I still need to deliver one more person. You're a person. By pushing you in, my work would be done. On the other hand, you did just save my life."

Omen nodded.

"Even after I tried to kill you, you saved my life. That was astonishingly decent of you, very brave, and profoundly stupid."

Omen nodded again.

"But should that bravery, that decency, that stupidity be punished? Can I do that? I've killed many people – many, many people – but how will I be able to look myself in the mirror tomorrow if I kill the boy who just saved my life? The simple answer is just not to look in the mirror in the morning, but that would make brushing my hair difficult. What do you think I should do, Omen?"

"Let me go and turn yourself in."

"What do you think I should do in the real world?"

"Uh... let me go?"

Chicane hesitated. He shook his head. Then nodded. Then looked unsure.

Finally, he just sighed. "Right, go on back to bed. If you want my advice, you won't tell any teachers or cops about this. Believe me when I say that you can't trust most of them."

Omen nodded. "OK. I won't. I promise."

Chicane lunged and Omen tensed, waiting for the push – but Chicane lowered his hands again.

"Ah, dammit," he said. "I thought I could surprise myself, but... ah, whatever. Good luck with the exams, Mr Darkly."

He walked away, and the wall sealed up behind Omen who did his absolute best not to collapse.

# 74

Three years ago...

"I don't want to hurt you," the sorcerer said, energy dancing between his fingertips.

Quell didn't respond. The sickle in his left hand dripped blood. The sickle in his right hand grew thirsty.

Blood dripped from the cut on the sorcerer's leg. It was a deep cut. He'd need medical attention if he survived the next few minutes. Quell doubted he would.

"I just want him," the sorcerer said, his gaze flicking to the mortal cowering on the floor behind Quell. "I just need him to return what he stole. I'm not here to kill anyone."

"I didn't steal anything!" the mortal whined. "I acquired it, fair and square!"

"You paid three mages to steal it."

"I acquired it once it had left your possession! That's called free enterprise!"

Quell didn't care about who was right and who was wrong. He was being paid to protect a wealthy mortal and protect him he would, because the job, the work, the *mission* was all that mattered. It had been this way when he'd been a Cleaver, and it was this way now that he was a Ripper. It was simple and it was clean.

Things had become less simple with Valkyrie. He'd lost his way while training her. He'd let himself become entangled. He'd lost focus. Lost sight of what truly mattered, and didn't notice the ways in which she was changing him. He'd liked being around her. He'd liked the times when they talked and the times when they'd been silent. He'd enjoyed the warmth that came with their relationship.

He wasn't used to relationships. He wasn't used to warmth. It was an odd sensation, the way it filled parts of him he didn't know were there, let alone that they needed filling. When he'd left to take that job in Spain, he'd missed it.

On that job in Russia, closing in on his targets – he'd missed it then, too.

The job in Scotland. The job in Australia. The job in Bulgaria. He'd missed it. He'd missed her.

No matter how many jobs he took or how hard he worked or how many targets he killed or clients he protected, he missed her.

Even now, back in the United States after over a year, he found himself missing her, and the thought struck him as the sorcerer lunged that maybe this was what Valkyrie had been talking about.

He ducked the energy stream and took the sorcerer's hand off at the wrist.

He loved her. The realisation hit him harder than he hit the sorcerer. There was a gap in his life, a gap in who he was, a gap that used to be filled by Valkyrie Cain. He loved her and he'd walked away because he hadn't understood that. But he understood now.

"Please," the sorcerer whimpered. "Please don't kill me."

"I won't kill you," Quell lied.

He lied so that there would be one more moment of hope in the world, and then the sickle blade passed into the meat of the sorcerer's neck at a downward angle, the tip lodging in the clavicle. Quell pulled the sickle free and the sorcerer crumpled.

Quell turned to the wealthy mortal. "I won't be working for you any more."

"But there are others coming for me," the mortal said, hurrying forward on his knees. "This isn't over! I'll double your pay! Triple it!"

But Quell was already walking away.

"Please! Without you, they'll kill me! Without you, I'm a dead man!"

But Quell kept walking.

# 75

Valkyrie looked pretty good as a blonde.

The dye she'd used – top of the line in magical cosmetics – could also be used to lighten eyebrows. The effect was startling. She looked so much less serious with lighter hair, as if the weight of the world – and the fate of the world – wasn't pressing down on her shoulders. It was a nice change to see herself like this – the new colour almost acting like a mask. It meant she could try out different make-up, different lipstick. It meant she could wear different clothes.

It was a nice day so she had her sunglasses on and she was in a cute skirt and a cute top and she had a handbag dangling from one shoulder and her shoes weren't her usual Stompin' Boots, as Militsa liked to call them. She took a selfie and wrote a little message, planning to send it to her girlfriend once she'd ditched the outfit.

Sending it while she was still wearing it would have been way too risky.

She bought an ice cream from the shop on the corner and licked it as she strolled through the Arts District. The tension in the city was entirely absent here. These people had money, and money bought a certain acceptance of the status quo. Nobody here wanted to see Roarhaven disrupted because nobody here would benefit from that disruption. Nobody here needed the change that a revolution would bring.

It was easy to put that stuff out of her head while wearing this disguise. It was easy to focus on the music drifting from the doorways, easy to smile at the men and women who smiled at Valkyrie as she passed – easy to be happy in this company.

Two officers of the City Guard walked by. One of them was busy checking his phone, but the other one looked her up and down and Valkyrie tensed, ready to lunge at him, ready to slam her forehead into the bridge of his nose before his partner knew what the hell was happening. But he gave her a wink, and she arched an eyebrow behind her sunglasses and walked on. She heard him mutter something to his friend and they both laughed, and she resisted the urge to inflict damage on him, and just kept walking.

She finished the ice cream and stepped on to a tram. A couple of teenagers tried chatting her up and it was the funniest thing she'd seen in a while, so that entertained her until they realised they'd missed their stop and begged the driver to let them off. When they tumbled out on to the pavement, she blew them each a kiss as they waved.

The tram reached Merciless Street and she got off and walked a few minutes south. There was no music here. No couples sitting outside cafés. No ice cream for sale.

The Necropolis was as quiet as – appropriately enough – a graveyard. Most of the buildings beyond the iron fence were cracked at best – half demolished at worst. But the new inhabitants didn't mind. They didn't need houses.

The Necromancers were still in the process of shadow-walking the dead over from the old Necropolis, but there were plenty here already. Shapes walked the streets, some with faces, some with human form, and some little more than a shimmering heat haze.

Valkyrie didn't look at them for long. She didn't know if it was in her head or actually happening, but she could feel their eyes on her. She was the one who destroyed their last home, after all. According to Uriah Serrate, that moment when she lost control of her magic resulted in tens of thousands of souls being petrified, somehow. Turned into glass.

She looked away, focusing instead on the sigils that were engraved into each of the fence's iron bars. One in particular seemed to be repeated at regular intervals.

"It's called the Gurahghul," said a stranger with Skulduggery's voice beside her.

Valkyrie glanced at him. "No way."

"What?" Skulduggery asked. The face he wore was amiable. It had sandy hair, a bit too long, maybe. But his clothes... He wore jeans and a T-shirt and sunglasses and leather bracelets on his wrist, and he completed the look with a pair of old tennis shoes.

"What the hell?" she whispered, grateful for the chance to think about something other than the accusing stares of the dead. "What are you wearing?"

"I could ask you the same thing."

"I'm wearing normal summer clothes that any girl my age would be happy to be seen in," she said. "Now what the hell are you wearing?"

"I'm wearing a disguise."

"You're wearing jeans."

"I've worn jeans before."

"When?"

He looked at her. "The 1870s."

"Were you in the Wild West?"

"I was, actually."

"It doesn't count if you were in the Wild West. You're wearing tennis shoes. And you have bracelets. You don't wear bracelets."

"It wouldn't be much of a disguise if it didn't depart from my usual apparel. I could mention the items you're wearing and point out the obvious incongruities, but I, unlike you, am a professional."

"A professional what, exactly? Surfer?"

"You look like you've..." He faltered.

This time, a grin broke out. "Oh my God. Oh my God, you've actually run out of things to say."

"No, I haven't."

"You were going to insult me and you can't. You've run out of insults. You're at a loss for words. Stay right there. Do not move. I want to carve this moment into my memory."

"You're being dramatic."

"This is the greatest moment of my life."

"You're exaggerating."

"I've won. You realise that, right? I was mocking you, I was slagging you off, and you tried to slag me off, but you couldn't. Do you know what this means? It means the dynamic between us has shifted, and things will never be the same again. This is a momentous moment. I'm just, I'm so happy."

"You're being ridiculous."

"You literally faltered in your speech."

"Yes," Skulduggery said, "but I didn't falter because I ran out of insults. I faltered because there was nothing to insult. You look happy and radiant and the blonde hair really suits you."

Valkyrie looked at him. Tried to think of a comeback.

"Nope," she decided. "I still win."

He looked back at the sigil on the wall. "As I was saying, this is the Gurahghul Sigil. It both generates and contains the death field that permeates the Necropolis."

"And how far does the death field go up?" she asked. "Does it stop at the top of the fence or does it keep rising? If it keeps rising, does that mean any plane that passes overhead will just plummet from the sky? And what about birds? If a bird flies into the death field, is it just going to drop dead? What if it tries to perch on a rooftop or something? How many birds and insects and animals is this thing gonna kill?"

Skulduggery walked along the fence and Valkyrie followed.

"This sigil here," he said, "and that one, and a few others, they look like they're designed to ward off wildlife. I'm sure there will be a few casualties at first until the system's refined, but, from what I can see, they're taking all reasonable precautions."

"And what if one of those ghoulie-ghoulie sigils is broken?"

"Gurahghul."

"What if someone smashes their car into the fence by accident? Or even on purpose? Will the death field spill out?"

Skulduggery hesitated.

"I don't like it when you hesitate," Valkyrie said.

"I'm just working through the possibilities," he responded. "There might be some leakage, yes, which means the fence will have to be reinforced, maybe even guarded. Having a Necropolis above ground has never been tried before – having a Necropolis within a city of living people has never even been contemplated. Mistakes will be made, I'm sure – but there's no reason why it won't be a success."

They stopped and looked across the street where construction was progressing on the new Necromancer Temple. The initial frame was up, secured to the foundations, and they watched the engineers grow walls within that frame, thick concrete that flowed upwards like candlewax melting in reverse. As the walls spread, the engineers made sure the pipes and cables and wires were in place, waiting for the walls to envelop them.

"Magic is handy," Valkyrie said.

"Magic is handy," Skulduggery agreed, and then his gaze focused on something behind her. "Don't make any sudden moves, but..."

Valkyrie took a moment, then flicked her hair and glanced over her shoulder to the corner of the street, where Savoir Fair was talking to Uriah Serrate.

"Whoa," she breathed, turning away from them again. "Wonder what those two have got to chat about."

"I think we may need to have a conversation of our own with Mr Fair," Skulduggery said.

"Stop staring."

"I'm not staring. I'm being casual."

"Try telling that to your eyes."

"Oh," he said, and made a concerted effort to look at her. "Sometimes I forget that the eyes follow my line of sight. When you see out of empty sockets, you can generally focus on whatever you like and nobody knows where you're looking. Oh, damn." The eyes started rolling in opposite directions.

"This is weird," Valkyrie said.

"Just give me a moment," he responded. The eyes swivelled, locked on to Valkyrie's chin and then dipped, and he shut them and squeezed them tight. He gave it a few seconds, then slowly cracked open the lids. "Is that better?" he asked, his eyes spinning.

"Kinda," she said. "Come on." She grabbed his hand, hurried to the other side of the road as a tram approached. She led him onboard, then sat him down on the back seat. While he concentrated on regaining control, she watched Fair and Serrate as the tram passed them. Neither looked up from their conversation.

Valkyrie settled back, crossed her legs, letting her shoe dangle from her foot. The tram only had half a dozen people on it, most of whom had earphones in.

The tram reached a junction and the different sections split apart. Their section flowed left, attaching itself to the back of another tram heading towards the centre of the city.

They got out and walked to Reign's nightclub, entering through the loading bay, stepping round trundling pallets of drinks. The house lights were on inside, robbing the place of its mystique, showing all the scuffs on the floors and the marks on the tables. The cleaning staff were in – mortals, from what Valkyrie could tell. She smiled at them as she passed, but they didn't meet her eyes.

A large man with a tablet walked by. He stopped tapping the screen long enough to frown at them. "Who are you?" he asked Skulduggery, and then he looked at Valkyrie and jerked his head. "You, in back. They're starting." He returned his gaze to Skulduggery. "Well? I'm waiting."

"I'm her friend," Skulduggery said, indicating Valkyrie. "I drove her here."

"How nice," the big man said, "but we don't allow friends backstage. Dancers only."

"Of course," Skulduggery said. He patted Valkyrie's shoulder. "Good luck."

"Cheers," she said without enthusiasm, and passed through a STAFF ONLY door. Another man indicated a set of steps and up she went, plunging into darkness and then emerging into the light on the edge of a stage with around twenty dancers, male and female, all paying rapt attention as Acantha spoke.

"To say this is a coveted gig is underplaying it," she was saying. "The party here for Feíle na Draíochta is going to be epic beyond a scale previously conceived by carbon-based life forms. Roarhaven will be alive with carnivals and costumes during the day, but at night – at night – Mr Reign wants all the focus here. On us. On you. Our regular dancers have been rehearsing for months for this show, but we need eight of you – eight of the best of you – for show-adjacent performances. You have fifteen minutes to warm up, then Raul will take you through the routine. If you can't hack it, you're out, no excuses. Any questions? Good. Dance well."

Acantha walked off and the choreographer took her place in the spotlight. Valkyrie moved round behind the dancers as Raul spoke, slipping into the shadows before she was noticed.

# 76

She followed Acantha between scaffolding and set dressing as music started to play, disguising the click-clack of her high heels.

Through another door, up some more stairs, and into Reign's empty office.

"Where is he?" Valkyrie asked, and Acantha yelped and whirled, pressing both hands to her chest.

"You almost gave me a heart attack!"

Valkyrie smirked. "Sorry."

Acantha recovered quickly, straightening up and tilting her chin in that insolent way of hers. "If you're a dancer, congratulations – you just failed the audition." She gave her a once-over, eyes lingering on her arms. "But, if you're interviewing for the door-staff position, we might have a place for you."

"I'm not looking for a job," Valkyrie said, coming forward. "I want to talk to your boss."

"Mr Reign is far too busy to..."

The realisation dawned, and Valkyrie gave her a smile.

Acantha whirled, lunging for the desk, and Valkyrie smashed into her, grabbed her before she could press whatever hidden button she was reaching for. Kicking off her shoes, she picked Acantha up off her feet and swung her round. Acantha hit the wall, dislodging a painting. She lashed out wildly and Valkyrie hip-threw her to the floor. She scrambled up, a ball of fire in her right hand, and Valkyrie let the energy crackle in her eyes.

They stayed where they were for a few seconds, and then Acantha closed her hand and the flames went out.

"OK," she said, "OK. You win. I'm not much of a fighter, anyway."

Valkyrie pulled her magic back in. "Where is he?"

"Mr Reign hasn't been into the club in days," Acantha said. "Ever since the attempt on your life. He knows you're after him."

"Where does he live?"

Acantha laughed. "I'm not going to tell you that. You can get mad and punch me if you want, but there's no way in hell I'm betraying Christopher Reign. He'll do a lot worse than kill me, and *then* he'll kill me."

"Did he hire someone to take us out?"

"I don't know."

"You're his assistant."

"In the club, yeah – not for his other businesses. I'm not involved in anything illegal – Mr Reign insists that I stay out of it."

"Then you're of no help to me whatsoever, are you?"

"Not especially, no. Are you going to beat me up now, or are you gonna just leave?"

"I suppose I'll just leave."

They heard footsteps approaching, and they both fixed their hair and their clothes and the door opened and Christopher Reign came in.

"Dammit," said Acantha, "she was just about to go."

Valkyrie raised her hands, energy crackling, and then something – Acantha's elbow, most likely – smashed into the back of her head. She stumbled and almost dropped, bright flashes and dark explosions going off behind her eyes, and looked up far too late to dodge Reign's punch. It hit her like a brick and all of a sudden Acantha hands were slipping up under her arms and clasping behind her head, and for a chick who wasn't much of a fighter she sure applied that full nelson pretty damn flaw-lessly.

Reign threw a left hook to the body and Valkyrie felt her ribs move. The right hook cracked something that she didn't have time to identify before the right cross knocked her head back into Acantha's nose. Acantha cursed and Valkyrie pulled free and Reign charged, arms wrapped around her, picking her up like she was a toy and then pitching forward. Valkyrie slammed into the ground and he slammed down on top of her and she tried to breathe and he reared up and hit her.

She ignored the cracked rib and the burning lungs and grabbed Reign's wrist with both hands as she wrapped one leg round his waist and the other round his head. She crossed her ankles and lifted her hips and moved his arm so that his own shoulder cut into his neck, shutting off his blood supply, then she pulled his head down and Reign scratched and scraped and pulled at her and she just held on.

She would have choked him out in seconds if Acantha hadn't run in. Valkyrie absorbed the kick with her upper arm, released Reign and crunched the ball of her foot into his face. He flew back and Acantha dived on her. They twisted as they grappled, rolling against the wall. Acantha hissed and snarled, her nails going for Valkyrie's eyes while her legs fought for the better position. She was a whole lot scrappier than she'd been letting on.

Valkyrie went for her throat with her teeth and Acantha jerked her head away, giving Valkyrie space to drop an elbow into the hinge of Acantha's jaw. Acantha sparked out immediately, eyes rolling back in her head, and Valkyrie sprang to her feet just as Reign's hand lit up. A blast of energy burned into her shoulder, spinning her round, and Reign had his hands on her again. He lifted her off her feet, held her over his head and then slammed her to the ground.

Valkyrie lay in a heap, struggling to breathe, struggling to move, struggling to think. Reign staggered against his desk, his hands at his bloody face.

There were running footsteps and surprised voices and, above them all, Reign yelling at his security team.

"You idiots! What the hell do I pay you for? She could've killed me in the time it took you to figure out what was going on! Goddammit!"

Apologies. They were apologising. Asking him if he was OK.

"Do I look OK?" he yelled back. "She broke my goddamn nose!"

More apologies. Questions now. They wanted to know what to do with her.

"Take her out back," said Reign. "Take her out back and kill her and dump the body. Don't take any chances with this one, you hear? Cuff her."

Valkyrie's arms were wrenched behind her and once the cold metal clicked round her wrists her magic left her. They picked her up, Reign's men, by her arms and legs and carried her out. Blood ran from her burst lip. The ground passed beneath her. Through blurry eyes she watched their feet as they moved behind the stage.

A door opened ahead of her. She felt fresh air and started to struggle. They gripped her tighter, cursed at her, told her to quit it. She shouted for help. Maybe the dancers would hear her. Maybe someone would come.

She struggled more and yanked her foot free, but someone else grabbed her leg and they just continued on, out of the door, into the shade behind the nightclub. They threw her down. She skinned her knees and her toes on the concrete and didn't feel it. Fell forward and turned, sat up, bringing her legs in, blinking up at them.

One of them took out a gun.

As he pulled back the slide, Valkyrie got up and she stood there, her hair a mess, her face all bloody. Nowhere to run and no chance to fight. But she wasn't going to die on her knees, not like she'd seen in the visions. If she was going to die today, then she was going to die standing.

The guy with the gun raised his weapon and pointed it right at her.

She was freezing cold. It was a lovely day, but she was in the shade and she was freezing cold. She was barefoot and her legs were shaking and she was going to die and she was freezing cold.

She grinned.

"What the hell are you smiling at?" asked the guy with the gun.

"I'm going to haunt you like no one's ever been haunted before," she promised him. "And when I'm done with you I'm going to haunt your friends here. I'm not gonna be a nice ghost, either. It won't be a fun time for you. I'm gonna tear your lives apart."

"You got guts, kid, I'll give you that," said the guy with the gun. "Close your eyes now."

She wanted to close her eyes and make the gun go away, but she kept them open.

"Holy crap," one of the others said. "That's Valkyrie Cain."

His friend frowned. "Valkyrie Cain's got dark hair."

"I'm telling you, man. It's her. Beau, it's her, isn't it?"

A guy Valkyrie had never seen before went pale.

"Why would Beau know if it's Valkyrie Cain?" asked the guy with the gun.

"He dated her."

The other men laughed.

"He didn't date Valkyrie Cain!" one of them howled.

"Yes, he did," said the other guy. "Beau, tell them."

Beau's pale face flushed red. "Yeah. I did. For a few months."

"Uh-huh," said the guy with the gun. "So what do you think, Beau? Is this your ex-girlfriend?"

Beau hesitated, then stepped forward, and made a show of

peering at Valkyrie's face. Then he stepped back. "It's her," he said.

The guy with the gun chuckled. "Hey, kid, that true? You Valkyrie Cain?"

She grinned again. "Take off these shackles and I'll let you find out."

They laughed at that, these men. They were starting to enjoy this. All except for Beau.

"And do you recognise this guy?" one of them said, wrapping an arm round Beau's neck. "Because he has been telling some wild stories about you."

More laughter. More enjoyment.

"Of course I do," said Valkyrie through her grin. "That's Beau. That's my ex-boyfriend Beau. We had some good times, didn't we, sweetie?"

There were cheers now, and Beau accepted the good-natured jostling with a bashful smile.

"One last kiss before dying," Valkyrie said. "Come on, honey. One last kiss."

Cheers and wolf whistles, and Beau was shoved forward. He swallowed nervously, and took another step, blocking the guy with the gun's line of fire.

Valkyrie dropped down to a hunkering position, scooped the handcuff chain under her heels and then rocked back, moving her hands up and in front of her and then everyone was shouting and Beau didn't know where to move and Valkyrie launched herself at him, crunching the top of her head into his chin, pitching him back into the guy with the gun. They grabbed at her and ripped at her and all she focused on was the gun, and she saw it and grabbed it and pulled it free.

She went down, all these guys on top of her, screaming into her ears, their hands everywhere, their panic building, and Valkyrie in the centre of it all, the gun pressed tight to her belly, turning it round in her hands, her fingers curling over the grip.

Right then.

There was a leg in front of her and she pressed the muzzle into it and fired. There was a scream and a scramble and she fired again, this time into an arm, and she turned and shot a foot, and then someone tried to grab the gun and she bit down on his hand and almost took a finger off and she fired again and again and she wrenched herself free.

She staggered into a wall, dimly aware of a guy with sandy hair and jeans, with leather bracelets on one wrist, tearing into what remained of Reign's men. The air rippled and people flew through the sky. Fireballs burst. Bones broke.

Many, many bones broke.

When Skulduggery was done, he turned to her. "Are you OK?"

She breathed out.

"Valkyrie?"

"I'm good," she said. She tossed the gun away and he uncuffed her and her magic came back. She saw her shoes on the ground – one of Reign's men must have carried them out. That was nice of him. Beside the shoes was her handbag. She limped over, removed the phone and the amulet and pressed the amulet to her chest and tapped it. The suit flowed over her body. It felt good to be wearing boots again. She pocketed the phone.

One of Reign's men moaned. She walked over.

"Hey, Beau," she said. "Stop lying to your friends about dating me." Then she kicked him in the face.

# 77

Crepuscular Vies stood with his back to Omen, looking across to the West Tower, his hat in his hand. The wind was stiff and cold up here so Omen stayed beside the wall, near the door.

"You should have let this Chicane fella fall," Crepuscular said. "He was going to kill you and, by saving him, you gave him another opportunity to do just that." He turned. "I'm glad you didn't let him fall, of course. Apart from anything else, you're not a killer, and nor should you have to be. But now someone out there knows you're a threat."

"I don't think he's going to come for me, though. Or send anyone else to come for me. It sounded like he was just going to walk away."

"And you're willing to trust that he won't change his mind?"

"I don't see that I have a choice. If he wants to kill me, he knows where I am. I think I've got to focus on the mission."

"On the mission Skulduggery Pleasant gave you."

Omen winced. "Do you mind? I know it'll probably be weird working with Skulduggery but not really working with Skulduggery. I don't want to bring up any bad memories."

"Bad memories?" Crepuscular said. "Like what? Like being his partner once upon a time? Like him dropping me into a vat of chemicals? Like the pain that seemed as if it would never end and the anguish that felt as if it would never go away? Like the memory of how my life fell apart and I wandered for years, piecing myself back together only to realise that I was building an entirely new person? Bad memories like that?"

"Yes."

Crepuscular gave a little wave. "It's fine. I'm over it. Turning Corrival Academy into one of these Pillars is not something Damocles Creed, with all his power and influence, is capable of doing alone. How did this city come about, Omen?"

"Like, originally?"

"Tell me the story."

"Uh, well, originally Roarhaven was a small village founded by sorcerers who wanted to stage a kind of, I suppose, a coup? They didn't like the Sanctuary in Dublin so they built another one out here, and then tried to—"

"Shorten the story."

"Um, it didn't work, and Roarhaven stayed a small village, and everyone here hated mortals, and they weren't very nice, and were quite, maybe, racist? Kind of? And it stayed like that for years—"

"Shorten the story further."

"And then the Dublin Sanctuary was destroyed—"

"Shorter."

"And Erskine Ravel paid this architect guy to construct an entire city in another dimension and then they shunted everything over and the city, basically, fitted on top of the old village and that's how we have Roarhaven today."

"And the name of this architect?"

Omen hesitated. "I want to say Brian...?"

"Creyfon Signate."

"Oh."

"Signate designed this city. He designed the Dark Cathedral and the High Sanctuary and he designed this school – with this so-called Pillar. I think we should pay him a visit. This Saturday, what do you say?"

Omen blinked. "Me?"

"We."

"But… me as well as you?"

"Why not?"

"I'm not really… Like, if you go and question him, then he'll take you seriously because, and I don't mean this in a bad way, you're a very scary person."

"I am," said Crepuscular. "This is true."

"But if we both go then I just think my being there will kind of dilute your scariness, in a way? It'll be like this big scary guy is taking his little brother along for a day out."

"I think you underestimate your scariness."

"I really don't."

"When Skulduggery first started taking Valkyrie Cain along on his investigations, she was younger than you are now."

"Yeah, but Valkyrie's Valkyrie. That's different."

"It's not different at all. She was young, in way over her head, always getting into ridiculously dangerous situations that no young person should ever find themselves in. Does that sound familiar at all? You, Omen Darkly, could be the next Valkyrie Cain, if only you believed in yourself. Maybe all you need is a partner to steer you through the worst of it. So what do you say?"

"What do I say to what?"

Crepuscular stuck out his hand. "To adventure. To proving to yourself that you can do it – that you can equal, even surpass, the accomplishments of your rival."

"Valkyrie isn't my rival."

"Of course she is. She's your rival just as Skulduggery is mine."

"But does it count as being a rival if she doesn't even know we're rivals?"

"It's not about her," Crepuscular said. "It's not about him. It's about proving to ourselves that we're worthwhile. This adventure, Omen. Accomplishing this task. You and me. Are you in?"

"I, well, I mean, I suppose so, if we're… if someone has to be in, then yeah, I could be the one that's, like, in."

Crepuscular grabbed his hand and shook it. "I am loving this enthusiasm."

"But I don't really have any interest in being a hero."

"That's OK, Omen," Skulduggery said from behind them, "neither does he."

They turned as Skulduggery walked up. No, not Skulduggery. It was his voice, but his skull was cracked, held together with metal staples, and he wasn't wearing a hat or a tie. His black coat was pretty cool, though.

Not-Skulduggery nodded to them both. "Hello, Omen. Crepuscular."

Crepuscular's whole body seemed to curl inwards, like a hand becoming a claw. "You know me?"

"Oh, yes," came the response. "And I know that right at this moment you're feeling an overwhelming urge to tear me apart."

"You think I shouldn't?"

"I'm not the man you want to hurt. I was, but no longer. You know who I am, don't you, Omen?"

"You're Cadaver Cain," Omen said. "You're Skulduggery from the future." He glanced at Crepuscular. "I meant to tell you about him."

"Skulduggery of the future or Skulduggery of the present," Crepuscular said, shrugging, "it doesn't matter to me."

"It should," Cadaver replied. "We are, after all, two distinct people. Skulduggery isn't the same person who left you for dead all those years ago, and I'm not the same person who's running around with Valkyrie Cain right at this moment. We change. That's what people do. I don't have to tell you that, surely."

"You talk like you know me."

"Oh, Crepuscular, I do know you. I know everything about you."

Cadaver held his hands up and the air started to ripple around the two men. Omen couldn't hear what was said within that bubble, but Crepuscular tensed, like he was expecting a fight.

396

Cadaver, however, merely lowered his hands and the rippling faded.

"Do you believe me now?" he asked.

Crepuscular grunted.

"I think back over our time together as partners," Cadaver continued, "and I regret my behaviour. I failed to appreciate everything you had to offer. I failed to value your obvious talents. That was a mistake. I apologise."

"You think an apology is going to make up for what you did?"

"No. That will be a process where I'll have to earn back your trust."

"You don't get to earn back anything," Crepuscular sneered. "You left me to die."

"I thought you *were* dead."

"Obviously, you were wrong."

"Obviously. It won't mean anything to you, but I'm proud of the person you've become. Taking on young Omen Darkly as a partner of your own is an inspired move."

"I know," said Crepuscular.

They weren't looking at him, but they did mention him, so Omen felt obliged to respond. "Thank you," he mumbled.

"You work well together," Cadaver said. "You're a better team than we were. There is genuine trust and affection between you. It reminds me of my time with Valkyrie."

"We're going to be better than you and Valkyrie," said Crepuscular.

Cadaver shook his head. "No. You're not. You won't get the chance, I'm afraid. In six days, you will both die, screaming, as your skin melts on your flesh, your flesh melts on your bones, and your bones melt on your internal organs. Which have also melted."

Omen cleared his throat. "We're, um, we're going to stop it."

Cadaver looked at him. "You'll try. I can see all possible futures, Omen, and, sadly, in the one we're heading into, you will fail. If it's any consolation, all that melting will happen in a moment or two, so you'll barely be aware of your failure before your thoughts shut down. Unless we change what's about to happen."

Crepuscular folded his arms. "You've come to us for help."

"No, but I have come to offer my help to you."

"Why do you need to help anyone? If you know everything, can't you just do what needs to be done on your own?"

"I have access to all knowledge – that's not quite the same as knowing everything. It takes time to sort through the – sometimes infinite – amount of possibilities. I could spend the rest of my days searching for a better way to overcome a single obstacle – or I could make a decision early on, and then fight to ensure that decision was the right one."

Omen frowned. "Your brain sounds complicated."

"I don't have a brain," Cadaver said, "but yes, it is."

"So you make a decision early on," said Crepuscular. "Out of all the ways you stop Creed, you picked what looked like the best one, and now we're on this path you want to help, is that right?"

"Yes."

"No deal."

"Um," said Omen, "maybe we should consider it?"

"No," Crepuscular responded. "We don't work with him."

"You partnered up with Omen here to prove a point," Cadaver said, his voice softening. "You wanted to demonstrate that the two of you were a better team than Skulduggery and Valkyrie ever could be. You needed to know that you could achieve more. You needed to be the type of mentor that Skulduggery never was to you."

"I didn't need a mentor," Crepuscular said.

Cadaver's head tilted. "Didn't you? Granted, you were a hundred and nine years old when you became Skulduggery's partner, but we never grow out of needing approval, do we? He let you down. It was a betrayal. And, because of this betrayal, you left your old name behind you – you abandoned it and

398

everything that came with it. Your family. Your heritage. You struck out on your own, but you could never quite escape him, could you? You could feel his shadow over you at all times, blocking out the sun, preventing you from growing into who you were meant to be."

"You claim you're not him," Crepuscular said, "but you sure like to hear yourself talk as much as he does."

"Yes, I do," said Cadaver, amused. "I'm here because your team will need my help to do what needs to be done. Skulduggery and Valkyrie are trying to save the world their way. I want to help you save the world your way."

Omen couldn't speak for Crepuscular, but he quite liked that little speech. He felt excited – inspired, even – despite the fact that all this would probably result in him being plunged into far more danger than he was comfortable with. Which was zero. Zero danger.

"What's your agenda?" Crepuscular asked, somewhat grudgingly.

"There are many players in this particular game. Damocles Creed wants his Activation Wave. Skulduggery Pleasant wants to stop it. Serrate wants his new Necropolis. The gangster, Christopher Reign, wants power. My agenda is simple: prevent the future from happening, no matter what."

"Well," Omen said, with some hesitation, "we are thinking of asking Creyfon Signate some questions—"

"—on Saturday!" finished Cadaver happily. "And I would love to accompany you!"

"Yay," said Crepuscular.

# 78

Sebastian sat in his favourite armchair, looking at the bloodstained couch where Demure had died. The house was quiet and still and it felt empty. Sebastian's insides felt quiet and still and empty.

The others had been and gone. They all had the same look on their faces – shocked. Distraught. Their little group was littler still, and shaken.

"I'm sorry," Darquesse said from the doorway.

Sebastian didn't look round. He just nodded.

"I didn't really think about what it would mean," she continued. "I didn't think about how it would hurt you. Or the others."

"Right," said Sebastian.

She came forward. "Would you like me to clean the couch?"

"Yes, please."

The couch rippled and then the blood was gone. Darquesse sat. "I'm really sorry. I liked Demure. I liked Tarry, too, but he was quiet. Demure was chatty and she talked to me about stuff I was interested in. I'm sorry I didn't save them."

He looked at her. "Why didn't you?"

She shrugged. He went to get up and she spoke quickly. "Because I didn't think it was important."

"You didn't think what was important?"

"Saving them," said Darquesse. "I don't see people the way you do. You have your..." She faltered.

"Go on."

"It's like you put people into boxes in your head. Like, this is Tarry and this is Demure, and Tarry is like this and Demure is like that. So they're in their boxes and their boxes contain what they look like and what their personalities are and... Everything you know about them is in their box, so that's how you think of them. But I don't have those boxes in my head, because everyone looks the same. Their bodies are made up of all these atoms and the atoms are the same wherever you go."

"But what about their personalities? Their memories and experiences?"

She gave another shrug. "I kinda don't think they matter, because they're so... fluffy."

"What do you mean?"

"Like fluffy, like... it's on top. It's fluff on top of something. That isn't them – not really. When I look at a person, I can see the real person – I can see the atoms and the energy and how it all fits together, and I can see how it'll come apart when they die and all that energy will go off and become something new. It's the energy that's important. The personality and memory are just bits of fluff. They don't last long; they don't change anything about the energy because the energy is deeper down, almost. They're just..."

"Fluff," said Sebastian.

"Yeah."

"Huh."

"Is that bad?"

He shook his head. "It's not bad. It's just different. I can't... I can't understand that."

"So it's bad."

"No," he said, sitting forward. "Hey, look at me. Just because I don't understand you, or I can't understand you, it doesn't mean you're bad. You just see things so very differently from the rest of us – sometimes it's hard for me to wrap my head around."

"But you wish I'd saved Tarry and Demure."

"I do. But that's just because I miss them."

"I miss them, too," Darquesse said. She lowered her eyes. "I'm just really sorry. I didn't think what it would be like for you. Or any of the others. I just thought about me, but that's selfish and I don't want to be selfish."

Not for the first time, Sebastian wished he could touch his face. He really wanted to pinch the bridge of his nose. He felt the situation called for some bridge-pinching. "I'm just going to need you to think things through in the future, OK?" he said. "Think about what would be the nice thing to do, and then do that."

She nodded.

"You OK?" he asked.

She nodded again. "Can I have a hug?"

He got up. "Of course you can," he said, and she hurried forward and they hugged.

# 79

Valkyrie washed the blonde out of her hair in one of Roarhaven's disused houses. She was sorry to see it go – it was almost like she was watching the chance at an alternate, happy life go swirling down the drain. At least the process was quick – the dye she'd used would have made a fortune in mortal salons were it not for those pesky, hard-to-explain magical elements.

The cuts and bruises from her recent beating were proving more difficult to get rid of. She hadn't been able to see a doctor so she chewed leaves as she showered in order to dull the aches.

Limping only a little, she dried herself off, put on the necronaut suit and her helmet, and rode her motorbike to the High Sanctuary. She parked on the Circle and sat there until the end of the day, when people began heading home. Savoir Fair was one of the first out – because of course he was. He came down the steps and a car pulled up and he got in the back, and Valkyrie flipped her visor down and followed.

She kept three cars between them at all times. Didn't break the speed limit. Didn't make any illegal turns. Didn't do anything that might attract attention. She followed the car into Meritorious Row, an affluent neighbourhood with ridiculously healthy trees lining the streets.

Savoir's house was a grand affair – a three-floored and many-windowed affair. The gates had stone statues scowling from atop each pillar. The car pulled up outside the front door and Savoir got out without acknowledging the driver. Valkyrie waited until the car had looped round and driven off before she gunned the engine and rode straight in.

Savoir, too busy reading from his phone, had his key in the front door and was only turning when Valkyrie braked, let the bike topple, and leaped off. She collided with him, powering him backwards into the house. He went sprawling and she slammed the door and whipped off her helmet.

He stared up at her – then turned over, jabbing at his phone.

Valkyrie threw the helmet at his head and he cried out in pain, and she kicked his phone across the hardwood floor.

The house was functionally wealthy. There was very little individuality to the decoration, but the floors were the right floors, the paintings were the right paintings, and the mouldings were the right mouldings. It was all very uninspired.

"Don't kill me," Savoir said.

Valkyrie glared at him. "Don't make me kill you and I won't."

"I had nothing to do with Rylent coming to arrest you," he said, getting to his knees with his hands out, palms open, to ward off any oncoming attacks. "That's not even my department. I have a fancy job title, but basically I work in a day-to-day administrative role, just keeping the High Sanctuary running smoothly."

She tossed him a pair of handcuffs.

"Oh," he said, trying to smile reassuringly, "no, these aren't necessary."

"Put them on."

"I assure you, Detective, I don't pose a physical threat to you in the slightest. I'm an Alchemist."

"You can turn lead into gold?"

His smile soured. "Sort of."

Her eyebrow arched, and he sighed.

"Turning lead into gold – turning practically anything into gold – is why I studied alchemy when all of my friends were learning how to be Elementals or Energy Throwers. I thought, *let them have the flashy powers – I'll take the one that'll make me rich beyond comprehension.*"

"But alchemy doesn't always work that way," Valkyrie said.

"I'm aware of that."

"Most things that you turn to gold will revert to their original state within hours."

"I am aware of that," he snapped. "I was young, for God's sake. I thought the rules didn't apply to me. I thought I'd be the exception. I mean, it's not only gold. I can turn mortar into water, and soil into stone. It doesn't have to always revolve around gold."

"But eventually most things do revert, right?"

"Right," he said grumpily.

"Sucks to be you, Savoir. Put the cuffs on."

"But I'm not a threat."

"I believe you." Her eyes crackled and he paled and cuffed himself. "Anyone else in the house?"

He hesitated.

"Savoir, I swear to God..."

"My family," he said. "My wife and children. Please don't hurt them."

"Where are they?"

"Probably having dinner. Look, what do you want? What do you need from me? I'll give it to you, whatever it is. We don't have to involve them. They don't even have to know you're here. That'd be safer, right? For everyone?"

Valkyrie took out her phone, texted their address to Skulduggery. "Tell me something, Savoir, are you the kind of person to hide himself away in his home office for hours on end, so much so that his family doesn't notice when he misses dinner?"

"It's been known to happen."

"Then lead the way."

He brought her to a large office lined with bookshelves she doubted he ever perused, and she sat him in the corner and opened one of the windows. A moment later, Skulduggery climbed through.

"You could have used the door," Savoir pointed out. 'Why wouldn't you use the door? What's wrong with—"

"Shut up," said Skulduggery. "Has he said anything?"

"Nothing useful," Valkyrie replied, picking up a fancy pen off the desk.

Skulduggery loomed over Savoir, who seemed to shrink in his shadow. "What are your dealings with Uriah Serrate?"

A moment passed.

"I've never spoken to him," Savoir said.

Valkyrie threw the fancy pen at him and it bounced off his cheek.

"Ow!"

"We saw you talking to him yesterday," she said. "You either tell us the truth or I go into your mind and bludgeon it out of you."

Savoir paled. "You can do that?"

"Want a demonstration? I'm not very good at it and I may damage something important."

"No," he said quickly. "No, please. My intellect is all I have."

"That's an embarrassing admission."

"Serrate approached a few months ago, requesting a meeting," Savoir said. "He's the Herald of the Dark, the Harbinger of Doom, the Something of the Everlasting Death and the King of the Dead – what was I supposed to do? Say no? Necromancers are serious people, and I didn't want to offend either him or the Order or the Necropolis. So we met. We talked. There's no crime in talking."

Valkyrie and Skulduggery waited.

Savoir cleared his throat. "The crime bit came later," he said.

"Knew it," said Valkyrie.

"It was an innocent favour he was asking for, but I knew if anyone were to hear about it they'd think the worst and accuse

406

me, yet again, of corruption. Detectives, I am not a corrupt man. Serrate asked for a favour, and, in the spirit of goodwill between Roarhaven and the Necropolis, I agreed."

"What did you get out of it?" Skulduggery asked.

"Nothing."

"What did you get out of it apart from nothing?"

"Money," he admitted.

Valkyrie grunted. "So this was less of an innocent favour and more of a quite obvious bribe."

Savoir made a displeased face. "Bribe is such an ugly word and yet it has dogged me throughout my career."

"Maybe if you quit taking bribes, that'd stop. What did Serrate tell you to do?"

"He wanted to move the Necropolis to Roarhaven."

"When was this?" Skulduggery asked.

"Three months ago."

"And what exactly did you do for him?"

"Nothing much," said Savoir. "He had other people to do most of the heavy lifting – I was mostly there to act as a go-between and to advise him on the various laws and rules he'd have to follow to get this done."

Valkyrie nodded. "I don't have to read your mind to know that you're holding something back, and I'm running out of patience."

Savoir frowned. "That was you being patient? Good heavens."

"I can barge into your head right now, if you'd like..."

He held up his handcuffed hands. "No, no, that's fine. There were obstacles to Serrate getting what he wanted. Sanctuary officials who wouldn't be as friendly as I was being. So I gave him a list of their names. Those who could be bought were bought. No harm done."

"And those who Serrate couldn't buy?"

"They were either persuaded to co-operate or they... vanished."

"They were killed?"

"I honestly don't know."

"But they were probably killed."

"It's possible."

"And you were OK with this?"

"No," said Savoir. "These were my friends. My colleagues. Sure, I knew rules would get broken, but I didn't think that anyone would get hurt. You've got to understand, I'm a pacifist by nature."

"Everyone's a pacifist until they're threatened," Valkyrie said. "Did you put anyone else's name down on that list of yours?"

"I'm not sure what you mean."

"The last time we spoke, when you came to see me in hospital – which was lovely of you, by the way – you told me you were blackmailing Skulduggery into investigating this disreputable crowd you were hanging out with, and you tried to get me to kill Reign. You strike me as someone who would take the opportunity – if such an opportunity presented itself – to have someone else take out your enemies."

"I don't *have* enemies," Savoir said. "The odd case of bribery aside, I'm a decent man, I assure you. As for Christopher Reign, he's a gangster and a killer and a blight on Roarhaven. For the good of the city, someone has to take him out."

"Uh-huh. And was Creed's name on that list?"

"No," Savoir said firmly. "What, you think I had something to do with his assassination? There was no chance I'd ever put his name on that list. And not out of some sense of loyalty to the man. I don't like him and I don't trust him and he may not be quite the man he was, but I *am* terrified of him. I had no idea Reign would send Coda Quell after him."

Suddenly the air rushed in Valkyrie's ears and Skulduggery was speaking like he was very far away.

"Who's Coda Quell?"

"You've never heard of Coda Quell, the assassin?" Savoir asked. "A Ripper, from what I can gather. He never fails. Or he never did fail, before he went after you. You've tarnished his record. I wouldn't say he's overly pleased about that."

Valkyrie needed to sit down, but her legs wouldn't work.

"You said Creed's not quite the man he was. What do you mean?" Skulduggery asked.

"Everyone's saying it, it's not just me," Savoir replied. "He's... I hesitate to say subservient, but that's what he is whenever Serrate's around. A few of my colleagues even suspect that the Supreme Mage is under Serrate's influence. The Necromancer brought him back to life, for goodness' sake – who knows what else he did to him?"

"That would explain why Creed is going along with this Necropolis relocation," Skulduggery said.

"That's what I was thinking, yeah," Savoir agreed.

"We're not having a conversation. Stop nodding."

"Sorry."

"Valkyrie, do you have anything else to ask? Valkyrie?"

She looked up. "No," she said. "Nothing."

"If I think of anything else," Savoir said, "I'll call you imme-diately. And not just about this. About anything. I'll be your inside man – what do you say? Your informant at the very heart of the High Sanctuary? We can be a team, taking down the tyrants from within and without. I like the sound of that. What do you say?"

He thrust out his hand, ready to shake on it. Instead, Valkyrie grabbed his wrist and, after twisting just enough to make him wince, unlocked the handcuffs.

"Thank you," he said. "Partner."

"We're not partners," she said. "We don't have a deal. But right now we don't have a jail cell, either."

"Understood. And I swear to you I'll behave from this moment on."

He grinned in a way that made Valkyrie doubt that, but she really didn't care, so she stuffed the cuffs back in her pocket and followed Skulduggery out of the house. She picked up the bike and wheeled it to the road.

"I think you should travel into the future again," Skulduggery said, handing her the helmet. "I know that it's risky, but all our avenues are being exhausted. We need to find out what exactly is involved in the Activation Wave, and we need to find out how to stop it."

Valkyrie nodded.

"You said that Cadaver mentioned China, yes? He implied she isn't pleased with how things have turned out? Then she'll be the one to help you. Valkyrie, are you listening?"

"China," Valkyrie said, nodding. "Travel to the future and talk to China. Got it."

"Are you OK?"

She looked at him. "Grand," she said. "I'm grand."

# 80

Trouble was brewing.

That morning there had been a protest in the Circle, just outside the High Sanctuary. Roarhaven citizens, concerned about the curfew, the mandatory church attendance, the oppressive introduction of the Sense Wardens, and even the illegal arrests of the mortal population, gathered in a group of maybe two hundred people and waved signs and placards and sang songs and chanted slogans. The City Guard and the Cleavers observed them, but made no move to stop any of it from happening.

Temper knew that wouldn't last long.

More protests were planned. Bigger protests. Even now, the organisers were compiling a list of demands, freedoms they'd lost that they wanted back. All very reasonable, all very straightforward. Roarhaven had been working pretty well up until now, they were arguing – so why change?

But Temper knew Damocles Creed, and he knew Creed was waiting for the protests to turn violent – anticipating it, in fact. When it came to whatever his grand plan was, he couldn't just make the leap from the first to the final stage – that would have been far too drastic, and the whole city would have erupted. No, he needed to move forward in smaller steps, steps he could frame as unfortunate measures necessary to ensure public safety. That was how the protesters were marching towards their doom – one step at a time.

One of these smaller steps was to have the City Guard roll right into the middle of the Humdrums. They'd jumped from their trucks and grabbed whichever mortal was closest, cuffing them, forcing them to their knees, making them wait there while they checked their IDs. Once they matched a name to their list, they hauled them up and threw them into the back of the trucks anyway. They weren't even being taken to be questioned – they were driven outside the city walls, to the tightly controlled relocation camp. No charge levelled. No crime committed.

That had all happened on Friday. Today was Saturday and things would be different now. It had been foreseen.

Temper rarely had time for the predictions of Sensitives – seeing into the future was a dangerous game fraught with difficulties and complications – but Onosa Tsira was an exception to all this. She approached her visions with a logical mind, sharp enough to cut through the contradictory nature of this aspect of her discipline. He'd worked with her before, back when her husband had been alive.

"He's still alive," Onosa said to him now as they waited in the café. It wasn't a particularly well-organised café – the owners had previously run a tavern in the Leibniz Dimension that had managed to burn down during a flood – but it offered them a good view of the wide-open streets, and that's all they needed.

"You're not supposed to read my mind without permission," Temper said.

"I wasn't using any magic," Onosa responded. "I just saw you looking at the jar."

The glass jar was on the table. It was very clean and very empty.

"I'm just trying to get used to the idea that you carry your husband's astral form around with you wherever you go."

"I don't carry him *everywhere*," Onosa said, "I have my own life, you know. I have friends. I have hobbies. But marriage is

412

about many things, and one of those is accepting your partner as they are, and not trying to change them to suit you."

"Right," said Temper. "And how does Jericho feel about living in a jar? I knew him as a big, tall man with a physical form. How's he coping with being what he is now?"

"He's fine," Onosa said, shrugging. "It was a bit of an adjustment at first – for both of us. He had to get used to being a non-corporeal entity living in a jar, and I had to get used to being married to one. It's been seven years, but every day it gets a little bit better. And how are you? I heard you're living with an assassin."

"Who told you?"

"Oh, people talk, Temper. You shouldn't be surprised to find yourself the subject of gossip – especially now that you've fallen in love with the sister of the man you were once prepared to die for. I've never met her, but I've heard stories, and I'm sure Kierre is a lovely girl, despite the many murders she's committed."

"Yeah, she's pretty great."

Onosa laughed. "We live such strange lives."

"Yes, we do."

They both looked out of the window. It was a fine day, but overcast. The streets were empty – the mortals staying home after yesterday's raid. Temper checked his watch. Only another few minutes and they'd have to get in position.

"It's all going to end," said Onosa.

Temper looked back at her. "Sorry? What's going to end?"

"This," she said, indicating the café around them, then nodding to the street outside. "That. Everything. It's all going to end."

"Like... eventually, or sooner?"

"Sooner," she said. "Much, much sooner."

He sat up a little straighter in his chair. "Is this a premonition thing? Have you had a vision?"

"I see oblivion," Onosa said. "I feel it around me. Just a hint, and then there's nothing. I see nothing, I feel nothing, I sense nothing. It's... blank. This world is going to just cease to be."

"Do you have a timeline? How long are we talking? Ten years? A hundred?"

"Maybe one," she said. "I can't see beyond that."

"One hundred?"

"One *year*, Temper. At the very most."

"Why? Why does it end? What happens?"

"I don't know," she said.

"Who's involved? Can you see anyone before it goes blank?"

"I'm afraid not."

Temper sat back. "Has anyone else seen this? Any other Sensitives?"

"I wouldn't know – I don't talk to any Sensitives except for Jericho. I don't know why he hasn't seen anything yet – but such is the nature of our discipline. It's not like throwing fire. It's not always straightforward."

"How concerned should we be?"

"That everything is going to end? Probably very."

"I mean, what are the chances of this actually happening?"

"Oh," said Onosa. "No, Temper, it's not one of those predictions. This is different. Special. I think that, no matter what we do, this will come to pass. It cannot be averted."

"So we have a year left before the world is destroyed?"

"I don't know if *destroyed* is the right word, but... yes."

"We should probably tell someone about this," Temper muttered.

Onosa raised her head slightly, and for a moment her eyes unfocused. "They're coming," she said.

They got up. Temper reached into his pocket, feeling the sigil carved into the back of his phone. He tapped it three times, sending the signal to get ready. Then he pulled on his mask and flicked up his hood, and Onosa did the same.

They left the café and Onosa nodded ahead of them. They walked in that direction while the City Guard truck sped into the street behind them. The truck braked and there was the sound of boots on the road as the officers jumped down. Shouted orders, and they came running.

Temper and Onosa dropped to the ground. A moment later, a blue pulse of energy rippled over their heads. Temper risked a glance, just in time to see the cops being flung off their feet. They were unconscious even as they landed, but there were still some jumping down off the truck.

Once they realised this was an ambush, they dropped their shock sticks and went for their guns, but Ruckus and Tanith and Oberon were there to take them down with energy streams and fists. Temper sprang up, bolted towards them, crashing into an officer he didn't know, kicked out his leg and kneed him in the face when he dropped.

Another officer got his gun out, but right before he fired, his arm jerked up. While he struggled to regain control of himself, Temper grabbed him, sent an elbow to his jaw four times before he collapsed. Another officer hurtled into a wall like he'd been swatted to one side. Onosa strode up, eyes narrowed with focus.

When all the cops were down, Temper searched the officer in charge and found the list of mortals they'd come to arrest.

"Find them," he said to the others. "Hide them."

# 81

She sat on the couch, her legs curled beneath her, reading.

That in itself wasn't surprising – Darquesse loved to read. What was surprising was that she wasn't flicking through the pages like she normally did, reading an entire novel in a few seconds and then reaching immediately for the next. She was taking her time with this one.

"You're looking at me strangely," she said.

Sebastian raised an eyebrow behind his mask. "How do you know?"

"I can still see you even if I'm not looking at you," she said, like it was the most obvious thing in the world.

"Enjoying the book?"

"Yes."

"You're not speed-reading."

Now she looked up. "Like you said, I'm enjoying it. There's a difference between absorbing something and experiencing it. You told me that."

"I didn't think you were listening."

"I'm always listening."

He sat in the armchair opposite and took his hat off. "Experiencing something—"

"—is what living's about," she finished. "You don't have to repeat

416

the inspirational little speeches you give me, you know. I remember everything you say. Even the stupid things."

He smiled. "Sorry. I just find it difficult to keep up with you, that's all. What age are you now? Twelve? Thirteen?"

"Twelve."

"See, you're the same age Valkyrie Cain was when she first set off on her adventures with Skulduggery Pleasant. And you look just like she did, right, when she was your age?"

"I'm letting myself get older naturally," she replied, "so yes, we look identical."

"And this was allowed to happen. That's the thing I don't get. People saw this twelve-year-old girl rushing from one life-or-death situation to another, and nobody said anything? Nobody pulled Skulduggery aside and pointed out how hugely irresponsible it was?"

Darquesse raised an eyebrow. "You don't think she could take care of herself?"

"Ah-ah, I never said that – but that's hardly the point. If you weren't you, if you were just a normal twelve-year-old, I wouldn't let you go out and get in fights to save the world."

She grinned. "You'd stand up to Skulduggery Pleasant, would you?"

"I would do my very best."

"Or maybe you're being slightly overprotective because you raised me?"

"It's not about me raising you," he said. "It's basic common sense. You still have all of her memories, don't you?"

"Up until I split off from her, yep."

"So you know the danger she was in."

"Lots."

"And the amount of times she almost died."

"Loads."

"All I'm saying is that maybe twelve years of age is a little too young to be thrown into those kinds of situations."

Darquesse considered it. "Yeah, probably." She went back to reading her book.

# 82

Technically, he really should have been studying. Omen knew that. He had three more exams – two on Monday, and one on Tuesday morning – and then the school year ended and the Draíocht celebrations began. He should have stayed in school with everyone else and revised. Instead, Never had teleported him to a small town just outside Dublin, leaving him to wait for Crepuscular, because there wouldn't be a lot of point in sitting his final exam if he was just going to melt later that day.

Also, and he acknowledged this with a quiet resignation, he had paid so little attention in class that he was pretty much destined to fail.

But failing an exam was one thing – failing to save the world was something else entirely.

Omen looked at the mortals wandering by, wearing shorts and T-shirts, and he wished he'd brought his sunglasses. Sometimes the world was way too bright for him.

Then the coolest car he'd ever seen pulled up.

"It's a 1969 Dodge Challenger," Crepuscular said as Omen got in. "Picked up two of these in California in 1971 and had this beauty converted to left-hand drive before shipping her over here."

People stared as they drove. It was awesome.

"Find some music," Crepuscular said, indicating the radio. "Something seventies. No disco."

It was an old-fashioned radio, the kind with buttons you pushed in and two knobs to twist. Omen had to skip past a whole load of news reports about whatever ridiculous thing Martin Flanery had said before he found music.

"He's unbelievable."

Crepuscular didn't take his eyes off the road. "I'm sorry?"

"Flanery," said Omen. "Martin Flanery. You know, the American president?"

"I am aware who Martin Flanery is."

"Sorry. Some sorcerers don't take any interest in mortal stuff."

"I never understood that," Crepuscular said. "We live in a mortal world, do we not? The bread we buy is mortal bread. The films we watch are mortal films. The news we read is mortal news. Yes, we have our secret magical society on top of all that and behind it and around it... but we're just as much a part of this world as any mortal."

"I suppose it's easy to lose track of that when you live in Roarhaven," Omen said. "There aren't any chain stores or whatever, you know? Every business is owned by sorcerers, even the coffee shops and bookstores."

"But it's still mortal money you're handing over, is it not?"

"It is."

"This is why I could never have joined Mevolent's army," Crepuscular said. "Apart from the compulsory worshipping of the Faceless Ones, I just could never understand anyone wanting to subjugate the mortals. I still can't."

"You were alive back then?" Omen asked.

"Oh, yes."

"When were you born?"

"In 1845. A bad year for Ireland's potatoes, but a good year for me."

"Did you have any brothers or sisters?"

"Many."

"How many is many?"

"I know him, you know."

"Who?"

"Flanery."

"What?"

"Oh, yes. I know him very well."

"How? And, like, why?"

Crepuscular chuckled. "I've found the best approach to take with dangerous people is to steer them in the direction of your enemies. They're going to do massive amounts of damage anyway, so why not have that damage benefit you as much as possible?"

"You steered him?"

"As much as a man like that is capable of being steered. I started by advising him, then resorted to threats. They worked better, as it turned out."

"What did you steer him to do?"

"Flanery had been speaking with Abyssinia. He thought their arrangement would guarantee him eight years of power – possibly more. Oh, that silly little man had grand plans. Abyssinia, of course, was going to betray him and launch an attack on the Sanctuaries and then the mortal world as a whole, which, again, seemed to me entirely pointless."

"So what did you do?"

A shrug. "I told him how to betray her first."

"So you saved the world, basically?"

"In a roundabout way – but it's somewhat less impressive when you're around people who saved the world on a regular basis."

"Even so... thank you."

"You're quite welcome."

"What's he like, anyway, Flanery? Is he really how he comes across on TV?"

"Oh, no. No, Omen. He's much, much worse."

The got to the road leading to Creyfon Signate's house and Cadaver Cain was already there, standing in the shade of a tree.

"We should walk the rest of the way," Cadaver said.

Crepuscular muttered something under his breath, and pulled the Challenger on to the grass verge. Then all three started walking up the narrow road.

"Why does the guy who designed Roarhaven live all the way out here?" Omen asked. "You'd think he'd have built himself a nice house in the city."

"Signate suffered a considerable backlash after everything that happened," said Cadaver. "At this stage of his life, he's largely left magic – and magic-users – behind, and retired to a life of peace and solitude."

"How's he going to feel about us barging in like this?"

"He won't be pleased. Before you arrived, I had some time, so I dismantled most of his early-warning systems and booby traps."

"Booby traps?"

"Just to keep people like us away."

"You dismantled most of them?"

"There are some that can only be dismantled from within his house, for which I require a diversion."

"Like a fire, or an explosion?"

"I was thinking more along the lines of you," Cadaver said, "knocking on his door and distracting him while Crepuscular and I sneak in the back."

"I'm not sneaking anywhere with you," Crepuscular said.

"Very well," Cadaver responded. "Although your appearance is quite distinctive and may alert him to the fact that you are, in fact, a magic-user."

They walked on in silence for a bit.

"Fine," Crepuscular mumbled.

"Wonderful," Cadaver said brightly. "Omen, you'll need to continue on this road until you come to a cottage and engage Mr Signate in conversation for precisely two minutes and thirteen seconds."

"What? What'll I talk about?"

"That's up to you."

"I'm not gonna be able to talk to him about nothing for two minutes and thirteen seconds. I can barely talk to someone about something for two minutes and thirteen seconds, let alone nothing."

"You'll be fine."

Crepuscular shrugged. "You'll be fine."

Then they disappeared into the trees and Omen walked on alone, dragging his feet until he came up with a ruse so simple that even he couldn't make a mess of it.

Signate's home was small and old, with a sagging roof that made it look like the cottage was shrugging. It had, Omen supposed, character. He knocked on the front door.

It opened, and Creyfon Signate peered out at him. He was a small man who looked around sixty, dressed in a painter's smock. His eyes twinkled with either mischief or unfriendliness – it was too soon to tell. "Yes?" he said.

"Hello," said Omen. "I was wondering if you'd like to sponsor me for a five-kilometre fun run I'm doing for charity. Even a few coins will do, if you don't have much to spare."

"For charity?"

"Yes. I've been training for the last two months, and I think I can run it in less than—"

"What's the charity?"

Omen's smile froze. "Sorry?"

"The charity," Signate said impatiently. "What is it? What's it for?"

"Children," Omen said at once, and then, for some reason, "and dogs."

Signate frowned. "Children and dogs?"

"Yes. Well, getting children for dogs. For sick dogs. It's an organisation that arranges a child for every sick dog. It's called, the organisation, is called, the name of it, the charity, is Sick Dogs United."

423

"Sick Dogs United?"

"Sick Dogs United with Children," said Omen. "SDUC for short, or Sidduck. That's what we call it, down at the... down at headquarters."

"Sidduck. I don't think I've ever heard of it."

Omen frowned. "Really? It's very famous. There are posters everywhere, and ads on TV. You know that famous Sidduck commercial, with the sick dog and the... the child? Hugging?"

"Can't say I've ever seen it."

"It's very famous."

"Can't be that famous, or I'd know it."

"Maybe you don't watch much TV."

"I watch a normal amount."

"It's always on right after the news."

"I always watch the news and I've never seen it."

Every part of Omen was telling him to shut up, but he kept talking, anyway. "Maybe you're having trouble with your memory."

"My memory's fine."

"Well, I don't know what to say. The commercial is always on. It's got the sick kid and the dog and they're playing in the field and it has that piano music and everyone knows it."

"I thought it was the dog that was sick."

"Hmm?"

"You said the child is sick. I thought it was the dog."

Omen shook his head. "Nope. You must have misheard. It's definitely the child that's sick."

Signate folded his arms. "Then why is the charity called Sick Dogs United with Children, if it's the children that are sick?"

"I don't know," Omen responded. "You'd have to ask them."

"Who, the sick children or the dogs?"

"The people in charge."

"You know something? I don't think you're collecting for charity."

Omen gaped. "How dare you."

"I think you're trying to scam money out of me."

"I have never been so insulted in my life."

Signate went to close the door.

"Wait!" Omen yelled.

"What?" Signate said, glaring.

"How long would you say we've been talking?"

"What's that got to do with anything?"

"It's just, would you say it's been two minutes and thirteen seconds yet?"

"I would," said Cadaver, suddenly appearing behind Signate, who screamed.

# 83

Creyfon Signate was quite a grouchy man once he'd calmed down. He sat on his floral-print sofa with his thin legs crossed, his slippers tattered, and accepted the cup of tea Omen made him without a word of thanks. Seeing as how they'd essentially broken into his home and were holding him hostage, though, Omen could see why he wasn't in the best of moods.

While Crepuscular and Cadaver talked over each other in an effort to bring Signate up to speed, Omen wandered round the living room. There was a half-finished painting on an easel beside the window, of a woman standing alone in a park. The brushstrokes were delicate, though her features were indistinct.

"You like poking around other people's belongings, then?" Signate said to him, interrupting Cadaver.

"Sorry," Omen said, blushing. "This is brilliant."

"It's fine," said Signate, sounding annoyed with himself. "I still haven't captured her the way I wanted to."

"Is she someone you know?"

"Someone I knew," he said. "My late wife, when she was a young woman, back when she lived in this cottage. She always seemed so sad in those days." He looked at Cadaver again. "You were saying?"

Cadaver resumed talking, and Crepuscular butted in, and Cadaver corrected what Crepuscular was saying, and Crepuscular apologised for how long it was taking Cadaver to say anything, and Omen waited for them both to finish.

When it was over, Signate slurped his tea for a long, gross moment, and then nodded.

"I see," he said, and looked at Crepuscular. "So you're not here to kill me."

"No."

He looked at Cadaver. "And you're not Skulduggery Pleasant."

"Not any more."

He looked at Omen. "And you. You're not anyone."

Omen nodded. "Exactly."

"Now it's your turn to talk," Crepuscular said. "Who did you think sent us to kill you?"

"There are many people unhappy with me for what they see as conspiring with Erskine Ravel all those years ago."

"But they're not the type to send someone to kill you. So who—"

"I can cut through a lot of this," said Cadaver, "as I already know everything Mr Signate is about to say."

Crepuscular frowned at him. "If you already know, then why are we here?"

"Because, if we weren't here, Mr Signate would never say the things I know he says," Cadaver said, strolling round the room. "Besides, events must unfold the way they unfold – but, every so often, I can nudge things along. Mr Signate, as we've said, we know about Damocles Creed's plans for the Pillars, and we know that you designed them. We want to know how that came about."

A grunt. "Erskine Ravel started it all off – came to me with the proposal. It was audacious, so spectacular, that I couldn't say no. To build an entire city – an entire *city* – on a parallel Earth and then superimpose it over a small town in the middle of nowhere? Not only did I have to oversee construction in another dimension, I had to ensure the town we were going to transport it on to had the infrastructure in place so that the joining would be seamless. It had to be perfect, down to the last millimetre. Hey. Hey, what are you doing?"

Omen looked round. Cadaver had picked up Signate's paintbrush. "Don't mind me," Cadaver said.

Signate stood up quickly. "That's my painting!"

"It's still your painting. I'm just adding some flourishes."

"Mr Signate, please try to ignore him," Crepuscular said. "He doesn't have anything to contribute right now so he's trying to show off."

"He's painting on my painting!"

"You said yourself you're not happy with it, so what do you care? Ravel got you to design and build a city in secret. How does Creed come into all this?"

Scowling, Signate sat down again. "He knew about it. I don't know who told him or how he found out, but he knew about it and he saw an opportunity to piggyback on top of Ravel's master plan. Creed gave me a design – Seven Pillars of power at very exact distances and angles from each other. I asked him what it was for – he wouldn't tell me."

"But you could guess," said Crepuscular.

"I knew it had to be something to do with the Faceless Ones, yes."

Omen frowned. "And you went ahead with it, anyway?"

"Creed gave me his assurance that were I to deviate even slightly from his instructions he would personally kill my wife in front of me. So I said yes to his kind offer."

"How does it work?" Omen asked. "The Pillar in the West Tower?"

"The Pillar isn't in the tower," Cadaver mumbled, focusing on the painting.

Signate scowled at him again, then looked back at Omen. "He's right. The Seven Pillars consist of three main Pillars and four adjuncts. Hand me that piece of paper."

Omen pulled a sheet from beneath a stack of books and Signate snatched it from him. He laid it on a clear space on the table and took a pencil from his jacket. He drew two dots side by side.

"This is the High Sanctuary, and this is the Dark Cathedral. Both of these buildings are boiling with obvious power – I didn't need to disguise much in either of them." He made four more dots on the page. "These are the adjuncts. They aren't required to handle as much power as the others so they're smaller Pillars, located on Carnivore Row, Wallow Street, Razorblade Alley and Suture Street."

Omen gasped. "They're churches! That's where they've built brand-new churches for Faceless Ones worshippers!"

Signate frowned at him. "Why are you shouting?"

Omen blushed. "Sorry. I just... I figured something out and I got excited."

"You're doing very well, Omen," Crepuscular said, patting him on the back. "Continue, Mr Signate."

Signate drew a square on the bottom of the page. "And this is Corrival Academy. With the Academy, I had to be subtle. I had to disguise its secret purpose." He made little dots at the corners of the square. "This is the courtyard in the centre of the school. The four towers at each corner are Tempests – do you know what a Tempest is, boy? A Tempest drains magic, holds it, and converts it into usable energy."

"That's why Chicane has been pushing people in," Omen said.

"And not just into the West Tower," Cadaver said. "He's been pushing people into all four towers over the last three years."

"As distasteful as it may be," said Signate, "that is how these Tempests are charged, yes. Once all the Tempests are powered up, they feed into the Pillar, here in the courtyard itself. As soon as all the Pillars are active, lines of energy are established, dissecting the city along its streets like so." He connected the seven points with lines of pencil, forming a sigil.

"And then we have the Mass Activation," said Crepuscular.

Signate shrugged. "If you say so."

"You could have asked for help," Omen said. "You could have gone to Skulduggery or even Erskine Ravel. Ravel would have been able to protect you and your family."

"There is no protection from Damocles Creed," Signate said.

"You could have done something. You didn't have to give him everything he asked for."

"Oh," Signate said, "I didn't."

"You have a way of shutting it all off," Omen said.

Signate nodded approvingly. "See? You figured something out and this time you didn't even shout."

"If you tell us how to do it, we'll make sure the Pillars are never used."

"And I'm in favour of that – but, before I tell you how to do it, I'll need to make final arrangements."

"Or you could tell us now to make sure that—"

Signate waved a hand. "Don't rush me. I'm the only person on the planet who knows where I've hidden it, so the least you can do is afford me the courtesy of waiting. Once Creed discovers that I've betrayed him, he'll send one of his killers after me. Don't worry, don't worry, turning off the Pillar at your school isn't a complicated process – it's as easy as pressing a button because that's exactly what it is. It's a big red button on a small black box. I don't have a hip and cool name for it, unfortunately – I just think of it as the remote."

"It's called the Zeta Switch," Cadaver said.

Signate looked annoyed. "It is not."

Cadaver shrugged. "That's what they'll call it in years to come."

"The Zeta Switch is needlessly dramatic. The remote will suffice."

"I actually prefer the Zeta Switch," Omen said, smiling nervously.

"Of course you do," said Signate. "You're a teenager. And apparently so is the skeleton over there. *Will you please stop ruining my painting?*"

Cadaver added another few brushstrokes, then stepped back, tilted his head, and nodded. He turned the painting for the others to see. Omen didn't know how he'd done it in such a short amount of time, but he'd transformed the woman on the canvas into a haunted figure, quite separate from the scene around her.

Signate walked over slowly, took the canvas from him. "How did you do that?"

"I can see into the future," Cadaver said, "and I can see into the past. Right now, I can see you and your late wife in this park – though she was only your fiancée at this point – and I can see her face. She does seem sad, you're right."

Eyes pinned to the painting, Signate wandered into the corner of the room, and turned. "She never told me what had made her so."

"It was another man," said Cadaver. "She had loved him and he'd loved her, but they couldn't be together."

Omen swore he could see the life leak out of the old man. "I... I thought as much."

"I can't see into people's minds and I can't see into their hearts," Cadaver said, "but I know the things she told her friends years later, and she was genuinely glad she met and married you. If that's any consolation."

"It is," Signate said, looking up. "Thank you. I've been trying to capture that sadness in a painting for years, and I just didn't have the skill."

Cadaver put down the brush. "I know. I thought it was the least I could do, seeing as what's about to happen."

"I'm sorry? What do you mean?"

Something moved in the shadows behind Signate.

The Necromancer, the one who'd brought Damocles Creed back to life, took a single step out of the corner and was suddenly looming over Creyfon Signate with a glaive in his hands. It didn't occur to Omen to shout out a warning. It didn't occur to Omen to do anything but stare.

He snapped out of it when that glaive came down diagonally and sliced through the old man from right shoulder to left hip. It was disturbing how the two parts of him flopped to the ground.

The painting fell, too, the canvas neatly divided.

Crepuscular leaped at the Necromancer – Serrate, that was his name – and Cadaver threw a fireball and Omen stepped towards Signate's remains. The old man's eyes were open wide and his mouth gaped, like he'd been caught peeing in the pool. The blood was leaving his body at a leisurely, yet admirably persistent, pace. It spread out across the carpet. There was so much of it.

Omen looked up as Crepuscular crashed into the wall next to him. Cadaver wrestled for control of the glaive, but once he'd torn it from Serrate's hands it turned to shadows that flowed back and reformed in Serrate's grip.

"Sneaky," said Cadaver.

Serrate lunged and Cadaver ducked and swerved away from the flashing blade. Any moment now, Cadaver was going to make a mistake and that glaive would find him. Unless Omen did something to save the day.

He pulled out the shock baton that Auger had given him, snapped it to its full length, gripping it tight to charge it. Then he hurled it, missing Serrate by a hand's breath, but making him jerk back anyway, giving Cadaver an opportunity to strike. He crunched a kick into Serrate's leg, taking it from under him and dumping him on the ground. Instead of finishing the fight, though, Cadaver just stood there, his head tilted, as if he was listening to something in the distance.

Serrate seized the initiative, kicked Cadaver away, and sprang to his feet. He swirled the glaive, enveloping himself in shadows, and when the shadows faded he was gone.

Omen hurried over to Crepuscular and helped him to his feet, and then they all stood round Creyfon Signate's remains.

"So you knew that was going to happen," Crepuscular said to Cadaver. "And you did nothing to stop it."

"Events have to unfold as they unfold," Cadaver answered.

Crepuscular shook his head. "And I thought I was ruthless."

"Oh," Cadaver said, "you still are."

Omen was a mass of conflicting emotions. On the one hand, he was sorry that someone had died. On the other, he was raging that Signate hadn't just told them where he'd put the Zeta Switch like they'd asked. But on another hand – presumably somebody else's hand – the loss of a life was surely more important than that. Yet, on the final hand, was it, though? Wasn't safeguarding the whole planet more important than the loss of an old man's life?

"We need to focus," Omen said.

"I am focused," said Crepuscular, picking up the shock baton and handing it back to Omen.

"I'm focused, too," said Cadaver.

"Then I need to focus," Omen said, coming perilously close to annoyance with them both. "OK, we don't have the device, but that doesn't mean we're beaten. We can still go back to Corrival on Draíocht and stop the Pillar from even activating."

Crepuscular frowned at him. "You're talking like we've failed."

"We haven't failed," Omen insisted. "This isn't over until we draw our last breath."

"Well now," Cadaver said, amused.

Crepuscular nodded. "That's very dramatic."

"You two can make fun of me all you want," Omen said, "but I'm not giving up and neither should you."

"As I was saying," Crepuscular said, "you're talking as if we've failed when we haven't. Creyfon Signate wasn't the only one who knows where the device is hidden."

Omen blinked at him. "Yes, he was. That's literally what he said."

"Just because he didn't tell any other person doesn't mean no one else knows."

Omen took a moment to puzzle it out, then his heart leaped

in his chest and he turned to Cadaver. "You know everything that's going to happen! You know where he hid the device!"

"Providing you're telling the truth," Crepuscular said. "Providing you really can see all possible futures."

Cadaver put on his coat. "Would I lie to you?" he said, and walked to the door. "Let's go save the world."

# 84

A constellation of blazing stars rotated in the living room, a galaxy of worlds and suns linked by continuous flashes of lightning. In the middle of it all, Darquesse, approximately sixteen years old and dressed in black.

"What is this?" Sebastian asked, his voice hushed as he walked in.

"It's you," she said.

He glanced at her and smiled. "You named a planet after me? It better be a handsome planet, I swear to God."

"This," she said, indicating the constellation. "It's you."

"I don't get it. What are we looking at?"

She pointed at where lightning had just flashed. "Did you see that? That was your question."

"I'm confused."

"I can tell. This is the inside of your mind. These are your thoughts. These are your synapses. Over here are your memories. Look." She poked a cloud of particles and he remembered that time when he was four years old, getting lost in the woods. "This is live," Darquesse continued. "A livestream of who you are right now. When we were talking the other day, and I was saying how someone's personality isn't really that important – afterwards, I started thinking that maybe I was wrong. It all depends on how you look at it, obviously, but..."

"I, uh, I don't know how I feel about this," Sebastian said.

She squinted at the constellation. "According to this, you feel awkward, and you're wondering if this is an invasion of privacy."

"You can tell that just by standing here?"

Darquesse laughed. "No, I could tell by your reaction. Am I right?"

"You are."

A grin. "I'm getting better at regular-people stuff, amn't I? Social cues and whatnot."

"It's all very impressive. But I can't fail to notice that my brainwaves are still being broadcast in the living room."

"Sorry," she said, and shrank the whole constellation down until it fitted in the palm of her hand.

He peered at it. It was an odd sensation. "What do you plan on doing with that?"

"I'm going to find somewhere to keep it."

"This is very, very weird, Darquesse."

"I know." She peered at him. "You have a question you want to ask."

"How can you tell that? I'm wearing a mask, for God's sake."

"I always look through the mask. What's the question?"

"Well, it's... I can't help but notice that you've got older. Your ageing is speeding up. Any particular reason why?"

She shrugged.

"Can I get a little more information?"

She sighed. "When I was younger, I was learning more, so I let that last longer. Now that I'm getting closer to the age I was when I started this, I can afford to let things speed up. That a good enough answer?"

"That's a fine answer, actually. Can I ask another question?"

"You're gonna ask which way I'm leaning when it comes to saving the world, aren't you?"

"I'm just curious. If the world was going to end tomorrow and you could do something today that would save it, that would save everyone on Earth, including me – and you decided not to, what would be your reason?"

"I told you that."

"In the conversation we had about energy and how personalities don't matter because they're just fluff?"

"Well, yeah."

"But you said you admitted you might be wrong."

"Sure, but... I mean, not wrong enough to change anything. A person's consciousness means nothing in the grand scheme of things and, like, the grand scheme of things is what I see."

"But, if you can save the world, why not just save it?"

"Because then I won't get to see what happens next."

Sebastian stared at her, and she sagged.

"And now you hate me."

"No," he said. "I don't hate you. I could never hate you."

"Well, you're not happy with me."

"I don't know what I am, to be honest. Above all else, I'm scared. I was sent to get you to save us when we need to be saved, and if you don't do that then everything I've done over the past few years will have been for nothing. I'll have failed, and everyone will pay for my failure."

"Oh, Sebastian," she said, walking over, hugging him, "if the world ends, it won't be your fault in the slightest. It'll just mean I don't care enough."

He hugged her back, unsure as to how to respond, and when the hug was done she vanished. A minute later, there was a knock on the door. Still frowning over her words, Sebastian answered it without wondering who it could be, and there was a flash and a moment of pain and then he was on the floor, gasping and unable to move.

Footsteps approached. Hands grabbed him. His arms were twisted behind his back. His wrists shackled. He was hauled up. Men in black uniforms.

His hat. His hat was on the ground.

Someone walked into his field of vision, picked up the hat, came over.

Commander Hoc peered at him. "Interesting outfit," he said. "Not sure about the mask..." He put the hat on Sebastian's head. "Make sure he doesn't lose that," he said to the men in black uniforms.

"Yes, sir."

"Yes, Commander."

Hoc gestured and said, "Go on," and they carried Sebastian out.

# 85

Cleavers were creatures of ritual. It was how they trained, how they practised, and how they performed their duties. Rippers may have laid down their scythes, abandoned the grey uniforms, but they couldn't abandon a lifetime of conditioning. Rituals soothed the mind in troubled times, after all.

Coda Quell's ritual was performing combat sequences as the sun set, bleeding over the sky. Valkyrie would watch him from the window in her kitchen back in Colorado as he flowed from one technique to the next perfectly, the elegance of the movements disguising their real-world applications. This sweep of the hand would break a jaw. That simple step would shatter a knee. Those moves would snap a neck. But Coda, and fighters like him, made the techniques look like a dance, fluidity punctuated by moments of hyper-rigidity.

Valkyrie knew him well enough to narrow his ideal dance floor down to six locations. Four could prove problematic if someone were to discover him, which left her with the two others. She picked one, a rooftop on Drowning Man Street, at random, and waited on an uncomfortable perch nearby. Right before the sun hit the horizon, the roof access door opened and he walked out.

He hadn't changed since she'd seen him last. Still had the same close-cropped brown hair, the same clean-shaven jaw. He took off his jacket and his shirt. Still had all the same muscles.

All the same scars. He stood with his feet together and bowed to the sun, then settled back into a wide stance, and began the first sequence.

Valkyrie stayed where she was, and watched.

When he was halfway through the sequence, when she was sure his attention was directed inwards, she launched herself into the air. She came up behind him, sent out twin bolts of lightning. But he dodged, ducked, flipped, and she was missing with everything she threw at him and passing him now, as he pulled something from his bag and fired.

A binding bullet struck her on the hip and her magic went away and she fell, rolling across the rooftop. She came to a stop against the lip of the roof. Quell walked over to her like he was out for a Sunday stroll.

"Where'd you get that?" she grunted, sitting up.

The rifle was clunkier than the versions she'd seen in the future, and less powerful – her necronaut suit was still active. It did the job, though, she had to admit that.

"It's new," Quell said. "There are only a handful in existence."

"And you managed to get your hands on one of them."

He put the gun down carefully, as if he couldn't stand to see it damaged. "How are you?" he asked.

Valkyrie got up. Didn't even try to pull the ink away. "I'm grand," she said. "I'm great. Nothing to report here. Anything new with you?"

"I missed you."

"Not from where I'm standing."

"I meant emotionally."

"I know what you meant, but, before we go skipping through the cornfields of our memories, let's not stray too far from the fact that you tried to kill me. I mean, I'm no stranger to an ex trying to kill me. Caelan tried it. Remember me telling you about Caelan, the vampire?"

"I remember."

"What happened to him?"

"He died."

"How did he die?"

"You killed him."

"So this is the second time this has happened and, while I doubt I'll ever truly get used to it, the shock value fades with familiarity, y'know? But Caelan at least hated me by the end. He had a reason. What's your excuse?"

"I didn't try to kill you. If I'd wanted to kill you, you'd be dead."

"You shot me multiple times. You hit vital organs."

"If I'd wanted to kill you, I would have shot you in the heart and in the head."

"So why didn't you?"

Quell hesitated. "I had never loved anyone, Valkyrie. I thought I was incapable of it. You knew this. You knew this when we started. I warned you, but you needed me to fulfil a function. You needed to love someone who didn't love you back. Have you ever asked yourself why? I think it was just another way for you to torture yourself."

"I don't need your opinion on my motivations," Valkyrie said. "I just need to know why you agreed to kill me and then why you decided not to. I mean Jesus, Coda, why are you even here?"

"I'm here because I love you."

This made her pause. "You don't love anyone."

"That was true, once. Then I met you and then I left you, and when I was on my own I realised what I'd been denying. I did love you, Valkyrie. I do love you. I went back to Meek Ridge, but you'd gone. You'd left. I thought my chance at happiness had evaporated – but when Christopher Reign hired me to kill Damocles Creed, I took it as a sign. You were always talking about signs. Do you remember? *If it's sunny today, I'll go for a run. If it's raining tomorrow, I'll work out indoors.* You were always looking for the universe to show you what to do."

"I was being silly," Valkyrie responded. "It was just something I said."

"Oh," said Quell. "I didn't know that. I thought you believed in signs, and so I took Reign's offer as a sign that I should travel to Ireland and reconnect with you."

She made a face. "Reconnect?"

"I've been reading books on relationships."

"Oh, God."

"I arrived in Ireland seven months ago, but you weren't here."

"Seven months ago I was in Dimension X."

"I accepted some other jobs in Europe while I was waiting for Reign to issue the kill order, but I was in Roarhaven when you returned. I fought by your side. When you came through the portal, I fought by your side. My face was hidden, though. You didn't know it was me. I saved your life."

"I'll take your word for it."

"I planned to announce my presence when things calmed down," he said, "but then I saw you with Militsa Gnosis."

"And... what? You're angry about that? Coda, you dumped me. You left me. I got over you, I came home, I fell in love with Militsa and I found something that resembled happiness."

He nodded. "And my happiness fell away from me."

"That's your own fault."

"I accept that."

"So what are you doing here, Coda?"

"Christopher Reign gave the kill order. The arrangements had been made, the weapon was in place – all I had to do was pull the trigger. When it was done, I left it a few days, then returned to get paid. I was in the nightclub when you visited."

"How much did Reign offer you to kill us?"

"Taking into account the risk – not only posed by the targets, but also by the impromptu nature of the task – he tripled my fee from the Creed hit. I borrowed a weapon from one of his men and a sledgehammer from the construction crew, and intercepted you. If I hadn't taken the job then and there, he would have hired someone else to do it."

"And they might have succeeded where you intentionally failed."

"I intentionally failed with you," Quell said, "but I had fully intended to kill Skulduggery Pleasant and I regret my failure. He's not good for you, Valkyrie. I think you'd be better off without him in your life."

"I'm struggling to process why you would think your opinion means anything after you were paid to kill me."

"I wasn't paid," said Quell. "I failed the task, remember? Christopher Reign called off the hit when he went into hiding. I think he regrets his rash decision."

"The poor guy."

"I love you, Valkyrie."

"Stop saying that."

"It's the truth. I love—"

"Please," she said. "Stop. Coda, I don't love you any more. I'm not sure I ever did. I think I saw you as someone I could use to punish myself, so I placed all my love with you. That's... that's not the same as loving you. I'm sorry."

He said nothing. Valkyrie took the small spray bottle from her pocket and squirted the ink. It dissolved and her magic came back.

Quell frowned. "What is that?"

She didn't answer him, just put it away again. "I have to go," she said. "Someone probably saw me and they've already called the City Guard. I'm... I'm glad you can love, I'm glad you've broken through all that Cleaver training, and I hope you find someone. It just can't be me."

Magic gathered and she stepped off the rooftop and flew.

# 86

Three years ago...

Valkyrie was gone.

Quell watched from afar as a removal company packed her stuff into a van. She was gone and she obviously wasn't coming back. This hurt him. It drove a spike into his middle and churned his guts. He didn't like this. She was supposed to be here, and he was supposed to walk in the front door, and things were meant to go back to the way they were before he left.

But she was gone. Even the dog was gone, the puppy she'd named Xena. He'd never taken the time to get to know the dog. Maybe he should have. He doubted it would have made a difference, though – he'd been the one to end the only slice of happiness in his life, not Valkyrie.

He watched someone talk to the removal people. He recognised him. The mortal who owned the store in Meek Ridge – Danny somebody. He called round every week to drop off the groceries because Quell didn't know what to buy and Valkyrie didn't want to go into town. Quell had never actually met him, and Valkyrie had only exchanged a few dozen words with him – but maybe things had changed. Watching Danny issue instructions, Quell thought he looked like he was very comfortable on the farm.

When the removal van left, Danny locked up the house and

drove back to Meek Ridge. Quell followed a few minutes later. He parked outside the store and waited for it to reopen. Once the sign on the door had been flipped, he got out of the truck and walked in.

Danny was stacking shelves. "Hi," he said. "Anything you need help with, just ask."

Quell pretended to look around while he formulated what he was going to say. It was odd, though – his thoughts were backing up in his head, tumbling and jumbling, as anger rose like flood-water from the depths to block the pathways to his usual reassuring rationality.

Danny moved behind the counter. Quell couldn't delay any more without drawing suspicion, so he walked up to him and said, "Where's Valkyrie?"

Danny paled, and Quell saw instantly that he had something to hide. His anger blossomed into jealousy and it screamed, but he kept it all beneath the surface and waited with the patience that had been trained into him.

"I don't know who that is," Danny said. "Sorry. Is that even a name? Did you mean Valerie? I don't know any Valerie, either. Sorry."

"Where has she gone?" Quell asked.

"I really don't know who you're talking about," Danny said, attempting a chuckle. "Actually, do you mind? I have to close up."

"You just opened."

"And now I have to close again. Real sorry."

Quell didn't budge. Danny licked his lips. His mouth was probably dry. Quell had heard that sometimes happened when people were nervous. Or guilty.

It may not have taken Valkyrie long to move on after Quell left. Danny might have been an acceptable substitute. He was wearing a T-shirt featuring one of the music groups Valkyrie liked to listen to. They would have had things to talk about that didn't revolve around combat. They would have had shared interests.

Danny looked normal. They would have been able to talk about normal things.

"What did you do to her?" Quell asked softly.

The guilt had to come from somewhere. Quell doubted that Danny could have hurt Valkyrie physically, but there were other kinds of pain, as he was just discovering. Jealousy was a type of pain he'd never experienced before now. It tore at him.

"I don't know what you're talking about and I'm asking you to leave," Danny said.

Quell dragged him over the counter. Danny panicked and flailed and Quell threw him against the wall.

"How did you hurt her?" he asked.

"I didn't hurt her," Danny said. "I didn't hurt anyone. I don't know what you're—"

Quell hit him. Danny leaned away from him, hands over his face. Didn't make a sound for a few seconds.

"Who are you?" Quell asked.

"I own the store," Danny answered.

"Who are you?"

"I'm Danny. I own the store."

"Where is Valkyrie?"

"I'm... I'm not gonna tell you."

This was untrue.

Quell hit him twice more and Danny fell to his knees, gasping.

"You hurt her," Quell told him. "She wouldn't have left otherwise. Were you her boyfriend? It's OK – you can tell me. I won't be mad." It occurred to him that he should have said this before he started inflicting pain. "You drove her away from here, didn't you? Where did she go? Did she even tell you?"

Danny lunged at him, swinging a fist. Quell caught his arm and flung him into the shelves. They toppled, sending their contents spilling across the floor.

"Tell me where Valkyrie has gone," Quell said as Danny scrambled backwards. "I won't be mad."

Danny had taken Valkyrie's love, the love she'd had for Quell, and he'd used it against her. Once, Quell would have had to imagine the pain she'd felt – but now he understood it. Now he shared it. It was a muddled pain, acute but confused, the type of pain that stopped you from thinking. He'd had dreams of returning to Valkyrie and picking up where they'd left off. Now those dreams were gone. Smashed. All because of this man. All because of Danny, with his stupid T-shirt and his stupid store.

Quell closed his eyes and breathed out, letting the tension leave his body. There was no point getting carried away. That wouldn't solve anything. That wouldn't get him the answers he sought. He opened his eyes and Danny was right in front of him and Quell's hands were around his throat.

Quell hesitated, then laid Danny on the floor. He'd made a mistake. He'd lost control. It was a stupid thing to do.

He set fire to the store and left Meek Ridge.

# 87

Near the top of the hill there was a cave, and the cave became a tunnel that lit up with a series of lights embedded in the stone floor as they moved through it. They got to a small cavern and Cadaver started patting his pockets, as if he was looking for something.

There was a table in the middle of the cavern, and on the table there was an Echo Stone. They neared, and an image of Creyfon Signate flickered up before them, frowning.

"You're not me," he said.

"Uh, no," Omen replied. "The other you, the real you... I'm afraid that he died."

"Oh, dear."

"I'm very sorry for your loss."

Signate's image slumped his shoulders. "I'm sure he was happy to pass away peacefully."

"He was murdered."

"Oh, my. Horribly?"

"Pardon?"

"Was he horribly murdered or murdered horribly?"

Omen hesitated. "I'm not sure I know the difference."

"Horribly murdered is when the method of your murder could be described as horrible," said Cadaver.

"And murdered horribly is when the misfortune of your murder outweighs the method," said Crepuscular.

Omen blinked. "Then I – I suppose he... Can I say that he was horribly murdered horribly?"

"You could," said Cadaver.

"If you wanted," said Crepuscular.

"Then he was horribly murdered horribly," Omen said to the image of Signate. "He was just about to bring us here when he died to give us the Zeta Switch."

"I'm sorry?"

"The remote-control thing for deactivating the Pillar at Corrival."

"Ah," said Signate's image. "Yes. That is indeed here."

"Could we have it?"

"Of course."

"Thank you."

"You're welcome. But first you must solve three puzzles, each one more fiendishly difficult than the last, in order to unlock three clues which will aid you in your quest for—"

"It's over here," Cadaver said, pulling a thick block of clay from inside his ribcage. Rebuttoning his shirt one-handed, he walked right through Signate's image and slapped the clay against the wall, where it stuck. He poked a metal pin into the clay and walked back again.

"What is that?" Signate's echo asked.

"Plastic explosive," said Cadaver. "I picked it up on my way here to save us all some time."

"But... but the fiendishly difficult puzzles," said the echo. "The clues. The hidden booby traps."

Cadaver took a detonator from his pocket. "Afraid not," he said. He pressed the button and the wall exploded and Omen jumped and the echo shrieked, and a moment later a small black box with a big red button came floating through the swirling dust and fell into Cadaver's hand.

"But that's not fair!" said the echo.

"I'm terribly sorry," Omen said, backing up as Cadaver and

449

Crepuscular walked into the tunnel. Signate's echo faded to nothing with a look of indignation on his face, and, when Omen turned to catch up, Cadaver tossed him the Zeta Switch. He yelped as he fumbled the catch, but managed to pull it into his chest before he dropped it.

"Be careful with that," Cadaver said. "It's important."

"So why am I holding on to it?"

"Because I don't trust him to do it," Crepuscular said, "and I barely trust me to do it. You'll be fine. Just don't break it."

Omen held the Zeta Switch in both hands. "So what do we do now?" he asked Cadaver.

"It's best if I don't tell you," Cadaver answered. "The less you know about what you're going to do, the more likely you are to do it, and the more likely you are to do what you're going to do, the better our chances of success."

Omen nodded. "I get that. Absolutely. It's what they always say about prophecies and visions – knowing the future changes the future. But maybe, like, just a rough outline about what we should maybe be thinking of doing?"

He heard a smile in Cadaver's voice. "I'm afraid not, Omen."

Omen looked to Crepuscular. "What do you think we should do?"

"As much as it pains me to say it," Crepuscular responded, "Pleasant and Cain had the right idea. We have the Zeta Switch to shut down the Activation Wave if it gets going, but killing Creed is the surest way of ensuring it doesn't flow in the first place. The problem is, Pleasant and Cain gave up too soon. As my old Scout teacher would have said if I'd ever been a Scout, if at first you don't succeed, try and try again."

Omen frowned. "So you're saying assassinate Creed for a second time? What's to stop Uriah Serrate from bringing him back?"

"Here's where my intricate plan gets intricater, Omen. Pay attention now – it's complicated. We kill Creed *and* we kill Serrate. See how that works? Two birds, one bullet. Or many bullets, and

450

maybe a big rock for smashing. Hell, I'll do it. I've always had a thing for killing Necromancers. It's quietly satisfying to pulverise pretentious people."

"We should stay away from Serrate," said Cadaver.

"Nobody asked you," Crepuscular said.

"I'm merely volunteering information. I've seen multiple scenarios in which Serrate is killed before the Activation Wave, and very few of them turn out well. The path we're on right now, this is the route to take."

"And we just trust you on that, yes?"

"Trust me or don't trust me – it's the way the future unfolds." They emerged from the tunnel and Cadaver rose into the night sky.

"Before you go," Omen said quickly.

Cadaver turned and looked down. "Yes?"

"Uh... I was wondering, because you've seen all the possible futures and everything, if there was any chance that you'd, that you could possibly, tell me what the questions will be in my remaining exams?"

Cadaver's head tilted. "In the English exam, the poets will be Keats and Seamus Heaney. In the Mortal History exam, you'll need to focus on the Molly Maguires and De Valera in America. And in your Magic Practical you'll be required to levitate."

"I suck at levitating."

"I know," said Cadaver. "Good luck, Omen Darkly, and not only with the exams. The fate of the world depends on you."

Omen stared up at him. "I don't want the fate of the world depending on me."

"You'll do great," said Cadaver. "Though not in the exams." And they watched him fly off.

"Could've offered us a lift," Crepuscular mumbled, and started the walk down the hill.

Omen hurried to catch up. "Looks like he's been telling the truth all along."

Crepuscular grunted.

"You don't think so?" Omen asked.

"He might be telling the truth about seeing the future," Crepuscular said, "but that doesn't mean we can trust him. For all we know, this road we're on leads to our agonising deaths and his glorious triumph. We're not all in this together, Omen. Keep that in mind."

"OK," Omen said, "just as long as you keep in mind that Cadaver might be telling the truth about everything, and he actually is here to help."

"Are you really that naive?"

"Yes," said Omen. "Yes, I am."

# 88

Sebastian was relatively sure it was morning.

He'd woken up in this cell, his wrists shackled to the wall. This was not the first time he'd been placed behind bars, and familiarity, it was fair to say, breeds contempt. But at least this time he had some company as, one by one, the members of the Darquesse Society were led in and chained up on either side of him.

When the last of Sebastian's friends had been secured, the men and women in black uniforms stood back, and Damocles Creed walked in, Hoc trailing after him.

The Supreme Mage went straight over to Sebastian, hunkered down and peered into his eyes. "And why is this one dressed as a plague doctor?"

"We're not entirely sure," Hoc said. "The mask is proving difficult to remove. Give me the night, Supreme Mage, and I will peel it away."

"I don't think that's necessary," Creed said. "Once he's dead, I'm sure it will be easier to take off." He reached out, tapped a thick finger against the glass lens over Sebastian's right eye. "Who are you, I wonder?"

Sebastian clenched his jaw. "You won't get anything out of—"

"It was a rhetorical question," Creed said, standing up. "I don't care who you are. All I care about is that the Darquesse child cares about you. She'll track you down, I trust? Come to your rescue?"

Sebastian glared. "I don't know what you're—"

"No use lying!" Tantalus said, bounding in with a delighted smile on his face. "I told him everything! Every last thing – *Sebastian Tao*! I told them your name, I told them it all! You should have killed me – you know that? You should have."

"How could you do this?" Kimora asked. "You worship Darquesse just as much as we do."

"More!" Tantalus screeched. "I worshipped her more! I founded the Darquesse Society! I was your leader! But you betrayed me, and by doing so—"

Two of Hoc's men grabbed Tantalus. "What?" he said. "Hello?" Despite his struggles, they led him to the wall without much effort and chained him there. "Supreme Mage, what is the meaning of this? I demand—"

"Hush," said Creed. "I don't care about anything you have to say. Literally anything."

"But... but, Supreme Mage!" Tantalus cried. "We had a deal! Supreme Mage! Our deal!"

Creed closed his eyes. "I have a headache," he said. "I've had a headache ever since I came back. I don't know what it is. I don't know why. Maybe it's a side effect of returning to life. Maybe it's something else." He opened his eyes. "I haven't been myself lately. Again, I don't know why. I've been agreeing to things without questioning them. That is unlike me. This is worrying. And so I find myself seizing each and every opportunity I can to attempt to reassert myself – to reassert the old me. This is one such opportunity. Mr Tantalus, the old me would have ordered you shot by now, simply for raising your voice. You'd better hope the old me stays hidden."

He walked out. Hoc and his agents followed. A gate clanged shut and Tantalus fell into a shocked silence.

Sebastian leaned forward so he could see him down the far end. "Had a deal, huh?" He leaned back. "How's that working out for you?"

# 89

Two days until Féile na Draíochta. Two days until the Activation Wave. Two days to save the world. Valkyrie had been in tighter situations.

Creed had people watching Grimwood and her family's house, and the Sense Wardens were making it impossible to lower her guard in Roarhaven, so they returned to room 528 of the City View Hotel in Meath. As Valkyrie slipped the DO NOT DISTURB sign over the door handle, Skulduggery put the Jericho Candle on the desk.

"Wow," Valkyrie said. "There is not a whole lot of that left."

"There isn't," he agreed. "So you travel to the future, you talk to China, and you get back as soon as you can. No dawdling."

"No dawdling. Got it," she said, but before she lay down on the bed she turned to him. "I have something to tell you that I didn't want to tell you, but I have to, because if I don't then I'm being stupid, and it's important, so I have to and I know I have to, and I know I'm babbling, but I'm kinda hoping that the babbling will lead to me actually saying what I have to say because I don't want to give myself a chance to have second thoughts so I basically dated Coda Quell for about two years."

Skulduggery tilted his head.

"And I talked to him," Valkyrie said. "Last night. We chatted."

"You dated him?"

"In Colorado, yes."

"You went on dates with him?"

"OK, maybe 'dated' is a bit misleading. We didn't go out for dinner or to the movies or anything, but we were together as a... a couple, I suppose."

"You," Skulduggery said, "and an assassin."

"Yeah."

"An assassin that then tried to kill you."

"In my defence, I was going through a lot back then so my decision-making might not have been the sharpest. Also, he wasn't really trying to kill me, apparently. He was trying to kill you, though, so... I don't know, I'm conflicted. Anyway, the amount of legs you've got to stand on here is exactly none. You dated a mass murderer, remember? Did you hear me judging you when we all found out about Abyssinia?"

"Yes."

"But only because it was really funny."

"Do you still have feelings for him?"

"No. God, no."

"And does he have feelings for you?"

"Apparently, he loves me."

"Did you tell Militsa about him?"

"She knows all about him."

"Does she know he tried to kill you?"

"She doesn't know that part."

Skulduggery nodded. "OK, that's very interesting. I'm not sure that it changes anything, but—"

"But that's not the point," Valkyrie said. "I just needed to tell you. Now I'm ready to go."

She activated her necronaut suit and lay on the bed, and Skulduggery clicked his fingers and lit the candle. Valkyrie closed her eyes and breathed in the aroma. The voice in her head, the voice of all her worries and anxieties, got steadily quieter.

"Tell me your intent," Skulduggery said, his voice soft.

"I want to travel into the future," Valkyrie replied.

"Why?"

"To find out how to prevent it."

"You've seen yourself in this future," said Skulduggery. "You've seen yourself with claws and fangs and wings. Picture that person. Keep that image in your head. Your future self is all that matters."

Valkyrie remembered the way the harpy had snarled, and she froze that moment in her mind. She remembered the narrowed eyes, the cracked lips, the long, dirty hair. She remembered the fangs.

And she found her; she felt that connection – immediate and strong.

"Got her," she whispered.

"There's a rope tied round your waist," said Skulduggery. "It's pulling you towards her. Do you feel it?"

"Yes."

"It's pulling you. You're getting closer."

"Yes."

"Let it take you. Let it take you away."

The rope – she could feel how it dug into her waist – tugged her up off the bed and she left her body behind and it was a wonderful feeling, an exhilarating feeling, and she was moving for the wall but also beyond the wall, beyond this moment.

Her body followed her and lightning took it apart and Valkyrie's thoughts scattered and she wasn't herself any more: she was something bigger and smaller and different and the same. She became a meteor storm that streaked through time and space and collided, and Valkyrie stumbled as she re-formed, falling to a wooden floor in the gloom.

The world rocked and rolled around her and she stayed very still, her eyes closed, waiting for it all to stop moving.

She looked around. She was in a small attic. The floorboards were old. A chill wind whistled through the gaps in the walls. She was up high, in a tower somewhere. She glimpsed blue skies outside.

The gloom was heavy, gathering in sections. Dust motes danced in shafts of sunlight that only darkened the shadows. Valkyrie filled her hand with energy and did a little exploring, found the harpy's... bed? Nest? Whatever it was. A bundle of rags and old, smelly blankets in one corner. The harpy wasn't home. That was probably a good thing.

She squeezed out through one of the gaps in the walls and flew straight up, into the light clouds to hide her from view. Positioning herself over Corrival Academy, she cut her power and fell, only using her magic to steer herself back on course and manage her plummeting speed. She landed – heavily – in a back alley nearby, and crept to the corner where she watched the school, looking out for anyone she might know. At lunchtime, a few dozen students walked through the gates, chatting and laughing and generally behaving like normal teenagers. Valkyrie watched some staff members leave, too, but no one she knew, no one who would do her any kind of a favour, no one who would—

Then she recognised a face. It had to be her. Out of all the sorcerers she knew, it *had* to be Arabella Wicked.

Valkyrie followed at a distance, keeping her head down. Those ridiculous cars, like the one that Cadaver had been driving, passed on the road with barely a whisper. Elementals flew overhead, chatting as they went. People looked pretty happy, all things considered. Then Miss Wicked went into a church.

It wasn't one of the biggest churches that Valkyrie had seen in her time here, but it wasn't one of the smallest, either. She hesitated at the door, then scowled and went in.

The church was like any Christian church she'd ever been to. It had pews and a pulpit, and behind the pulpit was an altar. Instead of a crucifix, there were two intersecting circles with a line through them both, symbolising something Valkyrie had no interest in. The walls were decorated with terrifying paintings, but she couldn't tell if the figures in those paintings were being rewarded or punished. Everything was fire and pain and blood.

Above and below the paintings were mouldings depicting screaming human faces and a whole lot of tentacles. It was unnerving, to say the least.

There were only a handful of people here, and Arabella sat in a pew alone, her eyes closed, her back perfectly straight, her blonde hair perfectly done. Valkyrie sat right beside her, making her frown in annoyance. When she opened her eyes to glare, Valkyrie smiled.

Arabella jumped up and Valkyrie grabbed her wrist to keep her from running.

"Not a word," Valkyrie whispered, letting enough energy crackle between her fingers to make Arabella's arm buzz unpleasantly.

Arabella paused, then settled back into the pew and Valkyrie released her grip. "So it's true."

"What's true?"

"It's you they're looking for. Your face has been plastered everywhere, but they won't say what happened. They won't say how you recovered. The last I heard, you had wings."

"It's a long story," said Valkyrie, "one which I have no intention of sharing with you. How have you been, Arabella? Still a teacher, I take it? After seventy-two years? Ever get the feeling that you're stuck in a rut?"

"What do you want, Valkyrie? Whatever you're planning, I can't help you. I won't, in fact."

"I never thought for a moment that you would. I'm just looking for someone to fill in a few blanks, actually. Do you have time? A quick chat and then I'll be gone, I promise."

"You don't know anything that's happened since...?

"The Activation Wave, no."

Arabella nodded slightly. "Then you won't have heard what happened to Militsa."

Valkyrie's smirk abandoned her. "What happened?"

"She fought back. She joined the resistance, rose up against

459

Malice. Creed killed her. Well, his people killed her, but it was Creed's order. I think it was a Necromancer, actually, who did the deed. You know, for years I hated you for that. If she hadn't loved you, maybe she'd have been able to see what the rest of us saw, that defying the new world order was futile. I blamed you for her death for... I suppose for close to thirty years."

She shrugged. "But time heals. I grew less angry. I reasoned that if I was blaming you for her death because she loved you, then I should really blame myself for her death because I failed to keep her before you ever came along. And, if I did that, then where would it stop? So I came to the conclusion that we can only be responsible for our own actions."

"How enlightened of you."

"Fletcher's dead, too. Fletcher and the Darkly brothers and Tanith Low and Dexter Vex... most of your friends. Do you know what happened to Skulduggery?"

"I've met Cadaver Cain."

"I wouldn't trust him if I were you, and if my advice means anything."

"What about China Sorrows?"

Arabella gave a little shrug. "China Sorrows is like me – she saw what was coming and she decided to stay alive."

"Where is she?"

"She won't help you. Whatever you're thinking, whatever you're planning, China Sorrows won't help you."

"Tell me where she is and let me worry about that."

Arabella's confidence evaporated. "That's what you're after," she said. "You want China. No. I won't tell you. Get away from me."

She went to move off, but Valkyrie took hold of her wrist again. "Arabella, I just need to know where to find her."

"If they find out I helped you, they'll kill me, Valkyrie. You don't know what they do to traitors. They torture them first, outside the Dark Cathedral, in front of a crowd. It doesn't matter if you've already confessed, they still torture you. Sometimes it lasts for days. And the execution? The execution would be a blessing if they released your soul, but they don't. They trap it. They feed it to the Faceless Ones. Let me go. Please, Valkyrie, I am begging you." There were tears in her eyes. Valkyrie had rarely seen someone so terrified.

But she tightened her grip. "If you don't tell me," she said, "I'll stand up and thank you for all the help you've given me. I'll make sure everyone in here knows what an asset you've been."

Arabella shrank into herself and Valkyrie hardened the part of her that felt sickened at what she was doing.

Valkyrie stood.

"OK!" Miss Wicked whispered. "OK, I'll tell you!"

# 90

When she returned to the harpy's tower, squeezing through that gap again, leaving the warmth of the sunlight for the chill of the gloom, she knew instantly that the harpy had returned. It wasn't even a psychic thing – she just knew, with everything that was in her, that she wasn't alone in the darkness.

"I'm not here to hurt you," Valkyrie said. "I'm here to talk. Can you talk?"

She heard a growl.

Valkyrie turned as the harpy leaped on her, got her arms up to keep those fangs away from her face, but she was driven back and suddenly there was no floor. They fell, plunging into darkness, slamming on to old stairs that splintered beneath them, and tumbled down, went sprawling.

Too dark to see so Valkyrie switched on her aura-vision and the harpy reared up in front of her. She launched herself backwards, blasting as she went, lightning hitting the harpy square in the chest and it fell, shrieking.

Valkyrie's hip banged into something, a banister that threatened to give way. She found stairs, switched off the aura-vision halfway down. There were windows in here, windows without glass. The wind howled. The city sat pretty and indifferent beyond.

The harpy came down the stairs and Valkyrie backed off.

"Stop, please. I don't want to fight. Please don't make me fight you."

Another hiss, but the harpy didn't take another step.

"Do you know me?" Valkyrie asked. "Do you know who I am? If you know who I am, nod your head."

The harpy snarled loudly.

"Was that a yes?"

Another snarl.

"I think you're saying yes. I get it: you're not a nodding kinda girl. It's cool if you like to snarl. So you know who I am. I'm you, but I'm you from the past. Did you sense me when I first arrived? Is that why you attacked? Hey, I get it – things you don't understand, they can be scary. But you know I'm not here to hurt you, right? I'm you from before the Activation Wave. Do you remember that?"

The harpy snarled, but less angrily.

"I'm trying to change what happens. All this, the world around you... I'm trying to change it. I want to make a new world instead."

The tiniest of snarls.

"Malice wants to stop me. Everyone wants to stop me. But I can't let them, and I need your help." Valkyrie hesitated, then tapped the amulet and the suit flowed off. She stood in front of the harpy with her hands down. Vulnerable. The harpy's hand twitched.

"Scared," the harpy said.

Her voice was tortured. A mangled whisper dragged through a cheese grater.

"I'm scared?" Valkyrie asked.

The harpy shook her head, tapped one of those talons against her own chest.

"You're scared," said Valkyrie. "What are you scared of?"

The harpy made a show of looking around.

"Everything," Valkyrie said. "You're afraid of everything. I

463

understand that. It must be horrible living here. And very confusing. Do you have any friends?"

She shook her head.

"I'll be your friend, if you like."

"Hurt me," said the harpy, and shook her head.

"I won't, don't worry. I won't hurt you. I promise."

The harpy studied her for a few seconds. Then said, "Help."

"You'll help me?"

The harpy gave a ridiculous little snarl, and Valkyrie laughed.

The Roarhaven Library rotated slowly in mid-air above its foundations. Valkyrie crouched on a rooftop beside the harpy and pointed to the guards.

"I need you to lead them away," she said. "Can you do that? If we fight them, more will come. Malice will come. Do you understand?"

The harpy frowned and looked away, as if she was searching for a word. "Decoy," she said.

Valkyrie grinned. "Exactly! Decoy!"

The harpy grinned wider, showing all those magnificent fangs. Then she said, "Friend."

Valkyrie blinked. "Yes. I'm your friend. Are you my friend?"

The harpy nodded.

Valkyrie reached out slowly, and the harpy watched her hand come closer until it touched her arm. "When we do this, I'll go back to my time and then all this, all of it, will be different."

"I die?" said the harpy.

"No," Valkyrie said, alarmed. "No, you won't die. You'll... you'll change, but you won't..."

The harpy nodded. "I die."

Valkyrie sagged. "Yes. You'll die."

The harpy snarled, and hugged Valkyrie. "Thank," she said, and then she dived off the rooftop, her wings unfurling, and with three great beats of those wings she was snatching one of the guards from his post and carrying him, shrieking, into the sky.

The other guards flew after her.

Valkyrie still had her arms out for the hug.

"Huh," she said.

# 91

The library was vast. Bookcases stretched from floor to ceiling on every level.

Valkyrie found China Sorrows at the very top, sitting in an armchair that was almost a throne, looking out of the large window. There was a small table beside her on which sat an elegant teapot, a cup and a saucer. The cup was empty. No steam rose from the teapot.

Valkyrie approached her from the side. "China."

A light sigh as she withdrew from her thoughts, and China stirred.

"China," Valkyrie said again.

This time, China heard her, and recognised her voice. She got up quickly, her startling blue eyes wide, her perfect lips pulled back over perfect teeth, her perfect features marred by three perfectly parallel scars across the left side of her face.

Valkyrie faltered midstep, as much because of the hatred in China's eyes as the scars on her face.

China tapped the invisible sigils on her palms and they glowed red.

"China, wait," Valkyrie said quickly. "It's me. It's Valkyrie. I'm not going to hurt you."

China frowned. "You talk now?"

"I'm not her," said Valkyrie. "I'm not the harpy. Look at me." She turned slowly, 360 degrees. "No wings."

China didn't drop her hands. Didn't cancel out the glowing sigils. "How did you do it?"

"I'm not cured, China – I'm literally not her."

A slight relaxation of China's shoulders. "Different dimension?"

"Same dimension, different time. I, uh, I'm a time-traveller. When I'm from, we still have a few days before Creed generates the Activation Wave."

The sigils stopped glowing and China slowly lowered her arms. "You actually travelled in time?"

"I actually did."

"So you're the Valkyrie I used to know?"

"Yes."

"Oh, my dear," China said, and embraced Valkyrie so tightly that Valkyrie doubted she could have broken free even if she'd wanted to. "I tried so hard," she said, her face buried in Valkyrie's shoulder. "I tried everything. I stepped into arenas of magic I never knew existed. Nothing could heal you. Nothing could bring you back."

A quick kiss on both cheeks and China was stepping away, perfectly composed once again.

"It's very good to see you again, my dear."

Valkyrie smiled. "Likewise. Where'd you get the scars?"

China laughed. "As blunt as always, I see."

"I'm sorry. Was there a politer way of asking that?"

"Probably not," said China. "You gave me them, actually. I had one idea left, one thing that might cure you, and it failed. You broke free of your restraints and made your displeasure known."

"Oh, China... I'm so sorry."

"It's my own fault, my sweet girl."

"Can't you go to a doctor? Get them healed?"

"Your talons leave a lasting impression, Valkyrie. They defy the best doctors. I could have surgery, I suppose, or cover them with a façade, and I was considering it until I spent an hour or two just looking into a mirror at my reflection. I've spent my whole life being flawless. I've spent my whole adult life dealing with people who think they've fallen in love with me because of how I look. It was fear that made me consider surgery – fear and a kind of destructive pride. But do you know something? I like my scars. I think they're beautiful."

"You *do* wear them well."

"Don't I? I like how they feel, too."

"May I?"

"Please."

Valkyrie trailed her fingers over the ridges. "Rough," she said.

"Yes."

"Rough and interesting."

"Yes," China said again, her eyes gleaming. "Exactly."

"I've got scars." She showed China the palm of her right hand. "Billy-Ray Sanguine's straight razor. Other scars, too. Knives, scythes, bullets... I used to be self-conscious on holiday, didn't want to wear bikinis." She shrugged. "But the scars are a part of me."

China smiled. "To be alive at all is to have scars, as Steinbeck once wrote."

"I'll take your word for it. How're you doing, China?"

A flicker of something across her features before she smiled. "I'm doing wonderfully," she said. "Everything is splendid. The world is as it should be."

"Yeah," Valkyrie said doubtfully. "I just remember all those threats you used to get from various disciples promising all kinds of nasty things for, as they said, traitors."

"Oh, yes," said China, "but did I deserve anything less? I turned away from the Faceless Ones, Valkyrie. I stepped out of their shining light, turned away from the warmth of their love.

468

The worst kind of blasphemer is the one who turns their back on their gods."

"I suppose so."

"But they are merciful," China continued. "That's one of their qualities that we'd lost sight of. Look at my home. Isn't it wonderful? I live in peace, I live in luxury, and I'm surrounded by books."

"It's a nice home."

"I've welcomed my punishment, actually. I think it's made me a better person."

"What was it?"

"I'm sorry?"

"Your punishment. What was it?"

China hesitated, but the smile didn't dim. "Pain," she said. "They hurt me. The disciples. The loyal ones. They hunted me down and locked me away. Took away everything. I thought they were going to leave me to die. And no less than I deserved!"

She laughed.

"But once things had settled, once the mortals had been dealt with and the uprisings put down, the Faceless Ones announced their forgiveness – through your sister, actually. Malice was their voice. She came to me and she let me out of my cell herself. She told me that despite everything I'd done, despite all my sins and transgressions, the Faceless Ones still loved me, and there was still a place for me in the world they'd built. All these books? Impossibly rare editions that I had never been able to find by myself – and they furnished my house with them."

"That was very thoughtful," Valkyrie said.

"Oh, no," said China. "This is part of the on-going punishment. You see, they did something." She tapped her head. "In here. They moved things around, turned things, twisted things... They took away my ability to read. Took away my ability to learn. The things I prize above all else."

"Oh, China..."

"I am most unhappy, Valkyrie. Most, most unhappy."

"I need your help."

"I don't think I'll be of much use to you, I'm afraid."

"I need to know how Creed did it. How he generated the Activation Wave."

"Oh, no. No, no, my dear Valkyrie. You can't stop what's happened. You can't get rid of this. If you change the past, what happens to me?"

"You'll be happier, I'd imagine."

"But that wouldn't be me. The woman standing before you wouldn't exist. I'd be someone else, someone with different memories, different experiences. You're asking me to help you kill me."

"For the greater good."

China stepped back. "No, Valkyrie. Absolutely not. Furthermore, what you're suggesting would harm the Faceless Ones. I cannot allow that."

Valkyrie held up her hands. "OK," she said. "Forget I asked."

"I'm sorry, but that's just not possible. I... I have to report this."

"What? No, you don't."

"I have to. If I don't, and they find out, they'll punish me again. They'll take more from me."

"China, I want you to calm down for a second, OK? If you report me—"

"You have to be punished," said China. "You have to be."

"It's OK, China," Malice said, walking in. "I'll take it from here."

# 92

Valkyrie bit back a curse as China fell to her knees.

"Forgive me!" China cried. "She wouldn't stop talking! I wanted her to stop talking, but she wouldn't!"

"I heard everything, don't you worry," Malice said, keeping her eyes on Valkyrie. "I told you not to make trouble. I told you there'd be consequences."

"Creed has to be stopped."

"It's too late for that. It's already happened."

"I can change it."

"I'm not gonna let you."

"Alice, I'm giving you another chance to be happy."

"First of all, and for the last time, it's Malice. I don't go around calling you Stephanie, do I? Malice is my taken name. Respect it and use it. Second of all, you want to give me a chance to be happy? You, the one who killed me when I was a baby? The one who tore my soul into bits? You're the last person I would ever trust to bring me happiness, Valkyrie. You made me the way I am."

"I'm sorry. I'm sorry for all of that, for everything. I did it—"

"I know why you did it. I know your reasons. But you still did it. It's still done."

"Help me," Valkyrie said. "We're sisters. Let's fight on the same side. We can help people. We can save the world."

"The world doesn't need saving. I don't need saving. I'm the most powerful human being on the planet. You wouldn't be saving me – you'd be killing me. If you change the past, I won't exist. There'll be some other version of me running around. Maybe she'll be better than me or maybe she'll be worse, but she won't be *me*. Even if you somehow convinced me to help you change how things worked out, I still wouldn't do it – because it's suicide. I have to stop you."

"I don't want to fight."

"I don't want to fight, either, but you are literally planning to destroy the world. You're the bad guy here, Valkyrie."

"I want you to think very hard about this, Alice—"

"My name is Malice!" Malice yelled, catching her with a punch that sent the world tilting on its axis.

Valkyrie tried using her lightning to keep her away, but Malice just seemed to move through it, and then she was on her.

# 93

Valkyrie would have collapsed into a groaning, painful heap were it not for the grip that Malice had on her collar.

"You'll see the truth," Malice said. "You'll see this way is the best way. A few days in the Enlightenment Chair and I'm sure the Faceless Ones will accept you. They'll have to. You share my blood. You're one of us."

China hurried forward, stumbling over the wreckage of smashed bookcases. "You can't."

"Leave the room, China."

"You can't do that."

"You do not tell me what I can do!" Malice screeched, the air around her shimmering.

China staggered back, then dropped to her knees, pressing her forehead to the floor. "Forgive me! Forgive me, please!"

"You are alive only because I want you to be alive!"

"Thank you, Mistress! Thank you! I just wanted to say that if you keep Valkyrie here then that would change the past, and, if the past changes, the Faceless Ones might never return."

The shimmering slowly faded, and Malice took a deep, calming breath. "Yes," she said. "You're right."

"I'm so sorry," China whispered.

"Don't be. It was brave of you to come forward. Thank you."

"Yes, Mistress."

"Valkyrie," Malice said, "you conscious? You are. I know you are."

"Ow," Valkyrie mumbled.

Malice smiled and stepped away, letting her stand on her own. "Sorry for hitting you all those times. In my defence, you're very stubborn and incredibly annoying."

Valkyrie managed a nod. "It's been said." China got up and helped her stay on her feet.

"You have to go home now, OK?" Malice said. "I wish we could talk, there are so many things I want to say to you... but you have a habit of pushing my buttons. If you stayed, we'd just get into another argument, wouldn't we?"

"Yeah, probably."

"I don't want to fight you. I love you."

"I love you, too, Alice."

Malice glared, and Valkyrie grinned a bloody grin, and eventually Malice laughed. "Go back to your own time and stay there. I mean it. If I see you here again..." She sighed. "I'll have to kill you. You're going to be transformed into that damn harpy any day now, so I'd actually be doing you a favour. Do we understand each other?"

"We do."

"Are you OK to travel?"

"I'm good," said Valkyrie. "I'm fine. I can already smell the candle."

"Well, I have no idea what that means, but could you say hi to the folks for me? Tell them I love them?"

"I will."

"Thanks. Maybe tell Skulduggery not to be so much of a pain in my neck, too."

"You don't have to worry about that right now," Valkyrie said. "Cadaver managed to hitch a ride with me back to my time. I don't think he's even considered how to get back here by himself."

Malice frowned. "Cadaver's in the past?"

"Skulduggery isn't impressed, as you can—"

"You can't trust him," Malice said.

"We don't."

"Valkyrie, no. You cannot trust Cadaver Cain. If I'd have known it was even possible for him to..." She faltered. "But he knew. Of course he knew. He knows everything."

"We're not trusting him, don't worry."

"He wants to end life," Malice said.

"Sorry?"

Malice gripped her hands, held them tightly, and looked into her eyes. "He wants to end life, Valkyrie. All life. All life everywhere. What did he tell you? Did he tell you about the Viddu De?"

"Yes. Malice, I have to go. The candle's not going to stay—"

"They're his masters, Valkyrie. Cadaver acts like he's independent, like he's working to his own agenda, but he isn't. When he was Lord Vile, when he was Deep Venturing, when he met them – they showed him their secrets and they recruited him."

"I'm not sure I—"

"The Viddu De are gods in a universe that has never known life. Life is impossible there. I've spoken to Necromancers who made the journey, but didn't dare go as far as Vile did. They describe a world, a universe, where death permeates everything. It's a... an energy field. They called it the death field."

"I know about the death field," Valkyrie said. "It's what makes the Necropolis possible."

Malice nodded quickly. "There's no surviving it, not without a necronaut suit. The Viddu De's entire universe is this death field, and it's quiet and nothing ever happens... and then they meet Lord Vile – this dead-but-not-dead being. This sentient creature. Small, yes, practically insignificant, yes... but a sentient creature. And these death gods, they haven't seen a sentient creature in eons – probably not since the gods went to war with each other."

"And they shared their secrets with Vile," Valkyrie said. "I know this. Cadaver told us the story."

"They didn't just share their secrets – they recruited him. They want us, Valkyrie, and they want our universe. They want to bring their death field *here*. They want to kill us, to transform us into the living dead, like Skulduggery. Dead-but-not-dead. All of us. This world and every world."

"And they recruited Vile to help?"

Malice nodded. "And Vile looked into the future, and he saw what he needed to do to achieve this, and no doubt he's been doing that ever since."

"Skulduggery doesn't know anything about it."

"Vile hid it from him – hid it from himself, I mean. Then his *future*-future self remembered and now he must be continuing with the plan."

"But what is the plan? How's he going to expand the death field so that it covers the whole universe?"

"I don't know," Malice said. "Valkyrie, I get that you don't want me to be Activated, you don't want this future to happen – but, if Cadaver Cain manages to stop Creed, then it won't be the Faceless Ones ruling the universe, it'll be the Viddu De. At least with the Faceless Ones, there are billions of people alive on the planet. If the Viddu De take over, they'll kill everything and everyone."

Valkyrie broke away from her. Walked a few steps. Turned back. "What's the point? Cadaver can see every possible future – he's seen us talking right now. When I get back, he'll be waiting."

"There are things he doesn't know," Malice said. "I've worked for years to hide myself from him, and with the Faceless Ones' help I've become invisible in time. He can't predict what I'm going to do, he can't see what I've already done – I'm a blank spot to him. I think I'm the only one, but I can't be sure."

"So he's not able to see us talking right now?"

"Which means, when you go back, he'll have no idea that you

know what he's really after. But the moment you tell Skulduggery, Cadaver will know you know."

Valkyrie nodded. "I'll stop him. I can stop him."

"I know you can."

Valkyrie fixed her with a look. "But I'm also going to stop the Activation Wave."

Malice smiled. "You can try. Take care of yourself, Valkyrie. It's been so good talking to you again. I love you."

"Yeah," said Valkyrie. "I love you, too."

She settled her thoughts and focused on the faint traces of the candle, growing fainter every moment. She reached back with her mind, and the energy began to swirl round her.

"The Eye of Rhast!" China shouted. "Don't let him get the Eye of Rhast!"

Malice roared, lunged at China, pulled her head off her shoulders and dived at Valkyrie, but Valkyrie was already streaking backwards.

# 94

"The Eye of Rhast," Skulduggery said, leaning back in his hotel-room chair and steepling his fingers. "Obviously, this Rhast is the monster we've been wondering about."

Valkyrie popped another leaf in her mouth and nodded. Slowly, the aches were dulling.

"This is good," he continued. "We have a solid lead on a way to stop the Activation Wave. We also have a major problem. The very fact that you've just told me what you've learned of Cadaver's motives—"

"Means that now Cadaver knows that we know," she finished. "You think he's going to come after us?"

"Maybe," Skulduggery said, "but his options are limited. He can't kill me – that would be suicide – and I doubt he'd want to kill you. Over the years, we have developed quite a soft spot for you, despite your many shortcomings."

"Oh, cheers."

"You remind us of an adorable puppy."

"Cheers again."

"Besides, it obviously suited his purpose to have us get to this point. It may even suit his purpose to let us continue. The fact is, when faced with an all-knowing opponent, you must always continue forward, anyway. To second-guess our own instincts is tantamount to failure. And we do not fail, Valkyrie."

"We don't?"

"We may stumble, but we do not fall, and we may fumble, but we do not fail."

She smiled. "That's cool. Is that from something?"

"My mind."

"It's suddenly less cool."

"My future self poses a problem," Skulduggery said. "But once we stop Damocles Creed and the Activation Wave, we can worry about Cadaver Cain."

"So the Eye of Rhast."

He nodded. "The Eye of Rhast."

# 95

Omen waited in the darkness with Crepuscular Vies and they watched the West Tower.

"I should really be sleeping," Omen muttered. "I've got two exams tomorrow. Everyone else in my class is sleeping right now. Sleep is essential when it comes to exams."

"I'd say studying is essential," Crepuscular remarked, "but, since you haven't done any of that, sleeping's not going to do you much good."

Omen sighed. "This is all in danger of unravelling around us. Skulduggery and Valkyrie are wanted criminals, there are protests in the streets, we won't know if the Zeta Switch even works until the Pillars turn on, and here I am, keeping watch for killers, when I really ought to be resting before exams that I know I'm going to do really badly in. It's all going to go wrong, I can feel it."

"I agree," said Crepuscular.

Omen sagged. "Great."

"So I say we kill Creed and Serrate. It won't solve your exam problem, but it will sort out this end-of-the-world thing."

"We don't kill people, Crepuscular."

"Speak for yourself."

"You agreed. When all this began, you agreed that we wouldn't kill people."

"I said I wouldn't kill people if I could help it," Crepuscular corrected. "Killing those two would seem to me to be the only sure-fire way we have of preventing the Activation Wave from being triggered."

"Cadaver said it won't work out like that."

"We can't trust Cadaver Cain."

"He hasn't lied to us yet."

"We don't know that."

"He led us right to the Zeta Switch, Crepuscular. I think he's on our side."

Crepuscular held up a hand and Omen fell silent. He heard footsteps. Shuffling footsteps, and a muffled voice.

Omen peeked. Two figures, passing in and out of shafts of silver-blue moonlight, moving towards the East Tower. Crepuscular nodded, and they crept after them.

By the time they got to the corner, the figures were gone. They crept faster, Omen yanking off his trainers and continuing in his stockinged feet. Crepuscular's shoes didn't squeak. Crepuscular's shoes were cool.

They reached the far corner and peeked round just as the figure shoved the bound man through another hidden door.

"Dammit!" Omen blurted.

The dark figure whipped round and Crepuscular sighed.

"Very good, Omen."

"Sorry."

They stepped out into the middle of the corridor, and the dark figure stepped into the light.

"Hey," said Crepuscular, "I know you. You're Silas Nadir."

Omen knew who he was, too. Everyone knew who Silas Nadir was. The Charles Manson of magic. The Son of Sam of sorcerers. The dimension-hopping serial killer.

"And who the hell are you supposed to be?" Nadir said. "And what happened to your face?"

"My name is Crepuscular Vies, and as for what happened to

481

my face, it was a terrible accident, years ago. Why, what happened to yours?"

Nadir smiled without humour. "That's funny. You're funny. You're a funny guy. I guess you'd have to be to wear a suit like that."

"You wound me, sir."

"Not yet. But I will."

Crepuscular laughed. "This is fun. Isn't this fun? I'm having fun here. I insult you, you pretend to insult me by insinuating there's something wrong with my suit when we both know that my clothes are both striking and beautiful. This is what should happen before people fight. *Conversation.* Instead, folk nowadays just hurl themselves at each other without taking a moment to learn their opponent's name, to understand their motivation, to appreciate what it is they're fighting for. Thank you, my friend. You have reminded me that I'm not the only one who yearns for the decorum of yesteryear. You made my day just that little bit brighter."

"No problem," said Nadir, and pulled out a gun with a big, ugly silencer.

"That," said Crepuscular, "is disappointing."

Nadir fired. The first bullet went through Crepuscular's right arm. There was a spray of blood. The second bullet caught him in the thigh. His leg kicked out and he fell, turning over on to his back, hissing in pain. Nadir walked up and fired twice more into his chest, and Crepuscular went still and Nadir turned, but Omen was already running at him.

Nadir fired. Missed. Omen tucked his chin down and slammed his shoulder into Nadir's sternum and they went tumbling over each other. Omen saw the gun out of the corner of his eye and lunged at it, gripping Nadir's wrist with both hands. Nadir snarled as they wrestled. He was strong and vicious, but there was nothing in his movements to suggest training of any sort. This set off a spark of hope within Omen. He might actually have a chance of not dying here.

They rolled across the floor. All of Nadir's attention was directed towards regaining control of the gun. Omen didn't care about the gun beyond wanting to keep it pointed away from him. Every single one of Auger's combat instructors had said the same thing: invest no emotional attachment in the weapon.

They rolled again and now Omen was on top, putting all of his weight on to his left hand, which pinned Nadir's wrist to the floor. He curled his right hand into a fist and hammered blows down on to Nadir's face. Nadir roared, more in annoyance than pain, so Omen started dropping elbows. Nadir used his free hand to try to cover up. His nose broke. His lips burst.

And then Omen was tumbling back and Nadir was on top of him, spitting blood, both hands going for Omen's throat. Omen tried to suck in oxygen, but the killer's fingers were closing off his windpipe. He didn't have the gun any more, though, so that was a kind of victory. In a way. Nadir gritted his teeth as he throttled Omen, banging his head against the floor a few times just for the sheer hell of it.

There. Just out of reach. The gun. Omen stretched for it, fingers splayed.

His head pounded. His vision clouded. His struggles weakened.

He felt the air, felt how the spaces connected, felt the air around the gun. He pulled the air towards him.

The gun didn't move.

Omen brought his legs in, hooked one foot over Nadir's right ankle, closed a hand around Nadir's right wrist, and shot his other hand up into his chin as he bucked his hips and twisted. Nadir yelled as he flipped over on to his back, and Omen sucked in a breath as he landed on him.

"Get off me!" Nadir roared, doing his best to turn away. Omen let it happen, but he stayed over him, and the moment the opportunity presented itself he sneaked an arm round Nadir's throat and closed up the stranglehold. Nadir clawed at his arm, tried to throw him off, but Omen tucked his feet in and clung on.

Nadir stopped trying to pull Omen's arm away. Making weird noises now, he reached for the gun. Grabbed it.

He fired blindly over his shoulder and Omen flinched and Nadir was on top of him now, gasping. Omen gripped the gun barrel with both hands. He could hear Nadir's ragged breaths as he fought to angle the gun downwards, Omen summoning every ounce of strength he had left to keep it away. Nadir's face was a mask of blood and pure hatred.

Then there was movement, someone behind Nadir, grabbing him, hauling him off.

Auger.

He twisted Nadir's wrist, snatched the gun, swung it into Nadir's jaw. Nadir stumbled back, an agonised moan escaping his lips. He tried to shunt away, but merely flickered, remaining in this dimension where Auger caught him with a left hook to the body that undoubtedly broke some ribs.

He staggered backwards and Auger walked after him, dismantling the gun as he went. The silencer, magazine, springs, slide, and barrel hit the floor. Nadir had his hands over his mouth. His jaw was broken.

Omen scrambled over to Crepuscular. His eyes were open and blinking, his shirt drenched in blood. Omen got out his phone, dialled.

"East Tower," Omen said once the call was answered. "Need to go to Reverie's clinic. Now."

Nadir flickered – and vanished.

Never appeared down the corridor. She saw them and ran over. Omen put a hand on Crepuscular's shoulder and Never grabbed Omen's outstretched hand and then they were in the clinic and Omen was shouting for someone to help.

# 96

Crepuscular lay strapped to the bed while Doctor Synecdoche held her hands over his torso. His leg and arm were already bandaged and the bullets removed from his chest. Now the doctor's hands glowed warmly as the flesh and tissue beneath repaired itself. Crepuscular's body was a mass of scars, what looked like knife wounds, bullet holes, and burns.

When she was done, Reverie undid the straps and left quietly. Moments later, Crepuscular opened his eyes and looked at Omen.

"I take it I'm not dead, then," he said.

"You're in Doctor Synecdoche's clinic. You were shot four times," Omen told him. "She removed the bullets and all the fragments and fixed the damage."

"You saved my life."

"No, she saved your life."

"She healed me, absolutely, but you got me here. You saved my life. What about Nadir?"

"Escaped."

"Unfortunate, but these things happen." He sat up with a groan. "Who knows I'm here?"

"Apart from Auger and Never, just the staff."

"Do you think they can be trusted not to talk?"

"They're discreet. It's why we came here instead of the High Sanctuary. But why don't you want anyone to know you're here?

485

Is it because you're worried it might get back to Skulduggery? I just don't get why you'd want to stay hidden. You're his old partner. He'd be delighted to see you."

"Before I announce myself, I've got to prove myself."

"Prove yourself to who?"

"The universe. Skulduggery. Me. Whoever's watching. Believe me, I'm itching to tell him who I am. Itching to tell him I'm still here. To confront him. Meeting Cadaver Cain was... interesting, but he's not the Skulduggery Pleasant that I knew. I'm looking at it like a practice run, but I've realised that I need my foundation to be solid before I approach him. Can you understand that?"

"I... I think so."

"It won't be for very much longer. Once our mission is complete, that's when I'll tell him. I promise."

"Yeah," Omen said slowly. "Crepuscular, I reckon we can take it from here."

"What? Draíocht is the day after tomorrow."

"And you've just been shot four times."

"And then healed."

"I can't ask you to risk—"

"You're not asking me to do anything," Crepuscular interrupted. "I might be a little sore, a little bruised, but this isn't going to slow me down. I'll be by your side, Omen. We're partners."

Omen smiled. "Thanks."

# 97

Monday brought a doubling-up of the City Guard engaged in relocation operations, which meant there were simply too many officers for Temper and his team to take down. They had to stand by, helpless, as mortals were beaten and thrown into the trucks that would take them to the camp outside the city walls.

So Temper had decided to retaliate in another way. Starting today, they would be targeting routine patrols, attacking swiftly and then melting away before reinforcements could arrive. His plan was to make every single City Guard officer fearful of leaving their headquarters.

He stood at the corner with Onosa, watching two of them turn on to Rainfall Road, their black motorbikes cruising by, making Roarhaven's citizens look the other way in case they were singled out for questioning.

"All clear," Onosa said. "The only things running through their minds right now are the most arrogant of thoughts."

Temper nodded, tapping the back of his phone to send the signal to the others to get ready. They were without Oberon Guile today – he'd had to return to the States to take care of whatever business he took care of when he wasn't rebelling in Roarhaven. But Temper still had Ruckus and Tanith – and Onosa, of course. More than enough talent to do what needed to be done.

He pulled on his mask. This would be an easy one. A short,

sharp strike out here in public, demonstrating to everyone that the Department of Roarhaven Security agents weren't nearly as untouchable as they wanted people to believe.

"Wait," said Onosa.

Temper turned. "Everything all right?"

She looked troubled. "I don't know, I... Their thoughts. Their thoughts are on a loop." Her eyes widened. "It's a trap!"

He went for his phone to send out the abort signal, and as he did so he saw a line of City Guard officers running in from behind. There were shouts, and gunshots, and he spun, saw Ruckus being swarmed on the rooftop above. Tanith came tumbling out of her hiding spot, wrestling with three cops.

The door beside him burst open and the swipe of a sword knocked his shock stick from his hand. He barely avoided the energy blast that followed, and then someone was wrapping an arm around his neck and pulling him backwards. He glimpsed Onosa falling to her knees as Sense Wardens closed in on her from all sides, and then a gun was pointed into his face and he stopped struggling.

Commander Hoc strode through the doorway, and pulled the mask from Temper's head.

"Temper Fray," he said, an eyebrow lifting. "You really shouldn't have come back here."

"I'd actually agree with you on that one."

An officer hurried up. "All targets have been apprehended, Commander."

"See to their transport back to headquarters," Hoc responded, and returned his attention to Temper. "I'm surprised. I didn't think you'd fall into my trap quite so easily. That's the problem, I suppose, with having a Sensitive who sees the future when I have Sensitives of my own who are powerful enough to make yours see whatever they want her to see."

"They're powerful, all right," Temper admitted. "That'll be all the drugs you're pumping into them."

A shrug. "I'll do whatever it takes to win. I pity you, do you know that? You could have been standing at the Supreme Mage's side during all of this. Instead, you ran, like the coward you are."

"That's me," said Temper.

"You squandered every possible opportunity you were born with."

"I tend to do that."

"And now you've involved yourself in a fight that has nothing to do with you. I want you to know that I will personally conduct your interrogation. I will break you apart and extract every last piece of information you possess, and then the Supreme Mage will Activate you so you can spend the rest of your life staring into space, nothing more than a mindless zombie."

"I accept the terms of your surrender."

"Take him away," Hoc said, and Temper's arms were twisted behind him, ready for the shackles.

The officer with the gun crumpled suddenly, an arrow lodged in his neck.

Hoc turned, cried out as an arrow thudded into his shoulder. Two more officers went down. Everyone else was shouting.

Temper opened his hand, let the tentacle with teeth dart out. The guy who was holding him screamed and released him and Gretel retracted into his palm even as Temper reached for the nearest gun. He fired at Hoc, but the sneaky little jackass dodged back through the doorway he'd emerged from, then he turned the gun on the Sense Wardens and pulled the trigger. One of them went down and the other two clutched their heads in pain. Temper didn't know much about Sensitive stuff, but he imagined disrupting a psychic link like that would hurt a whole lot.

Onosa staggered to her feet and Ruckus had got free, and he was throwing cops around the place like a whirlwind mainly comprising fists and feet. Another officer fell, screaming, from the rooftop.

Tanith was in trouble, but an arrow thunked into the back of one of the officers pummelling her, giving her enough of a reprieve to get her feet under her. She started throwing punches.

A big officer, his name was Gantuan, slammed into Temper and drove him backwards. They fell, rolled, scratching and scrambling. Gantuan's big hands closed around Temper's head and cracked his skull into the road. Bright lights exploded behind his eyes and for a moment he was lost, floating somewhere in a sea of sharp angles, and then Gantuan was standing, backing away from someone.

Kierre of the Unveiled, a sheaf of arrows hanging from her waist, a bow across her back, and a knife in her hand. Gantuan tried to defend himself, but he was too big and too slow and too clumsy, and Kierre was already crouching over Temper as Gantuan's body hit the ground.

"We have to run," she said. "They have reinforcements."

Temper looked back, saw a bunch of cops descend on Tanith. He tried to help, but Kierre pulled him back, and, as more cops opened fire, they got the hell out of there.

# 98

Valkyrie spent most of Monday sitting in the bath in her hotel room, submerged in piping-hot water that fizzed with healing properties. Her skin had long-since pruned by the time she towelled herself off, but at least her cuts and bruises had faded away. Her muscles felt better, too, and her energy was back to a normal level.

It was getting dark when the Phantom pulled up outside and Valkyrie got in. As they drove out of the car park, a passing driver slowed to gape at the car, and the driver behind her, who was also gaping, crashed into the back of her. That was the third time that had happened.

"This," Valkyrie said, fastening her seat belt, "is a dangerous car." They headed for the motorway. "Tell me."

"The only reference to Rhast I could find pointed me to an obscure book on the occult," said Skulduggery, "the Book of Shalgoth."

"So we read that, we find out who, or what, Rhast was, or is, and we take his eye. Easy. Gross but easy."

"Unfortunately, the Book of Shalgoth was destroyed by Mevolent hundreds of years ago."

Valkyrie frowned. "So we have nothing?"

"There might still be a way to find out what it said."

"Excellent. How?"

"The Book of Shalgoth was one of dozens of books and grimoires that would have been studied by a certain group of scholars down through the centuries."

"There you go," Valkyrie said, brightening. "So we find one of these scholars and they'll tell us what we need to know. Nice one."

"Unfortunately, all the scholars are dead."

"All of them?"

"Sadly."

"So there's no chance of finding out what was in the Book of Shalgoth?"

"None."

"Then why did you tell me there might be a way?"

"Because there still might. One of these scholars imprinted himself on to an Echo Stone."

"OK!" Valkyrie exclaimed. "Some good news! Some good news that you're not going to immediately turn into bad news, right?"

"Right. We've accessed this Echo Stone before, actually. Do you remember Oisin?"

"Oisin the rambling monk? The guy who told us about the Sceptre of the Ancients? That's great! I haven't seen him since I was twelve! He's an old friend! Basically. So who has the stone now?"

"After Ghastly died, his property was divided in accordance with his will. The collection went to one of his oldest friends."

"Is it you?"

"Ghastly had more than one friend, you know."

"So it isn't you. Is it someone you know?"

"It is."

"You're being hesitant."

"Am I?"

"It's someone you've annoyed in the past, isn't it?"

"It may be."

Valkyrie nodded. "Then we'll have something in common."

*

Uther Peccant was waiting for them at a big old tree on a hill. Four miles south of him, in the dark emptiness, Roarhaven stood invisible. They got out of the Phantom.

"Uther," said Skulduggery, "thanks for coming."

Peccant had the air of an old-fashioned headmaster about him – impatient and authoritative. Tall and broad-shouldered, he had a long face, severe but not unattractive – for an older guy. His hair was grey and impressively lustrous.

"It isn't as if you gave me any choice, is it? Urgent business, a matter of life and death, something-something about the end of the world, isn't that what you said?"

"Something along those lines."

"It's always so dramatic with you, isn't it?"

Things were getting decidedly frosty decidedly early, so Valkyrie smiled. "Hi," she said. "I'm—"

"I know who you are," said Peccant. "Everyone knows who you are."

"Right, well... I've heard a lot about you."

"Who from?"

"Your students."

"Who, exactly?"

She hesitated. "Omen Darkly."

Peccant grunted again. "That boy."

"He's a good kid."

"He's a daydreamer and a slacker who has decided he can never be good enough because of some ridiculous inferiority complex. Nothing gets my goat more than people who refuse to live up to their potential. Are you living up to your potential, Miss Cain?"

"I think so..."

"You are not," he growled.

"Oh," she said. "Sorry."

He took the Echo Stone out of his pocket. It was smaller than she'd remembered. Smaller than the other Echo Stones she'd seen. "This is what you're after, then?"

"It is, indeed," Skulduggery said.

"Even though it's damaged?"

Valkyrie stared, dismayed. "It's damaged?"

"It's got some damn fool imprinted on it, a blabbering, blathering monk, and he can't be erased. Not that I would erase him – he is quite a treasure trove of information regarding the Ancients and the Faceless Ones – but it's not an Echo Stone's purpose to keep one person's memories alive indefinitely. The point of memories is that they fade. It's part of the human condition."

"My memories don't fade," Skulduggery said.

"Well," Peccant replied, "you're not human, are you?"

Nobody said anything for a bit.

"You were a friend of Ghastly's, then?" Valkyrie asked, smiling.

"I was," Peccant said. "He was a good man. Unfortunately, he fell in with a bad crowd and it eventually got him killed."

"Erskine Ravel got him killed," Skulduggery said.

"Obviously, that's the bad crowd I was talking about. It's fully charged, in case you're interested. I didn't think you'd have a cradle on you, so I took the liberty."

"Thank you," Valkyrie said as he passed it to her. "I have a cradle, but it's back at home and—"

"And your home is being watched, yes? Because you appear to be an enemy of the state or some such nonsense."

"Pretty much."

"Well," Peccant said, "I hope this is all worth it. It probably doesn't need to be said, but don't use this out here in the open. That ridiculous car attracts attention, and you really need to be hiding right now." He didn't say anything else – just got in his perfectly ordinary car, flicked on his perfectly ordinary headlights, and drove off.

# 99

They drove to a secluded spot, parked out of sight of the road, and walked into the woods. Skulduggery, who didn't need light to see, stepped over every root and branch. Valkyrie, who did need light to see, did not.

"I think this should be far enough," Skulduggery said, coming to a stop.

Valkyrie tripped over something and stumbled into a tree.

"You are amusing," Skulduggery said, taking the Echo Stone from his jacket. His fingertips found the slight indentations in the stone's surface and an old man in a robe appeared before them, luminescent.

"Hello," Oisin said, smiling. "I'm here to help you with whatever questions you have about – ah! The skeleton! Yes! Once again, you have come to me for sage advice! And who have you brought this time?"

"I'm Valkyrie," she said, smiling. "We've already met, actually."

Oisin's eyes widened. "You don't mean...? You're not the little girl, are you?"

"That's me."

He clapped his hands. "This is delightful! This is wonderful!" He gazed at his hands. "Oh, my. I glow in the dark. I didn't know I glowed in the dark. This is most extraordinary." He looked up again. "The Echo Stone has been active three times since we first spoke, and each time had me conversing with Uther Peccant. Quite a humourless man."

"Ever so slightly," Skulduggery said.

"But even so," Oisin continued, "to me it seems like we first met only hours ago! And now look at you!"

"Now look at me," said Valkyrie.

"You've had adventures, yes?"

"Many."

"Oh, how I envy you! I always wanted to have adventures when I was a lad! I would have gladly spent my life as a swash-buckling pirate, sailing the seven seas, were it not for my deep and pathological fear of the open water and my chronic inability to wield a sword convincingly."

He looked away for a moment, then snapped back with a smile.

"But I chose the life of a monk and a scholar instead! In place of adventure and derring-do, I had my studies and my various and sundry chores – and I've never regretted it. Not one bit."

"Oisin, we were wondering if you could help us again," Valkyrie said. "Last time you were such a help. You helped us save the world."

His eyes popped wide. "I did?"

"Oh, yes," she said.

"I saved the world," he said softly, a smile spreading across his face.

"And we're hoping you can do the same again," Skulduggery said. "We're hoping that you've read the Book of Shalgoth."

"Ah," said Oisin, his smile fading, and Valkyrie felt her stomach plummet. "The Book of Shalgoth was not on the list of tomes essential to my work, I'm afraid. I was the expert on the Ancients – not the Faceless Ones."

"So you didn't read it?"

"I'm terribly sorry, but no, I didn't read it."

"Damn."

"... officially."

"I'm sorry?"

"It was my opinion," Oisin said, squaring his shoulders, "that, in order to understand the subjects of your studies, you must also understand their enemies. The other monks disagreed with me, claiming such reading would lead to distractions. But they were limited people, my brethren. No imagination."

"So you did read it," Skulduggery said.

"I did," Oisin said, grinning. "I tucked it under my cassock one night without anyone noticing, and took it to my chamber. I returned it when I was finished, of course. Nobody likes a thief. Monks, especially."

"What do you remember of it?"

"Oh, everything. I have a habit of remembering every word I've ever read – everything from main text to indexes, typographical errors to footnotes. It's my gift, and my curse. But mostly my gift. What do you need to know?"

"The Eye of Rhast," said Skulduggery. "We need to know what it is, where it is, and how to destroy it."

Oisin nodded. "I see. I can't help you on the second question, I'm afraid – I have no idea where it might be. The third question – how to destroy it – is difficult, but for reasons that will become clear, I imagine you would need a God-Killer – preferably the Sceptre of the Ancients – to destroy it completely.

"The first question, however, while being on the outskirts of my area of expertise, is something I can indeed help you with. Have you read the Book of Tears?"

"Yes," Skulduggery said.

"It's on my to-be-read pile," said Valkyrie.

"In the Book of Tears, it is claimed that the Faceless Ones already existed when the universe came into being. This is, from what the Book of Shalgoth tells us, a false statement. There *was* a race of gods who witnessed the birth of the universe, but the Faceless Ones only arrived afterwards, as did multiple other races.

"For eons, these gods lived together in relative harmony, punctuated by the occasional bout of deicide, until the Faceless Ones decided to kill all the others as part of something called the Great Betrayal. They had found Earth and they liked it and wanted it all to themselves. An unspecified amount of time later, the Ancients appeared and they rebelled against their gods, so the Faceless Ones sent down the Shalgoth – monsters, essentially – to hunt the Ancients and tear their bodies asunder."

"Lovely," said Valkyrie.

"While the Shalgoth were going about their business, the Faceless Ones sculpted lesser monsters out of clay and rock and meat – the Shalgoth Reth – and sent them forth to feed off the magic of the Ancients. But, once they'd been released, the Faceless Ones ignored them, and so these lesser monsters retreated underground."

Valkyrie frowned at Skulduggery. "Are they the things that are living in the caves under Grimwood?"

"Probably their descendants," he replied. "Rhast, Oisin. We need information on Rhast."

Oisin nodded. "Rhast was one of the Shalgoth. By far the most cunning, he watched the Faceless Ones abandon the Shalgoth Reth and he knew that, once the Ancients were gone, his gods would abandon him and his brethren also. So he led a rebellion against his masters, but that failed, and so he was imprisoned, along with his fellows, deep within the Earth.

"And what about his eye?" Valkyrie asked.

"Ah, well," said Oisin. "One night as he slept, before he rebelled, an Ancient crept up and cut out his eye. Once it left its socket, the eye became a jewel of tremendous transformative power."

"Transformative," Skulduggery echoed. "Could it be used to focus another kind of energy?"

"I'm no scientist," said Oisin, chuckling, "but yes, in my scientific opinion, I believe so. Until our research, the eye's history

498

had been lost over the millennia, along with the true nature of its power and its very name."

"So it isn't called the Eye of Rhast any more?"

"It hasn't been called that for over two thousand years," Oisin said. "Now I believe it's called the Crystal of the Saints. Have you heard of it?"

# 100

On a building site just outside Wicklow, by the light of the moon and the full beams of three SUVs, Rancid Fines took the Crystal of the Saints from his bag and held it up. His prospective patron stepped closer. Rancid had a good feeling about this one. He was a criminal, yes, but also a businessman, and so much better suited to a partnership than Kiln had been, or even Nocturnal.

"How do I know it's the real deal?" Christopher Reign asked.

"You don't," said Rancid. "You just have to trust me right now. I'll prove it to you once everything is agreed." He put the Crystal back in the bag.

Reign rubbed his chin. "Right. And what is it you're looking to agree, Mr Fines?"

"I'm not looking for payment," Rancid said. "I just want to continue my work."

"And what is your work?"

"The Crystal of the Saints is my work."

Reign nodded slowly, thinking it over, and Rancid glanced at all those thugs, standing around like a pack of dogs. They seemed disinterested, but Rancid had known people like them before. All they needed was an order to follow, and then they'd gladly slit his throat and go home and have their supper.

"I spoke to a mutual friend of ours, Mr Fines," said Reign. "Can I call you Rancid? It's such a nice name, I love to use it.

Rancid, this friend I spoke to, he said you haven't been too successful in your work with the Crystal. He said your work has been an abject failure."

"Who said that?" Rancid snarled. "It was Kiln, wasn't it? Christopher, do not believe—"

"Ah-ah. I get to call you by your first name, but you still gotta call me Mr Reign. It's a mark of respect, Rancid. You respect a man, you call him Mister."

"Yes," Rancid said, "of course."

"The rules change again for friends, but we ain't friends, are we, Rancid?"

"No, sir. Not yet. Mr Reign, I had an arrangement with Kiln. A deal. He gave me his word and I trusted him – but then he betrayed me, sir. He betrayed me! He planned to—"

Reign interrupted him again. "I know what he planned to do, and I commiserate. Kiln always has been notoriously untrustworthy. But what about you, Rancid? Can you be trusted?"

"My word is my bond."

"Oh, to live in a world where that would be enough. See, I've been looking into you. Investigating, you might say. You hooked up with Kiln because he had money and resources you could use. Before that, you hooked up with Christophe Nocturnal – because he had money and resources you could use. Before Nocturnal, you hooked up with – and this kinda blows my mind a little bit – you hooked up with Adolf Hitler. Why'd you go and hook up with Adolf Hitler, Rancid?"

"Because... because he had..."

"He had money and resources you could use?"

"Yes. Yes, Mr Reign."

"And was it also because, back then, you were a little bit of a Nazi yourself?"

Rancid swallowed. Didn't answer.

"What colour is my skin?" Reign asked.

"Sir?"

"My skin, Rancid. What is its colour?"

"Uh... it's a... it's a deep chocolate—"

"It's black, Rancid. The colour of my skin is black, and you're a goddamn Nazi."

Rancid shook his head. "No. No, sir. That's wrong."

"Are you, or have you ever been, a member of the Nazi Party, you little fascist creep?"

"I swear, Mr Reign, I only... I was forced into helping them."

"You were forced."

"Yes, sir. Oberste and Reinigen and Fruen, Mr Reign. They were terrible people. Terrible. They used to—"

"I know who they were," Reign said, "and I know what they were after, and I know they were Nazis."

"They forced me!"

"You wear a swastika, Rancid?"

He swallowed. "On a..."

"Yes?"

"An armband. But I wasn't one of them."

"You wear the swastika, you're a Nazi. That's kinda the rule."

"Mr Reign... have I made mistakes? Yes. I've made plenty. I've taken part in events that have hurt people and I never wanted that. I regret my actions and my past affiliations. But World War Two was a long time ago, and I'm a changed man. All I care about now is my work with the Crystal. It's my life, sir. It is all I have."

"And you wanna keep working on it, don't you?"

"Yes, sir."

"Which is why you came to me. Because I have money and resources you can use. So let me ask you a question. Why the hell should I agree to work with you?"

"The Crystal," said Rancid, "it has already unlocked so many secrets in magic, secrets that I have passed on to my partners. Christophe Nocturnal benefited greatly from my research. Kiln would have benefited, too, if he'd kept his word. You can also benefit, Mr Reign. You can reap the rewards."

"Until you get it working the way you want it working, and then you'll bring back the Faceless Ones. But you been outta the loop, Rancid. You are not, as we say, privy to new information that has come to light. You know who Damocles Creed is, Rancid?"

"Yes."

"He sent the serial killer to get the Crystal, didn't he?"

"Silas Nadir came to negotiate."

"Naw, man. You don't send a serial killer to negotiate. You send a serial killer to kill and take what you want. Pleasant and Cain, they saved your life, man."

Rancid shook his head. "Damocles Creed—"

"Damocles Creed is a very powerful man," Reign interrupted, "and, like all powerful men, he needs people like me to occasionally work in the shadows for him, doing the things he can't be seen doing himself. See, he's been looking for that Crystal you got, because he's got plans. Big plans. Plans that you, you little Nazi freak, would love. He wants to use that there Crystal of the Saints to bring back the Faceless Ones. Not next year, not the year after – but tomorrow."

Rancid stared, his heart filling with joy. "He can do that?"

"He's got everything in place, Rancid. He's just waiting for the Crystal."

"Bring me to him," Rancid said. "Bring me to him and he can have it! Let me stand by his side when that happens and the Crystal is his! I have to be there! I must be there when paradise comes to this world!"

"Calm down, calm down," said Reign. "You want paradise, do you? See, the thing is, I have my paradise right here. I have my club and my businesses. I have my influence and my power and I ain't got no one telling me what to do. Why, oh why would I wanna give that up to live in the shadow of a race of pernicious gods?"

"But... but Damocles Creed..."

"Damocles Creed thinks he's got everyone in his pocket," Reign said. "But he doesn't have me. So I'm gonna take that Crystal off your hands. I think it's had a negative effect on you after all these years. You're kinda like that little Hobbit, you know? Carrying around that ring? It's sad to see, but I'm here to help. Gimme the Crystal."

"What are you going to do with it?"

Reign shrugged. "Honestly? As powerful as it is, as much money as it's worth... I'm probably gonna just destroy it. Safer all round, y'know?"

"You can't," Rancid whispered.

"If you don't hand it over, I have zero issues with just killing you and taking it."

In the silence that followed, one of Reign's men coughed. A moment later, another laughed.

The man who had coughed sank to his knees, holding his belly, which was stained with something dark. The man who had laughed collapsed, and Rancid realised he hadn't laughed, he'd made the sound someone makes as they were being killed.

A Necromancer appeared behind another of Reign's people and his glaive flashed darkly, taking a hand that held a gun and then a head, and he swirled in shadows as gunfire erupted and Rancid clutched his bag to his chest and started crawling.

Headlights swooped over him. Reign had jumped behind the wheel of one of the SUVs and was reversing out of there. But the Necromancer didn't appear to have any interest in him. Once the people with the weapons were all dead, he stepped out of the darkness ahead of Rancid and stood there, looking down.

"Please don't kill me," Rancid said.

The Necromancer took the bag from him and removed the Crystal of the Saints.

Rancid went cold. "No. Please. That's my life's work. That's my life. Take me with you. Where the Crystal goes, I go. I won't be any trouble. I won't be any—"

The Necromancer dropped the bag and stepped back into the shadows and then he was gone, and Rancid sobbed.

# 101

After they'd let Oisin fade back into the Echo Stone, Valkyrie and Skulduggery stood there and didn't say anything for the longest time. They'd come so close to nabbing the Crystal of the Saints twice in the past few weeks. So, so close. And, each time it had slipped between their fingers, they'd shrugged because, hey, there was no rush. No reason they had to get it right there and then. No bloody reason at all.

Valkyrie turned to Skulduggery. "Can I scream?" she said.

"Sure," he said. "But do it quietly."

Valkyrie screamed and kicked leaves and branches and punched the air in sheer and unadulterated frustration.

When she'd finished, she flicked her hair back and smiled.

"Do you feel better?" Skulduggery asked.

"Not in the slightest."

They began to walk back, Valkyrie now holding a fistful of lightning to guide her way. "We could have taken it off the board," she said. "We could have taken it out of the game entirely. Rancid Fines and the Crystal of the Saints have been a joke to us for years. Years! Now it's too late. It is too late, isn't it?"

"We can't put our full energies into the search," Skulduggery said, "not when there's so many other things we have to focus on."

They emerged from the treeline. Cadaver Cain stood beside the Phantom.

"I miss the Bentley," he said.

"If you're here to tell us that the key to Creed's plan is the Eye of Rhast," Skulduggery said, "thanks, but you're a bit late. For all we know, Creed already has it."

"He does," said Cadaver. "Uriah Serrate took it from Rancid Fines seven minutes ago, denying Christopher Reign the chance to destroy it. He'll have handed it over to Creed by the time I leave, in thirty-nine seconds. I'm sorry. I couldn't tell you about any of it before you were due to find out for yourselves. Events must unfold how they unfold."

"You," Valkyrie said, "are useless."

Cadaver nodded, and rose up off the ground. "I'll see you later."

"But thirty-nine seconds haven't passed yet," Valkyrie shouted up after him. "And where do you see us? What's going to happen?"

He stopped rising, and looked down at them. "The Dark Cathedral," he said. "That's where Creed will be. That's where the Eye will be. That's where we'll meet again."

"What else?" Valkyrie asked. "Cadaver, come on, tell us how to beat him. Tell us what we're supposed to do. Tell us something!"

"You're going to lose," Cadaver said. "And that's thirty-nine seconds." He rose up into the darkness.

Valkyrie glared after him, then glared at the ground. Then stopped glaring. "Damn," she said.

They got in the car.

"Creed will be expecting trouble," said Skulduggery. "He'll be expecting something. When we make our appearance, we won't have long until Creed's people descend on us, so whatever we do it'll have to be quick."

"Like what?" Valkyrie said miserably. "We don't know how to turn off the Pillars. We don't even know if we can."

"That's up to Omen," Skulduggery said, starting the engine. "We're trusting him to come up with something, so our focus shouldn't be on shutting down the Pillars – our focus should be on destroying the Eye of Rhast."

They started driving.

"And how are we supposed to do that?" Valkyrie asked, putting on her seat belt. "Mevolent snapped the Sceptre of the Ancients in half. It's useless. It's..." She remembered her conversation with Militsa, weeks ago. "It's being put back together," she said.

Skulduggery nodded. "From what I've heard, it's in one piece. We just have to drop by and pick it up."

She stared at him. "Drop by the High Sanctuary? Where everyone wants to arrest us?"

"Yes."

A shake of her head and a shrug. "I mean, why not? Sure. Maybe this is how we lose."

"Don't listen to Cadaver Cain," Skulduggery said immediately. "We're going to turn this around. We've defied fate before, and we'll do it again. He doesn't decide whether we win or lose. We do. Are you with me? Valkyrie, are you with me?"

She held up her fist. "Until the end," she said.

He knocked his fist against hers. "Until the end."

# 102

It hit them just as the bell went that signalled the end of the final exam. It rippled through the students, through the staff, it rippled through Roarhaven and Ireland and it rippled across the world. The cosmos was in alignment. The Source rifts had widened. Magic poured into reality like someone had turned the tap on full, and it filled up every sorcerer and it was amazing.

Omen got to his feet – unsteadily. His fingertips tingled. He looked over at Never and Never laughed.

"Everyone stay calm," Miss Gnosis said from the front of the class. "You've all been told what to expect. We knew the boost was coming. Granted, nobody told us quite how wonderful it would feel..."

Everyone laughed.

Grinning, Miss Gnosis waved a hand to quieten them down. "If you'd been paying attention, you'd know that any state of euphoria you may be approaching will fade after a few minutes, but for the next twelve hours you'll be stronger than you were before, and more powerful, so I expect everyone to behave responsibly. Carelessness gets people hurt. Remember that. Now then, for those of you heading home today, I hope you have a wonderful summer and I'll see you in September. For those of you hanging around for the carnival and celebrations, please do stay away from the protests, have a good time, and I'll see you on the streets. Now go on – school's out!"

They cheered. Omen cheered. He'd messed up his exams and was probably going to get horribly hurt-if-not-killed tonight, but he cheered because right now he was safe, he was happy, and he was ever-so-slightly drunk on magic.

He joined the throng in the corridor, laughing with the others, and by the time he got to his dorm room he was practically giddy. The feeling subsided, however, as he got changed – replaced by a nervous energy. He pulled on jeans and trainers and a tight-fitting top – fighting clothes – then took the telescopic baton Auger had given him and slipped it into his pocket.

Staying well away from the crowds of students, he climbed the stairs to the fifth floor and got to the library before anyone else. The librarian, a small man with a wonderful white beard, was snoring loudly at his desk, allowing Omen to sneak past.

He got to the room at the back, crossed to the glass doors that led to the balcony, and let Crepuscular in.

"How are you feeling?" he asked, noticing the stiff way Crepuscular was moving.

"For a man who's just been shot multiple times, I'm doing surprisingly well," Crepuscular said, easing himself into a chair. "The Draíocht boost isn't doing any harm, I have to say. I should be back to normal by tonight, so don't worry about me. I'll be ready to fight when you need me."

"Thanks," Omen said, though the word lacked the enormity of what he was feeling. "I'll check on the others."

Crepuscular gave him a nod and Omen hurried back out to the library just as Auger walked in.

"What are you doing here?" Omen asked, frowning.

"Just dropped by to see how everyone's doing," his brother replied. "How's your friend?"

"He's good," Omen said. "Almost as good as new already.

Auger, listen... I didn't get to thank you for Sunday night. How did you know that I needed help?"

Auger shrugged. "Felt it. Led me straight to you. Must be a twin thing."

"Well, I'm glad. Obviously."

The librarian jerked awake – then muttered something and put his head down again.

Auger spoke more softly. "I'm sorry I let Silas Nadir escape."

"He shunted away," Omen said, shrugging. "It's what he does."

"No – I let him go. I could've stopped him and I didn't. I hesitated."

"That's not like you."

"I just saw the King of the Darklands," said Auger. "I saw the expression he had on his face when I stabbed him with the Obsidian Blade. I couldn't do that again. I didn't want to get into a position where I'd have to kill someone else."

"You don't have to apologise, Auger."

"And what about when Nadir comes back? Someone's probably healing his broken jaw right now, so he's going to walk away and murder whoever he's going to murder next. I mean, the guy's a serial killer, Omen. He's a serial killer and I could have stopped him and I didn't."

"Stopping Nadir isn't your job," Omen said. "Preventing him from killing anyone isn't your responsibility. The only responsibility you could possibly have had was to try to save your own brother – which you did. That's the only real responsibility either of us have. Nothing else matters."

Auger gave a smile, then winced.

"You OK?" Omen asked, frowning.

"Looks like the doctors were right," Auger said. "The boost is kick-starting my Surge."

"You're having the Surge right now?" Omen asked, his eyes widening.

"I think it's started, yeah. It's kinda overwhelming, actually.

You know in the textbook it says you might experience some mild discomfort? They're underselling it."

"You should rest."

"I got the rest of my life to rest. Today and tonight I'm with you. Whatever it is you're into right now, I'm in."

Omen shook his head. "If you're not going to lie down, then go enjoy the carnival. I've got this covered."

"I'm sure you do, but you could always use more help, right?"

"I suppose," Omen said, reluctance dragging at his words.

Either the discomfort passed, or Auger hid it really well. "One last adventure, then. I'll help you with this thing you've got going on, and then I'm dropping out and travelling the world."

"I can't believe you're really going to do it. I can't believe you won't be around for Sixth Year. I've never done anything without you before."

"And I've never done anything without you," said Auger. "It's scary, isn't it?"

"Scary? It's bloody terrifying."

Never arrived with Axelia, and a minute later Mahala and Kase joined them. They all moved into the backroom and Omen closed the door. Everyone sat at the round table, and looked at him expectantly.

"Thanks for coming, everyone," he said, trying not to sound nervous. "I know this is a day of celebration and everything – the end of school, the Draíocht carnival, the power boost – and I know we'd all rather be out enjoying ourselves with everyone else. But this is important, what we're doing, and we need all the help we can get. I'd like to formally introduce everyone to a friend of mine – Crepuscular Vies."

Crepuscular gave the room a slow nod.

"Crepuscular has helped me out in the past and I know him and I trust him. Crepuscular, you've heard of my brother Auger, obviously, and this is Never, Axelia, Mahala, and Kase."

Crepuscular tipped his hat to them all. "Greetings and salutations."

He received a chorus of *hellos* in return.

"Crepuscular," Omen said, "you should probably take over from here...?"

"No, no," Crepuscular responded, "you're doing great."

"Oh. OK." Omen paused for a moment to arrange his thoughts. "Right. There are Seven Pillars in Roarhaven. Once they're all switched on, a wave of energy will spread out and do horrible, horrible things to us, and to everyone we love. So we have to stop it by sabotaging the Pillar here, in the school." He held up the Zeta Switch. "This will do that. We just have to use it."

Axelia put up her hand. "It might be a stupid question, but why don't you use it now?"

"That's not a stupid question. That's a very good question. The Zeta Switch will only turn off the Pillar once it's been turned on. It won't stop it from being turned on in the first place."

"May I?" Mahala asked, and Omen handed the Zeta Switch to her. She peered at it, turning it over. "It's a big red button," she said.

"It looks simple," Omen agreed, "but it's actually very..." He paused. "Actually, no, it's probably just that simple."

"So how does it work?" she asked.

Crepuscular took that one. "Ever since the city of Roarhaven was established here, Creed's people have been killing sorcerers by throwing them into each of the four towers in the school. The towers are actually Tempests – generators that can absorb and store magic. When it's time, all of this stored magic will be released into the courtyard, forming the last Pillar. As far as we can tell, the Zeta Switch allows the Tempests to redirect all that magic, releasing it harmlessly into the wild."

Mahala handed the switch back to Omen. "I'm assuming there's a reason you haven't simply gone to Duenna with this information?"

"Duenna's working with Creed," said Axelia.

Mahala raised an eyebrow. "Can't say I'm overly shocked at that revelation. Who else is involved?"

"Mr Chicane," said Omen. "Silas Nadir. Probably others."

"*The serial killer* Silas Nadir?" Axelia said, going pale.

"Yeah," Omen said. "Sorry."

"We can't trust anyone," Auger said quietly. "Any staff, any students that look to be in lockstep with Duenna must be treated as potential enemies."

"The prefects," Never said immediately. "Filament Sclavi in particular."

"What do you need us to do?" Kase asked.

"We have to be at the towers at midnight tonight, ready to shut off the Pillar the moment it's switched on. Creed will probably send his people to each Pillar to make sure nothing goes wrong. Things could get ugly."

"Prettiness is overrated," Axelia said softly.

# 103

Tanith sat at the table in the small room with her wrists shackled and prayed to all the gods she didn't worship to keep her boyfriend as far away from her as possible. Oberon Guile was on the wrong side of old-fashioned, just enough to compel him to come charging to her rescue once he heard about her arrest. But Tanith didn't need him charging anywhere. She'd escaped from jails before and she would again.

A City Guard officer came in, sat opposite her, opened a folder and pretended to read it for a few seconds. She knew him. He was a good guy.

"Hello, Liege," Tanith said.

Liege shook his head. "I cannot fraternise with prisoners."

"That makes sense. You've got a difficult job to do and the fact that you know me so well will only make it more difficult."

"This brings me no pleasure," he said. "I've enjoyed working with you in the past. It's been a pleasure to lock up the criminals you bring in. The city, the country, and the world owes you a great debt."

"How nice of you to say so," Tanith said.

"A debt that now we'll never have to repay."

"A little less nice, that one."

"You are charged with conspiracy to assassinate the Supreme Mage. You are not being asked to enter a plea due to the incontrovertible facts presented. You are hereby found guilty and sentenced to seventy-five years' imprisonment. In three hours, you will be transferred to Ironpoint Gaol. When Coldheart Prison reopens, you will be transferred there. Ironpoint and Coldheart are maximum-security facilities, which means you will not leave your cell for the duration of your sentence. A prisoner statement will now be taken if the prisoner so wishes."

"Seems a bit pointless," said Tanith.

"Statements of contrition can sometimes get a sentence reduced," Liege said, "but in your case, yes, it does seem like a waste of time."

"Not the sentence," Tanith said. "I meant being shipped off to prison. If Creed gets to follow through on all his plans, it won't be long before prison doesn't mean a whole lot."

Liege closed the folder. "That's got nothing to do with me, I'm afraid."

"You're not going to let me out," said Tanith. "I know you're not. I am fully aware of this fact. But, if I didn't at least try it, then I'd be doing myself a disservice. Liege, let me out."

"No," said Liege.

"Ah, go on."

"I'm sorry, Tanith."

"No need to apologise – you're doing your job with precisely the level of professionalism that I expect from you. But you need to let me out now."

Liege stood. "The guards will be by to take you back to your cell to await transportation."

"Liege," Tanith said. "Liege, listen to me. Listen to me very closely. Let me out and I'll be your best friend."

"Tanith, stop."

"Well, maybe not your best friend," Tanith continued, "but a good one. An adequate one at the very least. I will never remember your birthday and I won't always want to meet up when you do, but, if you need someone to help you move, all you'll have to do is call me and I'll furnish you with the number of a removal company. Or you could just look it up yourself. There's no reason why I'd have to do everything in this friendship."

"I'm very sorry," said Liege, walking to the door.

"Friends help each other out," Tanith said. "They help each other out of bad situations, help each other out of dark segments of their lives, and, most of all, they help each other out of jail cells. Liege, if you walk out that door, I'll never speak to you again. If we see each other at a social function and you want to impress someone by saying hello to the cool chick in the leather, I will be positively cold towards you. Yes, I will pose for photographs, but I will not smile, or if I do you can be assured that the smile *will not reach my eyes*."

Liege left and the door clicked shut.

# 104

Sebastian sat with the rest of the Darquesse Society, his back against the dungeon wall, and felt slightly better about their predicament.

They had a plan. It wasn't a very good plan, and it wasn't a very smart plan, and it was literally the only plan they'd come up with as they were sitting there, chained to the wall, but it was their plan, and that was something. Not much, but something, and that was better than nothing, but only barely. Even Tantalus, the treacherous worm, the poisonous snake, was in on it. The plan was as simple as it was stupid: deny everything.

The gate clanged. Everyone straightened as best they could. They'd all been given their lines. They all knew what they had to do.

Hoc came in, stood there, looking at them. "Darquesse hasn't rescued you yet," he noted.

"I don't know what exactly Tantalus has told you," Sebastian said, "but I'm pretty sure he's exaggerated a lot of what—"

"He's lying!" Tantalus shouted. "They're all lying! They came up with a plan to deny everything, which is barely a plan!"

Everyone glared at Tantalus. Even Hoc.

"I'm loyal," Tantalus continued. "When I give my word, when I make a deal, I see it through. You can count on me, Commander. I don't belong here, chained to this wall with these idiots! I'm on your side! I'm on the Supreme Mage's side! Please, let me out!"

"As I was saying," said Hoc, "she hasn't rescued you yet, so we're going to hurry this along. Draíocht has started and we're all really busy, but we're going to start killing one of you a day until Darquesse comes to rescue you. Starting now."

He took out his gun and pulled back the slide, chambering a bullet. He went over to Tantalus and shot him in the head. Sebastian's whole body jerked sideways in shock and the others screamed and yelled and cursed and cried.

"I'll be back tomorrow for the next one," Hoc said, and left.

# 105

It was getting dark.

The sound of the carnival in the Arts District drifted through the streets, but by the time it got to the crowd that had gathered outside the High Sanctuary it was lost, trampled underfoot by the chanting and the shouts.

The City Guard formed a line in front of the High Sanctuary, keeping the protesters well back from the steps. They stood in silence, shock sticks in one hand, shields in the other. They wore their armoured uniforms with helmets that blocked out the upper halves of their faces, that only showed the tight-lipped grimaces and the clenched jaws. Behind them, lines of Cleavers, standing still, scythes on their backs, hands by their sides. Faces unreadable behind their visors.

The protesters kept their distance physically, but hurled their chants and demands like they were bricks torn up from the street. Fists punched the air. Signs stabbed the sky. They screamed their outrage.

Skulduggery and Valkyrie moved through the crowd. The officer in charge paced behind the wall of cops. He, too, was armoured, but he carried his helmet in his hand so he could glare balefully at the citizens that thronged the Circle. Whatever he was snarling was lost in the voices that rose against him.

Valkyrie watched him turn away, one hand cupped over his

ear. He nodded and spoke and listened again. Then he put on his helmet, fastening it tight under his chin.

The protesters didn't notice. They kept chanting, kept waving those signs. Didn't see what was about to happen.

The officer in charge said something into his collar and the cops leaned forward, tucked their chins down, bent their knees, gripped their shock sticks tighter. Now the protesters at the front could see what was coming. New shouts arose, warnings, telling people to move back, move away, move now, but there were too many behind them, and not everyone had seen the change in stance.

Valkyrie didn't hear the order when it was given, but the cops came forward like a wave, shields slamming into the protesters, causing a violent ripple that crashed into her on its way past. There were shouts of alarm from behind and roars of aggression from in front and an elbow cracked into her cheek and she couldn't find her balance, couldn't get her feet under her. She was lifted, carried backwards, terrified people tumbling beneath her, and she reached for Skulduggery, but he was gone.

A shock stick came in on a short swing, trailing blue energy. It hit her in the forehead. The impact alone would have made her reel, but the shock that accompanied it jerked her sideways and fried her thoughts, burning them from her mind.

Cops were moving past her, charging into the crowd. A fist struck her. Her lip burst. She fell to one knee and a boot crunched into her ribs. She tried to grab on to something, to anything, but her fingers slid off the shields. Another jolt from a shock stick. A jab. A crack, right under the chin. She fell, sprawling on to a wailing protester. The cops descended on her.

Valkyrie cried out in pain even as she pulled the amulet from her jeans and pressed it to her leg. She tapped it and her black suit flowed over her body and she rolled, yanking up her hood, pulling down the skull mask.

The shock sticks swung, but the suit dealt with most of the

pain and her thoughts came back to her, cold and detached. With the mask on, she could hear every shout and grunt, every cry and snarl. She could hear panicked breathing and people begging and cops cursing and she could hear shock sticks crackling and bones breaking and the rustle of clothes and all the myriad sounds of fists, boots, shields, and sticks coming into contact with human flesh.

She blasted the cop who was crouching over her.

She kicked at the knee of the next one, saw it bend sideways, saw him go down, screaming. She let her energy burst from her in all directions, hurling the City Guard away as she got to her feet.

She glanced over her shoulder. Some of the protesters were using magic, too, but they weren't fighters. They'd become Energy Throwers because it was an impressive discipline, but hardly any of them had ever been in a situation where they'd had to use it in self-defence. For many, fear clouded their minds and their magic failed them just when they needed it.

The City Guard had no such problems. They swept through the crowd, many of them abandoning their officially sanctioned shock sticks and instead blasting people at point-blank range.

One of the City Guard charged, his shield up to ram her. Valkyrie dodged at the last moment, jammed her shoulder into the very edge of the shield, felt him swing round and stumble past. He wheeled on her, shock stick arcing for her head. She lunged, trapped his arm, elbowed him in the part of the face that his helmet didn't cover, then put him on the ground and knelt on his neck while she broke that arm. He screamed and she left him there, stepping over injured protesters. The commanding officer had kept a few cops back and as she neared they formed a barrier – then they were lifted off their feet as the air itself shuddered. Skulduggery came forward, thrusting out his arms, flinging them away.

There were new orders now as the City Guards realised who

they were dealing with, but the protesters surged, colliding with the line of cops, and Skulduggery grabbed Valkyrie and they forced their way to the edge.

Cleavers saw them coming – and didn't do anything to stop them. They got to the doors and Skulduggery flexed his hand, ready to blast them apart, but they opened before they got there and the Administrator beckoned them inside. She closed the doors once they were through.

"Whatever you're here for," Cerise said, "you'll have to hurry. The building is about to be locked down. If you're found in here, the Cleavers will be forced to arrest you."

"We'll try to be quick," said Skulduggery, hurrying by.

"Thank you," said Valkyrie, following.

They got to the Research Wing without encountering anyone and approached the laboratory.

"Any particular strategy?" Valkyrie asked as they walked.

"I don't see any reason why we shouldn't stick with our default mode," Skulduggery answered.

"Maximum confidence, all of the time?"

"It hasn't let us down before."

"It's let us down a few times."

"Ancient history," he said, waving a hand. "I feel much better about the immediate future." He redirected the wave, and the doors flew open and they strode into the laboratory.

At this time of night, there was only one scientist working, and his head snapped up in alarm.

"Don't mind us," Skulduggery commanded as the scientist hurried over.

"Excuse me," he said. "I'm sorry, excuse me? You can't be in here."

"And yet here we are," Skulduggery responded, "thus completely contradicting your assertion."

"I mean, you don't have permission to be in here," the scientist said, jumping into their path.

Valkyrie stopped walking. "What's your name?" she asked.

"Reginald Regatta," he said, squaring his shoulders. "Professor Reginald Regatta."

"Professor, do you know who we are?"

"Yes."

"Then you know we're Arbiters."

"Yes."

"Then you know we have jurisdiction over anything we decide we want jurisdiction over."

He frowned. "Aren't you wanted by the City Guard?"

"Where did you hear that?"

"I could have sworn somebody told me," Regatta said. "Anyway, the fact that you're Arbiters still doesn't give you the authority to walk in here without permission. If you do not leave immediately, I'll be forced to call the Cleavers."

"The Cleavers are busy, Reginald," said Skulduggery. "Can I call you Reg?"

"No."

"Reggie, there's a full-blown riot going on outside. Can't you hear the shouting?"

They listened in perfect silence, and Skulduggery shrugged. "Well, this place has only the best in soundproofing so we shouldn't expect to hear anything much, but trust me, people are rioting. And with good reason. In fact, why aren't *you* rioting, Reggie?"

"What? Because I'm working."

"Which brings me to my next point – your work. We hear this is the place where you're putting the Sceptre of the Ancients back together."

Regatta stiffened. "I can neither confirm nor deny that."

"We need that Sceptre, Reggie."

"I can neither grant nor refuse your request to requisition an item whose presence in this laboratory I can neither confirm nor deny."

"I understand your position," Skulduggery said.

"I'm glad someone does," Valkyrie muttered.

"But this is a matter of life and death. You're a scientific man. You value cold, hard facts and logic, just as I do. The truth, no matter what, is that not the case?"

Regatta hoisted his chin a little more. "It is."

"There are two types of truth, Reggie. There's the simple truth, and there's a deeper truth. The simple truth is that we need the Sceptre to save the world. The simple truth is that you're unable to give us the Sceptre because we haven't followed the rules. The deeper truth is that simple rules don't matter when lives are on the line. The deeper truth is that the only code worth following is a code that values decency above all else. I understand your reluctance to break your rules, but you know what we do. What we've done. We came in just now fully intending to bamboozle you with bluster until you were forced to just give us what we need, but we don't have time for the usual games we play. And so I only have one question for you: do you trust us?"

Regatta hesitated. Then sighed. "You've both saved my life, and the lives of my loved ones. You've saved the world. So yes, I trust you."

"We need the Sceptre, Professor," said Valkyrie.

He considered it, then nodded, and led them through into another smaller room, where the Sceptre rotated slowly in a class case.

It wasn't the same Sceptre Valkyrie was familiar with. It was silver and metal and wood, the three materials twisting round each other, reaching for the black crystal, half the size of Valkyrie's fist, at the top.

"We tried putting the Sceptre itself back together," Regatta said, "but we had no idea what we were doing. The best we could manage was constructing a new Sceptre and transferring over the hirranian crystal."

"That's what it's called?" Valkyrie asked, peering closer. "I never knew that."

"You've handled it before, haven't you?" Regatta asked. "You've actually held it in your hand without specialised equipment? That's astonishing. We had to wear four layers of protective clothing and use insulated mechanical arms to even touch it. But you're descended from the Ancients, aren't you? That's what I heard, and I believe it. Only someone descended from the Ancients could touch the hirranian crystal and survive. Well, someone descended from the Ancients or the Faceless Ones, of course."

"Of course," Valkyrie said, her voice quiet.

"Have you been able to test it?" Skulduggery asked.

"Unfortunately not," Regatta responded. "The original Sceptre would only function for the person with whom it had bonded. This new Sceptre doesn't have that restriction. That said, we don't know for sure if it even works because nobody's been able to fire it yet. The crystal has remained inert. But now that Detective Cain is here..." Regatta tapped a code into a keypad and the glass case opened. "I must warn you," he said. "The moment you remove the Sceptre, an alarm will sound and the Cleavers and the City Guard will come running. This is something I can't deactivate, I'm afraid."

"Is there another way out?" Skulduggery asked.

"Normally, I'd say no. But both of you can fly, yes? There's a large air vent we use in the surprisingly common case of laboratory fires. That will take you outside in seconds."

"Then that shall be our escape route," Skulduggery said. "Valkyrie?"

She paused a moment, then reached into the open case and took hold of the Sceptre. As an alarm pierced the air, the black crystal began to crackle with power.

# 106

Omen and Never waited outside the underground car park, the one near the Dark Cathedral. It was almost ten when Valkyrie and Skulduggery landed beside them.

"Follow," Skulduggery said, leading the way inside.

Omen and Never did as they were told, with Valkyrie bringing up the rear.

"The Pillars are going to turn on at twelve minutes to midnight," she said. "Or that's when the Wave will start. Or hit. I don't know exactly – all I know is that twelve minutes to midnight is when something bad happens. Who do you have on your side?"

"Auger and Kase and Mahala," Omen said. "Axelia and one other. And Never, of course."

"And you," said Never.

"Me as well."

"So that's seven," Skulduggery said. "Seven's a good amount of people to have on your team."

"Seven against Chicane and whoever Creed will have guarding the Pillars," Valkyrie said, following them down the concrete stairs.

"Chicane's taken care of," Never said.

"That's right," said Omen. "He was gonna kill me, but I saved his life and I think he's decided to walk away."

"He tried to kill you? Are you OK?"

"I'm fine," Omen said. "It didn't work. I mean, I'm not dead. Obviously." He glanced back and for the first time noticed what Valkyrie was carrying. "Is that the Sceptre of the Ancients?"

"It is," she answered. "Though it probably can't be called that any more. Skulduggery, do you have an opinion on this?"

Skulduggery led the way across the underground lot. "The Sceptre of the Ancients was called the Sceptre of the Ancients despite it actually being constructed by the Faceless Ones – presumably in their humanoid forms. Just because this new version has been constructed by mere flesh-and-blood scientists shouldn't mean a name change is required."

"The Sceptre of the Scientists doesn't quite sound epic enough," Valkyrie mused, then nodded. "Fair enough. It keeps its name. Problem solved."

"Then we can all go home," Skulduggery said, opening a STAFF ONLY door. He entered the small room, stepping past the cleaning equipment stored here, and pressed his hand to one of the bare bricks. The wall rumbled and slid open, revealing a passage. He turned to Omen and Never. "Go back to Corrival. Gather your soldiers. There's no telling who Creed might assign to that Pillar, but we're counting on you to switch it off."

Omen nodded, searching for something to say in order to convey confidence.

"We got this," Never said.

Omen nodded again, and pointed to his friend.

Skulduggery hurried into the darkness and Valkyrie seized both of Omen's shoulders and looked deep into his eyes. "You can do this. You might doubt it, but I know you can do this. I believe in you, Omen."

He swallowed, and Valkyrie stepped back, and was gone.

# 107

Quell's talk with Valkyrie hadn't gone the way he'd planned.

That was his fault. Life as a Cleaver bolstered the imagination when it came to combat, when it came to finding physical solutions to physical problems – but the imagination required to plan for human interactions eluded him. It was a different beast altogether, one that demanded a kind of empathy that he was unsuited for. He had formulated one avenue of conversation, one argument, and one outcome. The Valkyrie in his imagination accepted his reasoning and they'd kissed and left Roarhaven together. The Valkyrie in the real world wasn't nearly so accommodating.

He'd never experienced love before Valkyrie, and he'd never experienced heartache. He'd never experienced rejection before her, either – but she'd rejected him now. Outright, and with no room for manoeuvre.

It occurred to Quell that he was as ill-prepared for rejection as he was for heartache. The complexities of the human experience once more threatened to overwhelm him, so he sat and meditated on the problem, and the resolution became clear.

The problem, once the complex human emotions were put to one side, was a physical one: there were two people standing in the way of his objective. As always, to every physical problem there was a physical solution: those same two people had to be removed so that he could reach his objective.

In this case, that meant he had to kill both Militsa Gnosis and Skulduggery Pleasant. Once those two obstacles were no longer blocking the path, Valkyrie would rush back into his arms.

When his meditation came to an end, Quell was satisfied that he had reached the right conclusion, and decided to kill Militsa first.

# 108

Valkyrie and Skulduggery flew through the tunnel, her crackling energy battling back the darkness. They touched down at the far end and Skulduggery pulled the lever and the wall parted.

No one around. Valkyrie hadn't expected there to be. This was a big night, after all.

They found the stairs and went up, encountering the occasional Cathedral Guard and either sneaking by them or choking them out before moving on. They got to the ground level.

"Are you sure you know where you're going?" Valkyrie whispered, sticking to the shadows.

"Positive," he responded.

"Then where are we going?"

He pointed ahead. "That way."

"I see. It's just, none of this looks familiar."

"No need to worry, I have everything under control. The nave is just round this corner."

They got round the corner.

"I don't believe it," Valkyrie said. "You've brought us to another wall."

"But just like last time," Skulduggery responded, "I am absolutely positive that on the other side of this wall is where we want to be. We just need to get through it, that's all. We just need... Why are you shaking your head?"

"If you're thinking of doing another Billy-Ray, you can leave me here."

"It'll be perfectly safe."

"So you've been practising, have you?"

"Well, no, but I have every confidence that I'll be able to pass through without leaving you trapped halfway in. Every confidence in the—"

There was a shout, and another shout, and then there were a load of Cathedral Guards running their way.

"No time for subtlety," Skulduggery said. "We need to get through this wall and destroy the Eye now."

Valkyrie ducked back as an energy stream sizzled by her head, and passed the Sceptre into her right hand. The crystal crackled. "I hope to God you work," she muttered.

She raised it at the wall and the crystal exploded in a flash of darkness, throwing her back against Skulduggery. She blinked madly, clearing her vision. The shattered pieces of the Sceptre lay strewn across the ground. The crystal itself was nothing more than tiny dull shards. And the wall was completely undamaged.

"Damn," she breathed.

Skulduggery and Valkyrie both turned at the sound of approaching footsteps. Uriah Serrate smiled at them as they got up.

"I must warn you," Skulduggery said, "that while you clearly bested us when we first met, things will not go your way a second time. Valkyrie and I have a tendency to learn from our mistakes – and we never lose round two."

Serrate became a streak of shadow that collided with Skulduggery, throwing him back. Then he whirled, his glaive materialising as it swung for Valkyrie. It exploded against her side in a burst of darkness and sent her sliding across the floor.

She came up on one knee in time to watch him leap, cracking a knee into Skulduggery's chin. As Skulduggery hit the ground, Serrate reached out and twisted his hand and the shadows around

Valkyrie convulsed, trapping her arms by her side, covering her face, forcing their way down her throat. She gagged, tried to bite down, but there was nothing except cold darkness between her teeth. She ignored the flash of panic and released her magic, the white fingers of crackling energy making the shadows recoil and draw back and she gasped, coughed, spat. Free again.

Skulduggery was on his feet, driving an elbow into Serrate's jaw. The glaive fell, becoming nothing but shadow the moment it left the Necromancer's gnarled hands. He grabbed Skulduggery, hit him, got hit in return, and back and forth it went until Skulduggery manoeuvred the fight so that Serrate's back was to Valkyrie.

She ran up behind him, blasted him, kicked out his leg, and wrapped an arm around his throat as Skulduggery twisted and broke his right arm. A stomp and Serrate's knee bent in a direction it shouldn't have and Valkyrie heard the distinct crack of a bone being snapped. She tightened her hold, cutting off both his air and his blood and he made a gurgling sound. He tried to pull her arm away with his good hand, but Skulduggery took hold of it and broke his wrist.

And then Serrate turned to darkness and Valkyrie was holding nothing but shadows that twisted around her neck and lifted her off the floor.

She dug her fingers into the noose, kicking her legs uselessly. Skulduggery tried using the air to dislodge the darkness. Fireballs flared but did nothing. Blood pounded in her temples. Her throat felt like it was caught in a vice.

Then she was spun, her boots crashing into Skulduggery, and she didn't even see him land she was spinning so fast, spinning from her throat, her vision darkening, the world growing quiet, and then she was free and she sucked in air and the wall smacked against her and she fell.

Before she could arrange her thoughts, there were hands on her, turning her on to her belly, pulling her arms behind her, and then that familiar rattle of a chain and the clack of shackles and the dulling of magic.

They hauled her up to her knees. Through the curtain of hair that fell over her face, Valkyrie watched the Cathedral security team kick and stomp on Skulduggery, even after the handcuffs were on.

She looked up as the shadows melted together to form Serrate, who stood over her, undamaged.

"You suck," she managed to say before they pulled her to her feet.

# 109

The last time Valkyrie had been in the nave, the tiers of pews that surrounded the platform on three sides had been full of worshippers. Now they were empty.

Cathedral staff were busy on the platform. They'd replaced the pulpit with a podium, and had run thick cables across the walkway that connected the platform to the stage. There was a large cage built there now, and a bank of six huge monitors beside it. Creed stood in the middle of all this, issuing commands.

Two Cathedral Guards escorted Valkyrie and Skulduggery down the steps. They'd reached the halfway point when Creed's assistant signalled them to stop. The guy escorting Valkyrie stomped on the back of her knee and she dropped. Skulduggery dropped beside her.

The assistant hurried over to Creed and stood on his tiptoes to whisper in his ear. Creed, his eyes on a computer tablet, tapped the screen a few times, swiped, tapped again, then finally looked. "What?"

Valkyrie glared and Skulduggery tilted his head, but Creed focused his attention on his assistant. "Why did you bring them here?"

The assistant paled. "I... I thought you'd like to—"

"To what?" Creed said. "Gloat? Explain my plan? Outside, there's a riot, and in here we're trying to change the world. I don't have time for this, idiot."

Creed strode back to his original position. The assistant flushed red, and busied himself at the monitor bank.

"I have to admit," Valkyrie muttered to Skulduggery, "I'm a little insulted."

"Me too."

"Like, are we suddenly not worthy of a gloating? Is he really so busy that he can't take two minutes to laugh in our faces?"

"He does look busy."

"Two minutes, Skulduggery. That's all it'd take."

They watched him issue orders to the technicians around him.

"Ah, maybe he's right," Skulduggery said. "Besides, if we've heard one gloating monologue, we've heard them all, right? We know how they go. *You interfering do-gooders have interfered for the last time. Once my Doomsday Machine is ready, I shall bring forth the end of the world and everything you know will crumble to dust, et cetera, et cetera.*"

"Yeah," said Valkyrie, "I suppose. But what's the deal with the jail cell?"

"*That's not a jail cell, you ridiculous simpleton.*"

"Oi."

"*That's a Faraday cage.*"

"And what's that?"

"*A Faraday cage is an enclosure built to block electromagnetic fields, you ignorant ape-person.*"

"Seriously, dude..."

"*But, instead of blocking electromagnetic fields, this particular cage will block the effects of the Activation Wave.*"

"So you all get to stand in that cool-looking cage, safe and sound, while the rest of the world turns into zombified Kith?"

"*Yes...*"

"OK."

"*...you moron.*"

"Skulduggery."

"What?"

"Stop insulting me."

535

"I'm not," he protested. "Creed is."

"Creed!" Valkyrie shouted. "Stop insulting me!"

Creed frowned over at them, then went back to work.

"You two are hilarious," their guard said.

Valkyrie grinned up at him. "We're at our best when we're in trouble."

"We're at our best a lot," Skulduggery muttered.

"You remind me of me and my friend," said the guard. "That is exactly our type of humour."

"Yeah?" said Valkyrie, and looked over at the other guard. "Is that you?"

The other guard glowered.

"Uh, no," the first guard said. "My friend isn't on duty tonight. His name's Puck. I'm Winger."

"Hey, Winger."

"Don't make friends with the prisoners," the second guard said.

"I'm not," Winger said, heat rising to his face. "I'm just making conversation."

"Why? They're going to be dead in a minute."

"We're just talking, Braylon. Jesus."

"The Supreme Mage told us not to talk to the prisoners."

"No, he didn't."

"Yes, he did."

"When did he say that?" Winger asked as Braylon clenched his jaw. "When did he say those exact words? Well? You can't answer because he didn't say that."

"It was implied in the briefing."

"A lot of things were implied in the briefing, Braylon. It was implied in the briefing that tonight would be amazing and wonderful and we'd all have a great time – but you're making that impossible."

"Just don't talk to them."

"I can talk to whomever I like."

"Then talk to whomever you like. Just don't talk to them."

"You're not my father, you're not my mother, you're not my wife, and you're not my commanding officer. So shut up."

"I'm getting so sick of you."

Winger barked a laugh. "Oh, really? You're getting sick of me? What have I done that's so annoying?"

"You're talking to the prisoners, and if you're not talking to the prisoners you're talking about Puck and about how great Puck is and isn't Puck hilarious and wait till you hear what Puck said this morning. I'm sick of Puck and I'm sick of you and you know what? When the Supreme Mage throws the switch, I might walk out of the cage because I would rather spend the rest of my life as one of those freaky Kith weirdos than listen to one more amusing anecdote about bloody Puck."

Winger stared at him. "What is your problem?"

"I don't have a problem."

"You obviously do."

"I just want to do my job. Can we please just do our jobs?"

"You've got issues, man. Unresolved issues."

"Yes, fine, I have issues. Can we drop it now and go back to being quiet? I like you best when you're quiet."

"Fine with me."

"Thank you."

"You're welcome."

"You're welcome, too."

Valkyrie winced at Braylon. "Oooh, weak ending."

"Shut up."

# 110

They were all here. The team. Omen's team. Everyone except Never, but that was OK. That was the plan.

What wasn't part of the plan was how dry Omen's mouth would be. It really was ridiculously dry. He peeked over the balcony, down at the water fountain in the courtyard. All that water. He licked his lips.

"Anyone have any water?" he croaked. Axelia handed him a bottle. "Thank you," he said, and gulped it down as Auger and Kase and Mahala held stencils to the walls and sprayed them with black paint.

"What are they?" Axelia asked, going over to peer at the perfect sigils they were leaving behind.

"It's a little trick we picked up last year," Mahala said. "They interfere with the mechanisms on automatic weapons, so, if the City Guard come, they won't be able to use their guns."

Axelia blinked. "They're going to be shooting at us?"

"They're going to try."

Axelia walked back to Omen. "These are cops," she said quietly. "Cops aren't supposed to even want to shoot at us. This isn't just another fight, Omen. This is... We're going to be fighting our own side here."

"No," Crepuscular said from nearby. "The City Guard are not

on our side. They're no longer police, so you have to stop thinking of them like that. The City Guard are the enemy."

"They're the *cops*."

"Axelia," Omen said, "he's right. If you think of them as the good guys, you'll hesitate. But they won't, and they'll kill if you give them the chance."

She stared.

Never teleported in beside him. He looked pale.

"Are the City Guard here?" Omen asked.

Never nodded.

"How many?"

Never hesitated. "Lots."

Crepuscular nudged Omen. "Go on."

"Go on what?"

"Inspirational pep talk," Crepuscular said. "Let's have it."

Omen realised everyone was looking at him. "Wait, me? Why me? No. You do it."

Crepuscular shook his head. "It won't mean anything coming from me. You're the reason we're all here."

"But I don't know what to say." Omen turned to Auger. "You do it. You're good at these speeches. I've heard you."

Never nodded. "You are good at them."

Mahala shrugged. "You're pretty inspirational."

"And I would love to," Auger said, his face pale and drenched with perspiration, "but I'm really not feeling the best right now. The Surge is really doing a number on me and, besides, I'm just a helping hand. Omen, this is your fight. You've got to find the words."

"OK," Omen said, "OK. Um. Right. You're all looking at me because we're about to get pretty badly hurt, if I'm being honest, and you want to know that it'll be worth it. Well, it will. We either stop the Pillar from turning on or some of us get our minds wiped and most of us melt into puddles, and then the Faceless Ones come back and, I don't know, probably slurp up the remains or something. But we won't care because, like I said, we'll either have had our minds wiped or else we'll be melted puddles of goo. But, just because we won't care when it happens, that's no reason not to care *now*. So we have to fight whoever comes to stop us, and we have to win. No matter what. Just, uh, remember that they can take our lives, but they will never take our freedom. Unless they take our lives."

"That," said Never, "was brilliant."

"Really?"

Auger squeezed his shoulder. "Truly awesome."

Omen grinned. *Hell, yeah.*

Then Principal Duenna and a bunch of City Guard cops came marching down the corridor and the grin vanished.

"What are you students doing out of your dorms?" Duenna said, astonishment written all over her features. "Return to your rooms at once. And who is this? Who are you, sir?"

Crepuscular took off his hat and laid it carefully on the floor next to the wall. "Nobody step on that," he said, ignoring Duenna completely.

"Sergeant," Duenna said, "please arrest that man for trespassing."

The sergeant nodded to a pair of cops and they came forward, mouths pressed into grim, thin lines.

"And so it begins," said Crepuscular, sounding unnervingly happy about it.

# 111

Four guards came to Tanith's cell.

"Your lucky night," one of them said as they shackled her wrists and ankles. "Your friends are causing trouble, so d'you know what you're gonna be? You're gonna be a hostage. They either surrender to us, or we'll kill you in front of them. Isn't that a laugh? Isn't it?"

"It is," Tanith said, watching them run a short chain from her shackles to a heavy belt round her waist.

"Let's go, gorgeous," the guard said, and Tanith shuffled out of the cell.

He talked a lot, this guard, made all kinds of jokes, all kinds of comments. She ignored them and kept her eyes open for Liege. Liege was a good one; he wouldn't let anything bad happen to a prisoner under his care.

"Where's Liege?" she asked.

"Been called away to help with the riot," said the guard, grinning. "You're all ours."

Then a wave of blue energy hit everyone from behind, throwing them off their feet, and Tanith went rolling, her shackles and chains rattling. She glimpsed an energy stream catching one of her guards between the shoulder blades.

She came to a stop facing the wall. Behind her, grunts of pain. The dull smack of people getting struck. She turned over, saw a woman in black kicking the hell out of the guards. Tanith's expression soured.

As the fighting continued, Tanith clambered awkwardly to her knees, and then her feet. She waited, watching China Sorrows dispatch the enemy.

When the enemy was down and out, China took a set of keys from one of the guards and hurried over.

"Are you OK?" she asked, unlocking the handcuffs.

"Fine," Tanith responded.

China hunkered down, unlocking the shackles around Tanith's ankles. "Sorry I took so long."

"Weren't you in a coma?"

"Medically induced. A detective revived me – Rylent. Do you know him?"

"I don't," said Tanith. "Remind me to send him a thank-you note."

"I picked these up for you," China said, passing over Tanith's coat and sword as she stood.

Tanith put on the coat, took out her phone and tapped her screen to check her messages. "Temper needs assistance," she said.

"Lead on," said China.

Tanith glowered.

# 112

The monitors clicked on. The first seven screens showed the Pillar locations – the Dark Cathedral, the High Sanctuary, Corrival Academy, and the churches on Carnivore, Wallow, Razorblade, and Suture – and the eighth screen was an aerial shot, a live shot, of Roarhaven at night. The streets around the Circle, around the High Sanctuary and the Dark Cathedral were filled with people as they clashed with the City Guard.

"Instigate the Pillar sequence," Creed said.

The technicians flicked switches and pressed sigils, and the floor began to vibrate. With each moment that passed, the vibrations grew in intensity, until Valkyrie could feel her teeth chattering.

There was a sudden whoosh from somewhere and the first screen, the one focused on the Dark Cathedral, showed the tallest spire opening and a column of energy surging into the night sky.

The riot paused so everyone could stare.

"The Cathedral Pillar is active," announced one of the technicians, pretty needlessly.

A moment later, the second monitor showed an identical column of energy bursting from the High Sanctuary.

"The Sanctuary Pillar is active," the technician announced.

Valkyrie had her eyes fixed on the third monitor – Corrival Academy.

"Stay dark," she muttered. "Stay dark."

# 113

The tower started to hum, light bursting from between the bricks. Not just this tower, either, but all four of them suddenly churning with all that salvaged magic.

Omen tore the Zeta Switch from his pocket and jammed his thumb on the button, but it did nothing to stop what was happening.

"It's not working!" he shouted. "It doesn't work!"

Crepuscular stopped beating a cop with his own shock stick just long enough to shout back, "Get closer!" and then went right back to enjoying himself.

Omen dodged round the grasping arms of a cop and ran to the railing, but a wall of air threw him forward. He rolled, losing the device, and slammed against the barrier. It took the wind out of him and he gasped, looking down and watching the light move to the base of the towers and then cross the ground, meeting at the fountain in the centre of the courtyard. The water instantly turned to a cloud of steam and the fountain cracked, crumbled, and a column of energy burst forth, puncturing the night sky.

# 114

"The Corrival Pillar is active," the technician said as another column of light shot up.

Damn.

"The Carnivore Pillar is now active," said the technician, and a moment later, "as is the Wallow Pillar. The Razorblade Pillar is... it's just been switched on, and so has the Suture Pillar."

The final two columns of light punched through the night air, and the aerial shot showed that same energy streaking through Roarhaven's streets, forcing both the protesters and the cops to scramble off the road. These massive walls of energy extended from one Pillar to the next – sometimes straight, sometimes curved – and pinged back and forth, forming a city-wide sigil that bled upwards.

"The Ensh-Arak Sigil is active," the technician announced.

Creed strode across the walkway to the platform, holding the Eye of Rhast in both hands.

"All personnel move to the Faraday cage immediately," the technician shouted. "There will not be a second warning."

Winger and Braylon glanced at each other and hurried to the cage, leaving Valkyrie and Skulduggery on their knees.

Creed placed the Eye on the podium, then walked quickly to the bank of monitors.

"Should we be doing something?" Valkyrie asked, keeping her voice down.

"I'm sure Cadaver Cain has some sort of last-minute move he has yet to make," Skulduggery responded.

"So we're waiting for one bad guy to stop the other bad guy?"

"Yes," he said, "and that is when we'll strike."

"Strike how?"

"I'm not sure," he admitted. "It will probably involve running over there and punching whoever's closest."

"How are we going to punch anyone with our hands shackled behind our backs?"

He looked at her. "Because our hands won't be shackled behind our backs. Because we have the keys to... Didn't you pick your guard's pocket?"

"What? No. No, I didn't. I didn't know we were meant to."

"We hadn't discussed it," Skulduggery said, "but I always find it helps." He turned slightly, and she saw him trying to manoeuvre the stolen key into the lock on his cuffs.

Valkyrie stared. "How did you pick someone's pocket with your hands behind your back?"

"I have many talents," he said, the key scraping round the lock. "This will just take a moment..."

Creed stepped away from the monitors, and turned to the Faraday cage. "Seventy-nine seconds," he announced. "Seventy-nine seconds and the Activation Wave will begin its journey. It will take three minutes to cover Roarhaven. If it encounters the Child of the Faceless Ones within the city's boundaries, it will transform a simple sorcerer into the messiah, and then it will retract. If it doesn't, it will speed up exponentially until it finds what it's looking for – even if it has to cover the entire planet. My friends, today marks the beginning of the new world. You may rejoice."

The people in the Faraday cage rejoiced like idiots.

Shadows swirled on the platform and Cadaver stumbled out and fell to his knees, his hands shackled. Uriah Serrate followed.

"Damn," Skulduggery muttered.

Valkyrie scowled. "So much for the great distraction."

Creed looked down at Cadaver, then over at Skulduggery. "Friend of yours? Relative maybe? I think I can see some family resemblance."

"He looks nothing like me," Skulduggery called out.

Cadaver shrugged. "My cheekbones aren't quite as high and my jaw isn't quite as square. He is, admittedly, much better-looking."

"His name is Cadaver Cain," said Serrate. "He claims to be Skulduggery Pleasant seventy-two years from now."

"You're from the future?" Creed asked, eyebrow raised.

"I'm here to stop you," said Cadaver.

"It works, then? What I'm about to do? It works?"

Cadaver nodded. "It works. You bring your precious Faceless Ones back. You murder billions. You corrupt the very fabric of existence."

"Oh, that is good to know."

"It's why I'm here," Cadaver said. "To stop you."

"Cadaver, is it?" Creed said. "Cadaver, how exactly are you going to stop me? I have you and your past self and Valkyrie Cain in chains. I have all the Pillars up and running. I have formed the Ensh-Arak and the Eye of Rhast is in place. There is literally nothing you can do now to derail my plans."

"Ah," said Cadaver, "but what if I knew all of this ahead of time?"

Creed smiled. "The knowledge of the future changes the future, Mr Cain. It's the first rule of prophecy."

"But I don't see just one timeline. I see them all."

"What a useless gift."

Cadaver laughed. "You still don't understand the sheer scale of what I can do."

"I'm sure I don't," said Creed, "but I am rather busy preparing to usher in an entirely new world. Serrate, kill this one. Once he's dead, kill Pleasant and Cain. And no more interruptions."

Creed turned back to the podium and the shadows formed in Serrate's hands, becoming the glaive. Cadaver continued to kneel there, like he knew something no one else did. Even when Serrate stepped behind him, glaive raised, he didn't seem particularly bothered.

The glaive came down and the handcuffs fell to the floor with the light clinking of chains.

Creed turned as Cadaver got to his feet. Serrate stood beside him.

"I see," Creed said quietly.

"Please," said Cadaver, "don't blame Uriah for this. I saw this play out hundreds of years ago when the Viddu De opened my eyes – such as they were – to what was to come. That's when I approached Uriah, and opened his eyes, too, allowing him to see as I see."

"This has been centuries in the making, Damocles," Serrate said. "There is no shame in being caught unawares."

"And the Necropolis?" Creed asked. "The souls of the dead who view you as their king? Do you actually care about them, or was that all just a lie, too?"

"They have fulfilled their purpose. They have provided the ruse we needed to distract you from our goal."

"So it was indeed another lie. You brought me back to life, Uriah. Of course, you were probably involved in my assassination, so I think that makes us even." His eyes narrowed. "But you held sway over me, didn't you?"

"I did," said Serrate. "I needed you obedient, Damocles, to agree to my requests without asking too many questions. If it makes you feel any better, my control over you was fast slipping away. You have an unusually strong will."

"This conversation doesn't involve me," said Cadaver, "and so

I find my attention wandering." He waved his hand and the door to the Faraday cage slammed shut.

"Um," said Winger, huddled inside with the others, "what's happening now?"

"This is what happens when I get bored," Cadaver said, tossing in a grenade. Valkyrie's heart lurched as it exploded with a dull whump, but instead of fire and shrapnel there was a bright light that pulsed for one moment, then shrank back in. The people in the cage dropped, their bodies hollow, their skin cracked and wrinkled.

Creed stared at their remains.

Cadaver shook his head sadly. "If you ask me, it's how they would have wanted to go."

"Murderer!" Creed roared, lunging at him. Cadaver stepped into the lunge, slamming his elbow into the side of Creed's neck. The bigger man dropped to his knees.

"In case you're wondering," Cadaver said, "I don't kill you. What a waste that would be. No, you're the first to be enveloped by the death field. I know you know what that is. I know you know what it will mean for you. You'll be the first of the New Dead. You can't see it now, but what's about to happen is an honour beyond anything you could ever have hoped for."

"I'll tear you apart," Creed mumbled.

"You won't. When the death field passes over you, you'll understand, and all this rage and all this hate you're feeling will disappear. You won't retain your individuality as I have, as Uriah has – but you'll still be content. Discard your old preconceptions about what it means to be living and what it means to be dead – they'll have no place in the universe to come."

"I must go," said Serrate, speaking to Creed. "Your City Guard officers have just realised that the resistance at the Corrival Pillar is proving more substantial than they'd anticipated. My help is needed."

"Burn in hell, Serrate."

"There is no hell, Supreme Mage. There's just here." He looked at Cadaver. "Life in Death, brother."

"Life in Death," Cadaver echoed.

The shadows swirled, and Serrate disappeared.

# 115

A cop gripped Omen, both hands curling into his shirt, and slammed him back against the wall, then drove a knee into his side. Gasping, Omen tried to break his grip, tried to counter, but this guy was way too strong and steaming mad, and all that anger was making him even stronger and Omen was pretty much finished.

Around him, Never and Mahala were holding their own, and Axelia was dragging Kase to his feet, and Auger was taking on three at once and Crepuscular was disappearing under an avalanche of City Guard uniforms, and there were more cops running in with shock sticks in their hands.

Omen's first real attempt at leading a team and it was a disaster. If anyone had been in a position to ask if he agreed with that assessment, he'd have shrugged and said, "Yeah."

And then he saw Uriah Serrate walking up and he suddenly got very frightened. His friends and his brother, they weren't just facing arrest now – they were facing death. He'd got them all killed.

"Please," Omen shouted. "We give up! Please!"

Serrate was coming straight for him, the glaive materialising in his hand. The cop saw Serrate coming and released him, and Omen staggered a little before straightening up.

"Take me," he said, "but please don't kill my—"

The glaive swished and took the cop's head off and Serrate spun, slicing through two more uniforms.

Ice water spiking through his veins, Omen turned, forced himself back on track, scanning the ground. He ran forward, got jostled and struck, but he grabbed the Zeta Switch and ran to the Pillar.

He held his arm out and mashed his thumb on to the button and the column of light spluttered.

# 116

One of the monitors started beeping and Valkyrie looked over, saw the column of energy emanating from Corrival Academy begin to flicker.

All of a sudden, the column vanished. The linking walls of energy around the city twisted and turned back on themselves, trying to complete the Ensh-Arak – but, without the lower-most point, it was no use. They flickered into dozens of new patterns, trying to find one that stuck, walls of energy searing through crowds of protesters.

"Oh, no," said Skulduggery.

"Such a pity," Cadaver said to Creed. "The Ensh-Arak is broken. Here you are, after all this work and effort, right on the cusp of success... and it's been snatched away from you. Do you know why, Damocles? Do you know how?" He hunkered down in front of him. "You've planned this for a hundred years. I've planned this for centuries." He stood. "Preparation, Damocles. That's what it's all about."

Valkyrie frowned at the screen as the six Pillars locked into a new pattern, a sigil she'd seen before – somewhere close by. Recently.

On the iron bars of the new Necropolis. It was the Gurahghul Sigil.

The death field.

# 117

Creed got to his feet, snarling at Cadaver. "Your dead gods will never dim the fire in my heart that burns for the Faceless Ones."

"Oh, they'll do more than dim it," Cadaver responded. "They'll extinguish it. And what's more they'll enjoy doing it. The Faceless Ones are to blame for all this, by the way. Would the Viddu De's desire to spread to this universe be so fierce if they didn't also see this as an opportunity for revenge? I wouldn't dare speak for them, but I doubt it. The Faceless Ones waited until their fellow gods were weak and wounded and then they stabbed them in the back – cosmically speaking. Now the Viddu De will strike, denying the Faceless Ones their way home. You reap what you sow, Damocles. As it is for us, so is it for our gods."

Creed swung at him and Cadaver swerved round the fist and hit him right on the hinge of the jaw.

"I've seen this happen," Cadaver said. "You don't have a chance."

Creed roared and swung again, and, as Cadaver dodged his attacks and responded with perfectly judged blows of his own, Skulduggery shuffled closer to Valkyrie and reached out, his hand hidden from view. A moment later, the cuffs sprang open and Valkyrie's magic flooded her system.

She immediately took out her phone, dialled Omen's number, and whispered into it. Then she stood beside Skulduggery. His hand was outstretched – he was trying to use the air to lift the Eye of Rhast from the podium. It wasn't working.

"Should have known it wasn't going to be that easy," he muttered. "Let's get down there."

Creed went sprawling across the platform.

"These are your last moments as a free person," Cadaver informed him. "I just want you to dwell on your imminent failure while I take care of this."

Valkyrie launched herself off her feet, flying straight for him, but Cadaver turned, using the air to smack her to the ground.

Skulduggery swept his arms in and Cadaver met that wall of air with one of his own. They crashed into each other and clung on, exchanging knees, elbows, headbutts. Skulduggery flipped Cadaver and Cadaver swept Skulduggery and they scrambled on the floor for the upper hand.

Valkyrie ran in with a kick. Cadaver reared back at the last moment, pulled Skulduggery into it instead. Valkyrie's boot collided with Skulduggery's ribcage and he grunted.

Rolling backwards on to his feet, Cadaver dodged Valkyrie's lightning blast and flung a handful of fire at her face. She barely got her arms up in time, but even as the flames exploded against her sleeves Cadaver was kicking at her knee, grabbing her shoulder, swinging her round to wrap her up in a chokehold.

He heaved her off her feet. She tried to take a breath, but there was no air there. No blood, either. Her head pounded. Skulduggery stormed up, but there was no way he'd be able to dislodge Cadaver in the few seconds of consciousness Valkyrie had left.

Skulduggery proved her wrong by kicking her in the chest. She flew back with Cadaver, landed on him, the chokehold abandoned, and rolled off, one hand at her sternum, tears of pain in her eyes. Cadaver was rolling, too, getting to his feet as Skulduggery closed in.

A punch to Cadaver's jaw. Elbow to Skulduggery's temple. Knee to the leg. Headbutt. Punch. Elbow. Grab. Throw. Faster and faster, harder and harder, degenerating into a mad scramble that saw Skulduggery's arm ripped from his sleeve.

Skulduggery cried out in pain and the air rippled and he hurtled away and went crashing into the pews. Cadaver whirled, freezing in place when he saw the energy filling Valkyrie's hands.

"You're done," she said.

Light rose through engravings in the podium and the Eye of Rhast began to glow.

"It's happening," Cadaver told her. "I know you can't see it now, but this is the right thing to do for the entire universe."

"You're going to kill everyone, Cadaver."

"Not everyone, and not in the way you think. You won't be lying-down-dead dead. You'll be walking-around-talking dead."

"But we won't be like you, will we? We won't stay as the people we are."

Cadaver tilted his head. "Is that so bad? Present company excluded, people aren't that wonderful."

"Who are they, the Viddu De? What did they say to you to get you on their side like this?"

"They offered me hope when I was hopeless."

"And now you're their slave."

"Call it what you will, I know I'm doing the right thing."

"Has anyone seen my arm?" Skulduggery called over from the pews.

"It's here," Valkyrie called back, and shook her head at Cadaver. "I can fry you where you stand," she said.

"I know," he answered.

"Did you see this happening?"

"I did."

"How does it end?"

"Not well for one of us."

Skulduggery joined them on the platform. "Take him out," he said, picking up the bones of his arm and feeding the humerus up through his sleeve first. "Don't give him a chance."

"You'll have to kill me," said Cadaver. "I won't stay down. You'll have to put everything into it. Turn these bones to ash. Can you do that, Valkyrie? Can you kill me?"

Skulduggery muttered in pain as his bones reconnected. "Do it," he said.

"Valkyrie, wait," Cadaver said. "You've got it all wrong. I'm Skulduggery. He's Cadaver Cain. We switched clothes and heads when we were fighting. Kill him, not me."

She looked at Skulduggery, who shook his head. "I'm not indulging this behaviour."

"Oh, go on!" Cadaver said. "It'll be fun. I point and accuse you, you point and accuse me, Valkyrie blasts one of us and she's not too sure if she got the right one until at the very end when—"

She blasted Cadaver off his feet.

"You're right," Skulduggery said. "That was fun." He looked around. "Has anyone seen my hat?"

Cadaver laughed painfully as he got to his knees. "You'll have to do a lot more than that, I'm afraid. You're really going to have to pour it on. You're going to have to fry me."

"Or we could shackle you," Valkyrie said.

"That won't work. But, to save you from worrying about it, you don't fry me. You just can't bring yourself to kill me. It's at this point, however, that you try to destroy the Eye," he said, a millisecond before she swung a hand towards the podium. "But that doesn't do any good. Sorry."

Keeping her right hand pointed at him as he stood, Valkyrie blasted the Eye of Rhast with her left. The fingers of energy scorched the podium, but the Eye itself remained undamaged.

And then it throbbed, and a bubble of shimmering energy popped out, surrounding it. The death field.

Valkyrie pulled up her hood and pulled down her mask as Creed ran to the Faraday cage, clambering over the bodies and slamming the door closed. The bubble pulsed and expanded, washing over Valkyrie.

Skulduggery reached for her.

"I'm OK," she said, and turned. The bubble almost filled the entire nave.

"The next pulse will cover the city," Cadaver said. "The one after that, Europe. Two more, it'll cover the world. And then it will keep expanding until the universe is as dead as we are."

"We're shutting it down," Skulduggery said.

Cadaver laughed. "As the saying goes, you and whose army?"

There was a sudden wind, a howling wind, and Valkyrie watched as the space behind Cadaver stretched and then suddenly bulged, as something tried to force its way through from a reality outside this one.

"Did I forget to mention that the Viddu De have been wanting to pay a visit to this place since they heard about it?" Cadaver said, almost shouting to be heard over the howl. A second later, the bulge started to tear.

Skulduggery looked at Valkyrie. "Suggestions?"

"Uh..."

"Eloquent as usual," he said. He shouted to Creed. "Damocles, I don't suppose you have any ideas?"

From the safety of the cage, Creed kept his eyes on the warping space, and didn't answer.

"Very well," Skulduggery said, shrugging to Valkyrie. "Then I suppose I'll go say hi."

She tried to hold him back, but he was too fast, and he flew straight at the tear in space and disappeared into it.

# 118

Auger broke a cop's arm, grabbed him by the throat, and then smashed his head into the wall. The cop crumpled and Auger doubled over, clutching his stomach.

"You OK?" Mahala asked, kneeing another cop in the face.

"Fine," Auger gasped. "Just... cramps."

"Is that it?" Omen asked as he got back to his feet. "Is it done?"

"The Pillar's off," Axelia said. "We won, right?"

"Not yet," said Silas Nadir, leading another bunch of City Guards round the corner. He sneered at Auger and showed him the knife in his hand. "You ready for round two, slugger?"

"This man is a serial killer," Auger said, straightening up and backing off. "The rest of you are cops. You're cops! You know this is wrong! Do your duty!"

"They were doing their duty," Nadir said. "They were busting the heads of protesters and rioters, and they want to get back to that. So what do you say all of you just lie down and..." He faltered when Uriah Serrate walked up to him. "Ain't you supposed to be with us?"

"Things change," said Serrate, the glaive forming in his grip.

Even more cops turned the corner, their numbers giving strength to Nadir's smirk. "You picked a terrible time to switch sides, but I guess it's too late to back out now, huh?"

"I've already seen what happens," Serrate said. "I've seen this conversation. I've seen your next move, and the move after that and the move after that, when you lose your hand – and then I've seen your death. But you are correct – it is indeed too late to back out. Your last chance to emerge from this alive came fourteen seconds ago."

"You've seen what I do next, have you?"

"Yes."

"Well," Nadir said, "isn't that—"

He lunged and Serrate dodged the knife and dodged the knife again and then he brought up the glaive and it sliced through Nadir's wrist.

Nadir shrieked and clutched at his ruined arm and the cops parted and let him stagger back and fall to the ground, still shrieking.

"I've seen what happens next," Serrate said to the shocked officers. "In forty-two seconds, Temper Fray will arrive with a team of fighters and one of the Unveiled. You will be quickly overpowered. I've seen who lives and who dies. It should surprise no one to learn that most of you die – but I do not want you to fear death. You will be rejoining the Great Stream – for however long it may last."

One of the cops yelled a war cry and charged, and Auger hurled a shock stick that struck him full in the face. He went down, knees buckling beneath him.

"That's one you don't have to kill," Auger said to Serrate.

Serrate frowned back at him. "This is not how it's supposed to happen."

Auger shouted a warning as two other cops leaped forward, but Serrate was too slow to stop them from plunging their swords into his chest.

Serrate gagged, and dropped his scythe, and fell.

"Didn't see that coming, did you?" Crepuscular muttered.

Just like Serrate had promised, there were running footsteps and Temper Fray came round the corner with a guy Omen had never seen before and China Sorrows, sigils rising all over her body. Running upside down along the ceiling above them came Tanith Low, sword in hand.

They slammed into the City Guard and Omen roared and led his team forward.

# 119

The wind threatened to topple Valkyrie off the platform as she stormed over to the Eye, went to snatch it off the podium.

"Don't!" Cadaver shouted. "The power it's putting out, it'll eat through your glove and eat through you before you even start to feel any pain. Please, Valkyrie, just... just don't touch it."

She left it where it was and rounded on him. "Turn it off," she called. "Turn it off and bring Skulduggery back."

He held up his hands in surrender, his coat flapping round him. "I can't bring Skulduggery back. That's up to the Viddu De now. They're explaining the situation to him as we speak."

"Will he be back?"

"Yes," said Cadaver. "In the next twenty seconds. I promise." She pointed at the Eye. "Turn it off."

"No."

She raised her hand, ready to blast. "Turn it off!"

"We both know you're not going to kill me," Cadaver said. "Furthermore, you can't kill me. We're in the death field, Valkyrie. Death as you knew it is no more. Life as you knew it is no more. Take off your mask and you'll see."

"Screw you, bonehead," she said, and blasted him right in the face.

Cadaver spun head over heels through the air just as Skulduggery came hurtling back through the tear in space and they bounced off each other and went sprawling, and she saw Creed laugh in the Faraday cage. She hurried over to Skulduggery, helping him to his feet. "Are you OK? Skulduggery, are you hurt?"

Then the podium powered down.

Cadaver sat up quickly. "What?"

The glow from the Eye of Rhast faded and the death field withdrew with a rush of tingling that passed over Valkyrie's flesh like a rash. The tear in space collapsed, taking the wind with it.

Cadaver leaped up. "What? No. No, this isn't how it happens." He turned to Skulduggery. "What did you do? *What did you do?*"

"He didn't do anything," said Creed, stepping out of the Faraday cage. "I tinkered with the podium yesterday. Nothing too extravagant – just an automatic shutdown if the wrong energy is detected. What's wrong, Mr Cain? Didn't you see this particular future?"

Valkyrie watched Cadaver's fists unclench as he forced himself to calm down. "How are you doing this?"

"I am able to do this because you have a lacuna," Creed said. "A blank spot that you can't see. A person filled with a power that allows them to remain undetected in any future you look into."

"I have one that I know of," Cadaver said slowly, "but I left her behind when I came here."

"You left her behind, did you?" Creed said, smiling, as the door behind Cadaver opened and Alice Edgley walked out on to the stage.

Valkyrie tried to bolt forward, but Skulduggery restrained her.

"Alice!" Valkyrie cried. "Alice, run! Run as fast as you can!"

"How many times do I have to tell you?" the little girl said, smiling at her sister. "My name is Malice."

# 120

Valkyrie switched on her aura-vision, watched the swirling energy that coursed violently through her little sister's body.

"Get out of her," Valkyrie said. "Leave her alone." Her voice rose to a shout. "You don't know what you're doing to her!"

"I know exactly what I'm doing," Malice said in Alice's voice. "And I'm not going to harm her. I *am* her. She's in good hands."

She stopped beside Creed and smiled up at him. "Hiya, Uncle Damocles."

"Hello, child," he said, smiling back.

She looked at Cadaver. "Hey."

"You followed me," Cadaver said.

She shrugged. "I hitched a ride, just like you did. I figured if some dumb skeleton could manage it then it'd be no problem for the Child of the Faceless Ones. I didn't need to make myself a body when I got here, though. This one fits just fine for now."

Cadaver grunted. "I admit I didn't see this coming."

"Outmanoeuvred again, eh? It must be getting sickening by now, always being beaten. I don't know how you keep that smile on your face, I really don't." She looked over at the cage. "You've been busy."

"I have."

"What was that, a life-force grenade?"

Cadaver shrugged. "Just something I've been tinkering with. Abyssinia's design."

"All those poor dead people," Malice said, and looked back at Cadaver. "And, for all your intelligence, it never occurred to you that they're all completely replaceable. I told Uncle Damocles what you'd probably try to do, and I got him to build another Faraday cage for the important people – you know, the ones we *didn't* want to see killed quite yet."

"You're a clever one, Malice."

"I am," she said. "And, if you're wondering if my power has been compromised in this adorable little form, you're about to find out."

Cadaver shook his head. "My plan certainly seems to be in tatters."

"The Viddu De are not going to be happy with you."

"They're not, this is true."

"You can apologise in person," she said, energy crackling round her hand as she raised it.

"A final request?" Cadaver asked.

"Denied."

"A last word?"

"That was it."

"Tables," said Cadaver. "They do tend to turn."

"Don't they just?"

Valkyrie stalked forward until she was standing in front of Cadaver. "Stop. *Stop*. Alice – Malice – whatever, you are not killing him while you're wearing my little sister's body."

"Stand aside, Valkyrie."

Valkyrie pulled up her mask and pulled down her hood. "I won't let you do this."

Alice laughed. "You're cute," she said, and started blasting.

# 121

Temper knew most of the officers he was punching.

He'd already put down two who he knew for a fact were on the take, and he'd helped Ruckus take down a third who dearly loved to beat his prisoners when they were handcuffed. Another one, an officer by the name of Graft, tried tackling him, but Temper spun him to the floor and hammered at his jaw until he lost consciousness. Graft wasn't a bad cop – he'd just chosen the wrong side.

All around him, the City Guard were getting their asses kicked. Tanith and China carved their way through them. Axelia and Never and Kase were out of the fight, but Auger and Omen and Mahala, despite being exhausted and bleeding, weren't stopping any time soon. There was one fighter who Temper didn't recognise – a tall man with a messed-up face – but he fought with the focused economy of a trained killer.

The new guy, however, had nothing on Kierre of the Unveiled, who flitted and spun between opponents like a ribbon caught on the breeze. Every move was physical perfection and every strike landed the way it was supposed to land. Cops fell and dropped and slumped and stumbled away from her. It was a thing of beauty, it really was.

The last of the officers staggered from Auger to Omen, and, once Omen's right cross put him down, the fight was over.

There were no cheers to celebrate. Just heavy, heavy breathing. Omen took out his phone, tapped the screen, put it on loudspeaker.

Valkyrie's voice came on. "Serrate and Cadaver are working together," she said, before the call was cut off.

"Huh," Omen said, then tapped the screen again and held the phone to his ear.

The new guy, the guy with the messed-up face, pointed at Auger. "You," he said. "You're the key."

Auger winced at him, but didn't answer. He was in pain, though Temper couldn't see any injury apart from a few cuts and bruises.

"Cadaver Cain doesn't notice you," the new guy said. "You don't factor into the futures he sees."

"I'm sorry," said China, "but who are you?"

"Valkyrie's not answering," Omen said, putting the phone away and crouching by Never. "Crepuscular, what are you talking about?"

"After Serrate killed Signate, he fought Cadaver," Crepuscular said. "You threw that baton thing at Serrate and it made Cadaver hesitate, like he hadn't seen that happening. It surprised him. That's the baton Auger gave you, right?"

"Yeah," Omen said, stirring Never to consciousness.

"And Serrate was doing great against the City Guard just then until Auger threw that shock stick."

Auger narrowed his eyes. "He said that wasn't how it was supposed to happen."

"And then he was killed," said Crepuscular. "They can't see the consequences of your actions. If Cadaver reckons he's figured out all the angles, you're the key to stopping him. You're the angle he can't see."

"You gotta go," Temper said. "You gotta get to the Dark Cathedral. Never, can you teleport?"

"I'm woozy," Never said, "but I think I've got one or two jumps left in me."

Auger took his hand. "First, we go to my room," he said, and Never nodded and they vanished.

"Oh," said Omen, his shoulders slumping.

"What?" Tanith asked. "Why are they going to his dorm room?"

"Because he's getting the Obsidian Blade," Omen said. "He's going to kill Cadaver."

# 122

Valkyrie groaned.

She tried to get up and couldn't.

Skulduggery lay somewhere behind her, Cadaver somewhere in front. Valkyrie was curled up on the platform, eyes blinking to clear the tears.

Alice stepped over her.

"Wait," Valkyrie whispered.

"No more waiting," said Alice, placing her hand on the podium. She poured her magic in. Valkyrie didn't understand what she was doing at first, but of course the podium was connected to the Seven Pillars, and energy could flow both ways.

"The Corrival Pillar is active," Creed confirmed.

Valkyrie sat up, watching the monitor as the Ensh-Arak Sigil re-formed across the city.

"Maybe I will leave you alive, Cadaver," Malice said, walking on to the stage. "You've been such a pain for the last seventy-two years, I think I'd quite enjoy knowing that you'd witnessed this glorious future you've seen fade away from you." A Soul Catcher materialised in her palm and she turned, and smiled. "Valkyrie, I'll see you soon."

Then every trace of Malice's energy flowed into the Soul Catcher and Alice took a step, her eyes rolling back in her head.

Creed caught her as she fell and grabbed the Soul Catcher before it hit the ground. He laid Alice gently on the floor.

Valkyrie got to her feet. Skulduggery and Cadaver did the same.

"It's up to you two," Creed said to Valkyrie and Skulduggery as he walked back to the Faraday cage. "Cadaver's going to try to re-establish the Gurahghul Sigil. If he does that, we're all dead. At least with the Activation Wave you can fool yourselves into imagining you have a chance at convincing Malice to go along with your way of thinking. How are you going to convince death to do anything?"

Valkyrie glanced at Skulduggery. "He has a point."

Cadaver shook his head. "Don't you see what she's trying to do? Don't you see that she's trying to get you to stop me?"

"Yes," said Skulduggery.

"Just checking."

Cadaver hit him. Threw a fireball at Valkyrie. Slammed Skulduggery into the ground. Dodged a lightning blast. Punched. Struck. Blocked. Hit.

Valkyrie fell.

Skulduggery got back up, fists raised. "You know I'm not going to stop," he said.

Cadaver nodded. "Not until I find some ingenious way to put you down without killing you."

"And have you?"

"Yes."

Skulduggery lowered his fists a little. "You have?"

"Of course."

"How?"

"A device, the size and shape of a sheriff's star, inspired by the Deathtouch Gauntlet. Temporarily scrambles your life force. Not enough to shatter your soul, but enough to take you out of the fight for a few minutes. I've tested it on myself, so I know it works."

"I see," Skulduggery said. "And the fact that you've explained all this to me means that—"

"I've already slipped it into your pocket while we were fighting, yes," said Cadaver, taking a slim box from his jacket. "By the way, this is going to hurt."

Cadaver pressed the button and immediately seized up and toppled backwards. When he hit the platform, his skeleton pulsed, as if it was going to break apart, and then changed its mind. He lay there, barely moving.

"The last time we engaged in fisticuffs, you stole my gun without me noticing," Skulduggery said, adjusting his tie. "Did you really think I wouldn't learn from that mistake? I felt you slip that star into my pocket, and so I slipped it back into yours."

"You are very sneaky," Cadaver mumbled.

"I'd have to agree."

"But that's all right. Just as long as you didn't feel me slipping in the second one."

He pressed the button again and this time Skulduggery seized up and toppled back, his skeleton barely holding itself together when it hit the platform.

Cadaver got up slowly. "You can train yourself to withstand the worst of the effects," he said, "but only with enough practice. Are you doing OK down there?"

"I hate you," Skulduggery said, his voice weak.

"I totally understand," said Cadaver, taking the silver star from Skulduggery's pocket and putting it in his own.

Valkyrie tried getting up, but collapsed again. "Give me a second," she mumbled. "Stay there. Don't do anything." She heaved herself to a sitting position and Cadaver waved his hand and a wall of air slammed into her.

As she was rolling, someone else leaped on to the platform, his knee crunching into Cadaver's back, sending him sprawling.

Auger Darkly, bleeding and sweating and looking like he'd

crawled through the nine circles of hell to get here, faced Cadaver as he got to his feet.

"Now this," Cadaver said, "this is interesting."

"Your friend is dead," Auger said. "The Necromancer. You can do what he did, right? See all the possible futures?"

"Indeed I can," Cadaver answered.

"Hope you're better at it than he was."

Cadaver's head tilted. "Me too."

Auger jumped at him, fists blurring, spinning and whirling with kicks. Cadaver dodged or blocked most of them, but a punch caught him across the jaw and he backed off.

"Very interesting," he murmured.

Auger circled, but his face suddenly tightened and he stumbled slightly and Cadaver snapped his hand at the air and Auger went flying, head over heels, into the pews. He groaned, and got up, and came back.

"You're another lacuna," Cadaver said, watching him climb back on to the platform. "How is that possible? Malice is the only one with the power to hide herself from the eyes of the universe, but you... you're invisible in certain futures. How are you managing that?"

"Come closer and I'll tell you," Auger said, drawing a knife from his belt. It was the Obsidian Blade, or a piece of it, anyway: a shard of black still sticking out of the handle.

Auger lunged and Cadaver veered back, the remains of the blade slashing the empty space. Cadaver pushed at the air, but Auger rolled beneath the attack, coming up into a crouch and swiping at Cadaver's leg, barely missing.

Valkyrie got to her hands and knees.

"Walk away, Auger," Cadaver said. "You're not well, boy. I can see the weakness in the way you move."

Auger came at him and Cadaver blocked and trapped and tried to disarm him, but Auger backed off.

"I can see you in the past," Cadaver continued, "up until the night you faced the King of the Darklands. You stabbed him with that knife. I can see everything up to that moment, to the knife sliding into his flesh – and then you vanish from my sight."

"I am sneaky like that," Auger muttered.

"What happened, Auger? The knife broke off when you stuck it in him, but what happened? It changed you, didn't it? You're not the person you were. Your skin is paler. You're tired. Not sick, exactly, but…" Cadaver's head tilted. "When the Obsidian Blade broke, did it cut you? Or maybe a sliver went into your mouth? Your eye, perhaps?"

Auger hesitated. "What if it did?"

"I don't know," said Cadaver. "But it has infected you, Auger. You know that, yes? You can feel it? Changing you?"

"Yes," Auger said.

Valkyrie stood, got ready to focus her magic into lightning. Energy started to crackle round her hands.

"One cut from the Obsidian Blade wipes you from existence," Cadaver said. "But I don't know what happens to someone infected with a splinter."

"So I'm probably dying," said Auger. "The splinter's going to wipe me away, and wipe away all my plans, and all my dreams. I suppose that's fitting. I'm the Chosen One, after all. If anyone's going to have a weird death, it'll be me."

"But it's not death, is it? There'll be nothing left of you. No soul, no energy, nothing. Simple oblivion."

Auger doubled over, gasping, and Valkyrie realised he was having his Surge, right there and then. "Yeah, well," he muttered as Cadaver moved in, "save me a seat."

He lunged.

Cadaver grabbed Auger's wrist, chopped down on the elbow with his other hand and plunged the broken blade into Auger's chest.

"No!" Valkyrie yelled.

Auger staggered back, eyes wide, and Cadaver stepped away.

A blackness spread outwards from the wound – angular, glinting. The Obsidian Blade itself was latching on to him, disintegrating his clothes even as it flowed over his skin. It covered his belly and his chest and ran down his legs and his arms and up to his neck and then it was flowing over his face and his hair and within seconds there was nothing left but an obsidian man. He opened his mouth and even his tongue and his teeth were black. He opened his eyes and even his eyes were black.

They stared, all of them, as the obsidian man looked at his own hands, flexing his sharp, angular fingers.

"*Ohhh,*" Cadaver whispered, "damn." He stepped back until he was behind Valkyrie. "If you want my advice," he said softly, "you won't let him touch you."

Valkyrie licked her lips, held out her hands. "Auger?" she said. "Auger, can you hear me? Are you all right?"

The obsidian man didn't respond. Didn't look up.

"We can help you," Skulduggery said, managing to sit up. "Whatever's wrong, we can find a way to reverse it. Auger, we're not leaving you. You're not alone."

Now the obsidian man did look up, but not at them. He was looking at something beside him, something Valkyrie couldn't see. He reached out, hooking his fingers round empty space. Valkyrie winced, a headache piercing her skull. The obsidian man pulled that empty space to one side, and within it was a hillside at night. He stepped through, and the space closed over and he and the hillside were gone.

Valkyrie blinked away the headache.

"I can't help but feel partly responsible for that one," Cadaver said.

"What'll happen to him?" Valkyrie asked, struggling to keep her anger in check.

Cadaver hesitated. "Nothing good. Nothing good for any of us. The futures are..." He shook his head. "This can't be right. The futures are falling away."

Valkyrie grabbed his arm and let her power flow and Cadaver jolted back, out of her grip. He fell and stayed down, and did nothing to stop Skulduggery shackling his wrists behind his back.

Skulduggery stood and turned, and froze.

"Valkyrie," he said.

The Eye of Rhast was glowing again.

# 123

Valkyrie picked up Alice, and Skulduggery wrapped an arm round her waist and flew them both over the pews, landing by the door. He hesitated, then waved both hands and Cadaver hurtled after them. He landed badly. Valkyrie didn't care.

The Eye of Rhast pulsed and energy rippled like the surface of a lake, covering the whole of the platform. It pulsed again and the energy field doubled in size. Accompanied by the sound of static, incredibly loud, it pulsed again and grew twice as big. At this rate, it would overtake Roarhaven in minutes. It would reach Haggard not long after that.

Valkyrie put Alice on the floor.

"Don't," Skulduggery called to her.

"I have to."

"There's always another way."

She turned to him, pulling down her mask, shouting now to be heard. "You have to stop me! If I go bad, you've got to stop me before I hurt anyone!"

"Valkyrie, no!"

"We don't have a choice! We've tried everything we could think of and nothing worked and the only thing we can do to avert the future is if I go down there!"

He gripped her arm. "I won't let you!"

She filled her hand with crackling energy and pressed it to his chest. There was a crack of power and he flew backwards and immediately she turned and dived, energy sparking all around her, and she flew low across the pews, the nave blurring into incoherence, her eyes focused on the podium and nothing but the podium as the Eye pulsed again and Valkyrie crashed into it, hugging it to her belly as she rolled and tumbled and the Wave...

The Wave enveloped her.

# 124

Valkyrie blinked to clear her vision. She was on her hands and knees. The Eye of Rhast was beside her – dull and blackened and inert. No more pulsing energy. No more wind. No more noise.

She stood. Pulled up her mask. Pulled down her hood. She felt weird. Her skin rippled with gooseflesh and her insides buzzed. Her mouth was dry.

The Faraday cage opened and Creed rushed out, and froze when he saw her. "Valkyrie," he said. His brow furrowed. "What have you done?"

She would have answered if she'd been able, but something was wrong with her voice. Something was wrong with her eyes, too – they were streaming tears. The muscles in her calves started to cramp. She felt sick and her head hurt. Her gut twisted. Her fingers curled.

Skulduggery landed beside her. He held out his hands. She looked at him.

The pain started in the base of her spine and exploded outwards. It hit her so violently she stumbled. Every muscle in her body contracted and she roared. Screeched.

Lightning danced from her skin, lifting her off the ground.

Her bones snapped.

Her lungs and her liver and her kidneys ruptured.

Her eyes burst. Her heart burst. Her brain boiled.

The lightning faded and her corpse hung in mid-air.

Then she dropped to her feet and she was healed.

"Valkyrie?" Skulduggery said, his voice quiet.

She worked her jaw a little before speaking. "I'm OK. I think. I think I'm OK."

He hurried forward and hugged her. She hugged him back. She couldn't think of what else to do. She was very confused.

"What happened?" asked Creed.

Skulduggery broke off the hug, watching Valkyrie as she answered.

"I'm not sure," she said. "There was a... a whole lot of pain. I mean, a whole lot."

"I'll have my doctors examine you," said Creed.

"They're not your doctors any more," Skulduggery responded. "You're under arrest."

"Don't be ridiculous."

Skulduggery's gun was in his hand. "Damocles Creed, I'm placing you under arrest for attempted genocide."

Creed didn't look impressed. "Skulduggery, please, don't embarrass yourself. You can't arrest me. Everyone in a position of power in this city is there because of me. Practically every Sanctuary around the world does what I tell them. What do you think will happen? You'll put me in a cell and they'll let me stay there? They won't fall over themselves in their eagerness to set me free? Let's not be childish now, not when Valkyrie is in need of our attention."

"Valkyrie's fine."

Creed laughed. "She's more than that, Detective. She is wonderful. She is superb. She is divine. She is, after all, the Child of the Faceless Ones."

Skulduggery grunted. "What do you have to say about that, Valkyrie?"

"Not much," she replied. "It affected me, sure, and it hurt like hell, but... it was the suit. The suit stopped it from changing me."

"You've failed," Skulduggery said to Creed. "Your grand plan is over. Maybe it would have worked with someone younger, maybe it would have worked with someone weaker – but Valkyrie was ready for you."

"Is all that true, Valkyrie?" Creed asked. "Has my plan failed?"

"I'm afraid so."

"Well, at least I tried. You can see yourselves out, yes? And take Cadaver Cain with you."

"You're under arrest," Skulduggery said.

"Build a case, Detective. You won't be able to find a Sensitive strong enough to break into my mind so you'll have to collect evidence and witnesses. When you have all that, I'll come quietly, you have my word." He looked at Valkyrie. "As for you, you'd better take your little sister home. I suppose, in a way, you have spared her from what's to come, but you've also robbed her of something it was not your place to rob." He shrugged. "Such is life. My door, Valkyrie, is always open."

Humming to himself, Damocles Creed walked off the platform and disappeared through the doors.

Valkyrie turned to Skulduggery. "We won, right?"

"I think so," he replied.

"It's just... it doesn't feel like we've won."

"We won," he said. "We definitely won."

They looked around.

"Are you sure you're feeling OK?" he asked.

Valkyrie hesitated, thought about it, and shrugged. "Nothing's different. Nothing's changed. I think."

Skulduggery nodded. "That's good enough for me. You go get your unconscious sister, I'll pick up my future self."

She smiled. "What a life we lead, eh?"

"What a life."

# 125

The trick to killing someone was not to break in through a window and wait for them to come home. People, Quell had come to realise, were finely attuned to the frequency of their dwellings. An open window disturbed the airflow, altering the pressure throughout the house. While this might not be acknowledged consciously by the occupant, it succeeded in creating a sense of vague uneasiness that put them on edge and made taking them by surprise a good deal more difficult.

The trick to killing someone, therefore, was to strike in an environment where things like pressure, airflow, and unusual sounds would not be a factor. Outdoors was preferable.

He could have struck half a dozen times as he followed Militsa Gnosis through Roarhaven, but the city was unquiet tonight – the Draíocht boost had seen to that. In one district, people were celebrating. In another, they were rioting. Some of the streets had filled with an energy that carved up the roads and burned anyone who got close. Nobody knew quite what to make of that – and Quell didn't care.

None of it would have stopped him from sliding a knife into her back, but Quell wanted to speak to her before he killed her. He felt Valkyrie would like to know Militsa's final words. Maybe they would help her get over the loss quicker.

He watched Militsa talk to some of her fellow Necromancers

by the temple that was being built beside the new Necropolis. The exchange, from what Quell could tell, was cordial, if unenthused. Thanks to the surveillance devices he'd planted in Militsa's apartment, he knew that she didn't get along with others in the Order. Even so, she was curious about the new temple, and the entire city was curious about the Necropolis.

She left the Necromancers to their construction site and walked the perimeter. Quell waited until she'd turned the corner on to an empty street before taking the helmet out of his bag and putting it on. He stepped into the light ahead of her and she stopped, eyes widening. Then she took in a breath.

"If you scream, I'll kill you now," Quell said. "If you run, just know that I'm faster than you. If you fight, I'm stronger."

"You can have my money," she said.

He ignored that. "You're not worthy of her."

"Worthy of who?" She frowned. "Valkyrie?"

"You and the skeleton. You aren't good for her."

"I don't know what you're talking about. Who are you? What do you want?"

"She loves me."

"I doubt that very much."

"She told me."

Those wide eyes narrowed. "You're Coda."

"She told me she loved me, but I didn't understand at the time that I loved her back. Now I understand. Now it's time for you and the skeleton to step out of the way."

Militsa shrugged. She was relaxing now. "Hey, if you want to make Valkyrie choose between you and me, I'm fine with that. I am. We should call her. Maybe not right now. She's kinda busy right now. Tomorrow then. She'll make a choice and the loser leaves. Agreed?"

"I have to kill you."

The slowly building confidence vanished. "What?"

Quell took the sickle from beneath his jacket. "If you have anything you'd like me to pass on to Valkyrie, tell me now."

"You don't... you don't have to kill me. This isn't what people kill each other for."

"You're in my way."

"If you kill me, Valkyrie will never forgive you."

"You don't know her like I do."

"Please, Coda, I love her. I love her and she loves me. I didn't steal her from you. I didn't do anything. I just fell in love with her. Please don't do this."

"OK," Quell lied, "I won't kill you."

He said that to be nice, so she wouldn't spend her last few moments scared. He swung for her throat so fast she didn't have time to blink.

# 126

But the shadows were already wrapping round him from behind. They snagged on his wrist and his sickle flew from his grip, barely missing Militsa's shoulder.

"Are you serious?" she yelled. "You attack me, outside, at night? I'm a Necromancer, you bloody idiot! The darkness is my whole entire *thing*!"

He tried to grab her, but the shadows were everywhere, tangling themselves round his limbs.

"And, what, you didn't think Valkyrie told me about you?" Militsa continued, raging now. "You didn't think she told me that you lie right before you kill people? We communicate, ya wee bampot! A loving relationship is all about communication!"

The shadow tentacles tried to lift him off his feet, but he struggled, and the more he struggled the more Militsa panicked, and the more she panicked the less control she had over her Draíocht-boosted power. All at once, Quell was free and he lunged at her. She yelped and fell back and the shadows convulsed and slammed into him, much harder than she'd intended, and he went spinning through the air. He died the moment he passed over the iron fence, into the Necropolis, and his empty body hit the ground, rolled three times and came to a sprawling, lifeless stop.

# 127

It had taken seventy years, but Martin Flanery had finally met a real, bona-fide monster.

Dressed in hospital scrubs and a long white coat, it was so tall that it had to stoop to come through the laboratory door.

"Mr President," Perfidious Withering said, "this is Doctor Nye. The doctor might not be human, but it has been carrying out experiments on humans for centuries, so it literally knows us inside out."

"Mr President," the Nye creature said in greeting.

Revulsion rippling over the back of his neck, Flanery shook its hand, its ridiculously long fingers closing weakly over his. "What kind of experiments?" he asked.

"I have been searching," said Nye. "Searching for the soul. I found one, years ago. I opened the subject up and there it was – but ever since then the souls of my patients have proven... elusive. I think they can smell it on me, what I did."

Perfidious stepped up. "Isn't that marvellous? The meeting of two great minds like this should be documented for prosperity. Sadly, the camera roll on my phone is already full, otherwise I would be snapping away. Mr President, you're probably wondering why I brought you here. The fact is, I think you could be useful to each other. Doctor Nye needs volunteers – soldiers, ideally – to continue its work."

"And what do I get out of it?" Flanery asked.

Nye held up a square of paper. "This is called a Splash," it said, "a piece of absorbent paper soaked in a chemical solution into which a sorcerer's magic has been diluted. When ingested by other sorcerers, they experience a significant energy boost. It can be quite addictive."

Flanery looked at the square of paper, barely bigger than a thumbnail.

"Splashes have been doing the rounds in magical communities for a few years now," Perfidious said, "making Doctor Nye a handsome profit along the way. But profit has never been the doctor's goal."

"The Splash was merely a test run," said Nye. "Some users had a bad reaction – some got sick. Some died. This was all useful. All the data went back into the project."

"And what project is this?" Flanery asked.

Perfidious and Nye walked to a window looking into a darkened room. Flanery scowled and followed.

"Tell me, Mr President," said Perfidious, "do you recognise this person?"

The lights inside the room flicked on. Sitting on a chair, looking tired and scared, was a man Flanery had seen before.

"That's Senator Rooker," Flanery said, alarmed. "What are you doing with him? Why do you have him?"

"Senator Rooker," said Perfidious, "the Democrat?"

"Yes."

"The annoyance, you mean? The man who regularly goes on the morning shows and slates your policies and insults you personally, even when you're doing a terrific job?"

Flanery looked at him. "Yes."

"The same Senator Rooker who disappeared from his home three days ago? Did you know about this, sir?"

"His disappearance? Yeah. The FBI are searching for him."

"I just wanted to make sure," said Perfidious. "I just wanted to be certain that we had the right man. Senator Rooker here has been injected with Doctor Nye's new formula for the last three days. I asked you here so that you could witness the results."

Perfidious pressed the button again, and the door opened and two men entered. Immediately, Rooker was on his feet, hands out, pleading with them to stay back. The men had knives. Rooker started crying.

One of the men lunged at him and Rooker thrust his hands out and the upper third of the man's body twisted round the other way. Skin and clothes tore and bones flew and there was blood everywhere. Rooker screamed in horror and the other man dropped his knife, took out a gun and shot him dead.

Flanery stared.

"The senator was not magical," said Nye.

It took a moment for Flanery to process what had just happened. "What?"

"The senator. He had trace amounts of magic in his system, which is to say nothing that could ever be used. He was thoroughly average, the same as most mortals."

"But three days of injections," said Perfidious, "and look what he was able to do."

"The man killed him," said Flanery.

"But not before he'd used magic. Mr President, do you understand what this means? Your soldiers can have this power. Your police. You can sell this to whoever can afford it – at whatever price you decide to set. Sir, you would go down in history as the president who changed the world."

The possibilities tumbled through Flanery's mind too quickly to grasp – but he found a question somewhere in all that excitement, and held on to it. "And what do you get out of it? Why would you want to do this? I know how much the wizards want to keep magic a secret. Why do you want everyone to know about it?"

Perfidious smiled. "I am merely a go-between, Mr President. Suffice it to say, Crepuscular Vies isn't finished with you yet."

# 128

Roarhaven was holding its breath.

That's how it seemed to Commander Hoc. The riot had been subdued and the protesters had returned to their homes. Maybe some of them were waking up this morning, blaming their disobedience on the effects of Draíocht. Others, he knew, had been waiting to riot all this time. It would be interesting, if nothing more, to gauge how many citizens returned to stage another protest after the violence of the previous night.

His City Guard were ready for whatever happened.

Some people were already leaving the city, citing safety concerns, but not enough to matter. The rest were waiting to see what would happen next – Hoc among them. But, until whatever was to happen next happened, he intended to go to work each morning and do his job, because what else was he going to do?

And there was plenty to keep him occupied. Supreme Mage Creed had insisted that the Corrival students who'd assaulted his officers should not face reprisals, but Hoc was free to hunt down Temper Fray and his gang of dissidents, so that's where he was putting his efforts. He had to do something to salvage the City Guard's reputation after the drubbing they'd received in that damned school. When the whispers of discontent started again – and they would, he knew that as well as he knew his own face – the people of this city would be questioning his competence.

He needed a win. He needed a win so big that no one could doubt his position.

The alert on his phone sounded and Hoc froze – then tore the device from his pocket and swiped and tapped for the live camera footage.

This could be it. If things went according to plan, then he'd emerge from this a legend, as the man who—

There. On his screen, he watched Darquesse walk through the locked door that led to the cells.

She didn't break it down. Didn't blast it open. She just walked through it like it wasn't there.

He tapped the screen and the shot zoomed in. This wasn't a child at all – this was *the* Darquesse, looking exactly as she did on Devastation Day when she'd razed sections of Roarhaven with barely a thought.

Hoc zoomed out again. His agents opened fire. Bullets and beams of pure energy sliced through her, but caused no damage. She waved and they turned to ash, and she looked around, no doubt searching for her friends.

One of Hoc's men ran up behind him. "Sir!"

"I'm watching," Hoc said, not taking his eyes from the screen. "Call everyone back. We don't need to lose any more of our people."

He watched the ground open up beneath Darquesse and switched cameras as she floated down. Her focus seemed to be on her friends. Hoc found himself holding his breath.

She walked through security doors, through gates, through walls, moving in a straight line. No hesitation. No doubt. Not even the briefest flicker. She was Darquesse, after all. A god. What did she have to fear from lowly sorcerers?

She passed into the room, walking with confidence. Got halfway across before the cage came down.

The sigils etched on to the bars lit up, bathing her in orange light. She stumbled, a frown on her face. The bars flashed with different sigils, different colours, dampening her magic the way a sodden blanket dampens a fire. She gripped the bars, tried to pull them apart. Hoc zoomed in on her look of sudden pain. Hissing, she fell to her knees, tried punching the floor. It cracked under her fists and for a moment – a *moment* – Hoc doubted the plan would succeed, but then Darquesse sagged, and crumpled, and it was done.

They had her.

# 129

A single Draíocht banner, attached by one corner, fluttered weakly in the warm breeze, an embarrassed reminder of a party that had been over for two weeks.

Beneath it, Roarhaven had returned to its own normality, the people focused again on their own lives, lost in their own worlds. They kept their eyes down and their minds on their own business. The Sense Wardens were monitoring. There were no more protests. No more riots. No more dissent. Freedoms were still being curtailed. Rights were still being restricted. Mortals were still being rounded up, jailed without charge, expelled from the city without reason, and the resistance was too busy evading capture to strike back in any meaningful way.

It was summer, and it was warm, and the sun was shining, and occasionally the clouds moved in and it rained, and then the clouds went away and the sun was shining again. It was all so completely routine that it sometimes fooled Omen into thinking that everything was normal. Nobody had knocked on his door and put him in shackles. He hadn't been hauled in for questioning and neither had Never or Axelia, Kase or Mahala. Their battle with the City Guard, their actions to shut down the Pillar, had gone unpunished. Whether that was an oversight or by design, Omen had no way of knowing. Every day he expected to be arrested. Every day had passed without that happening.

He didn't know if Creed had achieved what he'd wanted to achieve, but he'd watched from a pew in the church on Carnivore Row as the people around him went from mumbling unfamiliar prayers to reciting them with conviction, by heart. Omen didn't mumble. He just mouthed the words without speaking them.

He pretended a lot, these days – pretended to pray, pretended to worship, pretended to be OK with what was happening. He pretended to be fine, to not be scared, to not be anxious about what the future held. When he talked to Gretchen, he pretended that everything was all right, and that everything would be all right, and that he'd be able to apply to art college and be able to draw comics. He pretended he'd be able to be happy – and that Gretchen and all the other mortals would be able to be free.

He pretended that his heart wasn't broken, and that his brother could be saved.

His parents were having difficulty. Omen, at least, knew he was pretending. He knew that the pretence was a shield to slow down the truth, giving him the time he needed to come to terms with what had happened.

Omen's parents weren't facing up to the same reality. They insisted that Auger would be fine, that he could return to them. They didn't know of their favourite son's plans to abandon the family name, to walk away from their suffocating, selfish demands, to forge a life for himself out of their grasp. They didn't know and Omen didn't tell them. They needed to believe the things they believed.

High Sanctuary officials had spoken to him, made him promise to alert them if Auger made contact. Omen told them he would, even after they'd slipped up and referred to his brother as Obsidian. That's what everyone was calling him, apparently.

If Auger did make contact, it would be Crepuscular that Omen went to – Crepuscular and Skulduggery and Valkyrie. For reasons he didn't understand, the Supreme Mage had granted the Arbiters some kind of amnesty, even after they'd directly opposed him.

The resistance and China Sorrows had been forced to flee Roarhaven and were being pursued without mercy, but Skulduggery Pleasant and Valkyrie Cain were free to continue on as if nothing had happened. It was causing Roarhaven citizens to openly wonder if the Arbiters had come to some kind of secret deal with Damocles Creed. Their reputation as mavericks was being questioned. Their impartiality was being doubted.

But Omen didn't doubt them. He hadn't seen either of them in the last two weeks, but, if he had any chance at all of getting his brother back, he knew that Skulduggery and Valkyrie would be a big part of it.

And then, like the universe was actually paying attention, Omen passed Valkyrie in the street.

"Hi," he said, surprising himself by smiling. He hadn't smiled since Draíocht.

She stopped walking, turned, looked at him like her thoughts were tangled somewhere else and they needed a moment to settle.

"Omen," she said. "Hi. How are you?"

"I'm grand," he lied. "Are you on a case?"

"Sorry?"

"Are you on a case?" he repeated. "You and Skulduggery?"

"Oh," she said, "no. No, just out walking. It's a nice day and I thought I'd go walking. What about you?"

"Just walking, too. Haven't seen you in a while."

"No. Things, you know. Things were happening." She paused. "Militsa and I broke up."

"Oh, no."

She nodded. "We broke up. This morning."

"I'm so sorry."

"Did I tell you she killed Coda?"

"Who's Coda?"

"No one. Never mind. It doesn't really matter. But he tried to kill her and she defended herself and... She'd never killed anyone before. She took it hard."

"Is that why you broke up?"

She frowned. "How do you know we broke up?"

"You... you told me. Just then. Valkyrie, are you sure you're all right?"

Her smile was the saddest thing he'd ever seen. "No," she said. "No, I'm not."

He didn't know how to respond to that. "How's Alice?"

She brightened. She actually brightened. Usually, he said precisely the wrong thing, but not today. He was quite proud of himself for this one.

"She's good," Valkyrie said. "She's so good. She doesn't remember anything about Malice possessing her, doesn't remember anything at all about the Dark Cathedral... She still gets sad at weird moments, but that's OK. The important thing is that we didn't add to her trauma. The important thing is we didn't make her worse."

Valkyrie nodded, more to herself than to Omen.

"And," she said suddenly, getting some of her old energy back, "she has her whole life ahead of her. Her whole future is open. She doesn't have to become Malice. She doesn't have to go through what Malice went through. I mean, that's huge! That's all I wanted, you know? Before all this latest bit of craziness started, I just wanted her to have a chance at happiness, the same as everyone else. And she has that. So long as we continue to save the world."

"That's good news," said Omen. "That's really good news. But... I mean... aren't you the Child of the Faceless Ones now?"

The smile became strained, and then it dropped off completely. "Yeah," she said.

"So are you... y'know..."

"Am I evil?"

"Are you?"

"Do I look evil? Do I look like I suddenly turned into a bad guy?"

"Not especially. But then what does it mean, you being the Child of the Faceless Ones? What do you have to do?"

She didn't answer.

"Valkyrie?"

"Creed told me I'd be a receptacle," she said. "He said in this universe the environment isn't quite right. It isn't suitable for the Faceless Ones. There's not enough magic, apparently. He's doing his best to fix that. All those reports you hear, about the scientists studying the rifts to the Source? They're not studying them – they're widening them. They're letting more magic in, like the Draíocht boost only permanent, which means pretty soon every sorcerer around the world is gonna be stronger. More powerful. It also means the Faceless Ones will be able to exist here in their natural forms."

"But won't that send everyone mad?"

Valkyrie shook her head. "That's in their spirit state, according to Creed. Their natural forms, their physical bodies, are horrible and sickening and huge – but we should be able to deal with them. So that's good. That's another bit of good news."

"But what does it mean, to be a receptacle?" Omen asked.

"Well, Omen, I'll tell you. It doesn't require any effort on my part, which is nice, but apparently what's happening is that the entire race of Faceless Ones will enter this universe through me."

"I'm sorry?"

She tapped her chest. "They're in here right now. In my soul. Hundreds of thousands of them. Maybe more, I don't know. They fly around, squirming and wriggling, getting acclimatised to this reality – because they've been away for so long, you see. They need a little time to readjust. And, when they're ready, they'll fly out."

"Out where?"

"Out here," she said, waving her hands around. "Their home. They fly out and others fly in. My soul is kinda like the customs section in an airport, you know? You go through the checks, your bags get X-rayed, and, when you're cleared, you carry on to your destination. It'll take a few months to get through all of them, I reckon. I don't mind. It tickles."

He stared at her.

"And by the time they're all out," she continued, "the rifts will be opened up nice and wide, and they can reveal themselves to the world."

"Wait," Omen said. "Wait. You mean, they're already here?"

"Some of them, sure."

He went cold. He must have looked horrified because she moved in, hugged him.

"Oh, it's OK!" she said. "You're gonna be OK!"

He pushed away from her. "How can you say that? What do we do? How do we stop them?"

Valkyrie frowned. "Why would we want to stop them?"

He took another step back, and she rolled her eyes.

"Oh, don't be so dramatic! I can prove to you that they're not as scary as you think they are. I can prove it, OK? Come here."

She took him by the shoulders and turned him until his back was to her and he was facing north. She pointed into the distance. "See those clouds? Keep looking at them." Her hands went to his head. "This'll feel a little weird, but I'm just going to take a tiny, tiny step into your mind."

"No, I don't—"

"Relax," she said, laughing. "I won't be able to read your thoughts or anything. It's only a tiny step, just so I can let you see what I see. I call it my aura-vision. I keep meaning to come up with a cooler name for it."

Colour washed over the street. People passing by were surrounded by a wild array of different shades of orange. The magic, the energy, the sheer life of the world around him. It was breathtaking.

"Look up," Valkyrie whispered in his ear. "Look up at the clouds."

Omen looked up, into the distance, where she'd been pointing. He saw it, then, the creature he hadn't been able to see a few seconds ago. An impossibly huge thing, bigger than a mountain, with too many legs and too many eyes. Standing there. Just standing there.

Horrified, devastated, he looked away, to the east. Saw two more, as different from each other as they were from the first one. Standing. Waiting.

"Hundreds of thousands of them," Valkyrie whispered. "Millions maybe. I'm the Child of the Faceless Ones, but in a way? In a way, I'm also their mother."

And she sounded so happy.

She took her hands away and Omen's vision returned to normal, but, when he turned to her, her smile vanished.

"What's wrong?" she asked, with real concern in her voice. "Omen, what's wrong? Why are you crying?"